The Rogue's Runaway Bride

A Rogue of Her Own Series
Book 3

TARA KINGSTON

DRAGONBLADE PUBLISHING, INC.

ARE YOU SIGNED UP FOR DRAGONBLADE'S BLOG?

You'll get the latest news and information on exclusive giveaways, exclusive excerpts, coming releases, sales, free books, cover reveals and more.

Check out our complete list of authors, too!

No spam, no junk. That's a promise!

Sign Up Here

www.dragonbladepublishing.com

Dearest Reader;

Thank you for your support of a small press. At Dragonblade Publishing, we strive to bring you the highest quality Historical Romance from some of the best authors in the business. Without your support, there is no 'us', so we sincerely hope you adore these stories and find some new favorite authors along the way.

Happy Reading!

CEO, Dragonblade Publishing

**Additional Dragonblade books by
Author Tara Kingston**

A Rogue of Her Own Series
A Rogue to Watch Over Me (Book 1)
The Lady Needs a Rogue (Book 2)
The Rogue's Runaway Bride (Book 3)

Chapter One

London, 1896

OH, *BELLE, YOU simply must visit London,* they said. *You'll have the time of your life. And you might just find your very own prince . . . or perhaps a duke will do.*

Bracing herself against the damp chill, Arabelle Frost clutched the threadbare wool of a second-hand cape over her torn white dress. The flowing, once-pristine silk of the gown dragged over the cobbles as she trudged along the street. With each step of her thin-soled shoes against the hard, uneven pavement, echoes of her soon-to-be-former friends' words whispered in her thoughts. When—or if—she made it back to New York, she would certainly inform the Manhattan socialites they had been horribly mistaken. Not only had she *not* encountered a prince—or even a duke, for that matter—the scoundrel she'd happened upon had far more in common with a viper than with any fairy tale hero.

The clatter of a swift-moving carriage cut through the normal chaos of the city. Could that be Gideon? Had he tracked her path so easily? Spying a darkened doorway on the edge of an even gloomier alley, Belle tugged the hood of the cloak lower to conceal her features and dashed to her spur-of-the-moment refuge.

Twilight was settling over the city. In this moment, the impending darkness seemed both a blessing and a curse. Her pulse thundered in her ears as the rumbling of the carriage grew louder. Closer. Soon, it would be upon her.

For a heartbeat, perhaps two or three, she hesitated steps

from the arch of the unlit door. Eyeing the shadows, she prayed she would encounter neither vermin nor filth. But she didn't really have a choice, did she?

Belle gulped against her fear of what lay beyond the light and ducked inside the doorway. Her pulse thudded in her ears as the black Brougham rumbled past her hiding place.

Peering from the shadows, she spotted the distinctive crest on the carriage door. Her instincts had not failed her. Not this time, at least. The hulking driver held the reins. But if the man she'd fled with only the clothes on her back and the coins in her reticule rode within the conveyance, he had not peeled back the curtain to search the space. He had not looked for her.

Thank heaven.

The chimes of a clock tower sounded a new hour. It wouldn't be long before the light faded. Darkness would embolden the night creatures—both those that walked on two and four legs. She had to find a safe place to stay. Come morning, she'd flee both this city and the man who wanted to ensure she did not escape.

But for now, she had to make it through the night.

But where? Where could she find safe refuge? Who might take her in? While she'd had the presence of mind to snatch up her reticule before fleeing the luxurious townhouse where she'd been staying, she possessed only the coins in the small velveteen bag. Even if she might pay the cost of a night's lodging at a hotel, she couldn't chance being recognized. Or worse—tracked down by the heartless jackals and treated as though she'd gone quite mad.

Perhaps a small inn might provide respite for the night. If she kept the plain cloak bundled tight around her, the innkeeper might not notice her unusual attire. A shiny coin might very well buy her way out of this mess, at least for now.

Holding her senses on high alert, she made her way past an array of shops and taverns and cafes. Raucous sounds of music and conversation drifted from the pubs and music halls as, with each passing moment, more of the sun's light ebbed away and faint rays of gaslight left much of the street in shadows. Belle tugged the cloak tighter, as if she might ward off a shiver which had nothing to do with the chill in the air.

In the distance, lightning crackled against the darkening sky. A rumble of thunder followed close behind. Rain. Good heavens, could this night get any worse?

Another lightning strike, closer this time, made it clear she would not like the answer to her question.

Moving briskly over the pavement, she made her way toward an inn bearing a modest wooden sign. The tap of her soles against the cobbles could not drown out the beat of her pulse in her ears. Along the way, a far more brash sign caught her eye. *The Rogue's Lair.* The tavern's proprietor certainly made no secret of its desired clientele. For her part, Belle had had enough of rogues. If she never again laid eyes on a man who fit that description, she would count herself fortunate. When she returned to America, she would be quite content with a quiet life at her family's country home, living in peace with her books, her music, and the animals she'd taken under her wing.

As she hurried past the establishment, loud music—for lack of a better word—drifted to her ears from within the pub. Someone pounded the keys of a piano in a boisterous rhythm while a man sang along, his voice powerful and filled with enthusiasm, if not particularly on-key as he belted out the ribald lyrics.

Suddenly, her gaze was torn to an unexpected—and most unusual—sight across the road. A young boy scarcely older than a tot stood in the alley by a dimly lit café. Clothed in a ragged shirt and trousers that were much too big for his body, he looked cold and frightened. As their eyes met, he began to cry, his small voice wracked with fear and unhappiness. His little face scrunched up, red as a beet with the intensity of his sobs.

Oh, dear. Why would a young child be wandering alone and unprotected, much less on this busy street as the light waned around him?

Hiking her skirts to dodge a puddle brimming with muddy water, Belle darted across the road. With each step, she prayed that Gideon and his lackeys were now far from this place. Far from her. In any case, she had to take the chance. She simply could not ignore the child's distress.

Watching her with teary eyes, the boy backed away, even as his cries grew more insistent. Slowing her steps, she approached him with calm movements. It wouldn't do for him to take a fright and bolt away. Heaven knew she had no desire to chase him.

"What has happened to you?" she asked in a quiet voice. "Where are your parents?"

His head bobbed back and forth with uncertainty as he nibbled his lower lip.

"Come now," she coaxed. "Your mama must be near." She pointed to the café. "Is she inside?"

He shook his head. Fresh tears brewed in his eyes. "She . . . she told me to wait. But my mum . . . she didn't come for me."

A terrible suspicion crept into her thoughts. Surely the boy's mother would not have left a young child alone on these streets. Had she come to harm?

"How long have you been waiting?"

His small shoulders lifted and fell. "Don't know." One small hand moved to his belly. He raised luminous dark eyes to hers. "So hungry."

There was no telling how long the child had been without food. Given his tattered coat, he may have lacked for nourishment even before his mother walked away and left him here.

"If you come inside with me, I'll make sure you get something in your tummy."

"Would ye now?" The coarse male voice from the shadows in the alley startled Belle. Instinctively, she reached for the boy. Her heart raced. She'd do whatever it took to protect the tot from the lanky man whose features she could not quite make out.

But the child slipped out of her grasp. He darted away, his little legs carrying him at a pell-mell pace into the darkness of the alley.

"No," she called after him. "Stay with me. It's not safe—"

"Ye're right about that," the figure in the shadows said with a low chuckle under his breath. "But ye've no need to be concerned . . . not about my wee brother."

A young man—lad seemed a more apt description—emerged. He carried himself with the air of a street tough, but the light fuzz on his chin betrayed his youth. Why, he didn't look to be long out of boyhood. In another place, another time, she might have sponsored a gala to raise funds on behalf of the downtrodden. Like him.

But this youth, and the pair of hoodlums behind him, were not relying on charity.

No, they were prepared to take what they wanted.

Her breath hovered in her throat. Perhaps, with luck, they'd take one look at her bedraggled cape and dismiss her as too poor to be worth their time.

As with everything else that night, luck was most definitely *not* on her side.

The hooligan eyed her curiously, appearing to sense the apprehension she could not entirely hide. His gaze trailed from her cloak to the white silk now dragging upon the dirt of the pavement. His pale blue eyes narrowed, and his fingers brushed over the fabric.

Belle jerked back, and a curious look spread over his hard-beyond-his-years features. He shot his companions a glance. "That's quality, mates. Now, isn't this a puzzle?"

He reached for her again. This time, she smacked his hand away. The rotter flashed an ugly smile and brandished a blade he'd palmed in his other hand.

She took a step back, then another, until the wall of brick at her back boxed her in. Summoning her courage, she hiked her chin. An open show of fear would only embolden this young tough.

"Hand it over." He met her gaze. "Don't make me hurt ye."

Belle clutched her reticule tightly within her closed fingers as he caught the edge of her cloak and peeled back the fabric. "Ye're a generous miss," he went on, his tone brash and cold. "Ye wouldn't want *us* to go hungry now, would ye?"

With that, he snatched at the purse she'd tethered to her wrist by its braided cord. When she pulled away, he caught her arm, twisting hard until a soft cry of pain escaped her. Seizing the moment, he deftly sliced through the cord. A cold-eyed grin pulled at his mouth as he dangled the velveteen bag before her.

"You can't take that," she blurted out, shocking even herself with the force of her words.

He flashed the folding knife as he leered at her. "Ye're bloody lucky I don't take more."

Raw laughter burst out from the ruffians in the alley. The hoodlum flashed an ugly parody of a smile before he turned away, his prize in hand, and bolted down the alley. The young lad she'd believed lost ran along with the toughs as swiftly as his little legs could carry him until one of them scooped him up and they continued on their way.

Good heavens.

Belle's heartbeat hammered in her ears. Only then, after the ruffian had dashed away with her last shilling, did the shock of what had happened hit her with full force. She'd been in true danger—danger far beyond the loss of her meager purse. While she had faced the threat, her fear had lingered beneath the surface, not fully showing itself until now. Her knees felt suddenly weak. The sounds of her pounding heartbeat and the thief's crude laughter lingered in her ears. Thankfully, the ruffian and his accomplices had been concerned with stealing her coins and nothing more. She'd been quite vulnerable, more than she'd realized. If they'd had other foul deeds in mind, she might well have ended up cold and dead in the alley.

The very thought chilled her. She had allowed herself to be drawn into a trap. The sweet-faced tot had been nothing more than a lure.

Oh, she'd been such a fool. But how could she have ignored a young child, alone and teary-eyed? Truth be told, she worried over the lad, even now. What kind of life could a little boy experience on these streets, used as bait by a thief and his rowdy companions? Would the thief use the coins he'd stolen for food? Or would the stolen funds be used for far more nefarious purposes?

Thoughts racing through her mind, she dragged in a breath, and then another, as if that might calm her. A day earlier, she would have willingly pressed money into a hungry lad's hand for nourishment and shelter. But now . . . now she could not even afford a bed upon which to rest for the night. Nor a meal to fill her own empty stomach.

The door to the café creaked open. A woman with a tumble of gray hair pinned atop her head stood arms akimbo, eyeing Belle as though she were some sort of vermin set to infest the establishment.

"Move along, miss." Her voice was gruff and hard. "I don't need yer type bothering my customers."

Yer type? Belle blinked. What was this ruddy-faced woman insinuating? Hours earlier, the woman would've welcomed Belle into her modest café. But now . . . well, heaven only knew what she thought Belle was up to. Throwing a quick glance toward the dirt-crusted hem of her once pristine silk dress, she could scarcely fault the proprietor for the misunderstanding.

Another crackle of lightning lit the sky. "I've been robbed," Belle said, thinking she might inspire a touch of compassion. "Might I come in . . . until the storm passes?"

The woman stared at her. Her cold gaze raked over Belle. Seeming to assess the quality of the fabric in her dress, soiled as it was, she scrunched her nose and gave a dismissive shake of her head. "Stealing some fine lady's gown . . . I will *not* tolerate a thief. I run a quality establishment."

"I am *no* thief." Belle squared her shoulders, meeting the proprietor's cold gaze. "This dress was made for me."

The woman shrugged. "Made for ye, eh?" She chuckled. "And

I'm the queen's lady in waiting, disguising myself by stirring pots of stew every night."

Belle held her voice steady. "Please, you don't understand."

The woman's brows hiked. "I understand all I need to know." The coldness in her expression spoke louder than her words. "I meant what I said. Move along." She glanced behind her, at something or someone Belle could not see. "Before ye regret—"

As a fresh rumble of thunder drowned out the proprietor's words, Belle nodded her acceptance. Turning away, defeat washed over her.

My, she'd certainly gotten herself into a fix this time, hadn't she?

Behind her, lightning lit the sky. This time, the strike was nearly upon her. Far too close for comfort.

The faint rattle of wheels in the distance drifted to her ears. She glanced toward the sound. *Oh, my.* A large midnight-black coach headed toward her at a breakneck pace.

Another bolt of lightning crackled through the air. This time, the strike was close.

Too close for comfort.

Her heart and her thoughts raced. While lightning crackled against the ominous gray sky, the sounds of the carriage grew louder. Nearer. She could hear the clop of the horses' hooves against the cobbles. At this distance, she could barely make out the man at the reins, especially the distinctive feathered cap the driver had worn like a uniform.

A thunderclap seemed to shake the air itself. The dark gray clouds opened. Suddenly, cold, wet drops pelted her face. She clutched her cloak around her, but the thin wool was no match for the downpour. She'd soon be soaked.

But that was not the worst of her problems. No, the midnight-black carriage barreling down the street once again claimed the dubious honor.

She needed shelter. And she had to find a place to hide. At least until the coach and its occupants had barreled on its way.

Suddenly, the rowdy tavern across the road did not seem so unsuitable.

Pulling her hood lower to conceal her features, Belle hurried across the street. As she rushed toward the sound of the piano player and off-key warbler, she braced herself for the worst. There was no telling what she'd encounter in a pub whose proprietor described it as a lair. And for rogues, no less.

But that didn't matter. Not now.

Bundling her cloak around her, she pulled open the tavern's stout door and darted inside the alcove. And promptly collided with a man. With his broad, hard-as-stone chest, to be precise. But not just any man. *No.* Not on this night, when her fortunes continued to spiral from bad to worse.

Tonight, it had to be *him.*

She stared up at the tall, dark-haired man whose powerful, immovable object of a body had halted her frantic dash.

Jon Mason.

Good heavens. My luck cannot be this *bad.*

He'd rested his hands on her shoulders, gently stilling her. Those dark brown eyes of his were so very familiar. So very unforgettable.

For his part, he gazed down at her, seeming to regard her as if she had just arrived from another planet. Slowly, his brows lifted. Not quite to his hairline, but to the shock of coppery brown strands over his forehead that had escaped the style he'd neatly combed with just enough pomade. A slight semblance of a smile played on the full mouth she knew only too well.

After all, it wasn't all that long ago when she'd kissed those very lips.

"Hello, Miss Frost." He cocked his head in that assessing way of his, both infuriating and ridiculously appealing. "I must say, I am surprised to see you here tonight." His dark eyes narrowed. "And in such a beautiful ensemble."

This cannot be happening.

But it was.

Perhaps she could pretend he was mistaken. Would he fall for it if she claimed he'd confused her for someone else? Or perhaps . . . just perhaps . . . this might be a good time to feign a convenient case of amnesia.

No. She dismissed the panic-driven notions as quickly as they flitted into her brain. Jon Mason did not possess a gullible bone in his body. A West End thespian could not pull off a ruse on this man who prided himself on his razor-sharp logic.

So, as she usually did—before she'd met the scoundrel who now chased her through the streets of London, at least—Belle met the truth of the situation head-on.

"Hello," she managed through half-gritted teeth. "I am feeling a touch of shock as well."

His keenly intelligent eyes gleamed with curiosity as he tilted his head a bit more. At this rate, he risked getting a crick in his neck.

Dropping his hands to his sides, he took a step back and allowed his gaze to rather boldly sweep over her. For a moment, he idly stroked his chin, affecting the look of a man deep in thought. His attention settled on the delicate lace trim on the sleeves of the dress peeking out from beneath her plain cloak.

"Tell me this, Arabelle," he said, the faintest hint of amusement in his expression. "Are my eyes deceiving me, or are you wearing a . . . a wedding dress?" A little frown crinkled the area between his dark brows. "A rather soggy one, at that."

Good heavens. Every time she'd believed this night could not get any worse, it had done precisely that. Well, there was no point trying to evade the question.

"Why yes, as a matter of fact, I am." She lowered her voice even as she held her tone steady. "Given the pouring rain, I don't expect I will need to explain the *soggy* state of the fabric."

Nodding his agreement, he scratched his chin. "I suppose the detail that puzzles me is the very fact that you're wearing such a gown in the first place."

Through the leaded glass window behind Jon's broad back,

she caught a flash of black beneath the gas lamp. A sudden jolt of apprehension coursed through her. Had the driver spotted her when she made her way to the tavern?

"It's quite a long story." She dropped her voice nearly to a whisper and moved to stand by the window.

"Undoubtedly," he said, joining her there. "Looking for the groom?"

Raising up on her toes, she peered into the night. The telltale whinny of horses permeated the thick glass. *Oh, dear.* Her stomach sank. She could not see the conveyance. Had the driver maneuvered it out of sight?

The taste of fear rose to the back of her throat. If the driver—and the occupant of the coach—had concealed the carriage in the darkness of the alley, they likely knew she was here.

And they would come after her.

Her mind raced. A season earlier, Jon Mason had been the last man on earth she would've turned to for . . . well, for anything. She would not have asked the arrogant cad to pass the sugar bowl so that she might sweeten her tea. The man was a rogue—a rogue who'd kissed her breathless, then walked away to attend his precious business as if she'd meant absolutely nothing to him.

But that was then. Desperate times called for desperate measures.

At the moment, Jon was her best hope.

Heaven help her.

Chapter Two

I N HIS THREE decades of life, Jon Mason had seen his fair share of surprising sights. God knew he could fill time at the pub over a pint or two recalling his marriage-averse sister's escapades as she'd led the *heiress hunters* who had been the bane of her existence on a not-so-merry chase. Until Macie had exchanged vows with the one man on the planet she did *not* wish to outrun, her unconventional, suitor-repellent ensembles had raised many an eyebrow—including his own. But even she had never thought to make her way through London in a rain-soaked wedding gown, its silk hem caked with dust and dirt and whatever other muck was on the street.

In the days since he'd returned to the city from an uneventful trip to Cardiff, he'd heard talk that Arabelle Frost had made her way to London. After dodging merger-minded tycoons and down-on-their-luck dukes alike, the New York ice princess had finally embarked on the pilgrimage American heiresses were evidently obliged to make before they settled down to domestic bliss with some questionably lucky—and, of course, nobly titled—Englishman.

But what in blazes was she doing here, rain dripping from the tattered cloak that covered her hair, in a pub which bore no resemblance to the elegant restaurants she fancied?

She'd bolted through the door like a madwoman. In the first moments after she'd crashed into him, he had questioned his own eyes. Surely this was not the *never-a-hair-out-of-place* social butterfly he'd first encountered in Manhattan. The prim beauty he'd known would not have risked so much as a crease in her pristine—and expensive—taffeta and velvet dresses, much less drag silk through the grime of the London streets. He'd gazed down at her then, searching her face, not caring if he seemed uncouth.

One look in her sapphire eyes was all it took.

One look, and he knew the truth.

This woman in a soggy wedding gown and ragged cape was indeed the dollar princess he'd come to know as Belle.

Now that he knew who'd plowed into his chest with a resounding thud, the questions were even more confounding. By God's teeth, why had she rushed into the Rogue's Lair, of all places, with the devil at her heels?

And why, beneath the cool veneer she affected like a shield, was there fear she could not entirely disguise in those unforgettable blue eyes?

"Do you intend to tell me why you're here?" he asked, unconcerned if he came off as overly blunt. She already knew patience was not his strong suit.

She gave a quick nod, and he saw her throat constrict. "Eventually." Her gaze slid back to the window. "Now, I need a place to hide."

"What in blazes do you mean?"

Her attention darted to the tavern's stout front door. "Precisely what I said. I must find somewhere to go . . . somewhere I won't be seen . . . and quickly."

Through the thick window glass, he heard the sounds of horses shuffling with restless energy. Yet, he saw no carriage. Bloody peculiar.

A tall, stone-faced man in a caped coat came into view. Walking with brisk steps toward the tavern, he turned his head to say something to a burly man in a plain coat and a driver's cap who struggled to keep pace.

As she glanced toward the window, the color drained from her face. Clearly, she had recognized the men.

"I'll be in a true fix," she whispered. "I must go. Now."

"Come with me." He caught Belle's hand in his and ushered her through the alcove, past the painted door which led to the tavern floor. The pub was filled with their regular patrons. Some of the blokes were singing along with the piano player, while most of the others were engaged in boisterous conversation. Still, it wouldn't do for curious men to get a good look at the conspicuously dressed new arrival. Angling his body to shield her from question-filled eyes, he quickly led her to the back of the tavern and up the stairs to his private office on the second floor.

Despite her cumbersome dress, she made quick work of the steps. For the life of him, he could not figure out how women managed to maneuver the layers of skirts and petticoats without taking a tumble. But she moved at a feverish pace, unhindered by the abundant fabric swishing about her ankles.

As they reached the landing, the loud creak of the tavern door below had the effect of an alarm. She stiffened and turned to the noise. The notes of a deep, decidedly cultured male voice drifted to their ears.

Belle froze.

Her eyes widened, and she went unnaturally still. As an instinctive, rather confounding desire to protect her reared its head, he gently tucked an arm around her. Motioning to the room at the end of the corridor, he led her to his private office and escorted her inside. Since he'd become an investor in the tavern, he'd kept this particular space as a quiet sanctuary, a retreat from the chaos of his everyday life. Now, the small chamber would serve as a hiding place for a woman he'd never thought to see again after the morning when he'd boarded a steamer and sailed out of New York harbor.

Life was indeed bloody strange.

He closed the door behind him and turned to Belle. Her complexion had pinkened a bit, an improvement on her ghostly pallor. But the tense set of her features betrayed her fear.

"Who are those men?" he asked.

"One of them is the driver of the coach. His name is Roderick."

"And the other?"

She laced her fingers nervously, her gaze dropping to the loose knot of digits. Her lips thinned to a slash. "Lord Gideon Kentsworth."

The name was vaguely familiar, but he couldn't place it. Not that it mattered. He didn't give a damn about his title. Judging from the effect the smug-faced stoat had on Belle, the bastard had no place here. He wouldn't hesitate to toss him out on his pretentious arse.

"It's clear the man is not here to sample our ale." Jon searched her face. "What does he want?"

"Well, you see . . . he is the groom." She brushed a damp curl behind her ear and appeared to gulp a nervous breath. "And he's come after me."

GROOM. SELDOM HAD a word tasted as bitter on Belle's tongue as that single syllable. Lifting her chin, she forced herself to meet Jon's questioning gaze.

His brown eyes narrowed ever so slightly, as if he debated whether his own ears had deceived him. "The groom?"

"He intended to become a groom," she said. "But he has not yet succeeded . . . not this time."

"Not *yet*." Jon rubbed the back of his neck as if he'd developed a sudden ache. "And not *this time*."

"It's a rather complicated story. There's no time to explain. Not now."

His dark brows drew together. "But you are still . . . Miss Frost?"

"Most definitely," she said, allowing herself a little smile. "I would not wed the cur if he were the last man in London. On the planet, for that matter."

Jon nodded his understanding. "But he thinks to change your view on the subject?"

Gideon's chilling words before she'd fled the townhouse echoed in her thoughts. Belle dropped her gaze to her mud-caked shoes. Could she trust Jon with the whole truth?

Pulling in a low breath, she struggled to calm her thoughts. At this point, she had little reason to have faith in the man. When Jon had rushed her out of sight to his private office, he'd likely reacted out of instinct. Even rogues possessed a degree of gallantry, didn't they?

But he had no pressing need to know the ugly truth behind Gideon's pursuit. The less Jon Mason knew, the better.

"In a manner of speaking," she said without emotion.

Her attention drifted to the dirt on her once-white skirt. The dress had been beautiful, a symbol of her hope for a contented future. Now, hours after she'd stood before the dressmaker who'd sewn the final flourishes of lace on the gown, she could scarcely abide the sight of it. Foolishly, she'd believed Gideon's performance. She'd thought he'd seen more than her father's fortune when he looked into her eyes.

How very mistaken she'd been. Thank heaven she'd discovered the truth. Before it was too late.

Jon's brows knit together, the expression he made when he wasn't entirely pleased about something or other. Of course, he knew she wasn't telling him everything. Jon Mason was many things. But a fool was not one of them.

"I'll see what he's up to." Jon's voice was gruff as he went to the door. "Turn the latch. Do not unlock it for anyone except me."

A fresh rush of fear washed over her. She swallowed hard against it. "Do be careful."

"You've nothing to worry about," he said, confident as ever.

"I know his kind."

A knot in Belle's stomach tightened. "I don't think you do."

His gaze met hers and held for a long moment. "I do . . . better than you know."

Moments after the door closed behind him, Belle locked the door and went to the window. Concealing herself behind the thick curtain, she peered down to the street below, watching the ordinary comings and goings from the pub and its surrounding enterprises. The torrential rain had stopped, allowing a clear view from her vantage point. Suddenly, she spotted the carriage rumbling along the street. Gideon had gone on his way.

She was safe.

At least, for the moment.

Still, she peered into the night, watching for some sign of the coach's return. Gideon would not give up so easily. Of that, she had no doubt. Did he intend to search every hotel? Every inn? Any place where she might take refuge?

Gideon knew full well the predicament she faced. When she'd fled her aunt's home, she'd left nearly everything behind. Clothing. Spending money. Even her cherished, exceedingly worn volume of *Pride and Prejudice*. All stored within her locked steamer trunk, now well out of her reach in the plush appointed chamber in which she'd stayed as a guest.

She'd likely never see any of those possessions again. At least, not until her parents returned from their expedition to Egypt. Perhaps then, Papa would set the jackals straight. But then again, she didn't even want Papa to know the truth. She had been so very gullible. Mama would understand the longings of her heart. But Papa . . . now, he was another story entirely.

Belle toyed nervously with the lace at her throat, her fingertips brushing against the silver chain and paste-jewel pendant she'd carried for good luck. Her grandmother had gifted her the necklace on her thirteenth birthday, and even now, she couldn't help but smile as her fingers glanced over the faux sapphires. While the necklace would fetch very little in coin, its true value could not be measured. Thank heaven she'd had the presence of mind to snatch the cherished piece from her trunk before she'd made her escape.

A light rap at the door interrupted her thoughts. The low notes of Jon's voice followed, and she crossed the room and unfastened the latch.

"They're gone," he said without emotion.

"Thank heaven."

"You can thank Murray, the barkeep. He thinks fast on his feet, responded to their questions as though the pair of them were daft, and sent them on their way."

Belle continued to toy with the necklace. Since she'd been a girl, the very feel of it against her skin had soothed her anxious nerves. "Did they speak with anyone else? Any of the patrons who might've seen me?"

"The place was filled with our regular blokes tonight. If anyone spotted you with me, they'd have seen no reason to reveal it to a stranger, a high-and-mighty nob at that."

"Well, that is a relief."

"Unfortunately, I suspect it is only a temporary respite." His blunt tone was somehow comforting, if only for its honesty, its utter lack of artifice.

A twinge of alarm prickled over her skin. "You think they will return?"

"I don't expect they are about to stop looking. They'll likely be out until they've exhausted the logical possibilities." Jon went to the cabinet behind his desk, opened a crystal decanter, and poured a splash of liquor into a tumbler. "I would offer you a drink, but I suspect you haven't yet had a proper supper."

A proper supper. Goodness, when she'd run from Gideon and the scheming, sweet-faced jackal she'd so foolishly trusted, she hadn't had time for a hurried bite of a sandwich, let alone an actual meal. She'd had not given any thought to eating, not even when the child so movingly pleaded his hunger. But suddenly, she could not deny her stomach's own quiet yet insistent pangs.

"Your suspicion would be correct," she admitted.

He motioned to the plush settee between the window and a towering bookcase. "Please, make yourself comfortable."

She glanced down at her soggy dress and cloak and shook her head. "I wouldn't want to chance ruining the upholstery."

He regarded her thoughtfully for a moment. "It's only rain."

"Rain . . . and heaven only knows what else from the street."

He went to the low chest beneath the window, retrieved a knitted blanket, and splayed it over the cushions. "This sofa has been used for many a year. I suspect it will readily withstand the task of comfortably seating a slightly soggy American."

She followed him to the settee. "Thank you." Her fingers went to the fastenings of her cloak. "I suppose I should remove this scratchy thing."

"That would be wise." Jon took the cape from her hand. Holding it by the hood as if it were a curiosity, he draped it over a hook on a coat rack. A wry smile played on his mouth. "Somehow, this does not suit your usual tastes. As I recall, you possessed a fondness for fine wool and velvet." He plucked a wilted white petal from the edge of the collar. "There is a story here."

"There is," she agreed wearily. "I convinced a flower peddler to sell it to me."

Jon eyed the rough-woven wool. "I suspect she got the better of the deal."

"She was well compensated, but I was exceedingly grateful. I needed something, anything, to conceal this horrid dress."

His gaze glanced over her from the lace at her throat to the newly ragged hem. He rubbed his chin, looking as if a comment perched on the tip of his tongue. Still studying her, he raked a hand through his hair.

"So, are you going to tell me what in blazes is going on?" he said, eyes narrowing. "Or am I to pretend to enjoy the suspense?"

"It's quite simple, really." She forced herself to meet and hold his gaze. "The man intends to acquire a wife. At one point, I thought I was amenable to the idea. But . . . I've had a change of heart."

"A rather sudden one, I'd say."

"Not so very sudden," she admitted. "But my decision to finally follow my instincts came fast as a lightning strike."

"I must say this is a first—a runaway bride." His deep brown eyes flashed with interest. "How bloody original."

"As you can imagine, *he* was not pleased."

Jon rubbed his chin, as if to ease the tense set of his jaw. "Given the questions the high-and-mighty rotter was asking, I'd say it's not that simple."

Belle pictured the cold fury in Gideon's eyes when she'd made it clear she had no intention of spending her life with a cad like him. She gulped against the fresh pain of betrayal. "What *that man* wants does not signify. Not now." She pulled back her shoulders and faced him directly. "Not ever."

"We have some matters to discuss" He gestured to the settee, then took a seat in a leather wing chair and stretched out his long legs. Belle settled onto the cushions and arranged her cumbersome skirts around her.

Seeing the questions in his eyes, Belle squared her shoulders and met his gaze. "I do realize how very unusual this all must seem."

Especially to a man like Jon. Heaven only knew how much he prided himself on his orderly, methodical approach to life.

"That is one way to phrase it," he said, his tone confoundingly bland.

"In any case, I didn't plan to rush in here. And I certainly did not anticipate running into you." She glanced down at her folded hands. "I realize things did not end well between us."

He quirked a brow. "As I recall, our parting was amicable."

Amicable? Belle quirked a brow of her own as she mentally echoed his words. "I suppose that's one way to phrase it."

"Fate does indeed possess a sense of humor." He studied her over steepled fingers. "Or should that be irony?"

"Perhaps a bit of both," she managed, gathering her thoughts. "Well, I suppose I should get to the point. I really must be on my way. When I took refuge here, it was never my intention to pose a bother, but I'm in a bit of a fix. If I might make one request of you."

"And what might that be, Arabelle?" he said, enunciating her name with infuriatingly precise manner of his. "Might I see you to your residence?"

An invisible fist dug into the pit of her stomach. "I'm afraid that is not an option."

His mouth thinned as he nodded. "If you prefer someone other than me to escort you, I will arrange for a trusted conveyance to see you to wherever you're staying."

"It's not that." The raw truth felt like a burning in the back of her throat. "You see, at the moment, I have no place to go."

His forehead furrowed as his dark brows knit together. "Do you care to explain?"

She swallowed against the emotion welling within her. Now that the shock of the afternoon had faded, a dull ache penetrated to the bone. But still, she had her freedom. She would be no one's fool.

"I was staying at the private residence of a woman I believed to be trusted family." The grating notes of Gideon's taunting laughter played in her thoughts. "Suffice it to say, I was mistaken."

"I assume the situation is complicated," Jon said.

"That would be an understatement."

He nodded his understanding. "And your parents? Or your brother?"

"Mama and Papa are in the final weeks of a journey to Egypt. In her last telegram, Mama indicated they were about to embark on a tour of the Nile. Jeremy is happily keeping the family train on the tracks back in New York."

"So, you are here in the city on your own?"

"For the moment." She brushed away a flicker of doubt she

could not afford to dwell on. "As you can see, I find myself in a bit of a predicament. The same fate that displayed its rather trying sense of humor in bringing me here, of all places, has left me on the streets of London without a shilling—or even a penny, for that matter—to my name."

"A dollar princess without a penny." Jon fiddled with his cuff links. "Another first."

"Well, I see little has changed since we last met. You are *still* exasperating." Belle clipped the words between her teeth.

"Upon that occasion, I believe you used the term *vexing*. I rather prefer it."

Belle squared her shoulders. A flush of heat rose to her cheeks. If she were in New York—if she were surrounded by familiar sights and sounds, by family and friends—she would march out of this office and never look back. But the reality of the situation called for a cooler head.

"Exasperating. Irksome. Aggravating. Vexing. Nettlesome." She came to her feet, planting her hands on her hips. "Take your choice, Mr. Mason."

The faintest hint of amusement played on his mouth. "I believe you left out 'confounding.'"

"Indeed." A smile tugged at her lips, despite her best effort to suppress it.

For a long moment, he appeared to study her. The look of amusement faded, replaced by a far more serious expression.

"So, tell me this, Arabelle . . . the full truth. A man like Kentsworth is not likely to carry on like a lovestruck schoolboy." His gaze locked with hers, and he scraped a hand over the dark stubble on his jaw. "Why in blazes is the rotter chasing you all over the city?"

Chapter Three

GOOD GOD, *SHE is a beautiful woman.* Even a smudge of dirt on her face, the rain weighing down those long, honey-blonde curls, and an unflattering gown dulled by street grime could not hide that essential truth. Even now—as she glared at him with those gorgeous blue eyes, her rosy mouth taut with a touch of anger—Belle was a true diamond.

Bloody hell, why had he questioned her so bluntly? *Why in blazes is the rotter chasing you all over the city?* He'd phrased the question too harshly. Even to his own ears, his words came off as brusque. Perhaps even callous. He had not wanted that. He had not wanted to hurt her. Nor to anger her. But now, he'd managed to do both.

Sometimes, even he had to admit he was an absolute arse.

Well, there was nothing to be done about it now. Leaning back in his chair, he looked at the scotch in his glass. Murray would soon bring her meal, and perhaps the tension between them might ease. But for now, he took a drink as she uttered a terse reply.

"I've already told you." She glanced away, seeming to study the pattern on his carpet. "We had planned to speak our vows after my parents' return. But I had a change of heart."

"There's nothing more to it?" he pressed.

"Nothing more?" She let out a little sigh, a flicker of anger in her gaze. "Shouldn't that be enough?"

Jon took another drink. He'd seen the distress on her face, the way the question she posed seemed to cause her pain. "Evidently, not in the bloke's eyes."

"Quite so," she agreed, her tone a bit more relaxed. "He was utterly shocked when I refused to meekly follow his dictates."

Jon cocked a brow. "The man does not know you well, does he?"

"Truth be told, it was I who did not know him. Not at all." She spoke the words as though they revealed an ugly truth. "But that does not matter now. I do feel I can breathe more easily now. That chapter is over."

Jon studied her for a long moment, seeing the truth. Even she did not believe her own words.

He allowed her a moment's pause before pressing forward. "So, do you have any idea of what comes next?"

"Not precisely." She rose, turning about to take in all four corners of his office. As she met his gaze, a spark of inspiration lit her eyes. "Unless . . ."

"Belle . . ." He suspected he knew the direction of her thoughts. "What are you thinking?"

A smile brightened her face. "Perhaps I might stay here."

He regarded her for a long, speechless moment. "In my office?" he ground out finally.

She offered a hopeful shrug. "It might work." She gestured to the small sofa. "At least I would have a safe place to bed down for the night. After all, you've even laid out a blanket."

"My dear Miss Frost—" He rubbed his neck, kneading out a sudden ache. "Have you gone daft?"

She hiked her chin. "It is not such a farfetched idea. Not really. After all, I don't take up much space."

"The volume of space you occupy does not signify." He plowed his fingers through his hair. "I cannot vouch for your safety here. And I do not intend to spend the night sleeping on the floor, playing bodyguard."

"That would not be necessary," she countered. "I presume

the doors have stout locks."

"There are too many access points—too many panes of glass which could be broken by an intruder. You would be far too vulnerable."

"Gideon does not know I am here," she pointed out. "You saw him leave."

He shook his head. "It is out of the question."

"In that case, I shall have to find suitable accommodations at a hotel." She let out another little sigh. "However, as you know, I am currently penniless. If you might advance me the funds to cover my stay—likely no more than a fortnight—and a small amount to provide for meals and a new dress or two during that time, I would be in your debt."

He stood and walked to the window. Mulling the idea, he peered down into the night. "You think to hide in a hotel in London?"

"I see no other option."

"The bastard was determined to find you tonight. What makes you think he won't keep looking?"

"I suppose I shall have to take a chance." She pulled in a breath. "Now, will you assist me in reserving proper accommodations?"

Jon turned back to her. "Absolutely not."

Her eyes went wide, betraying that his answer had taken her aback. She nibbled her lower lip. "Very well, then." She looked to be holding back tears. "I suppose I should be on my way."

"I can't let you do that, Arabelle." He reached for her, placing his hand gently on her forearm. "I must insist—you're coming home with me."

BELLE JERKED AWAY from his touch as if his hand had transformed into a scorpion's stinging tail. "Coming home?" she repeated his words like a confused parrot. "With you?"

The slightest hint of amusement touched his lips. "Doubting your own ears again, are you?"

Squaring her shoulders, she pulled in a breath. "I do wish someone had informed me that you'd gone mad."

"Mad?" His gaze trailed over her dress. "Fine words coming from a woman running about London in a wedding gown."

"Well, this *woman in a wedding gown* is walking away. I knew you were quite full of yourself. But I had not believed you to be a complete heel."

He met her accusation with a deliberately bland look. "So now I am a heel?" he said. "I rather preferred mad. It's infinitely more interesting."

"Oh, you are mad as a hatter." She shot him a scowl. "But I'd never believed you were a scoundrel who would seek to capitalize upon . . . my desperate circumstance."

"Scoundrel? I rather like the sound of that." A faint smile curved his full mouth. "But we both know it would take more than this fix you find yourself in to drive you to desperation. You're like a blasted cat with nine lives."

"And I am only on my first." She snatched her cloak off the hook and went to the door, but he stood before it, blocking the space.

Why, the absolute gall of the man.

He slowly shook his head. "Leaving now would be a mistake."

"You think to stop me?" She planted her hands on her hips. "Have you forgotten you are not dealing with a fragile English rose?"

"Ah, an American princess, well-acquainted with the mean streets of New York." His voice was low and edged with gravel. "How could I ever forget?"

"Surely you do not think to keep me here against my will."

"Good God, no," he said as if the idea were the most idiotic notion he'd ever heard. "Nothing so theatrical."

Belle met his eyes. "Well, you don't have to act as if the possibility is so very absurd."

"The very thought of holding a woman against her will—any woman, much less a dollar princess from Buffalo—is bloody exhausting. If I wanted to keep you here with me, I could find a more efficient means of persuasion."

"You haven't changed a bit, have you?" She hiked her chin. "Always so very sure of yourself."

"One of my better qualities, or so I'm told."

Standing this close, she could detect the subtle notes of shaving soap on his throat, could see the bristles of new beard darkening the strong line of his jaw. "I'd hoped you might wish to help me, if only out of a sense of chivalry."

His eyes crinkled at the corners. "Do I look like a blasted knight?"

No, as a matter of fact, he did not. *Dash the luck*. Jon Mason was infinitely more appealing than any image she'd ever conjured of Sir Lancelot. With his lean and sleekly muscular physique, Jon wore his immaculately tailored linen shirt and wool jacket with an utter lack of conceit, despite the way the garments displayed the powerful build of his broad shoulders and chest. It tasted like too-tart lemon to admit it, even to herself, but the man was a dashingly handsome specimen of masculinity, a man who did not need to cloak himself in a suit of clunky old armor. But she certainly couldn't reveal *that* truth, now could she?

"My inclination to help you is not rooted in chivalry," he went on. "As far as persuading you to stay as a guest in my home, it would appear I have a simple technique at my disposal."

"Do you, now?"

"Before you further question my motives, I suggest you take a look." He crossed the room to the window. "But stand to the side, behind the curtain."

"Very well," she agreed. Slipping the drapery to the side, she peered through the glass to the street below. "There's nothing there."

"Look to the alley."

Her gaze tracked the street from the tavern to the café across the road. Gaslight illuminated what looked to be a large, exceedingly sturdy horse. Precisely the kind that pulled Gideon's carriage. Trailing her attention along the street past the café, she spotted the silhouettes of two men.

Oh, dear.

The driver with his substantial nose and distinctive cap stood out, even in shadow. Another man walked at his side. Not Gideon. This ox of a man was taller, broader, and in his hand, he carried what looked to be a patrolman's nightstick.

Her heart raced. For the first time that night, a sense of defeat washed over her. Gideon wasn't going to give up. And now, he'd enlisted a brute who might even wear a lawman's badge.

Suddenly, the room seemed to tilt beneath her feet, if only a bit. The cloak in her hand fell to the floor. Jon's hand pressed gently to her waist, his fingers splaying against her ribs to steady her.

"The finest hotel in London will not be safe. Not now," he said, leading her back to the settee. "Not until I arrange proper security."

"I suppose you're right," she admitted, nervously arranging her skirts as she settled upon the cushions. "This is worse," she managed. "Much more difficult than I'd expected."

He gazed down at her, his brow furrowed, but without a look of judgment. "When you left, did you think he would come after you?"

"I didn't *think.*" Swallowing against a fresh rush of emotion, she met his dark eyes. "I simply ran."

"Bloody hell," he murmured, more to himself than to her. "Are you going to tell me why?"

She couldn't speak the words. Couldn't share the ugly truth with this man who'd suddenly somehow become her safe haven in the storm.

"As I told you, I had a change of heart."

His eyes flashed, and he looked like he was trying not to scowl. "Then tell me the truth. Why is the blighter pursuing you?" His tone was low and gruff. "A man trying to win over a reluctant bride would not send two ruffians to hunt her down like a thief on the run."

Belle pressed her fingers to her temples to massage the growing ache. "I'd truly never imagined you possess a flair for the dramatic."

"You know blasted well that I'm right."

She glanced down at the third finger of her left hand. She'd tossed the emerald betrothal ring in Gideon's smug face.

She wanted nothing from him.

The cad had deceived her, well and truly. His promises had been empty. The tender words he'd spoken had been nothing but lies.

"I have no illusions. The man is neither lovestruck. Nor desperate," she said with a forced calm. "It's quite different from that."

"Then *what* is it?"

She pulled in a low, calming breath. "Gideon is not accustomed to defiance. He is a powerful man."

This time, Jon did scowl. "And judging from the look on your face . . . a dangerous one."

Goodness, he'd always been able to read her expression. And heaven knew she possessed little talent for hiding her emotions. Her brother had once advised her against playing card games where strategy and secrecy were factors. Her features blurted out the secrets she struggled to conceal.

"I suspect that may be the case." She gulped a small breath. "I do not wish to test the theory."

A sharp rap upon the door cut into her words. She jolted, alert for danger, but Jon's slight smile and brisk nod reassured her she had no reason for concern.

"It's Murray," a man announced in a brusque tone.

"Very good." Jon ushered in an older man who carried an

elegant silver tray laden with what appeared to be a late supper.

Tall and lean, with keen eyes and graying hair, the man's gaze swept over Belle's gown. He eyed her with a slightly puzzled expression, as if a question poised on the tip of his tongue. Giving a small shrug, he placed the tray on a side table and gestured toward the thick slices of bread, cheese, and a frosted glass brimming with tea. "I hope this is to yer liking, Miss."

"I thought you might be hungry," Jon explained. "I took the liberty of requesting something plain, but filling."

My, he'd remembered her fondness for simple fare. How very surprising.

"Thank you," she said to both men. "It looks delicious."

"You're quite welcome," the gray-haired man said with a smile. "Do let me know if ye require anything else."

"Thank you, Murray," Jon said as the older man went to the door. "Keep an eye out for the nob and his driver or any other unfamiliar ruffians. Let me know if they return."

"An unpleasant bloke by any measure." Murray's mouth thinned at his words. "Ye can count on me."

"Very good," Jon said as Murray closed the door behind him.

The aroma of food triggered Belle's hunger. Forgoing any pretense of a dainty appetite, Belle took a few hearty bites. While she ate, Jon went to his desk and began to quickly pen notations upon a thick tablet.

When she'd finished the last of the food, he looked up from whatever he'd been writing. Nibbling her chips, she studied his carved features. There was something about the intensity in his eyes that had always drawn her to him. And tonight, as he met her gaze, that intensity was as potent as she'd ever seen it.

"I have come up with a plan," he said in that direct way of his. "But you will have to trust me."

She took a sip of tea. "It would appear I have no choice."

"There is always a choice. But know this, Belle. You will be safe." He regarded her for a long moment, his expression unreadable. "He won't hurt you. On that, you have my word."

Chapter Four

A S A YOUNG man at university, Jon had engaged in numerous bouts of fisticuffs. In truth, brawling would've been a far better word to describe the sport. Bare-knuckled. Uncivilized. Fueled by ale and a need to work off the relentless steam of his existence. He had—for a time, that is—used his fists and the occasional elbow to best his most surly opponents. Rules be damned. Though he now preferred the more civilized environment of the gentleman's boxing club he and his business partner had established, he'd certainly taken his fair share of blows over the years. But now, while escorting Belle to his carriage to depart for his home, he wondered if those long-ago punches had led to some latent madness that might explain what he was about to do.

Not even in a fever dream would he have imagined the Frost Princess dashing through the door of the Rogue's Lair with the devil at her heels. For a moment, he'd marveled at yet another unexpected twist in his life—in the ironic sense of humor the universe possessed that had seen her end up nearly in his arms. Again.

Until he'd seen the fear in her eyes.

Belle hadn't fully explained what in blazes had driven her into the dreary London night—in a drenched bridal gown, of all the blasted things. But whatever had taken place in the hours before she'd sought refuge in the pub had forced her to put aside her *distaste for his very presence,* as she'd phrased it not-so-delicately nearly two years earlier when he'd walked out of her life. What had gone between them in the past was of no consequence now.

He would not leave her in harm's way. Whatever the man she'd run from was after, Jon knew full well that love had nothing to do with it. Over the years, he'd seen enough of the *heiress hunters*—as his sister had dubbed them in the days when she'd been pursued by greedy nobles—shamelessly chasing after a woman as if she were the golden goose.

At the moment, Belle sat across from him in the coach, draped in a coat far too large for her—his overcoat was the only thing on hand at the tavern that could possibly disguise her gown. She'd tucked her hair beneath the flat-brimmed cap the barkeep had offered to conceal her thick, honey-gold tresses. Glancing up from the tightly laced fingers she held in her lap, she met his gaze. Her rosy mouth set in a frown, her expression as glum as one of Henry VIII's unlucky brides on her way to the Tower.

The crack of the reins in the carriage driver's hands drifted through the closed window. Slowly, the wheels rumbled over the cobbles as they departed the tavern. For a time, they rode in silence, though neither was lost in their own thoughts. Rather, he couldn't think of a blasted thing to say. Pressing her on the nature of her predicament would be bad form, and the taut, unyielding set of her mouth made it clear she wasn't ready for anything resembling conversation.

Hours earlier, he could not have imagined this turn of events. Shortly after he'd taken dinner at his residence, he'd headed to the tavern for a brief respite from the newfound chaos that had upended his once orderly existence. He wasn't entirely surprised to encounter her in London. But the circumstances were certainly unexpected.

Given Belle's expression, her thoughts followed a similar path. No wonder, that. Nearly twenty-four months had passed since the days—and nights—when they'd enjoyed a brief interlude while he was in New York. When he'd informed her of his imminent return to England, departing on a steamer within the week, Belle had called him cold-blooded. She'd deemed him a stiff-necked bigwig, so utterly devoted to his family's enterprises that he would not—could not—open his heart to a woman.

Not even to her.

She'd been mistaken on that count. The invisible scar in the vicinity of his chest was proof of that. At times since he'd last laid eyes on her beautiful face—especially during the quiet times at night, when he was alone with his thoughts and a tumbler of whisky—the memories of what he'd left behind taunted him. But he'd learned how to drown them out. There hadn't seemed to be any other choice.

When Belle had bid him farewell, he'd heard the tremor in her voice. He'd seen the sheen of tears in her eyes, tears she'd refused to shed in his presence. He hadn't intended to hurt her. The sight and sound of her pain had cut through him like a dull knife.

But in the end, his parting with the lovely heiress had been rather civilized. No tearful pleas. No dramatic scenes. Nothing beyond a chilly dismissal from her presence.

At the time, he'd brushed aside his every doubt. He'd been so bloody certain he was doing the right thing. His responsibilities lay an ocean away from Manhattan. He'd been honest with her. He'd made her no promises. From the start, he'd made no secret of the fact that his time in America would not be long. Business was business, after all.

Perhaps more correctly, business was his life.

And his life ran best when it was free of complications.

Bloody hell. The sheer irony of the thought gave him a rueful chuckle. If the last months had proven anything, it was that life possessed a blasted warped sense of amusement. Since he was a lad, he'd strived to keep his path even and steady. While his heiress-hunter-averse sister's antics had no doubt brought about a few of the gray hairs on his head, his day-to-day and night-to-night existence had run as precisely as a Swiss clockmaker's gears.

Few detours and distractions. Even fewer surprises. His keen focus on the tasks ahead had kept his life on an efficient course.

Yet since the crisp mid-September day on which he'd marked his thirtieth birthday, the universe had tossed handfuls of sand into those once-precise gears. His orderly life had become anything but. And this—Belle's arrival at the tavern doorstep, dressed as a soggy bride on the run, no less—was the jam on top of the scone.

The carriage hit a rut in the pavement. The soft jolt stirred him from his thoughts. A ray of light from a flickering streetlamp fell over Belle's face, revealing widened eyes that suggested she'd also been jarred from an inner dialogue. She pressed her lips together, as she tended to do when she was deep and thought, then lifted her gaze to his.

"I do appreciate your assistance," she said, her velvety voice quiet. "I'm not accustomed to needing to be rescued."

"I would hardly describe this as a rescue," he countered. "Even if you had not run into me, I suspect you would've landed on your feet."

"I'd like to think so." The notes of uncertainty in her voice seemed very unlike the unflaggingly confident woman he'd known in New York. Her mouth pulled tight with a wry imitation of a smile. "I imagine my brother will enjoy the fact that I am suddenly the *scandalous one*."

Scandalous. He glanced away, out into the night, trying not to grit his teeth at the thoughts whipping through his mind. *Bloody hell.* Was she concerned the events of this night would tarnish her good name?

"What's the worst that could happen?" he said, keeping his tone light. "A proposal of marriage?"

Belle sat bolt upright on the bench, her only sound a little gasp he suspected she'd tried to suppress.

"From you?" she said finally, her tone as incredulous—and taken aback—as if he'd suggested they peel off their garments and jump into the Thames.

He wasn't sure why her shock at the mere thought of him

asking for her hand in marriage caught him off guard. He cleared his throat, affecting a bland tone. "You should not sound so surprised," he said. "It is a rational possibility, given the circumstances."

"Good heavens, that should not be necessary," she scoffed. Was that doubt in her voice? Or an attempt to reassure herself?

He could no longer make out Belle's features within the darkness of the carriage, but he imagined the set of her mouth, the slight thinning of her lips. How well he remembered that look. The last moment when he'd looked upon her face—the night in New York when he'd walked away from her for what he'd thought would be the very last time—she'd tried to hide her sadness with a tight-lipped glare. She had not succeeded. Even now, the regret-tinged memory dug into his gut.

"I shall do whatever is required to preserve your honor," he said, keeping his tone bland.

"My honor?" A rueful little chuckle escaped her. "You weren't so very concerned about such things before . . . in New York."

A heat he hadn't felt in quite a long time pulsed through him at the memory. Suddenly, the tie at his throat felt a bit too snug. He adjusted his collar. Once again, he cleared his throat, buying time, determined she would not rattle him. God only knew she had a talent for ridding him of his good sense.

"In Manhattan, we never slept under the same roof." He kept his reply matter-of-fact.

Another small sound like a sigh escaped her. She seemed to hesitate. And then, she responded with a boldness that caught him off guard.

"As I recall, in those days, you weren't interested in sleeping," she said in a hushed tone. Even though shadows still obscured her face, he could envision the half-smile on her mouth, the subtle curve and parting of her lips that might well tempt a saint.

Her softly spoken words unleashed a fresh current of awareness through his body. She'd certainly spoken the truth. In those days—and nights—in America, he would have entirely forgone sleep if it had meant another hour to drink in the smile in her eyes and the peal of her easy laugh. But that was then. It all seemed another lifetime ago.

He brushed the curtain back and peered into the gaslit street. "Allow me to put your mind at ease," he said, keeping his tone deliberately bland. "These days, I consider a peaceful night to be a luxury to be savored."

"Well, that is a relief." Folding her hands in her lap, she sat up a bit straighter. "And there I was so very worried about being ravished."

"Sadly, I doubt I could summon the energy," he said, countering her prim yet teasing tone.

"Understandable," she said coolly. "The duties of a tycoon must be quite exhausting."

"Indeed." *Though not nearly so exhausting as what lies behind the doors of my home.*

"Still set on conquering the world, one customer at a time?"

"Is there any other way?" he replied. "In any case, there's little reason to be concerned with scandal. You will not be the only female residing in my home."

Bloody hell. If that wasn't an understatement, he didn't know what one was.

"Such concern over my *good name.*" Belle sighed. "It's a lost cause, you know. If anyone spotted me dashing about town tonight, they'd suppose I'd gone mad. That's worse than a mere scandal, now isn't it?"

"You did what you had to do." He wanted to reach for her hand, to comfort her, but he stopped himself. "You'll be safe in my residence. And my housekeeper will be present at all times. She's quite vigilant in the pursuit of her duties."

And an utter busybody who won't miss a bloody thing.

"But what will she think when you return home with a woman—garbed in your overcoat, no less?"

"I'd assume Mrs. Gilroy will find it rather in keeping with recent events."

Her brows quirked, then relaxed as a little sigh escaped her. "I do realize how very unexpected this is."

Unexpected? He pondered the word. Given the events of the past weeks, the word had come to define his life. "I won't argue that." Jon allowed his gaze to sweep over her. "I'd imagine Mrs. Gilroy will be more surprised by the wedding dress than my overcoat."

"Yes, I imagine you've sacrificed your coat to keep some desperate woman or other warm on more than one occasion." She looked as if she fought against a smile. "After all, you are known for your chivalry."

"Do I detect a note of sarcasm?"

"Perhaps." Her lips curved, the slightest semblance of a grin.

"Ah, you wound me." He relaxed against the seat, feeling some of the tension ease from his bones. "Admittedly, you are the first woman in a mud-dappled bridal gown I've ever encountered."

"And perhaps more to the point, the first woman you've thought to *cover up* rather than attempted to inspire her to shed garments."

He cocked a brow. "Might that approach have worked?"

"Not a chance," she said without a moment's hesitation. "Though truth be told, I am looking forward to my first opportunity to be rid of this gown. Provided, of course, there is another dress to take its place."

"I'm sure Mrs. Gilroy will find something that will work, at least for the night."

"I would be ever so grateful for her assistance." Belle glanced down at a bit of tattered lace near her wrist. Jon's attention was drawn to the slight bit of fluff which dangled precariously, evidently held in place by only a few stitches.

"What happened there? How was the lace torn?"

Her brows knit together, and she nibbled her lower lip. "Honestly, I'm not quite sure. Suffice it to say, it has been a difficult night. I'd thought this gown quite lovely," she said, sounding a bit wistful. "But after tonight, I plan to never look upon it again." She turned to the carriage window, peeping out behind the curtain. "Might we discuss this in the morning? I feel an awful megrim brewing."

"Of course," he agreed. Her tone was weary. Sad. And perhaps, a bit angry.

She leaned her head back against the bench and closed her eyes. "All I want to do tonight is rest in a quiet room in a warm house."

Jon smiled to himself. "I must warn you—there is a possibility you may be disappointed."

"I find that highly unlikely," she said without opening her eyes.

"Do you, now?" He chuckled beneath his breath. "Would you care to describe your vision of my residence?"

"It's not much of a challenge, is it? I'd imagine your housekeeper is top-notch, tidy as they come. She undoubtedly keeps the furniture polished, the silver gleaming, and the floors without so much as a speck of debris. The only sounds one might hear are the swishes of a clock's pendulum and perhaps, the crackle of a warm fire in the hearth."

"And not a thing out of place," Jon added, completing the pleasant image.

"I'd think so," she went on. "Quiet. Orderly. A haven for a man who thinks, dreams, and lives for his enterprises."

He cocked a brow. "Is that so?"

"Of course," she said, sounding as if she'd bitten back a laugh of her own. "I cannot imagine there would be any hint of chaos. Unless your sister will be there, engaging in some shenanigan or other."

No, that chapter has closed. "Macie and her husband are gallivanting about Europe with that camera of hers. She is enjoying wedded bliss and driving Finn to distraction."

Belle's mouth dipped at the corners, not quite a frown. "I must say I'm disappointed. I would've liked to have made her acquaintance."

"You may just have your chance. She's expected to return within days."

"Very good," she said. "As for tonight, I've no doubt I shall soon enjoy a peaceful respite from this thoroughly blighted day."

"Or so one can hope."

Blasted shame he did not share her confidence.

Chapter Five

STANDING AT THE foot of the steps of Jon's Mayfair home, Belle studied the gaslit façade of the posh townhouse. Why, the place was just as she'd imagined. A sturdy entry door in gleaming ebony posed a perfect contrast to the precisely laid red brick and mortar walls, while the gleaming brass door knocker provided an elegant statement of refinement without appearing in the least bit ostentatious. A polished brass lamp illuminated the landing at the top of the stairs, revealing a space swept clean of any street dirt, as were each of the steps. The windows were dark—as was to be expected at that hour of the night—save for one window near the door which glowed with the light of a single lamp. All in all, his home was entirely what she had expected.

That was, until he opened the door.

A petite woman with a mass of silver curls spilling out from her frilled cap and a squinty gray gaze stood in the portal, her hand outstretched for the knob. She took a step back, grasping the carved handle of an ebony cane while eyeing them with what looked like a barely repressed scowl.

She slowly shook her head, the reproach in her expression nearly palpable. "Oh, dear. Not another one."

Another one? What in heaven did *that* mean?

"An enthusiastic greeting if ever I've heard one, Mrs. Gilroy." Jon's voice was surprisingly cheerful considering the woman's quietly scornful tone. He escorted Belle into the townhouse, past the woman who now stood with her hands planted on her hips, her well-lined features set with curious intrigue as she followed Belle's every move.

"Awakened from a sound sleep at this hour, I'm not inclined to be enthused about much of anything." Mrs. Gilroy wrung her hands in a knot. "At least this *houseguest* won't be gnawing on the rug." Her brows drew together. "Nor piddling on it, for that matter."

"Well, that is something to be thankful for, isn't it?" Jon replied lightly, his tone teasing.

Belle squared her shoulders and met the woman's cool gaze. She'd been through too much on this horrid night to be cowed by a woman who barely came to her chin. "Indeed, I cannot say I have a propensity toward either act."

"A bit of spirit, eh?" Mrs. Gilroy smiled. "I think I like her." Her eyes narrowed as the soft tinkling of a bell announced the presence of a small, furry dynamo trotting—or would galloping be more accurate?—into the hall. "Pity the same cannot be said of *him.*"

Jon raked a hand through his hair as the dog scurried to greet him. Crouching down, he patted the pup on the head. "Should I ask what he's ruined this time?"

"Nothing tonight." The woman's frown eased, if only a bit. "But I still haven't forgiven him for chomping on my favorite shoes."

Jon tapped a finger to his chin. "As I recall, I purchased a fine pair for you the very next day."

"That ye did," she agreed. "But I'd become quite attached to the others. They were my favorite, ye know."

Jon's gaze trailed to the feet poking out beneath the hem of the woman's flannel robe. "You're referring to the shoes you're wearing?"

"Indeed. The wee beast did not destroy them, but I certainly cannot wear shoes with teeth marks while I'm out and about on my daily errands."

A faint smile tugged at his mouth. "Mrs. Gilroy, since you are awake, I'm in need of your assistance."

"Are ye, now? Well then, that makes us even." The woman's keen-eyed gaze swept Belle, lingering over the formerly pristine white skirt of her gown. She pursed her lips. "I'm needing some assistance to understand why the Frost Princess is here, wearing . . . *that*, no less."

Belle met the woman's questioning gaze, even as she felt her own brows hike. "*Frost Princess*? I hadn't heard that one."

"Ice Princess . . . Frost Princess . . . something like that." Mrs. Gilroy pinned Belle with her hawklike gaze. "Ye're her, aren't ye?"

"My name is Arabelle Frost," she replied, suddenly intrigued. "Have we met?"

The woman regarded her as if she were daft. "Do I look like a society type ye'd be hobnobbing with at some ball or another?"

My, the housekeeper is a cheeky one, isn't she? Not at all what she'd expected. She'd imagined Jon would run a tight ship. But this crabby wisp of a housekeeper definitely did not fit the bill.

"It is possible I'd made your acquaintance," she replied with a little hike of her chin. "After all, I've done more than attend balls while I've been in London."

You certainly have. Belle's thoughts raced. *A charity soiree with some countess or other. A fundraiser for orphans and widows. An impetuous engagement to a scoundrel. And a frantic dash from that very scoundrel's grasp. Ah, yes, you've been a busy Dollar Princess, haven't you?*

"It's near as likely that I'd sprout wings and fly away from this place." Mrs. Gilroy shot Jon a glance. "One more person, or beast, to pick up after, and I might just do that, though I'll be in a carriage, firmly on the ground."

As Mrs. Gilroy uttered the words, the ball of fur on legs dashed over to Belle, sat on its bottom, and regarded her with beseeching brown eyes.

A dog. How very surprising. She'd no idea the business-and-nothing-but-business tycoon had a pet, much less one that possessed teeth capable of chomping down on shoes. Perhaps even more surprising was the large blue bow adorning the silver collar about the pup's neck. She'd certainly never expected to see such a thing on a dog belonging to Jon Mason.

"Come now, Mrs. Gilroy. You are likely the most well-compensated housekeeper in all of London." Jon flashed a smile that might've charmed an ogre. "You know this won't last forever."

"Well, I certainly do hope ye're right," the older woman said with an almost-grudging little smile. "As for ye, Miss Frost, I recognized ye from the morning edition. Yer picture was in yesterday's news. And the evening editions, at least twice. They can't get enough of yer good deeds." Her eyes narrowed again. "And yer engagement with the highbrow nob—as I recall, they dubbed him the Scottish Lord."

Belle gulped. *"That . . . that* was in the papers?"

"Last week, as I recall." Mrs. Gilroy's brow furrowed like a washboard. "Which makes it all the more of a puzzle that ye're here."

Belle nibbled her lower lip. *Drat the luck.* She'd had no inkling the press had been alerted to her impulsive response to Gideon's proposal. Had he—or her conniving aunt—planted the story in the papers? Why, she hadn't even informed her mother and father. They'd be stunned if they saw the news. And utterly relieved to discover the truth that she'd come to her senses before it was too late.

"Are you my new nanny?" The direct yet sweetly voiced query pulled Belle from her dismayed musings.

Nanny?

She turned to the archway behind her, to the precious moppet who'd uttered the question. Abundant curls in a shade of vibrant chestnut framed a round, angelic face. Clutching a stuffed rabbit made of calico against her small body, the girl stared up at Belle with wide brown eyes.

Mulling questions of her own, Belle met the child's inquisitive gaze. *How very interesting.* A tot was perhaps the very last thing she'd expected to find in Jon's home. Had he harbored a secret during his time in America?

"My name is Belle," she offered with a smile. "Might I ask your name?"

"Her name is—" Jon said, his tone gruff. Evidently, he had not expected to be greeted by the sleepy-eyed imp.

"Carrie," the child said brightly. Turning to Jon, the child flashed a little smile, as if to counter his stern expression. "I know my own name, silly."

"Silly, is it?" Jon's expression lightened, and he chuckled beneath his breath as he went to her. Belle thought he might hug the child, but instead, he offered a gentle pat on the head. "It's well past your bedtime."

"I was in bed. But I heard a noise," the girl explained, sounding as if the reason she was not sound asleep should be quite obvious. She looked up at Belle. "Are you my new nanny?" she repeated, sounding a bit more hopeful this time.

"You've no need of a *new* nanny," Jon said, seeming oblivious to Mrs. Gilroy's quiet *humph.*

The dog trotted over to the girl and plopped down before her small, slipper-clad feet. Evidently, the child had wrapped the furball on four legs around her little finger.

"But I *do* need a nanny," the girl said rather confidently.

"Now who's being silly?" he said gently as he softly tousled her curls with his fingers. He turned to Mrs. Gilroy. "Please summon Miss Pritchard from her chamber so that she might settle Carolyn back into bed."

"I would be happy to," Mrs. Gilroy said, looking as if she were biting back a little grin. "If she were still here."

Jon blinked. "*Still* here, you say?"

"Miss Pritchard is no longer in residence," Mrs. Gilroy said, leaning on her cane with each step as she made her way to the little girl. Bending closer, she took the child's hand in hers. "Wee one, would ye like to tell us what ye did today?"

"I had a tea party." The girl's beaming smile brightened her features. "With Heathy."

"Heathy?" Belle could not resist the question.

"The dog," Jon said, his tone weary.

"A rather unique name for a pet," Belle said, flashing a questioning glance.

"I had no part in choosing the little beast's name. He's not mine, you see."

"Another guest," Mrs. Gilroy muttered beneath her breath.

"One of my business partners and his wife were called away on an urgent family matter. It was not feasible to bring their dog along, so . . . here he is."

"Don't let his size fool ye, Miss," the housekeeper added. "Given the chance, he'll chew anything in sight. Except the cat. She's the one resident of this house he won't pester."

"Another guest, as Mrs. Gilroy likes to say," Jon added, his tone slightly wry.

Mrs. Gilroy slanted him a glance Belle suspected was deliberately weary. "Miss Macie thought it best not to tote a finicky pet along on her expedition. So, the cat has made herself comfortable here."

Jon glanced about the room. "Speaking of Cleo, where is she?"

Mrs. Gilroy's thin shoulders lifted and fell. "Bedded down somewhere, I'm sure. She's taken over the house, I tell ye. Thank goodness she has no fondness for tea parties. Or dirt."

Jon hiked a brow. "Dirt?"

"Wet dirt, to be more precise." Mrs. Gilroy turned back to Carrie. A touch of a grin played on her features. "Now, child, will ye tell us what ye served at yer little party?"

"Doggie and I had tea," Carrie said, sounding rather proud of herself. "Pretend, of course. And we made pies."

Jon's brow furrowed. "You made pies?"

"Make-believe pies," Carrie went on, sounding quite delighted with her little party. "We didn't eat them. But Heathy . . . he made a bit of a mess."

"Tell them how ye made the pies, child," Mrs. Gilroy urged.

Holding her cloth rabbit a bit tighter, Carrie nibbled her lower lip. "It was just a bit of mud. We were outside, in the garden. I poured a glass of water onto the ground and made tarts."

Jon nodded, taking it in. "Well, a little mess is to be expected with a child, I suppose."

"A *little* mess?" Mrs. Gilroy could not contain the amusement in her voice.

"But then Nanny came outside," Carrie went on. "She was cross with me."

"Nothing a bit of soap and water will not clean up, I presume," Jon said to Mrs. Gilroy, sounding hopeful.

The housekeeper's expression reminded Belle of the Cheshire Cat. "Ah, the soap and water worked quite well. On the wee lass, that is. But, ye see, Miss Pritchard's bonnet was another story."

"Her bonnet?" Jon rubbed his temples.

"I wanted Heathy to wear it to our tea," the girl explained matter-of-factly.

Belle bit back a laugh. "Oh, my."

"The woman had no reason to become upset," Jon said, as if to convince himself. "It goes without saying that I would replace the blasted bonnet."

"Oh, it gets better," Mrs. Gilroy said, not even trying to conceal her cheek.

"Better?" Belle could not contain her curiosity.

"Or worse, depending on your view of the matter," Mrs. Gilroy said.

"Promise you won't be cross with me, Cousin Jon." Clutching the stuffed creature even tighter, the girl regarded him with imploring eyes.

Cousin. A sense of relief washed over Belle as she chided herself for her momentary suspicion. Jon had left her in New

York . . . he had hurt her. That much was true. But he had not lied to her.

"I will not be angry with you," Jon said, his voice calm despite the tense set of his features. "You have my word."

"Nanny fell." Tears welled in the little girl's eyes. "And then, she was so very cross with me."

Belle could not stand by and watch the child's distress. Crouching low, she caught Carrie's small hands in hers. "It's all right, dear," she said, smoothing a wayward curl behind the girl's ear. "You were only playing."

The girl nodded and swiped away a tear. "Heathy didn't mean to . . . to make her fall."

"Good God," Jon muttered under his breath.

"I had a cup for Heathy. And for me," Carrie went on.

"Tea?" Jon plowed his fingers through his hair. "For the dog?"

"Not real tea." Carrie shook her head. "Just pretend."

"I should've known," he agreed.

"Nanny wanted me to come in. But Heathy was still drinking his tea."

Jon pressed his fingers to his temples. "He obviously didn't want to rush."

"She was looking for me." Carrie thrust out her lower lip, looking as though she fought against tears. "I thought Heathy looked pretty. But Nanny fussed about her bonnet."

"As ye can imagine, Miss Pritchard was not pleased to find the dog decked out in her finery. When she attempted to retrieve her bonnet—that ridiculous frilly thing with all the ruffles—the dog squirmed away," Mrs. Gilroy added.

"She chased him." Carrie's lip jutted out a bit further. "Then I chased him, too."

"Oh, dear," Belle said under her breath.

"Ah, it was a terrible commotion," Mrs. Gilroy explained. "Just as I made it to the terrace, Miss Pritchard slipped."

"She fell on my mud pies." Carrie sounded rather solemn.

"Good heavens," Belle said as Jon rubbed his temples again.

"It was a scene like no other, I tell ye. The prim shrew landed right on her bustle." Mrs. Gilroy recounted with a born storyteller's flair. "And then, to add insult to injury, Heathy pounced on her, muddy paws and all, and gave her a hearty lick on the cheek."

Carrie patted the pup on the head. "He was only trying to make her feel better."

"That he was, child. That he was," Mrs. Gilroy agreed kindly. "By the time Miss Pritchard made it to her feet, she was mad as a hornet. *Nanny* stormed inside and packed her bags. She won't be back."

Jon rubbed his temples as though they ached. "You're sure of that?"

"Quite so," Mrs. Gilroy said. "Trust me when I tell ye it is for the best."

Jon met the woman's tired gaze. "For the best, eh?"

Mrs. Gilroy gave a brisk nod. "There's a bit more to this story, but I will explain at another time. Such talk is not good for the wee lass's tender ears."

"Point taken." He scrubbed a hand over the edge of his jaw, over the dark bristles of new beard. "Now, I'll return to my initial request for your assistance, Mrs. Gilroy. Our guest requires a suitable night dress and a day dress for the morning. By any chance did Miss Pritchard leave behind some garments that might serve the purpose? While I'm purchasing the woman a new bonnet, I will certainly pay to replace a dress or two."

Mrs. Gilroy's keen gaze swept over Belle. She shook her head. "Yer eyes must be more weary than I'd thought. Nothing that scarecrow in skirts wore would fit Miss Frost."

Prim shrew. Scarecrow in skirts. My, the housekeeper had harbored no fondness for the child's governess. What had gone on between the women to cause such animosity?

Jon rubbed his jaw again. "You do have a point. Well, then, I'd imagine my sister has a dress or two in the closet. It wasn't that long ago that Macie was visiting, and you know how she always leaves something or other behind."

"I do believe I can find something suitable," Mrs. Gilroy said. "But first, I'll need to see the wee lass back into her bed."

Jon shook his head. "That won't be necessary. I'll tuck her in." He knelt down before the little girl. "Would you like that, Carolyn?"

"Very much." She rubbed her still sleepy eyes and turned to Belle. "Will you come, too?"

"Miss Frost is our guest. Not your governess." Jon clipped the words between his teeth before Belle could utter a reply. He scooped the child up in his arms. "Time for you to sleep."

"I wanted to tell her about Miss Bun-Bun," the girl said, reaching out to Belle.

"There's no time for that now. It's well past your bedtime. And mine." He held the child gently, yet there was a stern, no-nonsense air about Jon's manner. The little girl seemed to sense it, poking out her bottom lip ever so slightly. The hint of unhappiness in the child's eyes tore at Belle. She couldn't stop herself from reaching out to touch the girl's small hand.

"In the morning, you can tell me all about your rabbit," she said, brushing her fingers over the stuffed animal's little face. "She's quite a pretty one."

"Indeed," Carrie said with a wan little smile. "Night-night."

"Goodnight, Carrie." Belle blew the little girl a kiss, delighted by the child's small grin as she peered over Jon's broad shoulder while he carried her from the room.

Belle stared after the child. Should she have defied Jon and gone along to tuck the girl into bed? There would've been no harm in it. Would there?

But then again, she didn't expect to be here—in this house—for very long. With any luck, she'd have new accommodations by the next sunset. She'd no doubt Jon would arrange security for her at one of the exclusive hotels where he had connections. As soon as she could obtain a suitable dress and a place to stay out of Gideon's reach, she'd have no need to further distract Jon from his many responsibilities. Leading Carrie to hope she might actually take the place of the nanny who'd bolted so unceremoniously from the little girl's life would serve no purpose. Indeed, it might truly be unkind to give the child false hope.

Belle's heart ached at the very thought. The child was bright and sweet-natured, but there was such sadness in those big brown eyes. Who was this little imp? And why was she here—with Jon Mason, of all people? The man lived for the next endeavor, the next business deal, the next store opening. He had no wife. No experience with children. And very little patience with anything that impeded his efficiency.

"She's his cousin's child," Mrs. Gilroy offered, seeming to read her thoughts. "The wee lass is an orphan, ye see. This is her third home in little more than a year."

"Her third home?" Belle met the woman's careworn features. "Why is she here with Mr. Mason?"

"'Tis not my place to be carrying tales, but at the heart, it's rather simple. The wee lass had nowhere else to go."

The words plowed into Belle like a runaway train. How horrid it must have been to be shuttled about from one place to the next. She'd grown up surrounded by loving family and friends, never at a loss for someone who loved her. For someone who cared for her. Until tonight, when she was on her own in the city. She was an adult, an independent-minded woman, and yet, she'd felt so very alone. If the sense of having no one to turn to had left her feeling frightened and nearly desperate, how hard must it be for a child to endure such emotion?

"Of course, that will change soon enough," Mrs. Gilroy went on. "I don't expect Carrie will be here for long. When Miss Macie and her husband return from their travels, they'll take the child into their home. At least, this is the plan."

"He does tend to have a plan, doesn't he?" Belle mused aloud.

"That he does, miss." A thin smile played on Mrs. Gilroy's lips. "Always has. Even as a lad."

If only I could say the same, I might not be in this pickle.

"Somehow, that does not surprise me in the least."

"Come along, Miss Frost. I'll find ye something comfortable for tonight." She motioned to Belle to follow her to the stairs. "And don't think I've forgotten about my question. Tell me this, if only to put an old woman's mind at ease—ye are still *Miss* Frost, are ye not?"

"Yes," Belle said, bracing herself against a fresh wave of regret. And of relief.

"Ye're quite sure of that?" The woman's gaze settled again on Belle's gown.

"Most definitely." Belle met her eyes, seeing only caring within their gray depths. "You might say I came to my senses in the nick of time."

"And that's a good thing." Mrs. Gilroy gave a knowing nod, seeming to comprehend what Belle had left unspoken. "Ye're not the first lass to run from a man who was not meant to have her."

The undercurrent of pain in the older woman's voice touched Belle. What had she experienced to give her such understanding?

"Thank you." Emotion welled in her throat, and the two simple words were all that Belle could muster in the moment.

"Well, enough of that," Mrs. Gilroy said, her no-nonsense tone returning. "Let's see to finding ye something a bit more comfortable."

"Even Jon Mason could not have planned for this night," Belle said with a lighter touch.

"Do not underestimate him, lass." Mrs. Gilroy gave her head a weary shake. "He might not have had a plan when he left tonight for the tavern. But I'd wager my last penny he has one by the morning."

Chapter Six

NEARLY TWO YEARS before her desperate dash inside the tavern—a lair for rogues, no less—when she'd nearly crashed into Jon Mason's broad chest, Belle had first laid eyes on the man under vastly different circumstances. On the night they'd met, their connection had been electric. Undeniable. And utterly surprising.

Oh, she'd heard the tales, and then some. Jonathan Mason was a tycoon. A rogue. And a ladies' man of the first order. While the handsome Englishman was in New York investigating sites for a new venture, the first American location in his family's commercial empire, gossipy socialites—bored wives, winsome widows, and wide-eyed debutantes, alike—had been positively abuzz with excitement over his every move throughout the city. At the time, it seemed Belle was the only woman in Manhattan who was not over the moon at the prospect of encountering him at some ball or another. Weary of the talk that she simply *had* to meet him, she'd decided Jon Mason was most definitely *not* the man of her dreams.

Since the days soon after her first debutante ball, Belle had imagined a lover who would sweep her off her feet—a vibrant man who lived each moment as if it were his last. She'd expected to fall for a man who shared her passion for music and the arts and spontaneous adventures. Truth be told, she'd encountered her fair share of men who'd made an obvious show of being precisely what they thought she wanted. She'd honed an uncanny ability to see through their oh-so-earnest performances, to spot the dollar signs in their eyes as they attempted to impress her with their mastery of the latest dances and culture. So many poetry-spouting suitors saw an heiress when they looked at her. Not the woman she truly was.

Over time, she'd tired of the entire game. She'd turned away fawning earls seeking a dollar princess of their own, rejected second sons of industrialists in need of a marriage that would see them comfortably set for life, and coolly scorned a particularly irksome would-be seducer who thought to woo her with promises to pen a play in her honor. The gossipy biddies caught on quickly, their whispers dubbing her the Frost Princess. Behind her back, of course. She couldn't quite remember which newspaper had first adopted the name, but she rather liked it. The play on her name was amusing. And all too fitting.

She'd rather prided herself on her icy veneer. Until the moment when she'd spotted Jon standing across a Manhattan ballroom, and she utterly lost her ability to erect a shield of chilly indifference. Surrounded by the tony who's who of New York gathered for the charity gala, he'd cut a dashing figure. Tall, lean, and broad-shouldered, Jon had carried himself with an athlete's natural strength and grace. His black dress coat and trousers were impeccably tailored, while his crisp white shirt and bow tie were the height of elegance. And yet, there was no trace of the elite snobbishness that marked so many of the men who moved in her circles. There was something about him that warned he possessed both the strength and the confidence to make him a fierce competitor, both in the world of business and in the world at large.

He'd worn his dark hair parted and combed neatly back, the height of fashion. A sprinkling of silver accented the straight, sleek strands at his temples, which lent him a look of distinction. On another level entirely, the sight of him made her yearn to run her fingers through his hair.

She could still picture the way he'd looked at her when they'd first met. His dark eyes had lit with a slow-burning fire. Within days, she'd fallen for him. And she'd learned a lesson she would never forget: passion and love are not the same thing. Far from it.

And now, she was a guest in Jon's home. In spite of her gruff manner, his careworn housekeeper regarded her with both curiosity and a touch of concern. How very unexpected.

"It looks like ye've made a friend," Mrs. Gilroy said not quite cheerfully, pulling Belle from her thoughts as they proceeded up the stairs.

"A friend?" She noticed the tinkle of the bell then and glanced behind her. The little dog named Heathy navigated the steps at a jaunty pace. "I do hope Mr. Mason won't be upset."

The housekeeper chuckled. "That dog has the run of the house."

"You don't say," Belle said.

"Ye find that surprising, do ye, Miss?"

"A bit," she admitted.

"So do I," Mrs. Gilroy said, the words sounding a bit like a grumble. "The pup's a good-natured little fellow, but he's never found a shoe he didn't want to sink his pointy teeth into."

"I gathered as much," Belle said as they reached the landing. She glanced down at her hopelessly soiled shoes. "Fortunately, I'm not worried about these. A nibble or two on these won't do much more harm."

"Don't give him any ideas, Miss," she chuckled beneath her breath. "I do believe the little gent can understand English."

Chuckling beneath her breath, Mrs. Gilroy led Belle to a neatly appointed bedchamber. As she opened the door and lit the light, Belle's gaze fell upon wood furnishings that had been polished to a warm luster, the simple lines fitting Jon's no-nonsense style. But the frilly curtains and ruffle-edged quilt in shades of yellow, cream, and blue lent the chamber a distinctly feminine touch.

"Mr. Mason's sister had her say over the décor," Mrs. Gilroy explained. "Miss Macie stayed here quite a bit when she was a young lass, back in the days before she shared a flat with that flighty friend of hers. Now, of course, she's a wedded woman, but she still stays here from time to time . . . when she and her husband visit until all hours." She went to the massive wardrobe cabinet. "Let's see what she's left this time."

Mrs. Gilroy selected a walking suit in a rich shade of teal and held the skirt up to Belle. As she lifted up the white linen blouse, her lips pulled thin. "This might work for the morning. Miss Macie's not quite as tall as ye. But it's bound to be better than that gown ye're wearing." She turned to the cabinet, searching about for a few moments. "There's nothing here that would be comfortable for ye tonight. But I do have an idea." She patted the back of a wing chair. "Make yerself comfortable, lass. I'll be back in a trice."

Drinking in the first moment of quiet she'd had in what seemed like days, Belle glanced around the room. Gaslight from the wall sconce lent the chamber a soft glow. Fat pillows in colorful shams lay upon the bed, propped against the headboard, while silver-framed photos were displayed on the dresser. One in particular caught Belle's eye. She wandered over to it, lifting it in her hand for a better look.

A boy and girl—Jon and Macie, no doubt—decked out in what appeared to be holiday finery filled the frame. His mouth was set in a half-smile, his chin cocked at an angle she supposed he'd thought dignified, while Jon's sister smiled brightly for the camera, her dark hair spiraling in waves over her shoulders. Belle judged the girl's age to be around ten, while Jon, all lanky, long limbs and serious dark eyes, appeared to be a few years older.

Goodness, Jon had been serious for his years, even at that young age. Something in his expression tugged at her heart. He looked rather stern, but the slight crook of his mouth led her to think it had been an act, a role he'd evidently played quite well since he was a lad.

Her gaze wandered to another photograph. In this one, a tall, stern man with the same dark hair and eyes as Jon stood behind a chair bearing a lovely woman whose auburn hair framed her face. Her wide eyes brimmed with life and joy and laughter, quite the study in contrasts with her rather somber husband. So, this was Jon's and Macie's mother.

"Macie resembles our mother." Jon's voice from the open doorway startled her so, she nearly dropped the framed image. She turned to him, meeting eyes that regarded her with an expression she couldn't quite read.

He'd stripped off his wool jacket and loosened his burgundy tie. The strip of silk hung loose around his neck, not quite touching the vee of skin revealed by the open collar. She felt her breath catch. Perhaps the mere surprise of his unexpected appearance. Or was something else—an emotion she'd thought long dead?

"She appears to have your mother's expression as well as her features," Belle agreed, brushing away the questions she didn't want to answer, even to herself.

"They also share a similar temperament. While I have taken after my father in nearly every way." Jon's tone seemed rather ambivalent, as though he wasn't quite sure if that was a good thing.

"The fruit did not fall far from the tree. You are definitely your father's son."

He shrugged. "I'm not sure he would agree with you. But I certainly did inherit his hair."

She glanced at the image in the frame, then back to Jon. His dark hair was neatly trimmed and worn in the parted style that was the height of fashion for men of industry. At least, she supposed he'd combed in that manner earlier in the night, before he'd raked his fingers through his hair in weary exasperation.

"Indeed. Unlike your sister, you've not so much as a wisp of a curl." She reached up to brush an errant lock of chestnut brown hair off his forehead, then caught herself. Good heaven, what was she thinking? He was no longer hers to touch, even in such a casual manner.

He was no longer hers. Not at all.

"Well, then," he looped his thumbs under his suspenders, sweeping his gaze over the wrinkled white silk of her gown. He cleared his throat. "I trust Mrs. Gilroy has located something for you to wear."

"She found an ensemble that might work. I do hope she's right."

His brow furrowed. "If not, we'll find something else in the morning."

"There will be no need for that," Mrs. Gilroy said, making her way into the room with two dresses in her hand. "In her rush to leave for the journey with her husband, Miss Macie left these behind." Her gaze swept over Belle. "These should do."

Belle quickly sized up the colorful, high-necked dresses. They did indeed appear to have been made for a woman of similar—but perhaps less generous—proportions to her own.

"Thank you so much," she said as the housekeeper handed her another garment, a heavy flannel night dress with ruffles at the neck and wrists that looked very much like something her grandmother would have fancied.

"That one should do. It's not as if ye need something fancy for taking yer rest." Mrs. Gilroy hung the dresses in the wardrobe before settling a narrow-eyed gaze on Jon. "Now that that's done, I should ask what ye think ye're doing, intruding on a lady's quarters?"

A bland look of amusement pulled at Jon's mouth. "I'll have you know I am assessing the progress made towards providing Miss Frost with suitable accommodations for the night."

"So that's it, is it?" Mrs. Gilroy looked as if she tried to scowl but couldn't quite pull it off. "This is not one of yer stores. You'll find no need to supervise with me under this roof." Her eyes flashed with warmth and a hint of warning. "I have the situation well under control."

For the first time since she'd encountered him that night, the crinkles on Jon's forehead eased. He smiled. "So you do, Mrs. Gilroy." He turned to the door. "I never doubted it for a moment."

"I'll see that Miss Frost is settled in for the night," she said. "I trust the wee one is tucked in her bed."

He raked his fingers through his hair, feathered lines of tension crinkling around his eyes. "For the moment."

"I'll check on her later," Mrs. Gilroy said with a weary nod. "Before I lay down to rest."

"Thank you, Mrs. Gilroy," he said. "It's been a very long day . . . for all of us."

"Things will settle down soon enough," the housekeeper said.

"As a betting man, I would not like the odds on that," Jon said with a thin smile, then bid them a good night's sleep and closed the door behind him.

"Shall I run ye a hot bath, Miss?" Mrs. Gilroy offered, relying heavily on her walking stick as she made her way to light the small bathing chamber.

Hearing the weariness in the woman's tone, Belle gave her head a little shake. She certainly did not need to trouble the woman any further, much less at this hour. "Thank you, but that won't be necessary. I'll run it myself."

"Good enough, Miss," she said with a touch of relief. "Ye'll find clean towels on the shelf, and Miss Macie left behind a dressing gown."

"Thank you for your kindness," Belle said. "I realize this is quite an imposition."

"Think nothing of it, Miss. I should thank ye as well for yer kindness to little Carrie."

"I don't understand how anyone could be unkind to that darling girl."

Mrs. Gilroy hiked a brow. "Ye'd be surprised, Miss. As much as I shudder to think about trying to keep up with the wee imp on this cantankerous knee of mine, I cannot say I was sad to see her governess pack her bags. Some people simply do not have a warm heart for children. And Miss Pritchard was one of them."

"I once had a governess who had no fondness for me. Mama saw to it that she did not stay on for very long," Belle recalled. "I suppose some are drawn into the vocation due to circumstances rather than any nurturing heart."

"Indeed," Mrs. Gilroy said. "Carrie's governess was not cruel. I would not have allowed such a thing. But she was cold as ice, she was. And so very critical." She let out a low breath. "The child has been through so much. She deserves affection in her young life."

"You mentioned that she's been orphaned. How long has it been since she lost her parents?"

"It's been more than a year now. Her parents were killed in a terrible fire. With her last bit of strength, the child's dear mum got Carrie to safety. But the smoke had done its damage, and the poor woman succumbed not long after. Since then, the wee lass has been shuttled around from kin to kin. Mr. Mason would not turn his back on her. It's not in his nature, ye know. But the demands of his various enterprises leave little time for anything but his business. The man is gone more than he is here." She bent her head, staring down at the rug for a moment, seeming to collect her thoughts, then lifted her gaze. "Oh, dear, I've said too much."

"Not at all," Belle said. "I am acquainted with Mr. Mason and his dedication to, shall we say, meeting his responsibilities."

"Ah, ye do know him, don't ye, Miss?" The housekeeper made her way to the door. "If ye don't mind, I'll have ye sleep in here in Miss Macie's old chamber. The linens are freshly laundered, and I haven't had a chance to prepare the other guest room."

"I shall be entirely comfortable," Belle said with a smile. "Please, do get some rest. I don't wish to be any trouble."

"Thank ye, Miss. I suspect I will sleep like a rock tonight." Mrs. Gilroy scooped up the dog and made her way to the door. "Good night, Miss Frost."

"Good night," she replied as Mrs. Gilroy left the room with Heathy in hand. The door closed behind her with a snug click of the latch.

Venturing into the bathing chamber, Belle spotted a bottle of lavender bath salts on a shelf by the tub. How very nice. She ran a bath, liberally scenting the water with the fragrant crystals. Ah, the aroma was so very relaxing. For the first time since she'd bolted from Gideon, Belle felt she could let down her guard.

Peeling off the silk gown she now detested, she tossed it to the floor. She'd been such a fool. So very impulsive, wooed by sweet words and an all-too-convenient sharing of her interests, of her passions. She'd believed every lie from Gideon's mouth, her trust in the man nurtured by her scheming aunt. Never could she have imagined such betrayal from a woman Belle had considered a fond member of her family for as long as she could remember.

Never could she have imagined she'd be so vulnerable. For years, she'd kept alert for the lies. For the courtships motivated by a love of money, rather than her.

But when Gideon had swept into her life, she'd looked past the signs that he was too perfect to be true. When her aunt sang his praises, she'd never considered a motive other than a sincere interest in Belle's happiness. She'd looked past every hint of their conniving ways. Thank heaven she'd come to her senses. Before it was too late.

Stripping off her undergarments, she folded them and placed them on a small chair, then tested the water's heat with her finger. *Perfect.*

Easing into the tub, she leaned back against a folded towel and closed her eyes. She'd be safe here. How very ironic that of all the men in London—of all the men on the planet—she'd encountered Jon Mason. Goodness, she'd nearly run into his arms. Even then, as he'd gazed down at her with incredulous eyes, she'd known she could trust him. He'd said he would keep her safe. In her heart, she'd no doubt he would do just that.

At least, as long as he could.

In her mind's eye, she saw Gideon's expression as he'd blocked the door of her chamber at Aunt Vera's home. Anger had blazed in his gray eyes. And contempt. He'd closed her in and bolted the door from the outside. He hadn't counted on her desperation. Hadn't known the depth of her will to escape his control.

But would it be enough? Could she stay out of his grasp for a fortnight longer?

With a sigh, she stared up at the ceiling. A fresh foreboding crept through her thoughts. *Gideon is a powerful man. He knows what he wants. And he'll stop at nothing to get it.*

Easing lower into the water, Belle drank in the calming essence of lavender oil. She wouldn't dwell on her predicament tonight. For now, she would savor this brief moment of peace.

Still, her mind wandered. She left the tub, donned the flannel night dress that barely came to her knees, and made her way to bed. As she slipped beneath the quilt, another image entered her thoughts—a child's large brown eyes, filled with a keen sadness her sweet little smile could not camouflage. The little girl had endured such terrible loss in her young life. How very desolate the tot must feel in a life of being shuttled from home to home. From caretaker to caretaker. The girl was lonely. Vulnerable. And sadly, without anyone to show her true affection.

The very thought of it seemed a thorn pricking Belle's heart. If only there was something she could do.

Closing her eyes again, she mulled over Mrs. Gilroy's words of gratitude for Belle's small show of kindness to Carrie. The housekeeper had disapproved of the girl's governess, of the woman's sour attitude toward the girl. It seemed the old woman with her hobbled knee was the child's only true ally. Was it any wonder Carrie clutched her little stuffed rabbit as if it were her only source of comfort in the world?

Perhaps there *was* something she could do to ease the girl's unhappiness. She would speak to Jon on the matter. But he'd no doubt counter in that oh-so-practical way of his that the child did not want for anything. And she supposed he'd be right. He would see to it that Carrie had everything a child could need or want. When he'd bundled the girl off to bed, she'd seen the affection in his eyes. Jon cared for the child, and he would never deny her anything . . . anything he could buy, that is. She knew full well that he could not spare much time for Carrie. After all, the duties of his position at Mason Enterprises took precedence over most anything. She'd learned that bitter lesson when he'd left New York.

Fluffing her pillow, she allowed herself another sigh. She doubted Jon would ever be convinced to devote more time to the child at the cost of his business ventures. The very thought of it would be laughable if it were not rather sad. But perhaps—just perhaps—she could impress upon him the importance of selecting a nanny with a kind heart.

A kind heart. She smiled to herself, the words playing in her thoughts as she drifted off to sleep. *How very rare.*

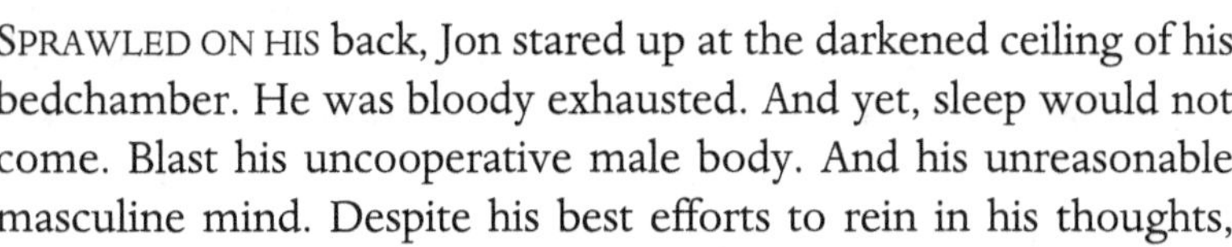

SPRAWLED ON HIS back, Jon stared up at the darkened ceiling of his bedchamber. He was bloody exhausted. And yet, sleep would not come. Blast his uncooperative male body. And his unreasonable masculine mind. Despite his best efforts to rein in his thoughts, his mind wandered to images of Belle. Again. And again.

He'd never slept under the same roof with Belle. Not even when they'd shared passionate kisses—and more—during those days and nights in New York. Memories flooded his brain. Holding her in his arms. Kissing Belle until she sighed with longing against his mouth. Her soft, velvet voice, telling him she wanted him. Only him. Just as he'd wanted her, and only her. But he forced the images aside, banishing them to the recesses of his thoughts. It was bad enough when they heated his dreams. But in his waking hours, he would not succumb to the longing he was determined to keep dormant. He'd put all that behind him. Hadn't he?

Not that any of it mattered. Belle was not here by choice. A moment of fear had driven her into the Rogue's Lair, a desperation compounded by the realization that the man she'd left behind was in active pursuit. She'd come here tonight out of need. Out of self-preservation. Nothing more.

He'd brought her here to protect her. Not to relive the past. Still, he'd been a fool to think he would be immune to the beauty of her soft smile. To the subtle aroma of lavender on her skin. To the memory of how it had felt to hold her in his arms, so close he could feel the rise and fall of her breaths. The mere thought that he'd have a moment's peace with Belle this close was bloody absurd.

Well, there was nothing to be done about it now, was there? He rolled onto his side, thumped his pillow, and closed his eyes. All the while, his thoughts swirled. The first thing he needed to do was plan for her security. He'd see to that in the morning. One of his business associates had opened a quaint hotel off the beaten path. Surely, she'd be safe there. Of course, he'd see to it she was registered under an assumed name, with an imaginary husband's moniker listed for good measure. And he'd arrange for a companion for her, a woman who'd draw little attention to herself and possessed the necessary skills to swiftly deter an attacker if the situation called for action. He knew just the person for that role. Now to hope that Mrs. Johnstone was in the country and wasn't still running about exploring some ruin or another.

He pounded the feather pillow again. Again, his mind wandered to Belle. This time, his thoughts took a different path, picturing the compassion on her face when she'd encountered little Carrie. She'd seemed to instinctively know how to comfort the child. Blasted shame he did not possess that talent.

With another thump on the pillow, as if for good measure, he flopped onto his back. In truth, what did it matter if he possessed a knack for comforting a child? It wouldn't be long before Belle's life had returned to her charity balls and Carrie would be off to another home, one far more suitable for a wee girl than his. Macie's correspondence had made it clear she and Finn would be happy to adopt the girl. And then, he could attend to his duties without even a slight touch of guilt. The child would be happy with his sister. And his life would be back to normal. The chaos would be behind him. Just as it should be.

Bloody odd how the thought brought him no joy.

Chapter Seven

*A*NOTHER SUNRISE. ANOTHER *day. Another adventure.*

Rays of morning light streamed between the curtains, rousing Belle from a restful sleep. For a long, luxurious moment, she savored the feel of the sun upon her face as her mother's morning greeting hummed in her memories. Throughout her childhood, Belle had awakened to the cheerful, slightly off-key notes of her mother's voice. *An eternal optimist,* her father had dubbed Mama in that gruff yet affectionate way of his. Mama was still a vibrant soul who saw the best in everyone, who hoped for the best in every situation. In her eyes, every dawn was the opportunity for a new start.

Another adventure. The words echoed in Belle's thoughts. She certainly would not have described the events of the day before as anything she had ever wished to experience. But perhaps there was a silver lining. She simply couldn't see it yet.

She pried herself out of the comfort of the feather mattress and quilt and set about preparing for her morning. Hopefully, Mama's ever-sunny outlook would be justified. Perhaps today would be the start of a new adventure, the first step in making her way home to the place where she belonged. Where she was safe.

She'd finished dressing when a light rap upon the door stilled her as she brushed her hair. Mrs. Gilroy called through the door. "Are ye up and about, Miss?"

"Up. About. And dressed in the lovely walking suit you found for me," Belle said as she opened the door.

Mrs. Gilroy's smile faded as her gaze landed on Belle's shirtwaist. On her bosom, to be precise. "Have ye tried the dresses?" she said after a moment of hesitation. "That blouse appears to be a wee bit . . . snug."

Belle glanced down at the mother-of-pearl buttons that appeared ready to pop their stitching at any moment. "I did," she said, feeling a sudden pinch of defeat. "I'm afraid they're not any better."

"I'd had a worry that might be the case. Ye've got a bit more at the top than Miss Macie."

Belle squared her shoulders. She certainly would not let such a small thing as a slightly—well, perhaps not so slightly—snug bodice put a damper on her prospects for the day ahead.

"I'll take care not to breathe too deeply," she said lightly, bringing a smile to the older woman's thin mouth.

"It's not the breathing that worries me." Mrs. Gilroy flashed a little grin. "Whatever ye do, Miss, do not sneeze."

BY THE TIME Mrs. Gilroy escorted Belle to the dining room, Jon was already seated at the head of a modestly sized oval table draped by a white linen cloth, a cup of tea and a slice of thoroughly browned toast by his left hand, the daily news in his right. Dressed in his shirtsleeves and a silver-gray waistcoat with wire spectacles perched on the bridge of his nose, he looked every bit the part of a well-to-do man of enterprise. An exceedingly handsome man of enterprise, at that. My, she'd tried to forget the way her gaze was drawn as if by instinct to his classically etched features. For a heartbeat, she allowed herself to drink in the sight of him—the firm, masculine edge of his jaw, the sensuous curve of his mouth, the small divot in his chin that added to his charm. He'd always looked especially dashing in his spectacles, the contrast between the civilized illusion he presented and the raw masculinity of the man beneath the proper and fashionable attire ever so tempting.

"Thank you, Mrs. Gilroy," he said without glancing up. As the housekeeper took her leave, he set the newspaper aside, removed his spectacles, and turned to Belle. "Good morning, Miss Frost."

"To you as well, Mr. Mason," Belle responded in kind, oh-so-very proper.

Taking a seat across from him, she held her breath as the linen of the shirtwaist pulled taut over her bosom. Mrs. Gilroy's sage words played in her thoughts: *It's not the breathing that worries me . . . do not sneeze.* Actually, the housekeeper might've been wrong about the breathing. She'd fastened the jacket of the walking suit to conceal the way the too-small blouse threatened to pop its buttons. That garment was a better fit, but not by much. Its braided ebony fastenings strained against their stitching with each breath.

Fortunately, Jon appeared entirely oblivious to her predicament. With any luck, he'd stay that way.

"I trust you slept well," he said, rather deliberately bland, as if her presence in his home—at his morning meal, no less—was quite an ordinary thing. The overt detachment in his tone chilled the embers of heat the mere sight of him had kindled. *Thank goodness.*

"Very well, indeed," she said, cool as could be. "The room was quite comfortable, and Mrs. Gilroy was a joy. So very kind."

"A joy?" He quirked a brow. "Are my ears playing tricks on me?"

"Not at all. She's quite endearing, in her own way."

"As I said, she likes you. Trust me when I tell you that is not the usual case."

"The usual case?" Belle quirked a brow of her own. "Before we met, I'd heard the tales. I suppose a woman at your breakfast table is not an unusual occurrence."

His dark eyes met her gaze. "More unusual than you might think."

Did he suddenly look a bit ill at ease? She smiled to herself. "Why, Mr. Mason, am I to believe you're no longer playing the rogue?"

"These days, I doubt I could summon the energy." He glanced at the door as Mrs. Gilroy returned. "Or a moment's privacy."

"I did not wish to disturb ye, but yer assistant, Mr. Bennett, is here." The housekeeper's dour expression made it clear she'd heard his comment. "He says it is important."

"Indeed, it is. Please show him in." Jon turned to Belle. "First thing this morning, I dispatched Mr. Bennet to make arrangements for your accommodations. He is also seeing to the matter of your security."

"Efficient as always, I see," Belle said, forcing a little smile.

He met her comment with a brief shrug. "Is there any other way to live one's life?"

Mrs. Gilroy reappeared in the doorway. Her mouth thinned with tension. "He says he needs to speak with ye privately."

"Very well," Jon said. "I presume he has matters squared away."

"'Tis not my place to question yer decisions, but—" Mrs. Gilroy met his words with a frown.

Jon's brow furrowed. "Might I ask which of my many decisions you are doubting?"

Her frown deepened. "I believe ye already know the answer."

"You've no reason for concern." Jon regarded her for a long moment, his expression weary. "I have everything well in hand."

As he rose to leave the room, Carrie bustled in. She greeted him with a wide grin and a cheerful "Good morning" spoken with a child's enthusiasm for a new day.

"Good morning to you as well." Jon smiled down at her, his expression losing its serious set for the first time that morning. "I will be back shortly."

The faint curve of his mouth faded as the dog trotted in, announcing his presence with a rather jovial bark.

"Heathy would like to say 'Good morning'," Carrie said, her tone fairly bubbling with cheer.

Jon's frown wiped away the girl's smile. "What did we agree about the dog and the dining room?"

Mrs. Gilroy offered a well-timed clearing of her throat. "Have ye forgotten about Mr. Bennett?"

"Blast—" Jon broke off his words.

"He did say it was a matter of importance," Mrs. Gilroy said, as if for emphasis.

"It is *always* important," Jon responded, not quite under his breath. With that, he briskly left the room.

Carrie pointed to the chair beside Belle. "I'd like to sit with you." She hesitated. "May I?"

"Of course. Please join me." Belle smiled as the girl scrambled onto a chair, an amazing feat of nimbleness considering the layers of frilly skirts in her way. The dog plopped down beside the spindled legs, making it clear he wanted to be with the humans of the household.

Reaching down to pet the dog, Carrie nibbled her lip. "I shall take him to my room." Her young voice sounded rather resigned.

"I see no need for you to do that," Belle said, as a vision of Jon's disapproving frown danced in her thoughts. "Not yet, at least." She decided to change the subject. "Where is Miss Bun-Bun?"

"Cousin Jon does not want me to bring her to the table."

"Now what could be the harm in it?" Belle said. "It's not as if she's going to nibble on anything now, is she?"

"Of course not," the girl said with a giggle. "She doesn't even have teeth. Not real ones, at least."

"Unlike the dog," Mrs. Gilroy said. "I'll take Heathy with me. Mr. Mason won't be pleased to see the wee chewing machine is still here."

"I'd prefer the pup stay, if only for a short while. He rather reminds me of my Angus. I do miss him so." Seeing Jon approach, Belle felt a sudden twinge of rebellion. "Besides, rules are made to be broken."

"Are they now?" Jon questioned as he rejoined them. "I'd have to say I disagree."

"Somehow, that does not surprise me in the least," Belle countered, adding a sweet smile for effect.

"I was just on my way to take the dog to the lass's room," Mrs. Gilroy spoke up.

"Thank you." His attention fell on Carrie before darting to Belle. "There is a children's table," he said, motioning to the small round table by the window.

Belle deliberately quirked a brow. "Unfortunately, there are no other children here. I see no reason for Carrie to sit by herself while we break our fast."

"You may have noticed the girl is not tall enough to sit properly at the table," he pointed out, sounding quite logical—as if logic truly mattered in this situation.

"I did take note of her child-sized stature," Belle said. "I suppose you do have a point."

His eyes flashed, betraying he'd taken note of her too-agreeable tone. "By thunder, I'd say today is a most remarkable day. Miss Arabelle Frost has decided to concur with me on at least *one* point."

"There is a small problem." She hiked her chin, meeting his gaze directly. "And I have a solution."

"Do you, now?" His words seemed a bit of a challenge.

"Of course." She plastered on a smile, if only to see his frown deepen. "It's actually quite an easy answer." She turned to Mrs. Gilroy. "Might you happen to have a throw pillow or two lying about that might be used to boost her height?"

"That I do, Miss. I'll fetch them from the parlor." The housekeeper looked to be biting back a little smile. "Come, Heathy," she called, then briskly left the room with the dog trotting happily at her heels.

Jon raked a hand through his hair. "I am not accustomed to being overruled in my own home."

She shrugged. "I would not regard a difference of perspective in that manner. Luckily—perhaps for both of us—you won't have to endure my hard-headed ways much longer." Belle turned to Carrie. The girl wove her fingers together in what seemed a sign of distress. The gesture tore at her heart. "In any case, Mr. Mason, might I suggest we continue this discussion at another time? We should not bore Carrie with our minor disagreements."

As he turned to the child, his expression softened. So, he'd also noticed the girl's fretting look. "Point taken."

"Now little one, let's have a chat while we wait for Mrs. Gilroy to return," she said, meeting Carrie's questioning eyes. "I trust you slept well."

Carrie nodded, her expression brightening. "Bun-Bun kept me company."

"Bun-Bun is a sweet friend, is she not?"

The child nodded again, even more enthusiastically. "Just like Heathy. You like doggies, don't you?"

"Very much so," Belle replied, picturing her own sweet pup. Angus had been a feisty little terrier, her near constant companion for more than a dozen years until he'd gone to his rest. Nearly twelve months had passed since the night when her furry companion had left the world, but the pain was still achingly fresh.

Carrie's eyes brightened. "Tell me about your doggie."

"Oh, he was a naughty boy," Belle reminisced. "Always getting into fixes."

"Heathy does too," the girl said with a little grin. "He chewed the lace on my nanny's shoe. She was very cross."

"It sounds like Miss Pritchard spent quite a bit of time being cross," Belle replied.

"That she did," Jon agreed, the slightest hint of a smile pulling at the corners of his mouth.

Suddenly, a small cry tore their attention to the hallway. Mrs.

Gilroy!

From the corridor, the raspy tones of Heathy's barking seemed a summons, not quite drowning out Mrs. Gilroy's hoarse cries for assistance. Jon leapt to his feet. "Stay here," he said, darting toward the commotion. "If anything happens, take Carrie to my study. She knows where it is. Lock the door."

A chill washed over Belle's nape. Good heavens, what was happening? Her pulse raced. Had Gideon tracked her down so quickly? Would he dare to intrude upon Jon's home?

Carrie squirmed off the chair, looking to the door. Belle took the girl's small hand in hers, stilling her. If there was any chance of danger, she had to ensure the girl was out of harm's way.

The tinkle of a small bell replaced the sound of excited barking. Heathy trotted back into the room, cutting a straight path to the girl. Was it Belle's imagination, or did the dog's features betray a look of guilt?

"Heathy!" Carrie cried out happily, enfolding the dog in her gentle embrace.

"The wee beast will be the death of me yet." Mrs. Gilroy's low grumbling drifted into the room.

As relief crashed over her, Belle exhaled a breath she hadn't realized she'd been holding and rushed to the doorway.

My goodness. Belle bit back a smile at the sight that further eased her anxious mind. Jon supported Mrs. Gilroy with one crooked arm as she slowly made her way into the dining room, tapping her cane against the floorboards with each unsteady step. Behind them, a cloud of what looked like feathers floated through the air.

"Good heavens, what's happened?" Belle asked, though she suspected she already knew the answer. At least part of it.

As Jon met her questioning gaze, Mrs. Gilroy grumbled heartily. Despite whatever had happened, her spirit had not been diminished. "That yapping ball of fur has it out for me, I tell ye."

"I hardly think the dog has engaged in a vendetta," Jon replied lightly, even as relief gleamed in his dark eyes.

"That's easy for ye to say. The pup is always underfoot," Mrs. Gilroy said with what looked like a deliberate little glare. "It would seem he has taken a fancy to my walking stick. Always wants to take a nibble. This time, he darted beneath my feet to get close to it."

"Oh, dear." Belle envisioned the scene as it must have unfolded.

"At least the pillows cushioned my fall. But my knee twisted—my bad knee, at that." Mrs. Gilroy glanced behind her to a pile of feathers and silk that used to be one of the aforementioned cushions. "Heathy got it into his wee head to hunt for whatever was inside the things that smelled like a goose. He's made quite a mess."

"Good heavens," Belle said as she looked over Mrs. Gilroy's shoulder to the still-airborne feathers amid shreds of silk. "Don't worry. I'll tidy it up."

"I'd be forever in yer debt, Miss." The housekeeper flashed a wan smile.

Belle shot Jon a speaking glance. "Might I ask why Mrs. Gilroy is still on her feet? Light as she is, you might have carried her."

"You think that did not occur to me?" Jon hiked his brows. "It would be easier to transport a wildcat."

"Carry me?" Mrs. Gilroy balked at the notion, backing up his words. "I am not helpless." She took a step, wincing loudly and undermining her point in the process. She cocked her chin. "Not at all, lass."

"You should rest," Belle said. "You mustn't chance making the injury worse."

"There's no time to rest," Mrs. Gilroy scoffed. "I need to be finishing up my work in the kitchen. Though I don't quite know how I'm going to manage." She leaned on the cane for emphasis. "Perhaps ye might help me serve the morning meal."

"Of course I will," Belle offered, eager to aid the woman who'd been kind to her. "For now, you need to rest. I insist."

"Ah, ye're an angel," the housekeeper said, her voice filled with as much sugar as a pecan pie.

"It's no trouble at all. I'm happy to help."

"Thank goodness ye're here," Mrs. Gilroy went on. "I don't know what I'd do without ye." Despite the syrup in her voice, she couldn't hide the determined glimmer in her eyes. "And please pour a cup of milk for the wee lass. The milkman brought a fresh bottle this morning. Ye'll find it in the ice box."

Carrie had been resting her chin on her hands, but she popped up in her seat, eyes wide with interest. "May I help?"

"Of course," Belle replied.

Jon sent the girl a speaking glance. She stilled in her seat. "That is *not* a good idea," he said.

"I see no reason why Carrie cannot assist in carrying a bit of food from one room to another," Belle countered.

Without another moment's hesitation, the girl slid from the chair and dashed toward her. "I'm a good helper."

"That ye are, wee one," Mrs. Gilroy said kindly, even as the note of doubt beneath the surface contradicted her words. "That ye are."

Even though Belle had known Mrs. Gilroy for less than a day, the housekeeper's suddenly sweet tone did not fit the crabby woman who had looked as if she might actually rap Jon with her walking stick moments earlier when he'd attempted to assist her. No, this was *not* the woman's natural state. What was she up to?

You've never wanted to see the worst in people. Now is not the time to start. Belle chided herself for her sudden cynicism. Not everyone was a conniver like Gideon. Nor a schemer like Aunt Vera. After all, what reason could the housekeeper—a silver-haired woman who now limped about with both her cane and Jon's strong arm to steady her—have to play upon her good nature?

Chapter Eight

*T*HANK GOODNESS YE'RE here . . . I don't know what I'd do without ye.

Questioning the veracity of his own ears and eyes, Jon stared down at the gray-curled woman who at that moment leaned upon him for support. When he'd come upon Mrs. Gilroy in the hallway—tangled in a twist of her own skirts as the dog looked on with a vaguely guilty look—she'd been the same cantankerous woman he'd known since he was a lad. How had she moved so quickly from cranky grumblings to saccharine displays of gratitude?

She was up to something. The only question was *what*.

"We should get you to the sitting room," he urged. "You should be comfortable on the sofa."

Her expression lost some of its sweetness. "I'm fine right here. Just help me to a seat." Her brow furrowed. "I should be near the kitchen in case Miss Frost requires assistance."

"I hardly expect that will be necessary," he said, realizing his own doubts even as the words left his mouth.

"Ye think not?" Mrs. Gilroy's wry tone sounded more like the woman he knew.

"At this moment, I don't know what I think," he admitted as he assisted Mrs. Gilroy to a chair.

"Mr. Bennett looked concerned," she said. "Is something wrong?"

"My plan for Miss Frost's security has hit a snag. Mrs. Johnstone has not yet returned from her European tour." His gaze settled on Mrs. Gilroy. "But you already knew that, didn't you?"

"I'd heard rumblings when I was out and about." Her expression became suddenly coy. "Ye'd be surprised how much one can learn at the market."

"Did you happen to hear *rumblings* as to how long she will be out of the country?"

"They say she's gallivanting about France, studying cooking of all things."

"A true Renaissance woman."

Mrs. Gilroy shrugged, her mouth thinning. "That's one way of putting it."

"Mr. Jameson at the hotel is willing to dedicate a member of his security staff to watch over Miss Frost during her stay. But there is another complication. An Italian soprano is making her debut at the opera house, and the who's who will be in London to attend her performances. Not a single blasted room is available. Evidently, the situation is the same throughout the city."

"Such a pity, that." Mrs. Gilroy sounded less than sincere.

"Jameson will notify me if a suitable room does become available. With any luck, the delay will be short-lived."

The housekeeper let out a quiet yelp as she rose to her feet, then plopped back upon the seat. "I've truly done it now, haven't I?"

"Mrs. Gilroy, you need to rest."

"But how? I've no idea how I'm to maintain the household."

"I will arrange for a maid until you're healed."

"Ah, that's a kind thought." Slanting Carrie a glance, Mrs. Gilroy sighed. "And what of the wee lass? I cannot keep up with the child. Not now." Flashing a slight scowl, she threw Heathy a glare. "Not to mention *him.* He'll be the death of me, I tell ye."

Jon kneaded the increasingly tense muscles in the back of his neck. "I shall contact the agency." Hopefully, he exuded more confidence than he felt.

"The agency that recommended Miss Pritchard?" Another well-timed sigh escaped her. "Do ye truly trust their judgment?"

The woman had a point. The agency's director had spoken highly of the dour nanny who'd walked away without so much as a day's notice. Their assessment had left much to be desired.

"So, Mrs. Gilroy, what would you suggest?"

"It is not my place to tell ye what to do," she said, making a show of her uncharacteristic hesitation. "But I'd suggest ye clear yer schedule for a few days . . . just until ye find a governess to assist with the child and the household."

"Clear my schedule?" If the woman had suggested he should find a bottle that housed a genie—a genie with an affinity for cleaning, cooking, children, and pets, no less—he might've been less surprised.

Once again attempting to rise, she contorted her features and added a dramatic wince. "I understand."

"You know I won't stand by idly while you're in pain," he said as she sank back to her seat. "I'll say it again—you need to rest."

"But how?" Her gaze trailed to the door leading to the kitchen. "Unless there's someone ye feel ye can trust . . . someone with a kind heart to watch over Carrie." A small smile tugged at her mouth. "Someone who can tolerate the ball of fur with teeth."

He tried to frown, if only to make the point that he didn't appreciate the old woman's scheming ways. But in his gut, he knew she was right.

"Someone with a kind heart, eh?"

She gave a slow nod. "What would be the harm in it?"

This time, his frown was genuine. "Where should I begin?"

"At least for a few days, until we can find someone else." Mrs. Gilroy slanted Carrie a glance. "Ye've seen Miss Frost with the wee lass. They took to each other from the start."

Mrs. Gilroy was right about that much, at least. Carrie had immediately warmed up to Belle. And Belle—well, she had a weak spot for little ones and wee creatures with four legs. But she'd demonstrated her compassion through her charities and such. What did she know about taking care of anything or anyone, including herself? By thunder, in Manhattan she'd had a lady's maid whose duties seemed to revolve around pinning Belle's hair into the latest styles and ensuring her taffeta gowns bore no wrinkles.

"You do realize she's never had to lift a finger in her life?" He pointed out what should've been obvious to his housekeeper. Belle was an heiress. Not a workman's daughter.

"She'll learn what needs to be done. She's got spirit, that one."

"Spirit?" That was one way of putting it.

"Miss Frost will be kind to the girl," Mrs. Gilroy went on. "I can see it in her eyes."

"She *is* fond of little ones. But she's never actually had to *take care* of one," he countered.

"The lass has a good heart. That much, I can tell ye."

Blast it, Mrs. Gilroy nearly had him convinced. But Carrie needed structure. She needed consistency. And for that, she needed a governess who would be there for more than a short time—more than the days he anticipated Belle might be in residence.

"Of course, ye could watch over the child until I'm back on *both* of my feet," Mrs. Gilroy went on. "She'd enjoy some time with ye, I'm sure."

"You know that won't be feasible. Not at the moment." The tension in the back of his neck returned with a vengeance. "I am in the midst of a major negotiation."

"In that case, I'll simply have to make the best of it, won't I?" Mrs. Gilroy tapped her cane to the floor as if to punctuate her thought, then added another perfectly timed wince.

Bloody hell, the guilt. The cagy old woman certainly knew how to drive her point home, didn't she? Perhaps he should bring her aboard in his most heated contract talks.

"I *will* figure out a solution," he said, keeping his tone even as he kneaded the ache in his neck.

"The solution is in the kitchen as we speak." A gleam lit Mrs. Gilroy's eyes. "Perhaps there's good reason why that pretty lass ran smack into ye last night. In all of London, she ran into ye."

"You're implying this is fate?"

"Fate. Luck. Call it what ye will," she said with a sage nod. "I've lived long enough to know very little happens by pure chance."

"This is madness." He slowly shook his head. "You know that, don't you?"

Glancing up, he met Belle's gaze as she returned from the kitchen, a silver tray bearing the breakfast Mrs. Gilroy had prepared in her hands. Her eyes narrowed, if only slightly. Had she overheard their conversation?

"That may well be, but I'm right. And ye know it." Mrs. Gilroy said, her voice low, yet pointed. "Unless ye have a better idea."

THE SOLUTION IS *in the kitchen as we speak.* Mrs. Gilroy's words played in Belle's thoughts as she sat down to the breakfast the woman had prepared before her unfortunate tangle with Heathy. Evidently, her suspicion that the housekeeper's transformation from crabby to molasses-sweet was rooted in an ulterior motive had not been so far-fetched after all. Even if the woman's plan was entirely well-meaning, the very idea that the housekeeper was speaking about her behind her back chafed a bit.

Unless ye have a better idea. She'd convinced herself Mrs. Gilroy wasn't a conniver like Aunt Vera. Perhaps she'd been mistaken. Again.

Her own *better idea* hovered on the tip of her tongue. My, wouldn't Mrs. Gilroy be shocked if the housekeeper could read her mind? *Madness, indeed.*

Diverting her thoughts from the twinges of hurt, she focused on Carrie as they made it through the meal. The child had retrieved one of the pillows that had survived Mrs. Gilroy's encounter with Heathy and now sat comfortably on her cushioned chair. At the moment, the girl was delighting in the taste of a scone with a bit of jam. Truth be told, she seemed to be the only one who was truly enjoying the delicious meal. The atmosphere seemed tense, as if much had been left unspoken in their half-hearted efforts at conversation.

She waited for Carrie to finish her meal before she broached the subject nagging in her thoughts. It wouldn't do to upset the girl. As for Jon and Mrs. Gilroy, that was another story entirely.

"I couldn't help but overhear a portion of your earlier discussion," she said, biting back a smile as he nearly choked on his tea. "As I play a part in a scheme that's evidently quite mad, I would be in your debt if one of you would tell me precisely what it is that you're proposing."

Mrs. Gilroy laced her fingers together and lowered her gaze. For his part, Jon narrowed his eyes, seeming to study her.

"I suspected as much," he said. "It's a rare occasion when you utter fewer words during the course of an hour than I have fingers on my hands."

"Is that so?" she replied. "Perhaps I shall continue to hold my peace until I'm gone from this place."

He turned to Carrie, his expression softening. "Heathy looks rather bored, wouldn't you say?" He glanced at the dog curled up on a small braided rug. "Would you take him to the garden to play?"

The girl grinned. "You'll come along, too?"

"Not quite yet," he said. When she poked out her lower lip, he added, "I shall join you shortly."

"Come, Heathy." The girl plopped from the chair to the floor. Within a few moments, she'd taken the dog from the room, skipping along the way.

"Well, we can speak freely now," Belle said, noticing the drawn, tense lines on Mrs. Gilroy's face. "That is, if you might be able to endure my chattering. Luckily for you, I will only remain within range of your ears for a few more hours."

"*Days* is more likely," he said, reaching for a scone. He slathered it with clotted cream while awaiting her reaction.

She blinked. Surely, she had misunderstood. "Did I hear you correctly?"

"Delays have arisen, both at the hotel and regarding your security."

"Oh, dear." She took a drink of cool water from her glass. "I had not wished to impose."

"It goes without saying that you will remain here until secure accommodations can be arranged."

She pulled in a low breath, taking him in. The coolness in his voice seemed unfamiliar. Not at all as she remembered.

"My, I don't recall you sounding . . . so very formal."

He studied her for a long moment, as if he didn't quite know what to say. But then, the words came. Very civilized. And so very cold. "Last night, I gave my word that I would keep you safe. I meant what I said."

Belle met his dark gaze. How many lonely nights had she lain in her bed, longing to look into those eyes again? Yearned to graze her fingertips along the hard edge of his jaw. To drink in the heat of his body, so close to hers she could feel each beat of his heart. And now she was here with him. Near enough to touch. Near enough to kiss.

But somehow, Jon had changed. This oh-so-proper man who spoke with the same cool lack of emotion as her father's lawyers was not the one she'd dreamed of all those nights.

"That's quite noble," she said. "But I never intended to stay under your roof. Not for more than one night." She squared her shoulders. "There must be somewhere . . . somewhere else for me to go."

"Arabelle, I will not see you in harm's way."

Arabelle. Once, she'd loved the way he pronounced her given name, uttering each syllable in a manner that seemed nearly a caress. But now, he clipped the words between his teeth, the sound nothing like the velvety tones he'd used all that time ago, when they were alone beneath the stars in Central Park.

"No." She gave her head a brisk shake, as if that might clear it, even as the slight ache in the vicinity of her heart told her she was in danger. She had to leave this house. Had to leave *him.* Before the bone-deep need flared again. "I simply cannot stay here." She gulped air. "I will not impose upon your good nature. Not you, of all people."

"Miss Frost, if I may be so bold . . . 'tis no inconvenience," Mrs. Gilroy spoke up, even as Jon shot her a speaking glance. "Truth be told, if ye would stay on for a bit, ye might be a great help. To me." Her voice gained strength with each word. "And the wee lass."

My, the old woman had gumption, didn't she? Her boldness intrigued Belle. "You're referring to the *mad* notion?"

"She is," Jon said.

"Something else occurs to me," Mrs. Gilroy went on. "I don't doubt one of the nosy biddies around here will soon realize there's a young woman at this residence. I'd imagine Miss Frost will want to go into the garden, if only for some fresh air. Ye'd be amazed at how fast the talk will travel. But if I can explain her presence, if I can say she's the new governess, no one will puzzle out her identity. Miss Pritchard made a show of leaving. It would make perfect sense to say that Miss Frost is her replacement."

My, the woman was quick on her feet, wasn't she? Belle sent her a glance of admiration. "That would quell the gossip, wouldn't it?" she agreed.

She turned to Jon just as his attention darted to the sight of the dog—now decked out with flowers adorning his silver collar—trotting back into the room with Carrie close behind. "And you will see that I am right. It is, indeed, mad."

Cutting a direct path to Belle, the girl presented her with a vibrant blossom she'd plucked from the garden. "Heathy wants you to have this," Carrie said with a wide smile. "He wants you to stay."

"Carrie, that is simply not possible." Jon's voice was gruff yet gentle as he reached for the child.

Even as he spoke, Mrs. Gilroy gestured to the child. "She's taken to ye, Miss Frost," she whispered. "Now that is *not* madness. Not in my book."

"Please, say you'll be my new nanny," Carrie said, proudly offering another freshly plucked flower.

Jon lifted the girl up and settled her back onto her cushioned chair. "Miss Frost is a guest in this house. She is most definitely *not* your governess."

Belle pulled in a breath. Perhaps Jon was right. Perhaps the notion that she might actually watch over this child was indeed ever so slightly mad.

Mrs. Gilroy sent her a look and a nod, an unspoken conversation Belle instinctively understood. The child needed someone to care for her. Jon was obviously quite fond of the little girl, but he was . . . well, he was *Jon.* He had his responsibilities. He had his business ventures. In his life, he'd left little room for anything else. In her heart, she knew that truth, far better than most.

Perhaps the idea was not so very mad. Not at all. For a time, at least, she could be there for this bubbly yet sad-eyed little girl.

"Not yet," Belle said, relishing the look of surprise in his eyes as she countered his words.

One of his dark brows hitched. "It would never work."

"You're quite sure of that, aren't you?" Belle challenged. "To tell the truth, I'd often thought I might enjoy the duties."

A spark that looked like amusement played on his mouth. "You, my dear Miss Frost, are unlike any nanny I've ever known."

Something in his tone chafed at her. For so very long, men had underestimated her. If she wished to become a governess, she certainly possessed the necessary qualities.

"I *would* be unlike any governess you've known. That much is certain." She flashed a smile. "I am equally certain that it would, as you put it, *work*. I'll have you know my training in etiquette is top-notch."

He shrugged. "I don't doubt that."

She hiked her chin. "In that case, I fail to see the problem."

"I would imagine you drove your own governesses to distraction," he went on. "There'd certainly be a cosmic irony in the reversal of the roles."

"I will admit to driving one—and only one—governess to her wit's end. As I recall, she was a rather strict shrew of a woman. Suffice it to say, she did not bring out the best in me." She squared her shoulders. "As for the others, they were pleased with my efforts. I was an excellent student."

"This has nothing to do with your qualifications." The glimmer of amusement fading from his eyes, he shook his head. "The very idea is unthinkable. I can only imagine your father's reaction at the very thought of you conducting yourself as a member of the staff."

"You're right. It might well be unthinkable, especially when you put it like that." An image of her father's expression upon discovering her new role—in Jon's household, no less—flickered into her thoughts, and she could not help but smile. This might prove interesting, indeed.

"Say you'll stay," Carrie looked up at her with beseeching brown eyes. "Please."

Ah, the little girl knew what she was doing, didn't she? The soft plea in her words tore at Belle's heart. Ruffling the girl's curly brown hair with her fingertips, she marveled that she was even giving thought to the notion. Perhaps Jon was right. Perhaps the idea that she would watch over this child, even for a short time, was ever so slightly mad.

A short time. Belle pondered her dilemma. Her stay in this house—in Jon's home, sleeping within a stone's throw of his bed . . . within a stone's throw of *him*—would be brief. Heaven knew even a few days would stir memories she did not want to face, emotions she did not want to feel. And even more importantly, was it fair to thrust the child into a situation in which she'd have to face watching someone she cared for walk away—again?

"Please stay," Carrie said in an earnest little voice. "I won't be any trouble. I promise," she threw in for good measure.

Trouble. The implication in the word pierced Belle like a thorn. The pinched-faced governess who'd made a blessedly few weeks of her young life miserable had used that word to describe Belle on a near-daily basis. Fortunately, her mother had taken note of the woman's mean spirit and sent her packing. But would Jon even be around to notice a governess instilling a sense of shame in the child?

Mrs. Gilroy's mouth thinned as she slowly nodded, her expression confirming the direction of Belle's thoughts. Her forehead furrowed in a look of surprise as Jon bent down and took the girl's small hand in his. So, he'd also grasped the undertone of the girl's promise.

"Carrie, you could never be trouble," Jon said, meeting her sad-eyed gaze. "You're a good girl. Don't ever let anyone tell you otherwise."

"But Miss Pritchard . . ."

He gave his head a hearty shake. "Miss Pritchard evidently ate something quite sour one day. Unfortunately, it turned her into a pickle," he said, his expression warming at the sound of the girl's giggle. "But let's keep that our secret, shall we?"

"Yes, we shall," the girl said with a wide grin.

Mrs. Gilroy's smile was the first look of true happiness Belle had observed on the old woman's careworn features. The housekeeper obviously cared for the child's well-being. And for some reason Belle couldn't entirely puzzle out, the woman trusted her.

Governess? She mentally dismissed that title in favor of another she much preferred. *Teacher.* Why, yes, that would do nicely.

Goodness, what would be the harm in it?

She might as well make the most of her time here. She would enjoy teaching Carrie about the beauty of nature and art and the fairy tales she'd loved as a girl. And if she was watching over the girl, perhaps—just perhaps—she'd be too preoccupied with her young charge to allow her thoughts to wander to the child's too-blasted-handsome guardian.

"As a guest in this home, I see no reason why I might not instruct the girl in proper manners and such while I'm here. Governess or not—such a title does not matter to me. Not one whit. Call it whatever you will," she said, summoning a resolute tone.

"Yes!" Carrie bounced excitedly to her feet.

She turned to the housekeeper. "And while I'm at it, should Mrs. Gilroy require a bit of assistance with her responsibilities while she is recuperating, I am certainly capable of lending a hand. Wouldn't you agree?"

Belle smiled at the undisguised surprise on Jon's features. He regarded her for a long moment, seeming to weigh his words carefully. "Am I to believe you actually intend to cook?"

"Of course," she said, hoping she sounded more confident than she was in that moment. After all, it wasn't as if she'd *never* prepared a meal. She was known for the delightful little finger sandwiches she'd bring to the meetings of the ladies' garden club. Well, she hadn't actually *made* the sandwiches. But she'd certainly taken note of the process her cook followed in putting the cucumber and bread together in such a tasty manner.

His brow furrowed. "And clean?"

"My apartment in Manhattan was spotless." *Surely, he had not forgotten that.*

"As I recall, you employed a maid."

She folded her arms at the waist and met his narrow-eyed gaze. "I tidied up . . . on her days off."

"You truly think you know what you're getting into, don't you?" Was that a smile curving his full mouth? Or a smirk?

"You should remember that I accomplish most everything I

set my mind to." As she spoke, the dog trotted over, begging for a bit of attention. Crouching down, she tousled his slightly shaggy fur. "Heathy, I do believe I'm going to enjoy getting to know you."

The dog yipped, a uniquely joyful sound. Carrie dropped to her knees to give him a hug. "You're happy, too. Aren't you, Heathy?"

Jon plowed a hand through his hair. He'd lost this minor battle. And the look in his eyes told Belle that he knew it. "Very well," he conceded. "I know when to fold."

"Interesting. I happen to be rather proficient at cards myself, and I'm feeling confident about this hand I've been dealt," she said, rising to meet his skeptical gaze. "In my life, I've met any challenge I've faced. And this one will be easy as pie. Wouldn't you agree?"

Chapter Nine

*T*HE DOLLAR PRINCESS, *the dog, and the tiny dynamo...* a combination Jon had never imagined, not even in his wildest dreams. The mix of players had the makings of a comedy of errors he might actually enjoy. If it were not playing out in his home, that is.

Leaning back in his leather wing chair, he resisted the urge to chuckle. Bloody hell, Belle had no idea what she was getting herself into. Her motivation stemmed from a tender heart for the young and the weak and the vulnerable. But the role of governess in this home entailed watching over a tiny whirlwind in curls. His precocious little ward had the sweet face of a young angel, but her energy, strong will, and penchant for mischief might well test the patience of a saint.

At the moment, Carrie and the dog had scurried off to her room. With any luck, she would not resume the creation of pretend pastries, of all the bloody things. At least within the house, he didn't have to worry about her making a colossal mess. Though he didn't doubt she might find something else to use in place of the mud that had been her creative medium the day before.

Mud pies. He couldn't help but smile to himself at the thought. What a ridiculous concept. Three short months earlier, he'd never considered that such a thing might even exist. But there was a silver lining to it all. The child had single-handedly managed to solve his dilemma over the employment of her governess. He'd found Miss Pritchard as sour as a ripe lemon, but he'd been loath to consider removing her from the position given the simple fact that he certainly wasn't capable of running his business *and* reining in the rambunctious child. If there was one good thing about the blasted *mud pies,* they'd been the final straw that had sent the stiff-upper-lipped nanny on her way and, as a result, forced his hand.

He'd assisted Mrs. Gilroy to the sitting room to recline and rest, if only for a few minutes. Knowing her as he did, he doubted she'd stay idle for long. His housekeeper was at least twice his age, but her energy—most likely the product of her desire to oversee every small detail of the daily tasks—might well prevent her from enjoying any significant rest.

Now, behind a not-fully-closed door in his study, he and Belle were alone. Finally. Somehow, it seemed a long time had passed since the carriage ride from the tavern the night before. So much had changed in less than twenty-four hours.

She'd settled upon a small sofa, perusing the daily news. The wool skirt of her suit brushed the floor. The rich blue color suited her, but she appeared a bit uncomfortable in the ensemble. He would have to see to obtaining garments which were more to her preference. But how? She couldn't be seen gallivanting about town, visiting the fashionable shops and such. He'd have to enlist someone to obtain the garments—someone he could trust. Who would know any blasted thing about women's clothing? It was a puzzle, but he'd figure it out. After all, he always did.

As she scanned the paper, Belle seemed more at ease, perhaps for the first time since he'd encountered her the night before. This morning, she'd pulled her long, honey-colored hair into a simple braid and secured it with a simple velvet tie. The unadorned style accented her perfect oval face and gentle features. God above, she was every bit as lovely as he remembered. No, he was wrong. With the morning sun streaming through the window, dancing over her softly etched features, she was even more beautiful.

When she'd taken on the role of governess to little Carrie, he'd wondered if she might be over her head. Suddenly, he knew the question could apply to him as well.

He couldn't deny he'd had doubts about bringing her here, not even to himself. But damned if he would leave her alone and vulnerable, on the run from a man she evidently feared. He would shield her from the bastard. He'd do whatever it took to protect her.

Blasted shame he'd never found the means to put the memories of her—and what they'd had—behind him. When he'd made the decision to leave New York, he'd made the logical choice. The only choice. Or so he'd convinced himself at the time. But as soon as she'd dashed into the *Lair*, his certainty had crumbled like a child's sandcastle facing off against the tide.

And now, she was here. In his blasted study, of all places.

Had she sensed him watching her? She lifted her attention from the paper, took a sip of tea, and met his gaze. "Penny for your thoughts."

Thoughts? So many blasted questions filled his mind. Questions with answers that might cause her distress. It wasn't the time. Not yet. He'd allow the moment of peace to linger. After what she'd been through, she bloody well deserved it. For now, he'd focus on the present.

"I can't help but wonder if you have any notion of what you're getting into by taking charge of my little ward."

"Ward?" She bit off the word as if it were somehow distasteful. "How very formal. The child is your kin."

"Indeed, she is. Carrie's father was my cousin. Fred was a good man, and his wife was one of the kindest souls I've ever had the privilege to know." He stared at the leaded glass in the window for a moment, collecting his thoughts. "The child was so young, not quite three, when her parents were killed."

"She's quite precocious."

"Indeed. The girl is exceedingly bright. And even more curious."

"Children are naturally inquisitive," Belle countered. "Curiosity is a good thing, is it not?"

"At times," he said. "But then again, you remember the old saying about curiosity and the cat."

"Personally, I believe inquisitiveness is a wonderful attribute in a child. Or in an adult, for that matter." Belle took another sip of tea, seeming to study him. He'd no doubt her last statement was aimed at him.

"I agree," he said, taking the bait, if only to see the glimmer of surprise in her beautiful eyes. "I consider myself positively overflowing with natural curiosity."

"You?" She cocked a brow. "I can't say that I recall *that* aspect of your personality."

He lifted one brow in reply to hers. "I don't know how you failed to notice."

A slight smile played on her lips. "I shall make a mental note to pay close attention you put your abundant interest in the world into play."

Ah, there was the Belle he'd known. Her natural wit could charm the most dedicated cynic, while her smile never failed to draw him in.

"Might we talk a bit more about Carrie?" she went on. "I'd like to consider how best to guide her during my stay. Since she has been here with you, what has most captured her interest?"

He mulled the question. The first word that came to mind was *everything*. But that certainly was not the answer Belle sought. In the weeks since the girl had arrived at his doorstep—with scarcely twenty-four hours' notice, no less—he had delegated much of her care to the governess he'd hastily arranged through the agency. Fortunately, Mrs. Gilroy had shown a clear fondness for the girl, her keen eyes and ears watching over the prim Miss Pritchard as the governess conducted her duties. He'd done his best to ensure the girl was well cared for, devoting attention to the child during the rare times when he was not in the office consumed with Mason Enterprise's most recent endeavor or overseeing the operations at the Rogue's Lair. He certainly didn't want to admit he was utterly stymied.

"My little cousin possesses an abundance of interest in the world around her," he said, vague enough to maintain his truthfulness. "From what I have observed, she is especially drawn to the dog."

"I noticed that as well," Belle said with a thoughtful nod. "Not surprising. I adored our family pets."

"Speaking of pets, you mentioned that you miss Angus." He gently broached the subject that had been on his mind since the night before. "Did you . . . lose him?"

"Last year." Her expression somber, Belle nodded again. "It was so very hard. I'd known he was old and didn't have much time left, but somehow, that didn't help. Not at all."

"I'm sorry," he said. "I know how much he meant to you." If he were sitting by her side, if it were still his place to hold her, he would take her hand and comfort her. He would do whatever it took to ease her sadness. But nothing in her manner or expression invited his touch. That time had passed.

Like a fool, he'd thrown it all away.

"Now, please, tell me a bit more about Carrie," she said, bringing his focus back to the moment at hand. "What activities does she prefer?"

"Activities?" Blast it, he was drawing from an empty well on that question. He had no bloody idea. But he didn't care to admit it.

"I take it she enjoys playing outdoors," Belle said.

"Well, she does seem to have a fondness for making creations out of the dirt in the garden."

"Ah, the infamous mud pies," Belle said, amusement in her tone. "I shall have to be careful to avoid taking a spill like her previous governess."

"I suspect you could not replicate that scene even if you tried," he said. That morning, he'd taken a look at where the child had been playing. How in blazes had the stiff-backed governess managed to end up bustle-first in a spot of mud not much larger than a serving platter?

"I've learned to never underestimate my own penchant for mishaps," she said brightly.

"Miss Pritchard's temperament was not well-suited to caring for a child as spirited as Carrie," he said. "She did not know how to channel the girl's energy. Or her intelligence."

Belle's expression warmed as she met his gaze. "She sounds like she takes after her cousin."

"She does. But that cousin is *not* me." He couldn't help but smile as he pictured his sister and her antics. "Carrie reminds me a great deal of Macie. My sister takes after our mum, free spirit that she is. When she was a girl, I suspect Macie drove more than one of her governesses to imbibe."

"Oh, you're exaggerating," she said lightly.

"Am I?" He reached for his own drink. "Macie and her husband are due back from their recent expedition by the end of the month. I'm sure she'll verify what I'm saying as the absolute, unvarnished truth."

"I will definitely enjoy making her acquaintance. If I'm still in London when she returns, that is."

Still in London. Why did the simple phrase feel like a kick in the gut?

"You'd asked about my little cousin's preferred activities," he said, refocusing the conversation, if only to distract himself from the sensations he didn't want to feel. "Mrs. Gilroy could tell you more on that subject than I can. I do believe she and Carrie are a bit fond of one another."

"I can see that as well," Belle agreed. "When I was a child, I enjoyed playing with my dolls. Does Carrie have a favorite?"

"She does have dolls. Quite a few actually," he said, picturing the carefully packaged delivery that had arrived a week or so earlier. "But I've only seen her play with that old cloth doll she's so fond of. It looks as if it should be destined for the refuse pile."

Belle's eyes lit with what looked like a memory. "The rag doll?"

He pictured the simple stitching on its worn linen face. "I suppose that's what you'd call it."

"Oh, I call mine Hildy."

His brow furrowed. "Hildy?"

"After one of my favorite aunts. Hildegard is a bit much for a three-year-old to manage, so my mother suggested we shorten the name. I'll have you know I still treasure that plain little doll." A gentle smile accented her words. "I suppose that may sound rather silly to you."

"Not at all," he said truthfully. "I'm assuming a sentimental connection."

"Ah, you know about such things, do you now?" She flashed a teasing look. "And there I thought you were a hard-boiled tycoon."

"Tycoon?" he scoffed. "My father can lay claim to that title. Not me."

She wrinkled her pert nose. "Many would disagree, you know."

"He would not. Of that, I'm quite sure." Somehow, the words tasted bitter on his tongue. "Now, tell me more about your doll. There must be a family connection."

"You are a clever one, aren't you?" she teased again. "Hildy has been in my family for generations. I'm told the doll was sewn nearly a century ago, while George Washington was in the White House and passed down through the generations. My great-grandmother gave it to my grandmother when she was a tot. Grandmama named the doll after her aunt, and choosing a special name became a family tradition. Eventually, Hildy made it to me. One day, I hope to pass it on to my own daughter. I suspect someone who loved Carrie may have given her the doll she cherishes."

"I hadn't considered that," he said, feeling every bit the dolt.

"Well, as I live and breathe," she mused. "Jon Mason admitting he may have overlooked an important detail . . . why, I never thought I'd see the day."

"A rare thing, indeed," he replied flippantly.

She hiked a questioning brow. "It must be difficult to live with the knowledge that you so seldom make a mistake." Her words might have seemed harsh if not for the playful glint in her eyes.

"Now that's where you are wrong, Arabelle. I make many mistakes. But I'm not inclined to admit it."

"Truer words have seldom been spoken," she said with a little grin. "I do hope it wasn't very painful for you."

He gave another shrug. "At least now I have a logical reason for refraining from tossing that threadbare doll of hers out with the rubbish."

"You do have a way with the little ones, don't you?" she chided.

"I make no such claim," he said, giving another shrug. "We've already established I have no experience with children. And that brings me back to my initial question. Do you truly know what you're doing, acting as governess to my exceedingly clever and curious young ward?"

"Of course," she replied quickly. Too quickly.

"You're quite sure of that?" he pressed lightly.

She lifted her pert chin, meeting his question directly. "You, of all people, know of my fondness for children."

"There's more to it than fondness, and we both know it."

"Watching over Carrie will be a new experience, but I will relish it. As I told you, it will be as easy as pie."

He could not hold back his skepticism. "Might I ask if you've ever actually baked a pie?"

"I'll have you know that apple pie is my specialty." Veiling her gaze with her lashes, she glanced down at her hands. *Interesting.* He knew her well enough to know the implication of that small gesture. She was being less than truthful in that moment.

"I shall remember that," he said, meaning every word. "Perhaps you will indulge my taste for sweets at some time in the near future."

"It will be my pleasure," she said, grazing her top teeth over her bottom lip. "When time permits, that is."

"Of course." He studied the way her teeth played with her lip and she fidgeted her fingers. Yes, she was definitely exaggerating her ability in the kitchen. But he wouldn't have expected her to back down. That wouldn't be the Arabelle he'd known, now, would it?

"You're quite confident that your experience with Carrie will proceed smoothly. Without a hitch, as they say."

Her teeth grazed her lower lip again. "My time here should be a pleasant change from my everyday routine."

"Ah, yes, taking tea with some railroad tycoon's bored wife and deciding upon a gown for your next ball must be utterly exhausting."

"It's not so easy as that," she said, hiking her chin. "In any case, I'm looking forward to every minute of my time here."

"Are you, now?" He studied her for a moment. Her intentions were good. Of that, he had no doubt. She genuinely wished to be of help. But Arabelle Frost had never had to lift a finger to cook, clean, or care for anyone other than herself. She was a quick study. But who might even be able to teach her?

"Of course," she said with a little grin. "If only to prove I'm right to a naysayer like you."

"Naysayer, eh?" He stroked his chin as an idea took shape. "Would you care to make it interesting?"

"Interesting?" she repeated, the grin replaced with a look of intrigue in her dark blue eyes.

"A wager," he explained. "Or, if you prefer, a challenge."

"And what might be the terms?"

He met her questioning gaze. "If a week passes and you continue to see no reason for me to bring in a governess from the agency to relieve you, I will donate to whichever of your charities you choose."

A smile played on her beautiful mouth. "I assume you're proposing a generous donation."

"Quite substantial," he agreed.

"And if, by some chance, I should lose this wager, we both know I have no money at the moment." Her brow furrowed. "What would you propose to receive as my forfeit?"

"What I'm thinking will not require so much as a penny from your purse."

The furrows deepened. "Then what?" She looked puzzled rather than wary. At least she still trusted him not to be an utter scoundrel, even now. That was something to be thankful for, at least.

"I shall expect to taste a delicious slice of your culinary specialty, an apple pie baked by you." He resisted the urge to grin. "For me."

Chapter Ten

BELLE'S FIRST MORNING as a governess—or teacher, or whatever title she wanted to claim—left her convinced she was made for the role. It wouldn't be long before Jon would see he had no chance of winning his wager. All she'd need to do was decide upon the charity which would receive his generous support. He'd departed for his office within minutes after he'd proposed the bet which now seemed certain to cost him a pretty penny. Such a shame he could not witness how very mistaken he'd been.

Her first hours with her new charge flowed so smoothly, Belle wondered why she'd ever had the slightest doubt. Carrie embraced the arrival of her new governess. The child was clever and cooperative, and evidently someone had taught the girl to watch her manners. Perhaps the not-so-endearing Miss Pritchard had performed a useful function in spite of her unceremonious exit. All in all, Belle's new role seemed an utter delight.

Pity Belle could not say the same of the hours immediately after morning had passed.

The afternoon had begun uneventfully. Mrs. Gilroy had put on a kettle of soup earlier that day. By noon, the savory aroma of herbs and well-seasoned chicken wafted through the air. When Mrs. Gilroy ventured into the kitchen to prepare their midday meal, Belle went with her, intent on lending a hand.

The housekeeper dished up the piping hot soup. "Do be

careful to wait for the broth to cool before ye serve the wee lass," Mrs. Gilroy advised as she placed two bowls on the serving platter.

With a nod of understanding, Belle reached for the bowl Mrs. Gilroy had left on the counter, but the housekeeper gave a brisk shake of her head. "I'll be taking mine in the kitchen."

"Are you sure you won't reconsider?" Belle asked. "I was hoping we might chat a bit."

The housekeeper's lips thinned. "Miss Pritchard did not think it proper for me to dine with the girl."

My, what a persnickety woman Carrie's previous governess must be. "Well, she didn't know what she was talking about, now did she?" Belle said. "I do hope you'll reconsider, Mrs. Gilroy. After all you've done to prepare this delicious meal."

"Ye're sure of that?"

"Of course." Belle mulled the question whispering in the back of her thoughts. "Might I ask what Mr. Mason thought of the governess's request?"

"I doubt he knew anything about it. He's so consumed with this deal he's working on, he's seldom been in the residence for his meals. The man works himself to the bone, don't ye know?" A hint of sadness tinged her voice at the revelation. "But if he'd found out, I do suspect he'd have thought it rubbish."

A sense of relief washed over Belle. At least Jon did not appear to secretly be a horrid snob.

"I didn't know if ye'd feel the same as she did," Mrs. Gilroy went on. A thin smile pulled at her mouth. "I suspected ye would not."

"Well then, we shall enjoy a stimulating conversation," Belle said. "There's so much I'd like to know about Carrie."

"I can't say as I've much to tell ye that ye don't already know, but I'll try."

"I would appreciate that." Belle glanced down at the woman's leg. "I'll be happy to assist you to the table before I bring the tray."

"Thank ye," the older woman said, "but I can make it on my own."

Mrs. Gilroy hobbled to the dining room with Belle following close behind. After setting the places for their meal, Belle made the short walk down the corridor to the room Jon had designated Carrie's playroom.

The girl sat on the rug, acting out a scene with a pair of stuffed rabbits. One of the bunnies had evidently suffered a fright from a threatening creature, and the other bunny was consoling it with a hug.

"That's a very kind rabbit," Belle said, smiling to herself.

"She's my nicest bunny," Carrie agreed. "And the prettiest."

"She is quite fetching," Belle said. "But now, it's time for our meal. Please put the bunnies on the shelf, out of Heathy's reach."

"Heathy likes the bunnies," the girl said, hugging the stuffed dolls. "He won't hurt them."

"I doubt he'd try to hurt them . . . not on purpose," Belle said gently. "But he is a dog, and we know that dogs like to chew, don't they?"

The girl offered a solemn nod, then placed the dolls on a shelf. "I'd like a real bunny," she said, reaching for Belle's hand.

"Perhaps you shall have one . . . someday."

"I do hope so." The child slipped from Belle's light hold, made a dash for the spindle chair in the corner, and scooped up a ragdoll into her arms.

Belle smiled to herself. So, this was Carrie's favorite.

"May I bring Anna?" The girl sounded rather proper as she proudly held out her doll for Belle to see.

"I see no reason why not." Belle studied the doll. Its hair consisted of a few fuzzy strands of faded red yarn, and while the velveteen dress on its cloth body might've been lovely in its day, it was a bit ragged with fraying lace at its hem. Studying the needlework on the doll's wide-eyed linen face, Belle leaned closer for a better look. The stitches that formed perpetually surprised blue eyes and a pert mouth appeared to have been crafted by someone who was not an expert seamstress, perhaps a girl learning to embroider. How touching that Carrie was attached to this old, simply fashioned doll when her room was filled with expensive creations decked out in expertly sewn finery.

"Mama gave her to me when I was a *little* girl," Carrie said.

"She's very pretty."

"Mama made her," Carrie explained. "When she was a girl."

"How very special that she gave it to you."

"Someday, I want to make one of my own. Just like Mama did."

"Perhaps we shall try very soon."

Carrie tucked the doll against her body, her sweet expression betraying the comfort she took from its nearness. From the memories it held. From the tender feelings its very presence evoked.

Belle blinked back tears. Goodness, she was a grown woman and the mere thought of losing her mother was painful. How very sad that Carrie had suffered such a tremendous loss at such a young age.

Taking the girl's free hand in hers, Belle led her to the dining room. The bell on Heathy's collar accented his jaunty trot as he followed along. While Carrie hurried to pet him, Belle noticed the expression on his canine features. Why, she might've described the look as guilty. Questions swirled. Where had the pup been? And what had he been up to?

There was no time to ponder the matter as Carrie quickly scurried up onto her chair. The girl's perch atop a pillow wasn't ideal, but it would have to do until she figured out a more permanent booster. She'd no intention of shuffling Carrie off to a separate table. Surely Jon would soon see the benefit of having the child take her meals with him, perhaps even after Belle was no longer a guest in his home.

"The soup is quite good, isn't it?" she said moments later as the girl seemed to enjoy her meal.

"It is very tasty," Carrie replied with enthusiasm.

"Mrs. Gilroy prepared this delicious food," Belle informed her.

The child turned to the old woman. "Thank you, Mrs. Gilroy."

Belle reached for a slice of bread and dabbed a bit of butter onto the hearty rye. Smiling to herself, she savored the sense of peace which surrounded her for the first time in what seemed a very long while.

Suddenly—without so much as a bell's tinkle of warning—a flash of black on four legs darted past the table. Macie's pet, most likely. Coming to a stop beneath the sideboard, the cat turned to face Belle, seeming to take her in with keen amber eyes. Jewels—perhaps genuine, perhaps paste—adorned the midnight black feline's collar.

"Cleo has finally stirred from her morning nap," Mrs. Gilroy observed.

"Such a beautiful name," Belle said.

"It's short for Cleopatra. Or some nonsense like that." Mrs. Gilroy chuckled. "I'm thankful Miss Macie bestowed the name on the cat and not a babe."

"It's pretty," Carrie said.

"I rather like it, too," Belle agreed.

She'd scarcely had time to utter the words when she spotted the reason for the cat's mad dash. Heathy charged into the room. Moving at a pace Belle suspected was as fast as his little legs could carry him, he chased after Cleo. The happy swish of his tail gave his pursuit a playful feel. But the golden-eyed feline was not amused. Rearing up, the cat let out a hiss.

And then, she took off.

If Heathy had ever learned that cats could jump far higher than he possibly might, he'd conveniently forgotten the lesson. He galloped happily after Cleo, but stopped in his tracks, appearing a bit perplexed as the cat leapt atop the mahogany sideboard.

"Heathy cannot be here," Carrie said with a tone of responsibility. She hopped down out of her chair. "I will get him."

"Carrie, stay here," Belle said quickly. "I'll take him to the garden."

But the child was fast. And determined. Intent on solving the problem at hand, Carrie scurried after the dog. Unfortunately, Heathy hadn't gotten the message that he was not allowed in the dining room. Rather than understanding that he was about to be unceremoniously shooed from the chamber, he met her approach with energetic wags of his tail. If anything, he evidently believed it was time to play.

And play, he did.

Heathy trotted toward Carrie, almost within her reach. But he darted under the table, avoiding the girl's grasp. And then, he turned and sped away, appearing quite amused by Carrie's attempt to catch him.

Up on her perch, the cat watched the pursuit with a bored gaze, as if the humans and the dog they were attempting to corral were quite silly. But then, Heathy's attention shifted. As if he'd suddenly remembered the cat, he bolted toward the sideboard.

Cleo's eyes widened. The cat looked rather incredulous and perhaps a bit annoyed. But then instinct took hold. And she ran.

The cat's ability to propel herself through the air might have put an athlete to shame. With a single leap, Cleo jumped from the sturdy sideboard to the table. The dishes rattled around her.

"Down, Cleo," Mrs. Gilroy scolded in a tone that made even Belle hesitate. For a moment, the cat actually looked as if she might heed the command. Gazing down at the floor, Cleo seemed to mull her options—encounter the wrath of an exasperated housekeeper or take her chances with Heathy.

Carrie hurried after the dog, who by this time had figured out how to bound onto one of the chairs at the table. "Oh, no you don't, Heathy." Bending forward over the chair, the girl wrapped her arms around the squirming pup.

Evidently realizing that Heathy was no longer in any position to chase her, the cat plopped down onto the carpet. Holding her tail high—arrogantly so—Cleo strolled by, throwing Heathy what looked like a feline smirk.

For his part, Heathy was not amused. In a feat of escape-artistry, he wriggled out of Carrie's hold and rushed pell-mell after the cat.

With feline agility, Cleo took another jump, landing soundly on the table. Heathy galloped after her. He attempted a leap, falling quite short of the tabletop. Then another.

This time, Belle caught Heathy. As she scooped him into her arms, Mrs. Gilroy's gasp of warning came a heartbeat too late.

"Oh, dear."

The old woman's shocked murmur made it to Belle's ears just as she'd lifted Heathy up—along with the tablecloth the dog had somehow snagged on his bejeweled collar.

Good heavens!

As the finely tatted white lace shifted beneath the table settings, dishes clattered. Porcelain cups quivered. Spoons rattled.

And the silver soup tureen upended.

Oh, no.

Broth splattered. On the tablecloth. On Belle. Even on the dog.

For a few breaths, Belle could only stare at the mess. And then, she met Mrs. Gilroy's sympathetic gaze.

She set Heathy on the floor, watching the pup shake himself off as she touched her fingertips to the drops of warm soup on her own face. A bit more had splashed on her apron. But the majority of the liquid in the large bowl had landed on her blouse. Glancing down at the formerly pristine linen, she saw a thin shimmer of broth and a handful of diced carrots that resembled orange polka dots. *My, she must look a fright.*

"Here. This will help, if only a bit." Mrs. Gilroy handed her a napkin. "I'll fetch you a clean towel."

A rasp of a cough—deliberately timed, or so it seemed—snatched Belle's attention to the archway between the dining room and the hallway. Jon watched her for a moment as Heathy danced excitedly around his trouser legs and Carrie tugged at his hand.

He fished a handkerchief from his jacket pocket. "Dare I ask?"

"There was a . . . minor mishap," she replied, forcing a pleasant tone as she dabbed broth from her face.

"Minor, eh?" Jon closed the distance between them, even as Carrie and the dog followed his every step.

"Cleo decided to put in an appearance. As you can imagine, Heathy's response was a bit rambunctious."

"That is one way of putting it," Jon said. He reached out, cloth in hand. "May I?"

"Thank you." She pulled in a low breath as he gently touched the linen pocket square to one cheek, then the other. The action was chaste, altogether innocent. And yet, there seemed an air of intimacy in his gentleness as he dabbed at her soup-spattered face.

"That's better." An inner warmth filled his eyes. "Now we can see your true freckles rather than bits of vegetables."

She didn't want to smile, but she couldn't quite help herself. Back in New York, he'd found the small freckles which dotted the bridge of her nose appealing. Once, he'd vowed to kiss each and every one, and given time, he might've made good on his promise. The memory brought a rush of heat to her face. Had her cheeks actually flushed?

"No harm was done." With some effort, she held her tone casual. "Other than a mess to clean."

It was at that moment that the action she'd so hoped to avoid occurred. A small tickle in her nose began to stir. Had a bit of seasoning from the soup landed above her lip? *Drat the luck.* Hoping against hope that the sensation would pass, she caught a breath, stilling herself. But the tickle grew more insistent. She tried to ignore it. And then, it happened.

She sneezed.

And with that simple, reflexive act, the button on her blouse that had struggled mightily to stay fastened came undone. Not only came undone, but popped off its stitching and sailed into the air, tumbling down to the carpet beneath their feet. Moments later, Cleo reappeared, rushing to bat the luminescent pearl button about as if it were a toy.

Easy as pie. Her own words played in her thoughts. She would not allow this moment, embarrassing as it was, to shake her confidence. For heaven's sake, less than twenty-four hours earlier, she'd dashed through the streets of London in a wedding gown, of all the ridiculous things. She'd weathered that, just as she'd push through this minor setback. A soup-soaked blouse was an inconvenience. Nothing more. She'd simply have to change into the snug-fitted dress Mrs. Gilroy had brought her the night before. She could make do, now, couldn't she?

If only Jon had not walked in when he did. He'd seen her looking so very frazzled. She certainly hadn't needed *that.*

For his part, he observed the scene with a notable lack of comment. As he diverted his gaze from her gaping blouse, Belle suspected his care for her modesty was rooted in a sense of decorum as well as the example he set for the girl in his care. He plowed his long fingers through his dark hair.

"Well, then, it would seem I've returned at an appropriate time," he said, keeping his attention on Carrie.

"Appropriate?" Belle could not help but balk at the statement.

He nodded, still appearing careful to train his gaze on something—anything—other than her soup-stained, modesty-challenged bodice.

"It's evident you are in need of a proper wardrobe. I've arranged for someone to help with that," he said, meeting her eyes. "Her name is Miss Blake, and you should expect her to arrive within the hour."

AT ANOTHER TIME in his life, Jon might've been astounded by the sight of an American heiress standing in his dining room, covered with what he assumed was soup, moments after he'd had to stop in his tracks in the hallway to avoid colliding with a frantic cat, a dog in hot pursuit, and a girl rushing to catch the determined pup. But given the utterly unpredictable arrivals that had landed at his doorstep over the last several weeks, the fact that Arabelle Frost had been doused with broth and bits of vegetable while pets and an energetic child ran wild in his home somehow seemed on par with everything else.

He'd tried to warn her, hadn't he? If Belle had thought his household—and his life, for that matter—would run as smoothly as a well-captained ship, she was sadly mistaken. That assumption might've proven valid if she'd arrived in London a few months earlier. But now, he could not lay claim to any semblance of order, not even within his own home.

Easy as pie, she'd said, her eyes flashing with confidence like brilliant sapphires. The scene might've possessed an ironic humor, but the look of mild horror on her face when she realized he was there just in time to see her in that state of soup-covered dishevel muted his amusement. She'd put on a brave front, but he knew her well enough to spot the tiny quiver of her bottom lip when she faced him. Not tears. Not quite. But a definite sign of unhappiness.

Never one to succumb to an affront to her dignity, she'd kept her head high. He'd always found that quality so appealing. She was certainly giving life in his chaotic home a go, he'd give her that.

He'd done his best to act as a gentleman when the button on her blouse had unceremoniously escaped its moorings. But he hadn't been able to avert his gaze quickly enough to avoid catching a glimpse of the lace of her chemise accenting her rounded curves. In truth, he'd seen very little of her bared skin in that fleeting moment, but it was enough to flood his mind with memories. And a renewed hunger.

By thunder, his sister's decision to load her traveling case with journals and books and such even if it had meant casting out a dress or two had turned out to be a stroke of luck. Macie had left the garments behind in a quest for trunk space after she'd pillaged his library for references to consult while she and Finn were on their journey. At the time, she could not have guessed she'd be providing a makeshift wardrobe reasonably well suited to his impromptu houseguest's figure. Belle certainly could not have fit into any of Mrs. Gilroy's dresses. The housekeeper was thin as a bird and, by his estimation, half a head shorter.

While Belle had gone to change into another dress, he settled Carrie into her playroom. As the child occupied herself with a set of colorful wooden puzzle blocks, he assisted Mrs. Gilroy to the sitting room where she propped her leg upon a footstool.

"Are ye planning to leave me here all by my lonesome? It doesn't feel right . . . me sitting about, playing lady, while ye're up and about."

"I'd hardly call this work," he said, getting comfortable in a chair by the window. Meeting Mrs. Gilroy's half-smile, he allowed himself a rare moment of relaxation.

"That's better," she said. "I know ye count on me. It's not in my nature to let ye down."

"You certainly have not done that," he said, stretching out his legs. "You've worked tirelessly to keep up with the changes about this place. I must tell you I appreciate that."

"What else would I do?" she questioned, her tone more gentle than usual. "I take pride in this household."

"Well-justified pride," he said as Belle joined them. She'd changed into a pale green dress he vaguely recalled his sister wearing the previous year. Of course, when Macie had worn the garment, its hem had skimmed the floor. But on Belle, the lower edge of the dress was a full hand's breadth from the floor.

Mrs. Gilroy's eyes widened as Belle crossed the threshold, and she seemed to hesitate. "My, doesn't that look nice," she said eventually, even as her brows lifted in mild contradiction.

"It is rather fetching," Belle agreed, her expression as doubtful as Mrs. Gilroy's had been. "Pity I can scarcely take a breath."

Mrs. Gilroy offered a sage nod. "Ah, ye could never tell, Miss."

"You wouldn't say something simply to make me feel better," Belle said, a faint smile tugging the corners of her mouth, "would you, Mrs. Gilroy?"

"No one could know it's too tight but ye, lass. But do stay away from the spices," the older woman said with a soft chuckle. "We wouldn't want another sneeze to come upon ye. Now, would we?"

"Most definitely not," Belle agreed.

"I think you look pretty," Carrie said. "Like a doll."

Jon rubbed the back of his neck, working loose a sudden knot in his muscles. He couldn't betray that his gaze was drawn to Belle like a magnet to iron ore. The modest, high-necked garment she wore was, as Carrie had said with a child's honesty, *pretty*. But the word didn't begin to describe the woman wearing the dress. Even now, standing there in a snug, too-short garment that was not her own, she was beautiful. By God, Belle was a true diamond.

"Thank you," she replied half-heartedly. "I suppose it will do."

"For the time being," he agreed. "I expect that Miss Blake will be helpful in remedying this situation."

"Miss Blake?" Scrunching her forehead, Mrs. Gilroy seemed confused. "Miss Macie's friend, the one who always seemed to be there when Miss Macie got herself into fixes?"

"The one and only," he said. "Eleanor Blake is . . . an original."

"That is putting it mildly," Mrs. Gilroy said. "I hope she doesn't get Miss Frost wrapped up in her shenanigans."

"Now that perks my interest." Belle's expression brightened. "I do believe I've heard of her."

"I wouldn't doubt it," Jon said. "She's drawn to society balls like a butterfly to a flower."

Mrs. Gilroy gave her head a slow, rueful shake. "'Tis not my place to speak my thoughts about the miss and her taste for mischief."

"Come now," he said with a smile. "When has that ever stopped you?"

"'Tis admittedly a rare occurrence." Her eyes twinkled with amusement.

"Regardless of a penchant for shenanigans, as you put it—the vast majority of which were instigated by my dear sister—Miss Blake is someone we can trust. At this time, that's the most important thing."

Belle nibbled her lower lip. "Does she understand the circumstances that led me here?"

He read the unspoken questions in her eyes. "She knows discretion is of the utmost importance."

"Heaven knows she should be good at keeping quiet," Mrs. Gilroy agreed. "After all, she kept Miss Macie's secrets from ye all those years."

Jon's attention darted to his housekeeper. *Macie's secrets?* He kneaded his neck again, deciding against pursuing the subject. God knew his younger sister had brought about more than one gray hair on his head. But if Miss Blake had been able to resist spreading tales of Macie's amusing exploits, he'd no doubt Miss Blake would be able to keep Belle's presence in his home a well-guarded secret.

"You can trust her," Jon said, turning back to Belle. "I would not have called upon her if I wasn't sure of that."

"I understand," Belle said. "So, she knows who I am?"

He nodded. "I'd considered employing an alias in the interest of security. But it was pointless. As soon as I described the situation, she deduced your identity."

"How did she know?" Belle's complexion paled. "Are you telling me my dash through London made the papers?"

"It's nothing like that," he explained. "Miss Blake is clever, so any attempt to evade the truth was bound to fail. She's exceedingly well-connected with the latest gossip running through the city.

That may prove helpful."

"Perhaps," she said, pressing her fingertips to her temples. "But I cannot help but wonder what she will think of my presence here."

As she grazed her teeth over her lower lip again, his gaze was drawn to her rosy mouth. In his mind's eye, he envisioned tracing the soft curves of her lips, drinking in the satin texture.

With ruthless efficiency, he shoved the thought to the back of his mind. Belle was not here to rekindle what had gone between them all those months ago. She was here seeking refuge. She was alone. And vulnerable. He'd best remember that over these next days.

Blast it, the desire to hold her, to offer comfort—or so he tried to convince himself—was getting the better of him. He had to return to his office, the sooner the better. He had work to accomplish, an appointment or two. Possibly a negotiation. There was no time to dawdle here.

At least he tried to tell himself that his need to leave was a matter of work. Truth be told, it was more than that. He had to leave while he could still think straight about something—anything—other than Belle.

Still, he wouldn't leave without easing her concerns. Even with his sparse explanation, Eleanor Blake had fully understood Belle's predicament. She would not judge Belle for taking refuge in his home. He'd known his sister's friend for years, and had come to see her as both kind and worthy of trust.

"She knows you've come here for your safety," he said truthfully, reaching out to take her hand in his. "She will not perceive a scandal where there is none."

Belle regarded him with uncertain eyes. "I do hope you're right."

Chapter Eleven

"GOODNESS, MY OLD eyes are seeing double. Could ye have a twin ye did not know of, lass?"

Mrs. Gilroy made her way to a chair and plopped down upon the overstuffed cushion. A slight smile played on her careworn features as she studied Belle and the young woman who'd arrived bearing a rolling trunk—presumably filled with clothing—Miss Eleanor Blake.

As she exchanged greetings with the visitor, Belle wondered if Mrs. Gilroy might well benefit from a new pair of spectacles. She and Miss Blake shared a superficial resemblance, though not nearly as dramatic as the housekeeper's observation. Miss Blake's hair—the color of fresh-churned butter, quite a bit lighter than Belle's honey-hued curls—framed her perfect oval face with soft golden waves, and her features were more finely etched, as if a fairy tale sprite had come to life. Her blue eyes gleamed with warmth and a hint of the mischief Mrs. Gilroy had described. For her part, Miss Blake's ever-so-slightly raised eyebrows betrayed she shared Belle's take on Mrs. Gilroy's remarks.

"It's delightful to finally make your acquaintance," Miss Blake said. "Since I returned from the continent, I'd heard so much about you. I was hoping we would eventually cross paths."

"I'd imagine you'd expected it might be under different circumstances," Belle said, managing a faint smile.

"Of course, I'd expected to find you at a ball or Lady So-And-

So's soiree. But this is delightfully unconventional, wouldn't you agree?"

"I suppose that is one way of putting it," Belle said lightly.

"Indeed," Mrs. Gilroy agreed. "I do hope yer aunt enjoyed her trip, Miss Blake."

"Please do call me Ellie. Miss Blake is so very stuffy."

"Ellie?" Mrs. Gilroy's brow furrowed. "I'd thought ye went by Nell."

"I did. But I've grown rather weary of that pet name. It's time for something new." The expression in her gaze hinted at a story she hadn't yet told. "You'd asked about Aunt Tilly. Oh, she had a grand time. So grand she hasn't come home." She punctuated her statement with a wink.

"I see," Mrs. Gilroy said. "Well, good for her. She's a kind woman. Always had a smile for me when she visited Miss Macie."

"Aunt Tilly is one of a kind," Ellie said. "I like to think I take after her."

"I'd say ye clearly do." Mrs. Gilroy stood and made her way to the sideboard. "Might I pour ye some tea?"

"Perhaps in a bit." Ellie turned to Belle. Her mouth curved up at the corners as her gaze drifted to the inches of Belle's shoes exposed by the too-short hem. "So, my dear, as it's not a grand idea for you to pay the dressmaker a visit at this moment, I've brought her wares to you. I presume you're in the mood to do a bit of shopping."

I CAN BREATHE again. How wonderful!

Gazing at her reflection in the bedchamber mirror, Belle pulled in a deep breath. The fabric of her blouse moved with the rise and fall of her bosom with a bit of room to spare. The white cotton was practical and comfortable, and she'd no longer have to worry about sending a mother-of-pearl button flying off like a projectile with every unpredictable sneeze. She twirled around once, twice, smiling to herself as she confirmed the hem of her new indigo wool skirt fell precisely in the right spot.

A ripple of sheer delight coursed through her. For as long as she could remember, trying on pretty new clothes had seemed a ritual of each season. Party dresses adorned with ruffles. Opera gowns with velvet capes. Pretty frocks for a spring dance. Over the years, she'd tried on more dresses and skirts and blouses and gowns than she could hope to recall. She'd endured so many errant pins pricking her skin in the course of dress fittings, she'd come to dread the very idea of paying a visit to the seamstress. But now, she was simply thrilled to have something to wear that fit her contours without quite literally threatening to pop at the seams. Something that was *hers*.

"I like it." Ellie regarded the simple ensemble with a look of keen-eyed appraisal. "The lace collar on the blouse truly suits you."

"I favor it, too." Belle ran her fingertips over the smooth fabric. "More than you might imagine."

"Oh, I think I have some idea," she said. "To be stranded with only the clothes on your back . . . how awful."

"It might not have been so bad if I'd been wearing something more practical at the time."

"Come to think of it, I had a dream like that one night. As I recall, I was stranded on some remote island. But as it turned out, I was not alone. The most deliciously wanton pirate had washed ashore with me." Ellie grinned. "Oh, my, I suppose it wasn't so bad after all."

"That could be a very promising circumstance," Belle agreed as an image of a dashing buccaneer strolled into her thoughts. Tall and broad-shouldered with deep brown eyes that drew her in, he was dressed in black from the bandana on his head to the tips of his polished boots. Even his hair was dark, save for the faint hints of gray at his temples.

Goodness. Her fantasy pirate bore a striking resemblance to Jon, didn't he? Quick as she'd conjured the image, she blinked it away. Perhaps the stress of her time in London had driven her ever so slightly mad.

"Try this one," Ellie said, displaying a demurely fashioned dress made of delicately patterned pale blue fabric. "I think it will look lovely on you."

Belle took the dress and stepped behind the screen to try it on. She'd no sooner slipped into the garment than the door creaked on its hinges, announcing an unexpected visitor. The cheerful *tinkle* of Heathy's bell accented each of his jaunty steps.

"Heathy, I'd forgotten you were here," Ellie said with undisguised delight. She reached down to pet the dog, who eagerly soaked up the affection.

"I take it the two of you are acquainted," Belle said as she buttoned the dress.

"Anyone who is a friend of Amelia MacLain gets to know Heathy. She adores that pup. Spoils him silly," Ellie said. "Amelia's husband, Logan, has developed quite a soft spot for Heathy as well. It's quite surprising to see the bond that grew between them."

"I presume Logan is Mr. Mason's business partner," Belle said, becoming acquainted with the names of those close to Jon.

"Mr. Mason, is it?" Ellie's forehead furrowed. "There's no need to be formal with me. He's been *Jon* to me since I was a girl in braids. And I have to tell you, I know that the two of you had, shall we say, a prior acquaintance." A sly smile tugged at the corners of her mouth. "Macie told me all about the American miss who'd nearly taken the starch out of her brother's shirt."

As a sudden awkwardness settled over her, Belle's breath caught in her throat. "It's true that Jon and I had known each other . . . some time ago." Collecting her thoughts, she toyed with the buttons at the cuffs of the dress. "But I could not say that *I* am the American miss in question. I'd imagine there were others."

"Oh, it was you. How could it not be?" Warmth gleamed in Ellie's eyes. "Macie will be delighted to discover her brother has risked causing a stir while acting the white knight. After all the worry he had over her so-called scandals, Jon Mason whisks an heiress away from a dangerous man. How very unexpected. And exciting."

"It has all been quite utterly unexpected." Belle considered Ellie's words. "But exciting is not the word I would use."

"Perhaps not," Ellie conceded. "But it is high time Jon took a chance on something not tallied on a balance sheet."

Belle continued to fiddle with her cuffs. "He is entirely devoted to his business endeavors, isn't he?"

"He is dedicated to seeing his responsibilities through. For years, he's been a major force behind his family's business ventures. Before he went to New York, he'd also been quite the rogue when he wasn't putting together some deal or another. But then, something changed. After he returned from America, Macie couldn't get over the change in her brother. He threw himself into the business with such intense focus, she was concerned about him for a time."

"That hardly seems a change from the man I knew during that short time when we were first acquainted," Belle said. "He was highly devoted to matters of business."

And, for an achingly short time, *her.*

"Macie felt he'd lost some of his spark, some of his wry wit," Ellie said as she offered Belle a walking suit in a beautiful rich plum hue. "I do hope I haven't said too much."

"Not at all," Belle said as she slipped out of the blue dress. "This suit is absolutely beautiful," she observed, hoping to change the topic.

"Oh, it is lovely. This ensemble will work well with your coloring. And it *is* modest. After all, you must pass as a proper governess," Ellie said, scooping up the dog to give him a rub behind the ears. "I take it Heathy has already developed a fondness for you. He doesn't trot after anyone he doesn't like."

"I'd say we've gotten along quite well." Belle smiled over the screen. "He reminds me of my old dog. Angus was such a good pup."

"Amelia adores dogs as well, as you can tell. I expect that the two of you will get along famously when she comes home from the Highlands."

"Will she be returning shortly?"

"She's expected back by the end of the month."

"How disappointing," Belle said. "By then, I will likely be on my way back to New York. I would truly enjoy making her acquaintance. And I cannot wait to meet Macie. I've heard so much about her."

"She is a true original," Ellie said. "I believe she may be home within a fortnight."

"I do hope so," Belle said. "I look forward to getting to know her."

"Jon claims his sister is the cause of each and every gray hair on his head. Not that he has *that* many. They make him look rather distinguished. Wouldn't you agree?"

"I suppose they do." Belle fought a smile as her imagination flashed back to her dark-haired, silver-templed pirate.

Ellie placed Heathy on the floor and sorted through the trunk again, bringing out an ivory linen blouse with long puffed sleeves. "What do you think? It complements the suit."

"It's beautiful," she said.

The minutes passed pleasantly as Ellie continued to pass her garments for her approval—dresses and nightdresses and undergarments and shoes. Donning a tweed skirt and jacket with a white pristine linen blouse, Belle studied her reflection in the mirror. The events of the past days had not changed her. Not on the surface, at least. But a sudden realization stilled her.

My goodness, she'd been born into such good fortune, and she'd taken it for granted, hadn't she? Now, that had changed. And she doubted she could ever go back to the blithe innocence she'd felt never having to worry over *things*. Never having to worry about a good, solid roof over her head, surrounded by people who loved her. Never having to feel the slightest pangs of hunger and to fear that she'd have nowhere to go. And now, it was as if that naivete had been shattered.

After she'd made her mad dash away from Gideon's grasp, she'd had a small taste of what it felt like to be without resources. She'd been tired and hungry and without a penny on her person. She had never felt so very alone in her life. If she hadn't rushed through the door of the tavern and straight into Jon, what might have come next? Would she have been forced to take refuge in some dank alley? Might she have encountered another man that night, one without Jon's innate sense of honor? The mere thought of it brought a chill creeping over her nape.

Since girlhood, she had never wanted for anything. Anything material, that was. She'd always possessed beautiful things. And in such abundance. Her mahogany armoire at home was nearly popping at the hinges with gowns and dresses and skirts and blouses, garments for every occasion one might imagine. And of course, she owned shoes and custom-made hats and beaded reticules to complement each ensemble. For so long, she'd felt appreciation for the lovely wardrobe her father's wealth had afforded her. In a sense, it seemed an utterly natural aspect of life as her father's daughter.

But she'd never had to face the feeling of needing and not having.

Oh, she'd certainly felt compassion for those in need. She was known for her good deeds, wasn't she? The charity galas she'd sponsored—lavish events at magnificent ballrooms where society types showed off their elegant gowns and finest jewels—had raised generous donations for orphans and widows and those who needed a helping hand. But she'd never tried to see things through their eyes. Not truly. Only now had she'd gotten a tiny, fleeting glimpse of what it felt like to rely on the kindness of others.

"What do you think of the tweed?" Ellie's question pulled Belle from her thoughts. "I think the pattern is subtle."

"I agree." Belle smoothed out a wrinkle in the snowy white linen blouse. "It's quite appealing."

Ellie looked rather pleased with herself. "It would appear we possess a similar fashion sense."

"I do agree. Every garment you've selected is lovely."

"I must confess I was a bit nervous when Jon reached out to me for assistance. I'd never selected clothing for anyone but myself. The message his assistant brought made it seem rather like a covert mission. But that would be Jon. Even as a lad, he had a plan for everything."

"So I've seen." Belle could not help but offer a knowing smile.

"You can imagine my excitement to be given *carte blanche* to select whatever I thought would suit you, and on his personal account, no less. The shop assistant at his store was ever so helpful, but the woman's eyes were wide as saucers when I requested a large trunk for my purchases."

"It *is* rather hefty."

"Jon tasked one of his employees with transporting it here." Ellie tapped her fingers against the elegant domed steamer trunk. "Thankfully, the driver was a strapping man, all brawn and muscles. Pity you didn't have the opportunity to observe him lifting it in and out of the coach. I must say, he accomplished the task with the utmost efficiency."

"Brawn and muscles . . . he sounds quite capable."

"*Exceedingly* capable, I'd say." The look in Ellie's eyes hinted at an unspoken meaning. "I do wonder if the shop assistants really believed the items in that trunk were selected on Macie's behalf, or if they'd formed a far different notion. One of the women was ever so pleasant, but she was something of a busybody, crinkling her nose a bit skeptically at times. I wouldn't doubt she suspected Jon was purchasing the items for me. Now *that* might be true fuel for the gossips."

Belle studied her for a moment. Could it be that Ellie was actually pleased at the thought?

"I do hope you're not drawn into the rumor mill."

"To the contrary, a little scandal would be just the thing. For me, at least." Ellie retrieved a pair of high-top black shoes from the trunk and presented them to Macie. "In my experience, few things better enhance a woman's appeal to the male of the species than the notion of a desirable rogue having eyes for her."

"I take it there is a certain *male of the species* you have in mind?"

Ellie nodded. "I've had my sights set on him since I returned from Paris. He's an American, like you."

"You don't say."

"As I understand it, he's from Texas. Very tall. Very handsome. And very wealthy."

"He sounds perfect." *For Ellie.*

"I've only met him in passing, so he could be quite a grouch behind that dashing smile. Rather like Jon these days."

Belle tugged at the laces on the supple new shoes as Ellie's words repeated in her thoughts. *Rather like Jon.* How very curious.

"You know him well, don't you?" Belle asked, eager for some insight into the man who suddenly saw himself as her protector.

Ellie pursed her lips, appearing to ponder the question. "I'm not sure I would phrase it that way. I've known Jon Mason for quite a long time, but I'm not sure anyone except Macie and his business partners, Logan and Finn, know the true man."

"I do believe I understand."

"Some men are simple," Ellie said. "Oh, they may be keenly intelligent. But there's no mystery. Nothing to puzzle out about their feelings and wants and needs. That certainly isn't Jon. From what I've observed, he is precisely the opposite."

"I'd say that's a fair assessment," Belle agreed.

"You may know him better than I do." Ellie paused long enough to hand her another pair of shoes, soft slippers for the house, then went on. "Over the years, I came to know Jon through my friendship with Macie. When I was a gangly young girl, he was kind to me, rather like the brother I'd never had. After we grew up, I think Macie might've harbored a hope that there could be more between her brother and me. But there was never the slightest spark."

A sense of relief Belle did not wish to admit, even to herself, washed over her at Ellie's words. "Tell me, Ellie, was he always so . . . serious?"

"No, not when we were young. Back then, Jon and Logan and Finn were like the Three Musketeers, always getting into some adventure or scrape. But then, they grew up. And Jon became the son his father wanted."

Picturing the young boy in the photograph, Belle took in Ellie's words. In that image, Jon had appeared far from mischievous. "I'd think his father would appreciate his unwavering dedication to the family business."

"I cannot speak to that. But I do know that Jon has set his mind to living up to his father's standards. But believe me when I say, it's a near-impossible task." Ellie selected a soft flannelette nightdress and robe from the collection she'd brought and handed them to Belle. "But enough of that. Let's enjoy this bit of shopping without a store, shall we?"

Belle gave a nod of agreement. "I must say, I'm amazed you've brought so many garments. There are far more than I'll need for my stay. I do appreciate what you've done for me."

"I enjoyed every moment. Why, I'd do it again tomorrow if I could, if only to see that gorgeous man carry the trunk with all those muscles flexing." Ellie flashed a grin. "That would really get the shopgirls talking, now, wouldn't it?"

"I do imagine a repeat day of purchases so soon after the last would draw some attention."

"The assistant's eyes would be wide as serving platters." Her grin faded to a more subtle smile. "Of course, there *is* a chance the employees will talk, even amongst themselves, about my visit today. Jon won't like that at all. He so detests a scandal."

Belle gulped a breath at the thought. Jon's pragmatic words in the carriage whispered in her thoughts. *What's the worst that could happen . . . a proposal of marriage?*

She let out the air hovering in her throat with a little sigh.

"With any luck, it won't cause a stir."

"Indeed. With luck." A coy little smile played on Ellie's mouth. "But it does occur to me that something rather curious has happened. Something quite unexpected."

"You aren't going to keep me in suspense, are you?" Belle said. "You must tell me."

"I'm surprised you didn't see it," Ellie said cryptically. "But then again, I suppose it did take me a bit of time to realize what he'd done."

"What he's done?" Belle searched for the answer to this peculiar puzzle. "I am truly at a loss."

"It's rather elementary, really. Jon avoids scandal at every turn. Surely the man understood the potential for, shall we say, raised eyebrows at a shopping excursion he personally funded. But he was willing to take that chance." She met Belle's gaze. "For you."

Chapter Twelve

*F*OR YOU. BELLE'S breath caught in her throat. The words were ordinary enough. And yet, their implied meaning stunned her. Ellie must've read something into Jon's actions that fit her own romanticized narrative. He'd sent her on the shopping errand because there was little choice. His motives were practical. As usual. Jon certainly could not have Carrie's teacher roaming about his house popping at the seams in his sister's too-small dress, now, could he?

"I'm of the opinion he had little choice in the matter," Belle said, summoning her most rational tone as she stepped behind the screen to change from the tailored suit into the practical yet pretty pale blue dress.

"There is always a choice," Ellie countered with an air of authority.

"I wouldn't be so sure," Belle said, easily closing the cotton bodice. After struggling with the too-snug dress she'd borrowed, donning a garment with fasteners which easily slid into place seemed quite the treat. "He couldn't simply stand by as I watched over Carrie while wearing blouses that quite literally threatened to burst their buttons."

"I sense a story there," Ellie said as a light rap upon the door announced Mrs. Gilroy's presence.

"Ah, there's a story all right," Mrs. Gilroy said as she entered the room with Carrie at her side. She turned to Ellie. "Isn't there always, lass?"

"I've had my fair share," Ellie agreed.

"Still not as many as Miss Macie," the housekeeper said with a touch of affection in her wry tone. "It still brings a smile to my face to think she's happily wed now—and to that rogue Finn Caldwell, of all people."

"Macie and Amelia are of the belief that rogues really do make the very best husbands," Ellie said with a knowing air.

"Well, I don't know about that," Mrs. Gilroy said, leading Carrie to a comfortably overstuffed wing chair in the corner. "But I'd never seen Miss Macie happier than the day she exchanged vows with Mr. Caldwell."

"She was absolutely radiant. After years of chasing off suitors, she found true joy with a rogue of her very own." Ellie's tone seemed a bit wistful. "The key is to find one who now has eyes only for you."

Was it Belle's imagination, or had Ellie slanted her a speaking glance?

"Oh, I do need a rogue of my own. But where to find one?" Ellie went on. "Now that is the question."

"Yer time will come," Mrs. Gilroy replied with a sage nod.

"I do hope so," Ellie said, turning her attention to a rather bemused-looking Carrie. She smiled at the child. "My, don't you look pretty today. And your dolly is . . ." Her eyes widened as she gazed down at the rather haggard rag doll. "Looking happy today."

"She isn't happy." Carrie shook her head and pointed to what appeared to be a fresh tear on the doll's hand. "Anna is a bit sad." She poked out her lip, looking as if she bit back tears. "I don't think Heathy likes her."

"I didn't want to disturb ye, Miss Belle, but the child was beside herself. I told her I'd help her with it, but she insisted on bringing the doll to ye," Mrs. Gilroy explained. "I'll mend it tonight."

Miss Belle. Well, that was progress. The housekeeper had

evidently warmed up to her.

Belle slipped the last tiny button on the dress into place and stepped away from the dressing screen. "Oh, that's not so bad," she said, taking the doll in her hands. "I'm sure Heathy didn't mean to hurt her."

"If I hadn't caught the wee beast in the act, the doll might be missing its hand," Mrs. Gilroy explained.

"Thanks to your quick action, Anna will soon be back to her old self." Belle examined the rip in the fabric. "Nothing a few stitches won't solve."

"Will you make her better?" Carrie asked with a sniffle.

Belle turned to Mrs. Gilroy. "Might I use your mending supplies?"

"Of course. But I am able to stitch it."

"I rather enjoy needlework, though I haven't had cause to thread a needle in quite some time." She held out the doll to Carrie. "Would you like to help me fix her up?"

The girl gave an enthusiastic nod. "She'll be all better."

"Of course she will," Mrs. Gilroy said with a smile. "I'll gather my sewing kit."

"Thank you." Belle turned to Carrie. "Please take Anna back to your playroom and I'll be there shortly."

"I'll put her on the shelf." The girl cast a little frown at Heathy. "Away from his teeth."

"That would be a good idea," Mrs. Gilroy agreed. "I'll go along with ye, child, and ye can help me in the kitchen for a bit." She tapped her fingers against the not-quite-empty trunk. "I'm sure Miss Belle and Miss Ellie would like more time to look through these pretty dresses."

"Thank you," Belle said as the housekeeper and the girl took their leave.

Something on the rug caught Belle's eye: a key tethered to a blue ribbon. Heathy appeared to spot the ribbon at the same moment, but Belle quickly scooped it up and hurried into the hallway.

Heathy's bell jangled as he took off after Carrie. At the sound, Carrie tugged on Mrs. Gilroy's sleeve, and the old woman turned just as Belle caught up to her.

"Mrs. Gilroy, I think you dropped this."

"I'm thankful ye spotted it," she said, tucking the key into her apron pocket. "I would've been in a dither searching the house for it."

"Heathy would've brought it to you," Carrie said cheerfully.

"I would not be so certain of that, child." Mrs. Gilroy took her hand. "Come along. Let's put yer doll in a safe place."

"Come, Heathy," Belle called the dog. She certainly didn't want Mrs. Gilroy to have to navigate her unsteady steps around the pup. Wagging his tail energetically, Heathy followed her down the hallway back to the bedchamber. After she settled comfortably on an upholstered bench, he plopped down contentedly at her feet.

Ellie leaned back in the wingchair. Holding the portrait of Jon and Macie in their youth, she appeared deep in thought as she studied the images. She drew a fingertip along the edge of the scrolled frame. When she glanced up, a look of nostalgia filled her eyes.

"This was taken at their country home," she said. "I have a portrait at home of Macie and me that was made when the photographer was visiting that spring. My, we were so very young."

"I can see the spark in her eyes."

"She's always had such a zest for life. I've never seen it dim." She pursed her lips, deep in thought. "Perhaps only once . . . when it looked as if she and Finn would part company. But as you already know, they figured it out. Happily ever after, as they say."

"I do so love the thought of a happy ending," Belle said. "It often seems the stuff of fairy tales."

"I'm not all that fond of those flowery tales. The notion of sitting around waiting to be rescued by a prince—charming or not—doesn't quite appeal to me."

"I, for one, do *not* have the patience," Belle said. "That is not to say I would object to a handsome knight charging to the rescue, but I doubt I could sit idly by and wait for him to ride up on his steed."

"I'd be content with the rescue. And perhaps a kiss—or two—to thank him for his courage."

Belle offered a nod of agreement. "Come to think of it, there's never any indication that the prince or knight or whatever has a brain in his skull. Why, the man could be a muscle-bound dolt, now couldn't he?"

"Not that a muscle-bound dolt might not have his, shall we say, purpose." Ellie's eyes flashed with mischief. "Fighting off a dragon or two would warrant sweet kisses. Perhaps, if he was particularly brave, I might even consider a scandalous touch. Or two." Her mouth curved into a sly smile. "But a lifelong commitment to a man I don't truly even know? I think not."

"Indeed," Belle concurred. "I much prefer Miss Austen's heroes, don't you?"

"Ah, Mr. Darcy," Ellie said. "Ever so much more appealing than a knight with all muscles and nothing between his ears."

"And no clunky armor to clutter up the house," Belle said with a soft chuckle. "I shudder to think about polishing all that tin."

Ellie laughed out loud. "I must admit, Belle—you are not at all what I expected."

"In what way, might I ask?"

"Oh, where to begin?" Seeming to stall, Ellie rose and placed the photograph she'd been holding back in its proper place. "I suppose I'd expected the *Frost Princess* to be a bit, for lack of a better word, *frostier*."

"Oh, I *can* be cool to those who don't deserve better. Since my debutante ball, I've stood my ground with people who mistook a kind heart for weakness. Some have portrayed my backbone as proof of a cold nature. That is their choice." A touch of pride rippled through her at her resolve. "I suppose I should detest that rather horrid name. Really, I should. But I don't." Belle smiled. A faint smile, but a smile nonetheless. "I actually rather like it."

"Really?" Ellie's eyes widened, if only a bit.

"I believe it all started in Manhattan. I'd heard one of the dowry-seeking snobs I'd shown the door—I'm not entirely sure which one, as there were *so* many—was in his cups at some high-brow tavern. While the oaf loudly bemoaned my supposedly frigid nature, a reporter at a gossip rag overheard what he'd said. The hack had a fine time making a play on my name. Truly, I find it rather silly. But the nickname captured interest, and the papers ran with it. Over time, it has proven to be rather useful."

Ellie rested her chin on her hand. "Do tell."

"Since the press spread the word that I am unapproachable, I've taken advantage of their warning. It has worked wonders with the men my mother and I call *Merger Hunters*," Belle explained. "For a time, you see, I was viewed as good *wife material* by more than one scion of powerful families."

"*Wife material?*" Ellie sighed. "How very tiresome."

"That's one way of putting it," Belle said. "I once entertained a courtship with a rather handsome man whose family controlled a lumber empire. He actually used those very words when he proposed that we unite our families."

"A true romantic," Ellie commented in a wry tone.

"I suppose he thought he was being quite proper. But the man simply did not have a tender bone in his body. He didn't possess the faintest inkling of what love is." Belle pictured the ruddy-faced suitor whose smile had so quickly turned to a scowl when he realized he'd wasted his efforts on the *Frost Princess*. "Just imagine a man whose idea of romance was to woo me with a recitation of the ways we might complement one another, including the fact that a merger between our family enterprises would prove advantageous."

"Oh, dear."

"When I gently turned down his proposal, the boor actually

had the gall to throw that name in my face. If he'd thought to wound me, he was greatly mistaken," Belle said, not entirely truthful. The words *had* stung. But not nearly so much as the prospect of a life with a man who viewed her as an asset to enhance his company's balance sheet.

"What a miserable dolt."

"He was used to getting his way in all things," Belle reflected. "He wanted a woman who would be meek and docile." She nearly laughed aloud at the idea. "A woman who was most definitely *not* me."

"Well, he was a fool. Now, wasn't he?"

Belle gave a little shrug. "In the end, he got what he wanted. I've heard he recently wed a pretty textile heiress. I do hope he and his bride have found happiness." She gazed down at the intricate pattern woven into the wool rug, allowing her thoughts to settle. "At least he wasn't as bad as the dowry hunters."

"Macie called them heiress hunters. She detested the chase."

"Oh, I do understand," Belle said. "Sadly, they're not so easily put off by a mere nickname. Greed—or perhaps a bit of desperation—makes them bold. And persistent. The *prospectors* are the very worst of the lot. But they soon learn that I am not the key to mining my father's fortune."

"Macie employed a bit of strategy to run off the heiress hunters."

"I've heard tales of her tactics. So very clever. I do admire her approach to setting the marriage-minded buffoons back on their heels."

"Jon claims her antics were the root of every silver hair on his head," Ellie said with a smile. "As I recall, he audibly sighed with relief after she spoke her vows with Finn."

"I can well imagine that. Sadly, I do not possess her flair for creating a perfectly timed scene."

"Neither do I," Ellie said. "Fortunately, my father is not a wealthy man, so I've seldom needed to make an attempt at Macie's methods. I've drawn my share of scoundrels, but of the ordinary variety. They're not nearly so persistent as fortune hunting bounders." Her attention drifted to the corner beside the bed, more specifically to the white dress Belle had carelessly tossed in a little heap with the dirt-spattered hooded cloak upon the floor. "That is a wedding dress, is it not?"

Emotion rose in Belle's throat, a sensation of dull pain she didn't want to face. Not quite yet. But she met the question directly. "It is."

"Yours?"

"Yes." The simple word seemed to echo in her ears. She'd come so close to making a disastrous choice. "For a brief moment. But thank heavens I came to my senses." She met Ellie's curious gaze. "Jon didn't tell you?"

"He told me only that you were in a bit of a fix . . . that you were in danger. And he made it clear that you would be safe here." Ellie slanted the discarded gown another glance. "As Mrs. Gilroy said, there is always a story. Do you care to tell me this one?"

Belle took a moment to collect her thoughts. She couldn't quite explain why she trusted Ellie with the truth. But she did.

"It's rather simple, actually. I met a man with whom I believed I could make a good life. But it was all an illusion." Belle pulled in a low breath, carefully working out her response. "I called off our engagement." She hesitated. "He made it clear that he had no intention of accepting my decision."

Even as it seemed a relief to confide in someone, actually uttering the words brought a fleeting stab of pain. Belle stared down at her hands. Her fingers were trembling. How odd. They weren't even quivering when she'd made her escape. Had her fear finally caught up with her?

"I see." Ellie's mouth thinned with concern. "You ran from him?"

"I saw no other choice." As she pictured Gideon's angry eyes staring into hers, a little shiver rippled over her nape. "He thought he could bend me to his will. But I wouldn't . . . I will not give in."

"I can only imagine how difficult this is for you." Ellie reached out to clasp her hand in hers and gave it a reassuring squeeze. "Well, you can count on Jon. You'll be safe here."

Gulping a breath, she confided another truth. "But I am concerned . . . I am bringing trouble to his doorstep."

"Don't worry about such things," Ellie said with a soft shake of her head. "He'll face down any challenge that comes his way."

"The man I'd thought to marry in that infernal dress . . . I fear he will continue to chase after me." The all-too-recent memory of Gideon's voice—smooth, yet tinged with razor-sharp anger—sent a wave of apprehension through her. "When he wants something, he is utterly driven. In this case, what he wants is me." Simply speaking the words churned a fresh dread within her. Never in her life had she felt the need to hide. Not from anything. Or anyone.

Until now.

"I hope you don't think me too bold, but a question does occur to me." Ellie's gaze softened. "Could it be that he is in love with you?"

You will not leave this place. How could you think I would allow you to walk away?

When Gideon had uttered the words, his eyes had been as cold and hard as his voice. There had been no trace of love. Nor passion. To the contrary, every word he'd clipped between his teeth betrayed icy rage at her defiance.

Belle braced herself against the chilling memory. Oh, she'd been a fool. So very naïve. How had she allowed herself to be swept into his elaborate charade?

"I know that is not the case." She swallowed hard against a fresh rush of regret. "He sees me as the key to my father's money vault. Nothing more."

Ellie nodded her understanding. "Belle, might I ask . . .?" She hesitated for a long moment, seeming to think better of voicing her thought.

Belle read the unspoken question in her eyes. "If you wish to know if I love the man, the answer is that I do not." She drew in a calming breath. "The truth of the matter is, I never did. Not truly." My, it eased the pain within her to speak the truth.

Ellie's eyes lit with comprehension. "This was not a love match?"

"We'd enjoyed what I'd thought was a true friendship. We had seemed quite compatible. Gideon and I shared many interests, and we got along famously. I'd hoped it might develop into more."

"But it did not," Ellie offered a nod of understanding.

"There was no spark. Not even a flicker." Belle felt as if a weight was being lifted off her shoulders. It seemed such a relief to speak to confide in Ellie. "To be quite honest, I was utterly surprised when he proposed—and in such dramatic fashion in the midst of one of the most elegant restaurants in the city. My first instinct was to turn him down gently."

"But you accepted his proposal?"

"I did." Belle knew her words sounded like a confession. But she had done nothing wrong. In her heart, she knew that. "When I looked at him that night, he seemed so very earnest. I simply could not bring myself to cause a scene that might have devastated him. And I did not wish to sever the ties between us. So, I tried to convince myself that I would be content with him. After all, many successful marriages have started without a thought to love, true or otherwise."

"You deserve better than that, Belle."

She drew in a slow, calming breath. "At the moment he proposed, I wanted to believe we might make a go of it. But in my heart, I knew I'd made a colossal mistake. I couldn't go through with it. But I wanted to find the right time . . . to gently call off the engagement. I did not wish to hurt him." She dropped her gaze to her hands, but forced herself to meet Ellie's questioning eyes. "But then, everything changed."

"Do you feel comfortable telling me what happened?" Ellie's

gaze softened with compassion. "What changed your mind?"

"Gideon showed his true colors." Belle could hear the ugly strains of his voice in her thoughts. *You will give me what you've promised. You will not make a fool of me.*

Ellie's brow furrowed as she appeared to ponder Belle's words. When she spoke, her tone was hushed. "I believe I understand."

"He is a powerful man—Lord Gideon Kentsworth."

Ellie's mouth thinned. "The name rings a bell, but I cannot quite place it."

"I suspect you may have seen the chatter in the gossip rags. The papers had a fine time plastering our names on their society pages. Ever so much innuendo."

"I'm afraid I must've missed the excitement," Ellie said. "You see, I've only recently returned from visiting the continent."

"It was much ado about nothing."

The furrows in Ellie's brow deepened. "I don't recall ever making the man's acquaintance. How very odd. I'd think we would have at least a passing familiarity, given the sheer number of balls and soirees Macie and I attended."

"He possesses no fondness for London society. His primary residence is away from the city, in Cornwall."

Ellie pursed her lips, deep in thought. "I shall ask my aunt what, if anything, she knows about the man. Aunt Cora is well connected with London's elite and possesses a keen ear for gossip. She gained a snobby title when she married and now fancies herself an expert on the who's who of the noble class. Especially the skeletons in their closets. She also keeps tabs on everything of note that goes on in the city. The juiciest scandals are of particular interest." Her lips curved into a sly smile. "It goes without saying that I shall be discreet. But it will be to your benefit to know if Lord Kentsworth is hiding any ugly and potentially dangerous secrets."

Chapter Thirteen

BELLE HAD ALWAYS enjoyed the twilight. As a girl, when her family spent summers on the shores of Lake Erie, she'd relished the sight of the setting sun over the magnificent lake and the quiet time in the hazy light. If she closed her eyes, she could remember the cheerful sounds of the frogs and crickets welcoming the night. But tonight, in the garden of a posh London home as evening shade fell over the city, the sound of her own pulse drowned out the pleasant tones in her memory.

Sitting on the garden bench beside a black cat who appeared to be rather bored, Belle watched as Carrie played in the flower garden. The girl danced about with a pretty, frilly doll with coal-black hair and a painted-on red mouth, while Heathy scampered about in canine bliss. Belle smiled at their innocent glee. If only she could find a way to silence her own racing thoughts.

Scandals. Skeletons. Secrets. The words played like a steady drumbeat in her thoughts. When Ellie had spoken the words, a sense of intrigue had colored her tones. Oh, Belle understood all too well. Gossip was stirring, even among friends. Especially when one was only an observer. But Belle was a participant in this bit of real-life drama.

She'd nearly been caught in a web of Gideon's making. Thank heaven she'd discovered his deception before it was too late.

Perhaps she should've advised Ellie there was no need to seek out her aunt's expertise on the subject of London's scoundrels and cheats. But she hadn't found the will to tell her the truth. Not the full truth, at least. Not one word she'd spoken to her new confidant had been a lie. But even though she trusted Ellie, she hadn't been able to reveal why she'd fled the man she had planned to marry. The reality was too painful.

Belle's heartbeat thundered in her ears. Why, she'd never run from anything in her life.

Until Gideon had given her no choice.

She knew his secret. She had seen his duplicity with her own eyes. She had heard his cruel, cutting words. And she knew beyond a doubt that he'd only wanted her as a means to attain a piece of her father's fortune.

The truth had sent her on a mad dash. She'd had to escape. From him. From the aunt who'd betrayed her. From a future of treachery.

What could Ellie's aunt possibly know about Gideon that she didn't?

Drawing in a calming breath, she pushed the unsettling thoughts to the back of her mind and fixed her attention on the child in her care. She had no experience as a governess, but at this moment, it was just as well. What Carrie needed most was affection and attention and someone who gave a fig about her.

My, she was a beautiful little girl. With her sparkling dark eyes and chestnut-brown hair, she could see a resemblance to Jon. Carrie danced about the garden like a little pixie, singing a happy, slightly off-key melody. In her soft, high-pitched little voice, she made up a tune as she went, blending bits of nursery rhymes together into one lyric. Such a clever child.

Despite the worries running wild in her thoughts, she met Carrie's innocent smile with one of her own. A smile from the heart.

For a moment, her mind wandered, drawing from the pleasantness of the scene. What would it be like to have a child of her own? A sweet girl with moppet curls who possessed a penchant for mischief. Or a boy with a sly sense of humor and a knack for wrapping his mama around his finger.

Someday.

She smiled to herself, soothing her aching heart with the thought. Someday, she would marry a man who would be the right one for her. *Someday.*

The steady tap of Mrs. Gilroy's cane gently brought her back to reality. "I thought ye'd want to know Mr. Mason has returned home." Mrs. Gilroy made her way onto the garden terrace, her expression brightening as she surveyed the scene. "I see the young lass has learned to amuse herself without making such a mess."

Belle motioned to the bench. "Won't you join us?"

A look of surprise flashed over the housekeeper's features at the invitation. She gave her head a small shake. "I've put supper on. I'll be on my way. I need to tend the stew."

"How might I assist with the preparations?"

Mrs. Gilroy's brow creased. "Ye meant what ye said, didn't ye, lass?"

It was Belle's turn to be surprised. "About helping out with the daily tasks?"

A faint smile tugged at Mrs. Gilroy's thin mouth. "After what happened with the soup, I'd wondered if ye'd have second thoughts."

Belle met the old woman's smile with one of her own. "I'm not a gambler, but I would wager that won't be happening again."

"I'd agree the odds are rather low," Jon said, strolling onto the terrace. "But I would not rule it out."

"Perhaps this time you will be the one in the danger zone," she replied.

"I will hurl myself in front of you to take the brunt of the assault," he quipped. "After all, I am a gentleman."

She cocked a skeptical brow. "And so very chivalrous."

Belle's gaze swept over him from his neatly clipped dark hair to his polished black boots. The shadow of new beard drew her eye to the strong lines of his jaw and chin, while his charcoal-gray suit, though tailored for a man in the world of business, could not conceal the power in his lean body. The cut of his jacket accented the breadth of his shoulders and the power in his muscular arms.

With a blink to clear her thoughts, Belle forced herself to look away, to stop herself from drinking him in. As he neared her on the garden bench, he paused and smiled down at Carrie. He crouched low, holding himself at eye level with the child. "Is that the doll I brought you from Scotland?"

The girl nodded enthusiastically. "I like her very much."

"I'm happy to see that." His grin seemed quite genuine. "You were a good girl for Miss Belle and Mrs. Gilroy today, were you not?"

Carrie nodded again, then slanted Belle a shy look. "Miss Belle read me a story, and I taught my dolly to dance."

"I did hear your song," he said, rising to his full height. "You remind me very much . . ." He raked a hand through his hair and glanced away. "I like to hear you sing."

Carrie reached out and wrapped her arms around him in a hug. "Will you tell me a story tonight?"

"If time permits," he said, the happiness in his eyes more muted now. He threw Mrs. Gilroy a speaking glance. "Would you be so kind as to see Carrie to her playroom?" He turned his attention to Belle. "Miss Frost and I have an important matter to discuss."

UPON HIS RETURN from his office, Jon had thought to go about his typical routine. On most evenings, he would retire to his study, pour two fingers of scotch, and allow himself three-quarters of an hour of peace and quiet reading over the evening edition of the newspaper. He'd check on the well-being of his young ward and take his supper. Later, after Carrie was settled in her bed for the night, he would depart for the Rogue's Lair, where he would remain until late in the night. With Logan and Finn traveling far from London, he needed to watch over the tavern. Logically, he knew that Murray, the head barkeep, and the other barkeeps and servers who'd been with the tavern for years were capable of running the place. But he felt a responsibility to oversee the operations.

But as he arrived home as the sun set on Belle's first day watching over the child, Jon was struck by an unusual sound. In recent weeks, he'd grown accustomed to being greeted at the door by a boisterous pup whose tail wagged so furiously, he wondered that the dog possessed the energy to propel it. At times, he'd been met by a sour-faced governess who looked as if she'd taken a sip of brine. At others, he'd faced an exasperated housekeeper upon his return. But he had never walked through the doorway and heard the sound of a moppet singing at the top of her little lungs about Mary's lamb, Jack's pail of water, and the demise of a clumsy dolt with an inexplicable penchant for sitting on walls.

He'd followed the cheerful, if less than melodic, song to the garden. Jon had expected to encounter Belle there with his little cousin. But he had not expected to find her looking more beautiful than ever.

In New York, he'd attended balls and galas with Belle. On those evenings, she'd been garbed in gowns made from the finest silks, her hair arranged in the most stylish fashion with elegant tiaras and fancy jeweled earrings to accent her lovely face. But now, sitting in the garden before the backdrop of the setting sun, she wore a dress of pale blue fabric, most likely cotton. The only ornamentation on the dress was a slight bit of lace at the collar. But the unadorned dress suited her. She didn't need frills. Didn't need yards of ruffles and bustles. Didn't need jewels.

By thunder, she didn't need any of it. She was breathtaking. A true diamond.

He'd cleared his throat and made an off-handed remark about the probability of being accidentally doused with soup yet again, if only to cover his own reaction to the sight of her. And now, they were alone. Mrs. Gilroy had made her way from the garden with Carrie holding her hand, moving at a snail's pace as she appeared to stall in order to hear what he'd say to Belle.

Moving to the door, he left it slightly ajar. Not that it really mattered. The very fact he was here with Belle was the stuff of scandal. But at least he might persuade himself that he'd tried to protect her good name.

The humor brightening her eyes when he'd first walked onto the terrace had faded, replaced by a look of concern. "Is something wrong?" she asked, holding her voice rather still.

"In a word, yes." He closed the distance between them, lowering his voice. If Mrs. Gilroy was indeed eavesdropping, it wouldn't do to alarm her. "The barkeeper at the Rogue's Lair is one of the best sources of information I have. Murray's hearing is keen as any spy," Jon said, deciding the truth was the best approach. "According to word on the street, the ruffians are still on the hunt and actively seeking your whereabouts."

"On the hunt. My, I'm not accustomed to feeling like prey to be tracked." Belle's complexion paled. "This . . . this isn't right." She laced her fingers in a nervous knot. "I need to find somewhere else to go."

Searching her features, he saw the flickers of shock in her eyes at the thought that someone—someone she'd trusted, no less— was searching for her as if she were an escaped prisoner with a bounty to claim. He'd seen the look of alarm flash over her features.

"Trust me when I tell you that I will shield you from those brutes."

"Those men will not hesitate to hurt anyone who gets in their way." She stared up at the darkening sky. "My presence here puts everyone at risk."

"The bastards will not dare to cross my threshold."

"I do hope you're right. But at this point, we don't know what they are capable of."

"I will keep you safe, Belle." He caught one of her hands in his, stroking his thumb over the satin-smooth skin. "I will see to the protection of everyone under this roof."

"I trust that you will. But at what cost?" She met his gaze with a look of resolve. "I won't be able to live with myself if anyone is hurt. I should leave this house."

She'd tried to disguise her trepidation, but he saw the truth in her eyes. And he knew she had good reason to be afraid.

Over the years, he'd seen betrothals called off before the exchange of vows. He'd spotted many a bloke at the Rogue's Lair drinking himself numb to ease the sting of a broken engagement. But Gideon Kentsworth was not downing tumblers of whisky at a tavern. The man had not retreated to his club to lick his wounds. No, the high and mighty rotter had ox-headed oafs combing London for a woman who didn't want to be found. The bastard was not seeking a tender reconciliation. Of that, Jon had no doubt. Rather, the jackal sought to reclaim her, as if Belle were a valuable possession. No man who truly cared for a woman would send those brutes in pursuit.

But even in the face of her own fear, Belle was concerned for the safety of his old housekeeper and the child. God above, she even worried over him. He could bloody well take care of himself in the face of a dandy and his hired thugs.

By thunder, she was willing to put herself in harm's way to shield the people under his roof. To shield *him*. The very idea crashed over him like a rogue wave. *How bloody unusual.*

He would not leave her to face the bastards who chased her like hounds after a fox.

"Do you trust me, Belle?"

She worried her lower lip again, even as she nodded. "I can't quite explain it, but I do." Her voice was hushed and smooth as velvet.

Jon studied her features, seeing the taut set of her mouth, the slight, tense creasing of her forehead. He drew the pad of his thumb over her soft, plump lower lip. "You're trembling."

"Am I?" A sheen of moisture darkened her blue eyes. It was as if he gazed into a stormy sea.

The sight of her tears felt like a fist twisting in his gut. "Belle, I can help you." He kept his tone quiet and even. "I need you to tell me what is really happening here."

"I have," she said, nearly a whisper.

"You haven't told me why you ran," he said, gentling his tone. "You said you had a change of heart. But there had to be something more. Something of such urgency you were compelled to bolt into the night."

"As I told you, Gideon is a very powerful man. He tends to get what he wants." She let out a low breath. "But he didn't count on my determination in the face of his anger."

Pride rippled through him at the strength in her quiet voice. Belle had not crumbled. She had not meekly complied with whatever demands the bastard made of her. No, she'd defied him. That was the Arabelle he'd known. A lovely face, a kind heart, and a will of steel. Thank God for that.

"When you darted into the pub, you'd run without even knowing a destination." He met her deep blue eyes. "Tell me this, Belle . . . did the bastard hurt you?"

"No." Her lip quivered. "I had to get away from him." She glanced away, as if the words were too painful to face. "Before it was too late."

Seeing the stirrings of emotion in her gaze, he tipped up her chin. Every instinct he possessed urged him to comfort her. But bloody hell, he wanted to kiss her.

She looked into his eyes. Her lips parted ever so slightly. Memories of her delicious kiss rushed unbidden into his thoughts. For all those lonely months that had seemed an eternity since he'd left New York, he'd longed for her touch. Longed for her, though he tried to deny it. Even to himself.

And now, she was so very near. Near enough to hold. Near

enough to kiss. Would she welcome his caress? Would she respond to his touch? Or would he drive her away?

Blast it, this was not the time. Belle was frightened. Vulnerable. He could not take advantage of this moment.

"Oh, Jon, I don't know what to do. If he finds me . . ."

"He won't." Jon believed the words as he spoke them. And if he was mistaken, he would deal with the bastard when the time came.

"I haven't gone far. He must suspect I'm still in the city."

"The man has no idea where you are," Jon said truthfully. "Of that, I'm quite confident."

Questions shone in her eyes. "But how . . . how can you be sure?"

"Come, sit with me," he said. Taking her hand, he led her to the chaise. "One of Kentsworth's hired oafs came into the pub again this afternoon. Nosing about the place, the bloke was out to weasel information from the barmaids, but they would not tolerate the buffoon's attempts to sweet-talk them. He then tried to find out what the barkeeper had heard about the runaway bride. For his troubles, Murray served the blockhead a wild goose chase that should set them off the trail for at least a day or two."

"I owe Murray a debt of gratitude." The faintest of smiles played on her mouth. "But it's not quite so simple as distracting those ruffians. Those muscle-bound oafs may not be our greatest concern."

Given that the men were ninety-five percent brawn and five percent violence-inclined brain, Jon was tempted to disagree, but he thought better of it. "You suspect another threat?"

"The rumor mill concerns me," she said. "I have no doubt my aunt will spread gossip about this situation . . . scandalous lies which may work to Gideon's advantage."

"Scandalous, eh?" He mulled the word. When he'd offhandedly mentioned the possibility of a proposal of marriage, if only to silence any whispers of impropriety, Belle's response had been incredulous. In all truth, she appeared somewhat horrified at the very thought. He doubted she had suddenly grown concerned over her good name.

"My aunt knows how to turn a situation to her advantage. It's only a matter of time before she plants a well-placed rumor that works to her benefit. But what will her strategy be?" Belle pursed her lips, seeming to ponder the question. "She *will* get involved. After all, she is Gideon's partner."

Bloody hell.

"Belle, what are you saying?"

"My aunt, the woman I'd long considered one of my dearest friends, is allied with Gideon. In fact, she is the one who drew me into this ugly scheme."

Chapter Fourteen

*W*E CANNOT ALLOW *her to leave. Belle's father will destroy me. And you ... you will return to your bored widows and penny schemes.*

Her aunt's treacherous warning to Gideon echoed in Belle's mind. Even now, the cold contempt in Vera's calm, precise tone rippled a chill over her skin. Allowing herself a slow, calming breath, she met the questions in Jon's dark eyes.

"You know of Lady Vera Willsbury, do you not?" she began.

His brow furrowed. "We have met in passing, at some infernal ball or another."

"She is my aunt, though not by blood. Vera wed my father's brother many years ago. At the time, I was a girl about Carrie's age." Belle pictured the woman she had once thought the world of, so vibrant and beautiful with a cascade of coppery red hair. "I always looked forward to her visits. Her arrival at our home always brought some new excitement. She would teach me something new—a fancy braid, a clever way to bring color to my cheeks, the latest in fashion from Paris. But then, my uncle suffered a heart attack, and Vera was left a widow. It wasn't long before she married an Englishman and moved to London. Years went by with only the occasional card or letter in the post. Until her husband collapsed at his club."

"As I recall, Lord Willsbury was not at an advanced age when he died," Jon said. "He was an upstanding man. Bloody shame, really."

"Sadly, I have reason to suspect Aunt Vera did not see it that way."

Jon's brows shot up. "What are you saying?"

"Only the truth." Belle touched the pendant at her throat, steadying herself with the comforting feel of her grandmother's gift. "Her grief was short-lived. Perhaps curiously so."

"Are you saying she had something to do with his death?"

Belle shook her head, though after seeing Vera's true colors, she would not have put it past her aunt to rid herself of anyone who'd stood in the way of her wants.

"I don't mean to suggest she caused his death. But her time of mourning was brief. Surprisingly so. It wasn't long before she returned to New York and became the toast of the town. During her last visit, she encouraged me to come to London and stay with her." She pulled in a low breath. "That was when it all began."

"Tell me what happened, Belle." His voice was a low, husky rasp as he caught her hands in his. His touch was warm and gentle, precisely what she needed to ease her through this pain.

"I'd only recently arrived in London when Aunt Vera introduced me to Gideon Kentsworth. At the time, I didn't realize how perfectly convenient his supposed return to the city had been. She claimed he was an old friend, a distant cousin to her late husband. Looking back, I can see how she carefully orchestrated every interaction I had with the man to prove that we were perfect for one another."

Perfect. What an utterly absurd word. Her relationship with Gideon had been anything but. From the start, everything she'd believed about the man had been a lie. So much deception. So many illusions.

As he took in her words, Jon set his jaw in a hard line, as if the words were difficult to hear. Perhaps they were. But she supposed he should know the true nature of her feelings toward Gideon. She glanced down at her hands, steadied within Jon's firm hold. So very reassuring. Yet without demand.

"Your aunt deceived you," he said, his expression speaking louder than his words.

"They both did," she said. "From the first time we met, Gideon pretended to share my interests. He played his part to a T." She braced herself to speak the truth. "But even before I discovered his duplicity, there was one problem that could not be overcome."

"And what was that?"

"He was not the man for me." Belle stated the truth directly, without hesitation. Meeting Jon's gaze, she saw the way the tension in his jaw seemed to ease, if only slightly.

Jon's brow furrowed. "Might I ask why in blazes you were wearing that blasted dress?"

Belle swallowed against a rush of emotion she hadn't realized she'd been holding in. She had never loved Gideon. Not truly. From the start, her doubts had felt like a rock in the pit of her stomach.

"Yesterday morning, I resolved to cry off the engagement. When I told my aunt what I planned to do, she dismissed my reservations as nothing more than cold feet. But I knew better. At that moment, I should have followed my instincts." She let out a low breath, attempting to clear her head. "But Aunt Vera insisted that the plans should not be altered. Not just yet. I needed more time to think it through, she'd said. And like a fool, I trusted her."

Jon nodded his understanding. "At that point, you had no reason to doubt her."

"Honestly, I sensed that something wasn't quite right . . . she was a bit too eager for me to marry. I did my best to drown out the nagging little voice in my thoughts. That afternoon, I ventured out to the modiste's shop for a final fitting of the gown." Again, her fingers went to her necklace, drawing comfort from the touch. "When I arrived at the shop, I simply could not go through with it. I thanked the dressmaker for her lovely work, instructed her to box up the gown, and took it with me."

"How in blazes did you come to be wearing it on a dreary

London night?"

"I suppose you could attribute that predicament to an unfortunate whim."

The ridges in his forehead deepened. "A whim?"

"A most poorly timed one, at that," she said. "You see, when I returned to my aunt's residence, I found myself alone in the house. As I looked at the ribbon-wrapped parcel that contained a dress I no longer needed or wanted, a peculiar mix of emotions washed over me. The gown was beautiful—or so I'd thought at the time. The design had seemed like something out of a fairy tale. So, I decided to try it on, if only to picture the alterations which might make it suitable for a ball or something of that nature. It seemed a shame to waste such a dress, and you know I'm actually quite practical."

"That is not a word I might've used to describe you. Evidently, I was not witness to that aspect of your nature." The slightest of wry smiles played on his mouth. "I shall have to take your word for it."

"I suppose you will," she said, mustering a prim tone. "In any case, I'd no sooner managed to fasten the last button when I heard my aunt return. But she was not alone. And soon, the shouting started."

He quirked a brow. "An argument?"

"One might call it that. Aunt Vera had arranged to meet a friend for an early tea, so she had no way of knowing that I had not stayed for the fitting. When she returned, she evidently did not realize I was in the residence and could hear the shrill notes of her voice."

"Kentsworth was with her?"

"Yes." The single syllable tasted bitter on her tongue. "At first, I didn't understand what was happening. I couldn't make out what she was saying. She sounded agitated, as if she were in a state of sheer panic. I assumed something was wrong and rushed to her bedchamber. The door was closed. But I could hear that she wasn't in danger." Belle pulled in a sharp breath. "They were having a lovers' quarrel."

"Bloody hell," Jon muttered under his breath.

In her mind's eye, she saw Gideon's angry scowl when he discovered she'd learned their secret. The image taunted her, even as the echoes of her aunt's icy attempt to convince her she'd gone a bit mad played in her thoughts.

"Aunt Vera tried to tell me that I was letting my nerves get the better of me. The shrew dared to insinuate that I was in an irrational state. When I told her I would take up residence in a hotel, she made it clear they would not allow it. I knew then that I had to leave." She stared down at the stone patio beneath her feet. "I had to escape."

Honestly, Belle, I am finding this all a bit tiresome, Vera had said in that low, breathy voice of hers. *It's high time you stopped pretending you possess an iota of virtue. You made a promise, and you are going to keep it. Gideon and I will not allow you to simply walk away. Perhaps the best cure for your fear of matrimony is a night with the man who will take you as his bride.*

The memory of her aunt's calm, poison-filled words was so very bitter, Belle felt a fresh whisper of fear. She could not bring herself to reveal the ugly details. Not yet. Not even to Jon. "So, I ran."

She hadn't realized the chill that had washed over her had unleashed an actual shiver. Jon pulled her closer, brushing his fingertips over her cheek. "You're safe now."

She nodded, even as a fresh wave of apprehension prickled along her nape. "Jon, they may be dangerous. I don't know what they will do, but they won't give up. Not until they have what they want. Everything they did, everything they said, was driven by their hunger for my father's money."

"Trust me when I say I will protect you, Belle. No matter what comes this way." Ever so gently, he drew one finger along the curve of her face. The sensation was so very familiar. So very comforting. After nearly two years apart, his tender, nearly chaste touch seemed natural. It seemed right.

"I do trust you." She allowed herself a little smile. "I suppose I always have. But if the jackals find me, something terrible may happen. My presence here may draw danger to your doorstep. There must be somewhere else . . . a secure place where I might rest more easily."

"If they find you, the blighters will bloody well have to deal with me. And I promise you, they will not like the consequences." His jaw set in a resolute, granite-hard line, he tipped up her chin. As the pad of his thumb brushed over her bottom lip, his eyes darkened, and he met the questions in her gaze. "You're safe with me." A hint of amusement brightened his features. "And I would not underestimate the value of Mrs. Gilroy's broom as a means of defense."

"Is that so?" she said, resisting the urge to smile at his wry tone.

"You think I'm not serious?" His forehead furrowed. "It wasn't long ago when that sprite of a woman chased off a cutpurse with only a loaf of crusty bread and her cane. She's a tough one, she is."

Again, she bit back a smile. "You are exaggerating."

"I would swear to it in a court of law." A sly grin played on his full mouth. "Of course, I cannot say that I actually observed the act. I heard the tale secondhand."

"From whose lips, might I ask?"

"Her own," Jon said. "But I still would not doubt it. I would not want to cross that woman when she's angry."

"Oh, I do understand. She has the capacity to be a force of nature," Belle said, relaxing into a smile. "But I am not being followed by a hungry thief out to snag a few coins. As you said, those men are *on the hunt.*" Even at that moment, even as Jon's touch comforted her, the words held the power to ripple a chill through her. "I've never before experienced this sense of being pursued, as if I were a rabbit chased by hounds. Why, the very idea of it cuts against the grain."

"The fact that those bastards are searching for you is all the more reason for you to stay right here. In this house. Under my protection."

The very thought of needing Jon's protection—or that of any man—chafed like a too-tight shoe. But there was nothing to be done about it, was there?

His brows furrowed into a stern line as he seemed to read her thoughts. "You understand the people you're dealing with, Belle. The rotters have too much riding on their scheme to be easily put off."

"I know what is in their treacherous hearts." She swallowed hard against the bitter truth. When her aunt dropped the oh-so-pleasant demeanor she'd used as a disguise, Belle had seen the stunning hatred in her eyes. "Truth be told, I may have more reason to fear my aunt than I do Gideon."

"It's personal for her, isn't it?"

"Yes." Since her husband's death, Vera had relied on Belle's family to support her lavish lifestyle. But her aunt had wanted more. Always *more*. "She won't rest until she gets what she wants."

Or until she silences me.

He gazed down at her for a long moment, seeming to study her. "Bloody hell, that settles it. You're staying here for as long as it takes."

She searched his eyes. "Am I now?"

"I don't care if they show up at the door with an army of oafs and a blasted dragon to boot. I will not leave you to face this on your own."

Was Jon acting out a sense of duty? Or was it something else altogether?

Something deeper. Something far more enduring.

"I see you've acquired a newfound sense of chivalry," she said, not quite teasing.

He seemed to mull over her words. "I've never had reason to play the white knight. Not until now."

"You have no duty to protect me," she reminded him.

He slowly shook his head. "How could I not protect a lady in the face of danger?" His voice was low and husky, so very appealing. "You may not agree, but I do consider myself a gentleman."

"How very civilized."

He regarded her with a slight frown. "Belle, if my sister was alone and in peril while your brother was in a position to provide assistance, I'd expect Jeremy to meet the challenge."

"I suppose he would," Belle said. "Though the endeavor would require him to consider something other than our family's business. Jeremy strives to keep operations functioning as smoothly as the gears of a fine Swiss watch, as he likes to say."

Meeting Jon's perceptive gaze, Belle felt a sense of relief. He had soothed her fears. Eased her apprehension. Yet a hope she hadn't even realized she'd been holding onto began to dim.

As she drank in the familiar scent of Jon's shaving soap, she suspected an ever-so-slightly bitter truth—his protective instincts had little to do with *her*. His motives were likely rooted in duty. In a determination to do the right thing. And to act as a gentleman, no less. Jon might well have done the same for another woman facing a desperate situation.

His mouth hitched. Not quite a smile. "And remember this, Belle—I can be bloody stubborn when I have cause to be."

"Stubborn? You?" She infused the words with a deliberately light tone. "Never."

"Once I've made up my mind, no amount of argument will change it. You know that."

"Well, we shall see." Belle relaxed, if only a bit.

"In any case, if you leave this house now, I don't think I could endure days of Mrs. Gilroy's frown, and I depend on that woman to cook my meals. A smart man does not irk the person who prepares his food."

"I rather think you would survive," she countered.

"Besides, she's counting on you to assist her with *the wee lass*. Not to mention the dog." His full mouth widened into a smile.

"And there is the matter of our wager."

"Surely you would not hold me to a trivial bet in the face of danger at the door."

He cocked a brow. "Trying to weasel out of it so soon, eh?"

She suspected his light tone was intended to distract her from her worries, to ease the awful tension of not knowing whether a threat would soon present itself. She allowed herself to relax. There was no harm in enjoying this simple moment now, was there?

"You know me better than that now, don't you?"

"I know this: I am looking forward to the aroma of apple pie baking in the kitchen."

"Perhaps not so much as I am looking forward to preparing said pie." *Pity I've no idea how to actually bake the infernal pastry.*

"Do I detect a lack of confidence?" Blast the man's perceptive gaze, seeing through her so readily.

She shook her head, perhaps a bit too quickly. "Not at all," she said, pausing to collect her thoughts. "But you must promise me that you will take swift action to protect Carrie and Mrs. Gilroy if there is any sign that Gideon's lackeys suspect I'm here."

"I will see to the protection of everyone in this house." He spoke with a resolve which comforted her. "On that, Belle, you have my word."

A RABBIT CHASED by hounds.

As Jon poured good scotch into a tumbler and settled into a leather wing chair in his study, he pictured the tense set of Belle's soft mouth as she'd put her current predicament into words. The fear in her voice was palpable. But she was strong of heart. Courageous. She wasn't about to be cowed by bastards like Kentsworth and his lackeys.

Damn the curs, trying to chase her down as if they were hunting dogs in pursuit of prey. What the hell was driving

Kentsworth? Belle had been ready to cry off their engagement, and the discovery of his relationship with her aunt had proven her instincts were right.

Many in the high-brow social circles of London looked upon Belle as an especially valuable trophy, an heiress who was as beautiful and clever as her father as wealthy. He knew what his sister had endured over the years with the bloody *heiress hunters* who chased after her fortune. Macie had managed to put most of them off with a well-timed, mildly scandalous scene or some other shenanigan. A rare few had conducted themselves without a bloody scruple to their name, pursuing her as if she'd been a bounty to be claimed.

What was the bastard's endgame? Was Belle the prize he sought? Or was it a matter of the funds the rotter might bleed from her father?

But now—now that Belle knew he'd been carrying on with her aunt—Kentsworth could no longer go through the motions of a courtship. He could not entice her back to him with pretty lies.

I had to escape . . . I ran.

Belle's words had cut like a rusted knife. He'd heard the distress in her hushed voice. The fear. *Escape.* Propelled by desperation. She'd rushed into the night. Into the unknown. Did the blighter intend to compromise her, to coerce her into speaking her vows? *Bloody hell.*

Belle had become a bit reserved after the revelation. In his gut, Jon knew there was much she had not told him. It had all been too fresh. Too hard for her to bear.

He hadn't pressed for more. Her trust was so very fragile. Not that he could blame her. He certainly had not proven worthy of it in New York, had he?

The only thing that mattered now was earning her confidence. As long as she had faith that he would be there for her, he could keep her safe.

Whatever it took, he would protect her. From Kentsworth. And from himself.

He couldn't deny his hunger for her, even as he stared down a bitter truth—they were tempting fate. By thunder, he wanted her. In his arms. In his bed. But giving in to desire would lead to consequences neither of them were ready to face.

But bloody hell, it was a challenge to pretend he wasn't absolutely mad for her. Since he'd become a man, he had encountered his fair share of women. Flirtatious socialites. Pretty dollar princesses. Sophisticated widows. But none of them—not a blasted one—could hope to compare to Arabelle Frost.

She was a diamond, a true treasure. In his eyes—in his heart—she was utterly incomparable.

At the moment he'd laid eyes on her, he'd fallen for her. Hard. And fast. He had always considered himself a logical man— a man who'd believed the notion of love at first sight to be sentimental drivel—but damned if he hadn't had the wind knocked out of him when he looked into her sapphire eyes.

He'd soon discovered she deserved better than a man like him. Their civilized but far from amicable parting had been proof of that.

But that was then. Now, Belle was here. He would defend her, no matter the cost. And perhaps he might truly repair the trust he'd so foolishly shattered.

Chapter Fifteen

FOLLOWING A QUIET evening and a restless night filled with dreams of a seductive swashbuckler—no doubt inspired by Ellie's talk of her own swaggering seducer—Belle awakened to two rather startling realizations. First, the pirate in her hazy fantasies had been the same tempting buccaneer who'd strolled into her waking daydream. While his face had been hidden by shadows, the mysterious raider's dark hair, broad shoulders, and husky voice bore an undeniable resemblance to the man who'd once shattered her heart. *How very maddening.*

And secondly, as she stirred from sleep, she became aware that the soft, rhythmic snoring drifting to her ears was not a product of her dreams.

She was not alone.

Sitting up in bed, she glanced about the room. *Good heavens.* Spying a lump beneath the bedcovers at the bottom of the bed, she chuckled to herself as she quickly identified the culprit. *Cleo.* Curled beneath the quilt, the cat continued to snore in what seemed to be feline bliss. Had she slept there all night?

Shaking herself out of the remnants of a light, drowsy fog, Belle slid from under the covers. Selecting a practical cotton dress in a vibrant shade of teal, she prepared for the day ahead, then went to assist Mrs. Gilroy.

The housekeeper was already up and about when Belle made it to the kitchen. Bustling about with pans and pots as she prepared the morning meal, Mrs. Gilroy appeared not to hear Belle as she approached. Standing in the doorway between the kitchen and the dining room, Belle watched with a growing sense of curiosity as the older woman moved about with steps she might actually have described as spry. *How very curious.*

Appearing to sense Belle's presence, Mrs. Gilroy startled, then spun abruptly to face her. "Oh, I'm so glad to see ye, lass," she said, looking as if she'd nearly dropped the empty pot in her hand. "Will ye be a dear and fetch my cane? I left it in the pantry and could not summon the energy to go back for it."

"Of course." Moments later, she returned with the walking stick in hand. Mrs. Gilroy flashed a quick smile, then made a slight wince as she leaned on it, favoring her left leg. "This dratted knee of mine."

Was it a trick of Belle's memory, or had Mrs. Gilroy's *bad* knee been on her right side the day before? She decided against giving voice to the question. With all that had taken place, she didn't doubt she might've mixed things up. Still, her curiosity nagged at her, if only a bit.

"If ye'd like to be of help, I'll ask ye to prepare these for tonight's stew," Mrs. Gilroy said, handing Belle a bunch of carrots.

"I'd be happy to," Belle said. Taking the vegetables to the chopping board, she searched her mind, trying to remember how her family's cook had approached the task. As a child, she'd watched Ginny slice and dice and peel vegetables with ease. But it had been such a long time since Belle had paid any mind to what went on in the kitchen.

Surely it could not be so much of a challenge. She pulled in a breath, as if that might invigorate her confidence, and set about the task.

Belle had chopped only one carrot—slicing it into thick chunks that truly did appear a bit too large for a respectable stew—when Mrs. Gilroy placed a gentle hand on her sleeve.

"Did ye forget to peel them, lass?" Mrs. Gilroy's brow furrowed. "Or do they not do that in America?"

Belle shook her head. Now that she mentioned it, she clearly remembered watching Ginny skillfully prepare the carrots she'd used in her recipes. "Drat, I did neglect that step, didn't I?" Peeler in hand, she reached for one of the chunks on the cutting board. "I'll fix it."

Mrs. Gilroy stilled her hand. "Lass, the way ye're holding that thing . . . well, ye're likely to slice yer finger. We wouldn't want that now, would we?"

Again, Belle shook her head. "Truth be told, I don't have much experience using a knife."

The older woman hiked her brows. "*Much*, dear?"

"Well, I do know how to use one to cut a cake," she said with a little shrug.

"Why don't ye come over here and help with breakfast while I prepare the carrots? We'll have ye do something that doesn't require ye to use a blade."

"That might be a bit more productive," Belle agreed. After all, cooking breakfast couldn't be that challenging now, could it?

Mrs. Gilroy motioned to a basket of eggs on the counter. "Mr. Mason has already departed for his office, so we'll only need a scramble for the three of us. The pan is already warm."

Belle stared at the basket. "You would like them . . . scrambled."

"Carrie's partial to them that way. But if ye'd rather fry them, I'll have no complaint."

"Then scrambled it is." Summoning a ration of optimism, Belle selected an egg and cracked it against the mixing bowl, just as she remembered Ginny doing.

The liquid white of the eggs dribbled over her fingers as a few clumps of shell fell into the bowl. With a few shakes of the fractured shell, she dumped the rest of the egg into the bowl. But fragments of shell floated in the mix. Not a problem, she told herself. She'd simply fish them out before she scrambled the yolks. She wiped the residue off her fingers and tried it again.

With one vigorous rap against the porcelain rim, the shell

cracked. Once again, gooey liquid dripped over her fingers, but she managed to add the egg to the contents of the bowl. If only the tiny bits of shell didn't cling.

Mrs. Gilroy scooted closer, peering around Belle's shoulder. "I'm thinkin' those eggs will have a bit more crunch than usual."

"Nothing to worry over. I'll strain out the bits of shell," Belle said, forcing a cheerful tone.

"Will ye, now?" Mrs. Gilroy quipped before she went back to chopping vegetables.

Refusing to accept defeat, Belle picked up another egg. A large, fine egg, if ever she'd seen one. *Crack.* This time, she placed more yolk and white in the bowl than shells. That was progress, wasn't it?

Mrs. Gilroy returned to her side. Her forehead creased, and the expression in her eyes softened. "Would ye like me to show ye something I've learned over the years?"

"That might be a good idea."

"I thought as much," Mrs. Gilroy said with a knowing nod. "Ye do not have much experience in the kitchen, do ye, lass?"

"Once, our family cook allowed me to stir the batter for my birthday cake." Belle couldn't help but smile at the expression on Mrs. Gilroy's face. "Does that count?"

Mrs. Gilroy's brow furrowed. "How old were ye at the time?"

"Seven, as I recall."

The older woman gave another sage nod. "Well, I must say, that is a relief."

"In what way, Mrs. Gilroy?"

"Ye're not hopeless," she said, not bothering to coat her words with sugar. "Ye've simply never been taught."

"I'd say that's a fair assessment."

A brief smile lit her features. "It's about time we change that."

I DO BELIEVE I'm getting the hang of domesticity.

Belle strolled through the sitting room, selected an anthology of poetry from the well-stocked bookshelves, and plopped down upon the chaise. Her day had been busy and productive, and now, a bit of rest was in order.

Under Mrs. Gilroy's tutelage, she'd managed to scramble the eggs for their breakfast and had diced a vegetable without so much as a nick of the blade against her finger. She'd even learned how to prepare the stew Mrs. Gilroy planned for dinner.

"Yer mum would be proud of ye," the housekeeper had observed.

"Oh, my, that would *not* be the case," Belle had replied with a half-hearted laugh. "Mother would be utterly horrified if she knew I had lifted so much as a finger in the kitchen."

"She never taught ye to cook, not even a bit?"

"I'd wager Mama has never so much as boiled water."

"Well, she might change her tune if she could taste the eggs ye made this morning. The seasoning was just right."

Belle smiled at the thought of it. Mrs. Gilroy was not one to toss out kind words she did not mean. A sense of accomplishment washed over Belle. She'd done it. She'd actually prepared a meal—at least, part of it. Now *that* was quite something.

Propping her feet up on a footstool, she opened the book. She'd settled Carrie in for a nap less than a quarter hour earlier, so she should have time to simply relax in the quiet chamber.

Taking in the gentle cadence of the verses, she turned from one page to another. After a brief time had passed with only the steady swoosh of the clock pendulum for company, she began to feel a bit drowsy. Each tick of the second hand lulled her into a peaceful state, until she drifted into that realm that was not quite asleep and not quite awake.

Crash.

The sound of metal colliding with the floor tore Belle from her pleasant rest. She bolted upright on the chaise, meeting Cleo's unblinking, golden-eyed gaze. The cat had scampered up onto a high shelf, positioning herself with enviable feline skill between a porcelain vase and a stack of books. The vase sat untouched, without so much as a quiver of movement.

The same could not be said for the silver candy dish that had landed on the floor beside the marble-top table it had occupied. The small, shallow bowl seemed to shiver with the force of its landing upon the polished wood planks.

Belle's attention darted to the culprit. *Heathy.* He stared up at Cleo, his playful demeanor undeterred by the look of sheer disdain in the cat's eyes.

She retrieved the silver dish and put it back in place. The bowl appeared to be no worse for wear. Thank heaven Heathy had not plowed into the sideboard, with its abundance of fine crystal that might've shattered into a thousand pieces.

She shot Heathy a glance she intended to appear cross, but he was utterly oblivious. Happily wagging his tail, he continued to gaze up at Cleo, as if he might manage to coax the cat down to play.

He was an adorable pup. Truly, he was. Belle couldn't find it in her heart to be upset with him. He'd only been playing, after all.

Her gaze shifted to the small, white, paw-shaped clumps on the floor leading to the bookshelves. And to the table. She blinked. Was that . . . could that possibly be . . . flour?

Turning to the open door, she saw Carrie standing in the hall, peeping inside the room. The child nibbled her lower lip, looking quite concerned.

Belle went to the girl. Her sweet round face was dusted with flour. As was her blue dress. What in the dickens was happening?

"Heathy wanted to play. But Cleo didn't want to," Carrie explained, sounding quite rational as she explained the situation. "I hope you are not upset with him."

"Not at all," she said truthfully, even as questions formed in her thoughts. "Carrie, I thought you were taking a nap."

The girl shrugged. "I didn't want to sleep."

Belle swiped a bit of the white dust from the child's cheek.

Flour. Just as she'd thought.

"Carrie, why do you have flour on your face?"

Once again, she nibbled her lip. "I wanted to surprise you."

Oh, dear. Belle suspected she would definitely not like this surprise. "How did you want to surprise me?"

"I wanted to make a pie," she said. "Not a pretend pie, but a real one."

Belle held her voice calm. "Will you show me what you made?"

"I didn't get a chance to make anything." Carrie raised her hands in a little shrug as Mrs. Gilroy limped toward them. Tears filled the child's eyes. "I didn't mean to make a mess."

"Oh, it is," Mrs. Gilroy whispered, standing with one hand on her hip and the other on her cane.

Belle's heart sank. Judging from Mrs. Gilroy's expression, the mess must be a real humdinger.

"I thought it had begun to snow in her playroom," the housekeeper added under her breath.

"The playroom?" Belle repeated. Surely she'd misunderstood. "Not the kitchen?"

Mrs. Gilroy shook her head. "Carrie came to me with the idea that I might make a *real* pie with her. I suppose the child has tired of romping about in the mud. I did not have time today, so I saw her to her playroom. When I left her, she was playing with one of her dolls. But she returned to the kitchen. She must've taken the canister while I was gathering supplies in the pantry. And now, the flour seems to have made its way throughout the house."

"Well, it cannot be *that* bad, now, can it?"

Mrs. Gilroy's slow shake of her head seemed rather ominous. "Don't say I did not warn ye, lass."

Belle took Carrie's small, flour-dusted hand in hers and led her to the playroom. Along the way, Belle could not miss the trail of white paw prints and child-sized footprints.

She'd reassured herself that she was right. I could not possibly be as bad as the housekeeper's expression implied.

As she entered the playroom, Belle stilled. She'd been mistaken. It was *that* bad. In truth, it was even worse than she'd imagined.

The floor did indeed look as if it had experienced a dusting of snow. The shelves had also been dusted with the flour, while Carrie's doll looked as if it were wearing a powdered wig.

Goodness gracious.

"Heathy was playing with the kitty. They ran in here," Carrie explained. "But he bumped into the flour." She pulled in a rather dramatic little breath. "And it all went *poof.*" The child gestured with her hands. "Everywhere."

"A bit of an understatement, I'd say," Mrs. Gilroy quipped.

"It's nothing that can't be tidied up," Belle said optimistically.

"Tidied up?" Mrs. Gilroy said with a wry chuckle. "That's one way of putting it."

Oh, well, there was nothing to be done about it now. Other than to clean the mess.

"Well, I shall simply have to get to work." Belle forced a pleasant tone into her voice, as if that might convince even *herself* that the task at hand would not be *that* daunting.

Picturing her ever-energetic grandmother, she imagined what the human dynamo of a woman would say. *This is no time to dilly dally, Belle. You'll get it done. After all, it's only a bit of grain.*

Squaring her shoulders and plastering on a cheerful smile, Belle got to work.

She swept. She dusted. She cleaned. Then she swept and dusted and cleaned again. And again. She repeated the process until the floor gleamed and the surfaces shined. Even though she'd made it clear that she would clean the mess—a task that had turned out to be *that bad,* if not even worse—Mrs. Gilroy had insisted on helping. For her part, Carrie joined in the clean-up effort, swishing a feather duster with a child's natural joy.

Finally, they were finished. Satisfied with their efforts, Belle joined Mrs. Gilroy in the kitchen for tea.

"Mrs. Gilroy, might I use the kitchen table for a little lesson with Carrie?" Eyeing the housekeeper a bit gingerly, Belle broached the subject on her mind. After their efforts to restore the playroom to order and remove all the bits of flour that had been tracked all the way into the sitting room, she didn't dare try to predict the housekeeper's response.

Mrs. Gilroy sent her a wary glance. Belle could see that she was worn out, and understandably so. Now, the old woman had stretched out her bad leg with a little groan. How very odd. Hadn't the housekeeper injured her *other* leg in her tangle with Heathy? Somehow, the achy limb seemed to have shifted.

Oh, dear. I am more tired than I'd thought. With a small sigh, she shook off the question of Mrs. Gilroy's injured limb.

Watching Belle over her cup of tea, Mrs. Gilroy took a sip. "A lesson, is it?" she said with the faintest of smiles. "Ye're a brave one, aren't ye?"

"Carrie is feeling a little down, so I thought I might teach her to make ornaments. You do know the kind I'm talking about, don't you?"

Mrs. Gilroy took another drink of tea. "I cannot say as I do."

"You've never made pretty decorations out of flour and salt?"

"I cannot say as I have," she said, echoing her previous response.

"Oh, it's great fun."

"Is it now?" The housekeeper appeared skeptical.

"My grandmother taught me when I was a little girl. It's very simple. And not very messy."

"Now that is music to these old ears."

"Might I trouble you for your cookie cutters?"

"I'll fetch them for ye," Mrs. Gilroy said. "What else might ye be needing?"

"A bit of salt," Belle said, then added with a smile, "And a few cups of flour."

"I'm not sure I dare." The old woman flashed a crooked grin. "But I trust ye know what ye're doing, Miss Belle."

"We shall see, Mrs. Gilroy." Taking a sip of tea, Belle pictured the trail of white prints on the sitting room rug. "We'll be working at this sturdy table. Hopefully, it's capable of withstanding Heathy's shenanigans."

Chapter Sixteen

"M R. MASON, WILL you be heading directly to the Rogue's Lair?"

"Not tonight," Jon replied to his assistant, Alton Bennett. "I expect to venture out later, after I attend to matters on the home front."

Bennett's forehead furrowed, but he kept his thoughts to himself. The man's reaction wasn't surprising. Not really. In the not-too-distant past, Jon had rarely felt a need to head home before midnight. He'd gone about his days—and nights—with very little inclination to spend his waking hours rambling about his house, essentially alone. That was, of course, before Carrie had come to stay. Since the child had been rather unceremoniously shuttled into his care, his habits had changed. He now made a point to return home most nights, if only to verify the child's wellbeing with her governess before he headed to the tavern for the evening.

An image of the girl's wide smile flashed through his thoughts. Truth be told, he had come to look forward to the child's enthusiastic greeting. By thunder, he'd even begun to enjoy her lively accountings of the dog's mischief, especially as it related to the pup's ability to leave Carrie's dour governess in a stir.

Recently, Carrie had often made plaintive requests for a bedtime story. In all honesty, he could not puzzle out why the little girl wanted to hear the tales in his gruff voice, but it seemed to matter to her. And so, he'd actually delayed his departure to read from a book of fairy tales, of all the blasted things, after the child had been tucked into bed.

He couldn't deny the heart of the matter. Since Carrie's unexpected arrival at his doorstep, he'd grown quite fond of the child. When she was happy, the light in her blue eyes might've buoyed the spirits of Scrooge himself, while the sadness he observed from time to time was like a fist to his gut.

In those moments, a dreaded sense of uncertainty tended to fall over him. In his life, he was the one people turned to when they needed a problem solved. From major negotiations that had gone off the rails to the minor crises within his family's enterprises that arose on a near-daily basis, *he* was the one that his father—and so many others—counted on. He was the one who found the solution, the one who came up with a way to make the issue go away. But a sweet-faced moppet's tears could leave him utterly confounded.

Truth be told, he didn't know the first thing about raising a little girl. Or a little boy, for that matter. It wasn't as if he could reflect back on his own childhood. It had been a bloody long time since his boyhood, and God knew he would not wish to raise a child with the same philosophy, for lack of a better word, that had guided his father. Over the years, he'd rarely spent time around children. One of his partners at the Rogue's Lair was father to a tot and a babe in arms, and his sister was expecting the birth of a child soon after she and her husband returned from their journey. He'd never thought to have any interest in being a father, beyond the duty to carry on the family name.

But that had changed with Carrie's arrival. He'd quickly come to care for the girl with her sweet, impish grin. The *wee lass,* as Mrs. Gilroy had dubbed her, had quickly mastered the art of twisting him around her little finger. She was an adorable sprite, and though he wouldn't admit it to Mrs. Gilroy, the child's earnest affection for the wild little dog and cantankerous cat who were currently in residence rendered the bit of chaos they'd brought with them worthwhile.

Carrie had taken an instant liking to Belle. No mystery there. When Belle looked at the girl, her rosy smile was utterly genuine, as real as the kindness in her heart.

"Is there anything else for today's agenda?" Bennett went on, ever efficient.

Shuffling through papers on his desk, Jon offered the man a perfunctory dismissal for the day and prepared to take his own leave. As he donned his overcoat, an image of Belle's smile flickered through his thoughts, bringing with it a peculiar sense of anticipation. He didn't want to admit it, even to himself, but the idea of Belle in his home—in his life—appealed to him far more than it should. Certainly far more than was prudent.

An hour later, as he walked through the door of his house, he was greeted once again by the sound of Carrie's high, not-quite-on-pitch voice, singing a tune about Mary and her lamb. This time, the song was coming from the kitchen. And the flawless notes of a soprano accompanied the child. Was that Belle? He'd known she could carry a tune, but he'd never heard the true beauty of her voice.

Intrigued, he followed the sound, confirming his suspicion that the lyrical notes were the product of Belle's voice. She sat at the kitchen table with Mrs. Gilroy and Carrie, cutting cookies out of dough while they happily recited the nursery rhyme verse set to music.

"Biscuits?" He decided to play the rascal. "I think I'll have a taste."

"Don't," Carrie said as he reached to take a small bit of the dough. "You won't like it."

"And why won't I?" He took a better look at the dough, seeing that it looked nothing like Mrs. Gilroy's shortbread.

"It's not for eating, Cousin Jon," she said with a tone of authority. "It's for art."

Art? He turned his attention to Belle, who at the moment was rolling out a bit of the mixture. Her cheek bore a streak of what looked like flour, while her chin was dotted with a smudge of the stuff. In all his days, he'd never met a dollar princess who wasn't too preoccupied with her appearance to ever be seen with a dusting of flour on her face. *How bloody appealing.*

"You should listen to her," Belle said lightly. "She knows what she's talking about."

"Or ye'll get a mouthful of salt. And flour," Mrs. Gilroy added.

"Might I ask what the three of you are doing?"

Belle slanted him a glance. "As Carrie said, we are making art."

"Michelangelo might well disagree."

"If I were a betting woman, I would wager that if he were alive today, he would agree that the three of us are engaged in artistic creation." Belle accented her words with a saucy little smile.

"I shall alert the Louvre."

"Would you like to make an ornament?" Carrie offered him a cookie cutter shaped like a star. "It's easy. You'll see."

"She's right," Belle said. "Will you show him how you do it, Carrie?"

"Of course I will." The girl sounded rather formal. "This is how I make my ornaments."

Carrie proceeded to demonstrate how she cut the design, then pressed her small fingers into the dough. "Poky-dots," she declared proudly.

"Ah, polka dots," he said. "Very creative."

"Will you try?" the child urged.

"My fingers are too large to make the dots," he said, finding a logical excuse.

Carrie was not convinced. "Just one dot."

"Yes, Jon," Belle said, her eyes teasing. "Shall we see how artistic you can be?"

"I do not possess a creative bone in my body," he countered, but unable to resist Carrie's encouragement, he chose a bell-shaped mold and pressed his thumbprint into the trimmed shape.

"We will paint them tomorrow," Carrie went on. "I think yours should be blue."

"An excellent choice," he agreed. "I'm counting on you to paint it for me."

"I will make it pretty," she said proudly. "I promise."

"I have full confidence that it will be," he said, ruffling her chestnut-hued hair.

Belle looked as if she were biting back a chuckle at his momentary awkwardness. "And we will have a grand time coloring our ornaments."

"This *is* fun," the child agreed with bright-eyed enthusiasm.

Watching Carrie manipulate the dough with her small, slightly clumsy fingers, he smiled to himself. The ability to create something of beauty—even the unsophisticated beauty to be found in a child's fledgling efforts—brought her such joy.

In his boyhood, he'd experienced the joys of simple pastimes. He'd enjoyed games and roughhousing and rollicking treks through the woods surrounding his family's country estate. For a time, he'd lived without a care in the world, other than whether or not he would best his cousins in footraces and their boyish scrapes. But then, days before his ninth birthday, everything had changed. His existence became focused on his studies and his father's near-daily talks on the value of duty. Of responsibility. Of the need to prepare to one day lead the family business.

Even so, he'd managed to wedge moments of reckless adventures and camaraderie between the lessons and lectures, especially during those summers when his childhood friend, Finn Caldwell, would come to visit. Thankfully, his mother, a free-spirited pixie of a woman who was evidently the only person on the planet who possessed the ability to soften his father's steely edges, saw to it that he had the opportunity to cultivate the friendship that endured to this very day.

Now, as he watched Carrie, he could not help but marvel at

the contrast between the child he saw today, happily engaged in an activity which allowed her young mind to flourish, and the descriptions Miss Pritchard had offered of the girl. The governess had painted Carrie as willful and disobedient, perhaps even incorrigible.

But that was then. That was before Belle had darted into the Rogue's Lair and back into his life. Since she'd first stepped through the doors of his home, she'd drawn Carrie to her with her caring heart. He could see the way Belle's kindness had brightened the child's smile.

The stark difference between Belle's cheerful smile and Miss Pritchard's cool gaze was impossible not to see. He'd little doubt Carrie had perceived the lack of warmth from the woman he'd employed to watch over her. Bugger it, he should've tossed the woman out on her scrawny arse before she'd had a chance to pack her bags. He now knew what to look for when it came to hiring on Carrie's next governess.

The *next governess*. The thought of it landed in his gut like a rock. In less than forty-eight hours, Belle's presence in his home had added a warmth that he'd forgotten to crave. She'd already won Carrie over, and the dog seemed to adore her. Good God, even Mrs. Gilroy could not maintain a frown when Belle was around. Only Cleo seemed unaffected. The cat seemed to pride herself on her highly cultivated feline indifference, but he sensed it was a matter of time before even the cat came around to Belle.

But it wouldn't be long before Belle had to leave. Once the threat Kentsworth posed was in the past, she would return to the life she'd known. Most likely, she'd leave London and return to New York.

Belle would leave him behind. Just as he'd left her. By hellfire, the realization was like another rock plummeting into his gut.

"Will ye be taking yer supper here? I've prepared a hearty stew," Mrs. Gilroy's question offered a welcome pause from his thoughts.

Jon glanced toward Belle. He needed to leave, if only to clear his head of notions that served no purpose. "Not tonight. I'll be off to the Lair shortly."

"I can keep it simmering on the stove until ye return," she offered.

"Thank you, but that won't be necessary," Jon said quickly, before he had a chance to change his mind. "I don't expect I will return before midnight."

TAKING THE REINS of his phaeton, Jon set a brisk pace on his route to the Rogue's Lair. The evening was foggy. No surprise there. But the full moon managed to show itself among the clouds. On this night when he felt strangely unsettled, more discontent than he had in ages, he wanted nothing more than a hearty drink and perhaps a few bites of food he knew couldn't possibly hold a candle to Mrs. Gilroy's stew.

He'd needed to leave the house. He'd needed to put distance between him and Belle. This was no time to think of what might've been—of what they might've had together. At this moment in their lives, she trusted that he would protect her. She was vulnerable. He could not take advantage of her, no matter what.

Jon had no sooner walked into the pub than a familiar voice greeted him. "Jon, I'm surprised to see ye here tonight." Logan MacLain stood by the bar, a well-filled stein in his hand.

"I might say the same," Jon replied. "I was not expecting you to return from the Highlands before the end of the month."

"I received word of a new opportunity, a possible partnership that might lead to an expansion." Logan motioned to the barkeep to bring a pint for Jon. "I'll brief ye on the details later."

"An expansion?" Jon considered the thought. "It may prove worthwhile."

"It will be," Logan said with his typical brash confidence. "I can feel it in my bones."

"I'm more interested in the financial projections than your creaky bones, but we shall see," Jon responded, pragmatic as always.

Logan shot him a muted scowl. "Sometimes, a man has to trust his gut."

"Indeed," Jon said. That particular strategy had worked well for Logan. Every venture the Scot touched had proved a rousing success. But Jon still trusted a logical analysis over any semblance of intuition.

Logan chuckled. "Ye still haven't learned to have faith in yers, have ye?"

"Only when it tells me I've eaten too many of Mrs. Gilroy's heavy dumplings," Jon replied as the barkeep placed a stein before him. "I take it Amelia and your son are well."

"Amelia—brave woman that my lovely wife is—has charmed the old lion." Logan smiled as he referred to his aging father. "She decided to stay with my family a while longer so Finnegan might have more time with his grandfather. Our boy melted my father's heart like nothing I'd ever thought I'd see."

Jon took a hearty draught of cold ale. "When you found Amelia, you struck gold, my friend."

"Aye, when I wake up with Amelia by my side, I still wonder at my good fortune," Logan said. He glanced about the room, then lowered his voice before he went on. "I suggest we continue this discussion in my office."

"That would be wise," Jon agreed.

Once they were behind the sturdy doors of his oak paneled office, Logan spoke freely. "I understand ye've had an unexpected visitor since I left for the Highlands."

Jon took another drink. "Are you referring to the child, the cat, or the woman?"

"When Macie wrote Amelia about the young lass in yer care, she mentioned ye're also looking after her cantankerous feline." Logan chuckled. "So that leaves the woman. Murray said she's an

American."

"She is." Jon felt a sudden tension in the back of his neck. "I presume he told you who she is."

Logan shook his head. "He said if I care to know, I should ask ye."

"Did he now?"

"He mentioned the lass was under yer protection, but he did not care to elaborate."

"Murray is indeed a man of few words," Jon said.

"Now that is an understatement." Logan took a seat in his wing-back chair. "Care to tell me what in blazes is going on?"

Jon settled into a chair and stretched out his legs. "A few nights ago, Arabelle Frost came through the door of this pub."

Logan's eyes narrowed. "The pretty lass ye knew in New York?"

Jon knew his friend had kept his description deliberately vague. Logan MacLain was one of the three people on the planet—including his sister and Finn—he'd allowed to see how bloody torn he'd been about leaving Belle behind.

"That would be the one. She was on the run," he said. "From a man."

"A cutpurse after her bag?"

"Nothing so simple as that," Jon said. "The man pursuing her was not a stranger."

"I think I'm getting the picture," Logan said. "She is an heiress, is she not?"

"Her father is one of the richest men in all of New York, if that gives you an idea."

Logan nodded his understanding. "What is the bastard after? A payoff?"

"It's worse than that," Jon said. "The cur has men actively searching for her. I suspect he intends to coerce her into speaking her vows with him."

"Definitely a more lucrative option for a scoundrel," Logan observed. "So, who is the rotter?"

"A Scottish lord by the name of Kentsworth."

Logan took a hearty drink. "Kentsworth, ye say."

"Gideon Kentsworth," Jon said. "When she speaks of him, Belle looks as if the devil himself was on her heels. Just as she did that first night."

A look of bitter recognition filled Logan's eyes. Bollocks, what did he know?

"Like the devil was on her heels, eh?" Logan drummed his fingers against the arm of the chair in a steady rhythm. "If she was tangled up with that rotter, the lass has gotten herself into a true fix. She has good reason to be frightened."

"At the moment, she is in my home. Under my protection."

Logan steepled his fingers, frowning as he often did when he thought through a problem. "That may not be enough," he said finally. "Obviously, ye cannot be with the lass every hour of the day."

"True." Jon considered his words. "I'd thought to hire on private security, but that presents its own risks. The more people who know she's at the house, the greater the chance word will make it to the jackal."

Logan nodded his agreement. "I have a suggestion, but ye will not like it."

"If you're thinking about Mrs. Johnstone, I've already pursued that option. The woman is out of the country."

"You're in luck, Jon." He smiled. "The Dragon has returned to London."

Chapter Seventeen

BELLE'S PLEASANT MORNING transformed into a decidedly eventful afternoon after the door chimes announced Ellie Blake's arrival at teatime. And this time, Ellie was not alone.

Peering out to verify the identity of the callers, Mrs. Gilroy spoke under her breath. "Well, well . . . the Dragon."

Belle hesitated for a moment. *Dragon.* Surely, she'd misunderstood. *How very odd.*

"Has Miss Blake arrived?" she asked finally.

"Yes," Mrs. Gilroy said. "It would appear Mr. Mason has arranged yer security. Miss Blake has brought the Dragon."

Security? Dragon? Belle silently repeated the words.

Appearing to read the confusion on Belle's features, Mrs. Gilroy's mouth pulled into a faint smile. "You'll understand soon enough, lass."

When she opened the door, Ellie strolled in, carrying a satchel in a vibrant black and red plaid. A strikingly pretty woman whose thick, dark hair was streaked with silver and topped with a tasteful black hat followed close behind. Tall for a woman, she wore a precisely tailored herringbone tweed walking suit in a rich blend of purple, cream, and black and charcoal gray gloves. In her left hand, she carried a bright yellow parasol, the only item in her ensemble which didn't quite fit the rest.

This lovely woman with refined tastes could not possibly be the Dragon. Could she?

As the newcomer glanced about the room, her assessing brown eyes appeared to take in the uncluttered, masculine aesthetics of Jon's townhouse. "I must admit, this is precisely as I'd expected," she commented to Ellie, who nodded in agreement.

"The dark woods suit him, I'd say."

As Mrs. Gilroy closed and bolted the door behind them, Ellie introduced Belle to the elegantly attired woman. An old, trusted friend of the family, Mrs. Johnstone greeted Belle warmly in a charming Scottish accent.

"'Tis my pleasure to make yer acquaintance," she said. "Ellie has spoken highly of ye."

"And with good reason," Mrs. Gilroy said, much to Belle's surprise.

"Indeed," Mrs. Johnstone said, even as her keen gaze settled on a spot near the length of carpet that ran the length of the entry hall. Her pert nose wrinkled. "Are my eyes deceiving me, or is that . . . a pawprint?"

Ellie followed the path of her gaze. She leaned closer. "I do believe it is. And it is precisely Heathy's size."

Belle and Mrs. Gilroy both saw it then, at precisely the same moment—the bits of flour they'd missed while cleaning up after Carrie's attempt at making a *real* pie. How in the dickens had the pup managed to drag the stuff all the way out here?

Mrs. Johnstone peered more closely. "That is flour, isn't it?"

"It is," Belle said. "There is an amusing story—"

"We had a bit of fun yesterday teaching the wee lass to make pretty baubles she might hang on the wall," Mrs. Gilroy spoke up.

Mrs. Johnstone's forehead creased. "It would appear the dog joined in as well."

"He is a playful little beast," Mrs. Gilroy went on, sounding unusually positive about the dog.

"As I recall, he can be a bit willful," Mrs. Johnstone replied as the dog trotted toward them, as if he knew he'd been the topic of discussion. Tail wagging, he cut a direct path to the woman who reached down to pet him with an easy familiarity. "He is a fiercely loyal little pup."

"One of his better qualities," Mrs. Gilroy said with a wan smile. "Might I bring ye all some tea in the parlor?"

"That would be lovely," Belle replied, thankful the housekeeper had changed the subject. "I'll come to help you with the tray."

"No need, lass," she replied. "I'll roll in the cart. I think it will be beneficial to exercise my leg a bit."

As Mrs. Gilroy took her leave, Belle led the women into the parlor. The dog followed along, plastered to Mrs. Johnstone's side. How had she developed a rapport with the pup?

The women began a conversation that remained lighthearted until Mrs. Johnstone's cheerful tone took a turn.

"Ye might be wondering why I've come today," she said, her expression growing more somber. "Jon feels I may be of help to ye."

Belle pulled in a breath as she folded her hands in her lap. "Thank you, but if you're here to assist me in watching over the child, there is no need." She made an effort to sound cordial even as she dismissed the woman's offer of assistance. "I have matters well in hand."

Mrs. Johnstone flickered a glance toward a few more bits of flour shaped like a paw, albeit smaller than Heathy's print. One brow hiked up in a speaking glance.

Drat. Belle resisted the urge to frown. Evidently, the cat had tracked the grain into this room as well.

The woman slowly shook her head. "Miss Frost, that is not why I'm here."

"It's quite exciting, really." Ellie's eyes lit with enthusiasm. "She is a woman of, shall we say, unique skills."

"Indeed." Mrs. Johnstone's manner was pleasant. Yet reserved. "You've much to learn."

Belle turned to her. "I am afraid I don't follow."

Before she could respond, Mrs. Gilroy ambled in with the tea service on a cart. Carrie assisted her in pushing the wheeled wooden tray. "Thank ye, child," Mrs. Gilroy said, and Carrie hurried to Belle's side.

Fresh from her afternoon nap, the girl fairly bounced with enthusiasm. She greeted Ellie and Mrs. Johnstone with a cheerful smile.

The women engaged the child in a light discussion of topics ranging from Carrie's preference for yellow and green dresses, the child's fondness for Mrs. Gilroy's fig jam, and a brief debate as to whether Heathy would look more handsome wearing a blue or violet bow on his collar. After a few pleasant minutes had passed, Ellie sent Mrs. Johnstone a speaking glance.

"Mrs. Gilroy, Belle and I have matters to discuss," Mrs. Johnstone said directly. "Matters not suitable for a child's ears."

"I figured ye might," the housekeeper said with a knowing nod. "Carrie, will ye show me yer new doll, the one Mr. Jon brought ye?"

"She's very pretty," the child said. "I know you'll think so, too."

"Ye can be sure of that," Mrs. Gilroy took the girl by the hand and walked a bit gingerly from the room.

As the door closed, Mrs. Johnstone took a sip of tea and sent Ellie another glance. "I know it must all seem a bit odd, with Ellie's talk of unique skills and such. But I'm here to assist with the matter of yer security. I understand ye've good reason to be cautious, given the situation."

"I take it he's informed you of my circumstances."

Mrs. Johnstone nodded. "As soon as I heard the name of the man who is looking for ye, I knew the danger ye'd faced."

"You've heard of him?"

She gave a somber nod. "A few years ago, I was involved in an investigation as an agent performing services for a certain detective bureau. It was all rather hush-hush, and discretion does not permit me to divulge the details of that particular case. But suffice it to say that Gideon Kentsworth is a very dangerous man.

Ye would not be the first young woman of means who became entangled with the scoundrel, only to regret it."

"Thank heaven you trusted your instincts," Ellie said.

"If I'd had any doubt that you were in danger, the information Miss Blake has learned only confirms my suspicions," Mrs. Johnstone said.

Tension gripped Belle's insides. "What is it, Ellie?"

"Since he arrived in London, Kentsworth has portrayed himself as Scottish nobility. But Belle, the man is a fraud."

Belle had already seen how very unscrupulous Gideon truly was. But this information still plowed into her with the force of a blow. "My, he did make a complete fool of me, didn't he?"

Ellie slowly shook her head. "He's been deceiving people for a long time. Most everyone he came across in the city believed him. After all, very few would feel inclined to research and verify one's title."

"Indeed," Mrs. Johnstone said. "Kentsworth has honed a talent for being a chameleon. He blends into an environment and characterizes himself in a way that does him the most good."

"He didn't have to try hard to convince me. I truly didn't care if he possessed a title or not." Belle reflected on the seamless manner in which he'd blended into her life, sharing her interests and dedication to aiding the poor. Why, he'd even made a show of sharing her love of poetry, even going so far as to recite verses of Walt Whitman and Ralph Waldo Emerson.

It had all been an act. Every last bit of it had been a bitter charade.

"In my heart, I think I knew all along. I saw through him, deep down. Even when I wanted to view him through a rosy lens."

"Ye can be thankful ye followed yer instincts." Mrs. Johnstone took a sip of tea and faced Belle directly. "Do ye care to tell me more of what happened the night ye ran from him?"

Belle gulped a swallow of tea and composed her thoughts. "It's rather simple, really. I'd already realized I could not go through it . . . I could not marry him. I had been staying with my aunt, Lady Vera Willsbury. You may have heard of her."

"I have," Mrs. Johnstone said without elaboration.

"I see clearly now that she'd done everything in her power to bring me and Gideon together. At the time, I truly believed she was hopeful that I would find the right man for me, especially after—" *After Jon took a piece of my heart when he returned to London.* But she certainly couldn't say that now, could she? "After I'd happily put myself on the shelf."

"She stood to benefit from your relationship," Ellie said as Mrs. Johnstone nodded her understanding.

"Yes, though I'd believed her efforts were sincere. Until I heard the two of them quarreling when she did not realize I was in the residence. Aunt Vera had flown into a rage. I don't ever recall hearing her voice so very shrill. So filled with anger." Belle took another sip of tea, collecting herself. The echo of her aunt's harsh tone in her thoughts still left her shaken.

"Belle, I know this is hard for you," Ellie said gently.

"For years, I trusted her as a dear friend. The truth was so bitter. That night, when I heard them, Gideon was much calmer than she was. He wasn't shouting, and it seemed he was trying to reassure her. But Aunt Vera was utterly furious."

She's having second thoughts, you fool. If Belle leaves . . . we'll be left with nothing. Aunt Vera's harsh tones echoed in her mind. *If she will not publicly speak her vows . . . I've found another way. But her father is a powerful man. We must ensure there is no way that he can challenge the documents. I don't care if you use persuasion. Or force. You cannot let her leave.*

Belle pulled in a low breath. "In Vera's eyes, he was letting the prey slip away."

The women's eyes went wide. "Good heavens," Mrs. Johnstone said.

"I knew then that I had no choice. I had to get away. They did not intend to let me go. I would be forced to marry Gideon. Or so they thought. Even if I refused, they could extort funds from my father in exchange for their silence."

"Oh, my," Ellie said, her tone hushed.

"I was able to create a distraction," Belle went on. "I escaped through the kitchen. And I ran." She sighed. "I kept going until I came to the tavern. Until I saw Jon."

"I doubt I could've been so brave," Ellie said.

"I was not brave." Belle shook her head. "I was terrified."

"Miss Frost, ye showed true courage," Mrs. Johnstone said. "And now, I am here to help ye to learn certain skills . . . skills ye may need if the jackals dare to come after ye."

Chapter Eighteen

JON RETURNED TO his home following a thankfully uneventful day to the sound of Carrie's cheerful voice singing a tune. But on this evening, the tune had nothing to do with a nursery rhyme. Rather, the child sang out the word "stomp," followed by a giggle and the word "kick."

Bloody peculiar, that.

He followed the enthusiastic, off-key notes to the sitting room. The door was open, so he watched the scene from the entry.

"Poke." Belting out the word followed directly by a giggle, she jabbed her bent arm backwards, as if to elbow an invisible person.

"Very good, Carrie," Mrs. Johnstone said. "Tell us what comes next?"

"Punch," she said, acting out the word with her right hand clenched into a small fist.

He propped an elbow against the doorframe and took in the scene. After Carrie followed her punching with another top-of-her-lungs rendition of the word *stomp*, he deduced what was going on. And he had to admit, he was bloody pleased to see it.

Mrs. Johnstone stood in the middle of a space created when the women had slid the furnishings to the perimeter of the room. Carrie stood before her, practicing her stomping and kicking and jabbing and punching with an imaginary opponent while Belle,

Ellie Blake, and Mrs. Gilroy looked on with pride.

Glancing his way, Mrs. Johnstone flashed a half-smile that told him she'd known he was there. "I see ye're impressed," she said as Carrie rushed up to him.

"Cousin Jon, did you see me stomp?" The girl gave him a hug. Thankfully, she did not utilize his feet in a demonstration of her new skill.

"I did," he said with pride. "Well done."

"As ye can see, we've been busy," Mrs. Johnstone said. "Carrie is a quick study."

"Indeed," he said. "I hadn't realized you could teach a child such tactics."

"I see no reason why the girl—and every woman in this house—should not have a means of defending herself."

"I am impressed," he said. "But I cannot say I am surprised at your capabilities. You come highly recommended."

"Is that so?" As Mrs. Johnstone smiled, he spotted Belle biting back a little grin. "It wasn't that long ago that yer new brother-in-law, Finn, also called upon my services."

"I recall Macie mentioning the instruction you provided."

She nodded thoughtfully. "Sadly, the instruction has been lacking in one aspect." She'd narrowed his eyes. Suddenly, he felt a creeping suspicion he was not going to like was coming, especially given the way she was looking at him the same way a lioness might eye up some unfortunate animal in her path.

"And what might that be?" he asked.

"A true demonstration with an attacker . . . a man-sized attacker."

Good God.

Finn had complained about his creaky back for a full three days after serving as Mrs. Johnstone's demonstration attacker. This was most definitely *not* what he'd had in mind.

"Will you be back tomorrow? I'll send my assistant. Mr. Bennett won't know what hit him."

"I don't think this will wait," Mrs. Johnstone said. "Ye're tall.

Fit. Reasonably powerful." Her eyes gleamed with humor as she put him on the spot. "I see no reason why ye would not suffice."

Suffice. What in blazes was she getting at?

"I can name one good reason," he explained.

"And what might that be?"

He flashed a grin that usually helped him out of a fix. "Well, you see, I have an aversion to pain."

"Ye will survive the experience. I assure ye of that."

"Here's another—my father taught me to never raise a hand to a woman. Now, given that, how can I attack you? Even in the name of self-defense."

"I guarantee ye will not have a chance."

"It's much too awkward," he said truthfully.

"We do need a demonstration," Belle spoke up as Ellie and Mrs. Gilroy looked on with subtle half-smiles on their faces. "For the sake of our training."

Blast it, she had gotten him good. She'd found his Achilles heel.

He couldn't let her down.

"By thunder, I'll do it." He sent Belle a speaking glance. "In the name of education."

"Excellent," Mrs. Johnstone said. "I was hoping ye'd see it that way."

Mrs. Gilroy and Belle looked at Carrie. Seeming to share the same realization, Belle nodded as Mrs. Gilroy took Carrie's hand. "Shall we go have a wee snack? I've made shortbread."

Carrie nodded enthusiastically, and Mrs. Gilroy led her from the room. Once the child was out of the room, Jon met Mrs. Johnstone's cool-eyed gaze.

"First, I'd suggest ye remove yer jacket," she said. "We wouldn't want to tear that fine wool, now would we?"

"I suppose not," he agreed. Shrugging off his coat, he laid it over the back of a chair.

"Now, when I count to three, I want ye to come at me," Mrs. Johnstone said. "Rather like a hooligan in some dark alley."

He studied her for a long moment. *Good God.* Was it possible she was toying with him? "I cannot take the chance that I might injure you."

"Why? Simply because I am a woman?" Mrs. Johnstone regarded him with a hint of taunt in her eyes. "A woman who is quite literally old enough to be yer mother?"

"I'd say that has something to do with it."

"Ye will not hurt me. I promise ye that."

"Very well," he said. "But don't think I'm going to give this my full strength."

"I am not concerned," she said with a sly confidence.

"I'll do what I can to assist you," he said, attempting to sound, at the least, civilized before he acted, to use her term, the hooligan.

"Again, attack when I count to three." She looked quite serious, other than the mischievous gleam in her eyes. "And by the way, the ladies told me ye still refer to me by that rather undignified name my dear nephew Logan came up with when he was an incorrigible young rascal. Oh, what was it?" Her smile was sly now. "The Dragon."

Bloody hell. He braced himself for what was going to come next. *Bugger it, this is going to hurt.*

OH, DEAR. BELLE winced as Mrs. Johnstone employed Jon as her model for teaching techniques for disarming, distracting, and essentially knocking the stuffing out of an attacker. Although it appeared the woman had used stage blows in most of the cases, Jon's foot had been stomped, his shin kicked, and his ribs jabbed. At one point, he'd landed on his back while Mrs. Johnstone demonstrated a martial arts throw, and he'd come uncomfortably close to suffering a particularly unfortunate strike from the woman's weighted umbrella.

Throughout the lesson, he'd been a good sport, and when it was done, he offered a half-hearted salute. With a quiet groan, he hobbled off, presumably to change into more comfortable attire.

"He's a gutsy one, he is," Mrs. Johnstone said. "Not many men would assist me in that particular task."

Ellie smiled, looking a bit wistful. "He did it for you, Belle."

"I find that rather doubtful," Belle replied as Cleo plopped down from her feline perch on a shelf. She'd been napping, but now she landed on the carpet and gave her head a little shake. She strolled over to Mrs. Johnstone, displaying an easy familiarity with the woman.

"Well then, we simply must agree to disagree," Ellie replied with a coy grin. "Perhaps we will carry on this conversation another time, over tea and scones."

"It would be my pleasure," Belle said. "As I will need to stay out of the public eye for a while longer, I do hope you and Mrs. Johnstone might enjoy paying another visit."

"Of course. We shall be happy to, and if any busybodies should happen to question my presence here, I will simply inform them that I am looking in on Cleo in Macie's absence."

"Good thinking," Mrs. Johnstone said. "I agree that it would be wise to remain out of sight until this problem with Kentsworth has been put to rest. The training I have provided ye is valuable, but ye do not want to make yerself an easy target. With any luck, ye will not have to put those tactics into play."

"Indeed," Belle said as Ellie nodded in agreement. "Perhaps I will ask Mrs. Gilroy to prepare some of her marvelous shortbread when you return."

"She is a master of the art of baking," Mrs. Johnstone said. She picked up her yellow reinforced umbrella. "Even while ye're here, in this house, do keep the tools I've brought ye close at hand. They're not foolproof. But they will buy ye time."

She toyed with the brolly, running a finger over its ribs lined with bits of stone and crystal and pebbles. "This is perhaps the most effective tool I've given ye. With a proper swing, it's quite possible to disarm an assailant. Aimed at the bridge of the nose or combined with a stout jab to the ribs, I've found it particularly effective."

"It would certainly offer a nasty surprise to someone bent on harm," Belle agreed.

Ellie unfolded the special handkerchief Mrs. Johnstone had given her. The tiny crystals and stones sewn into the fabric lent the cloth a vibrant shine. "This might prove interesting."

"It's quite effective, especially to create a momentary distraction. The pain of the burrs flung against an attacker's face would sting quite a bit, buying some time," Mrs. Johnstone explained. "It's especially useful because it is so small and easy to hide."

"I cannot tell you how much I appreciate your assistance," Belle said, grazing her fingertips over the silky, stone-reinforced cloth.

"It was my pleasure," Mrs. Johnstone said. "If it would not be an imposition, I would enjoy returning for tea, perhaps without the simulations of violence, as well."

"I would certainly enjoy that. Your journeys must've been truly fascinating."

"I will be sure to regale the two of ye with tales of my recent travels," she said with a little laugh. "Along the way, I met the most fascinating man." A soft smile pulled at her mouth. "Of course, no one could ever replace my dear late husband. But a clever man may certainly provide a delicious distraction."

"Oh, you are shocking," Ellie teased. "I love it!"

"After all the years that have passed since I lost my husband, I see no reason to be coy about my treasured friendships. I believe it unhealthy to pretend to be happy when one is not." A smile that looked rather bittersweet curved her mouth. "Since my Franklin died, I've made a point to be deliberate in seeking out my own contentment."

"Bravo," Ellie said. "I knew I liked you."

"Ye're a bit of a free spirit. Rather like me," Mrs. Johnstone said, then turned to Belle. "I don't suppose you've had the opportunity to make Amelia's acquaintance."

"Not yet," Belle replied. "But I am hopeful our paths will soon cross."

"Ye would so enjoy her company," Ellie said. "She has established a wonderful library. Tell me, Belle, have you read Miss Braddon's latest?"

"Not yet, but I am looking forward to getting my hands on a copy."

"In that case, I shall make a point to visit Amelia's lending library and obtain a novel or two for you. I'll be sure to see if her work is available."

"I suspect I will enjoy anything you might select," Belle said with a smile of appreciation.

"Shall I bring a book or two that you might read to little Carrie?"

"Absolutely. I would be in your debt."

"It will be my pleasure. I cannot imagine Jon has anything in his personal library that would be of interest to a child." Ellie shrugged. "Or to anyone who doesn't particularly have a taste for the business reports in the papers."

"I've noticed a few volumes of poetry," Belle said. "As well as a few of the classics."

"I'd imagine the poetry anthologies belong to Macie," Ellie said. "I cannot imagine Jon Mason would spare time to read verse of any sort."

"Ye might well be surprised," Mrs. Johnstone spoke up. "In the years since he first visited my nephew Finn in the Highlands, I've seen there's more to him than ledgers and profits."

Ellie regarded her curiously. "Have you now?"

Mrs. Johnstone nodded without a trace of amusement. "I first met Jonathan when he was still a lad, only twelve or so. He was not so serious-minded then, but over time, he became the son his father expected him to be."

She threw Belle a speaking glance. Moments later, a rhythmic rap upon the wooden door was followed by Jon's cool tones.

"It is not locked. See yerself in," Mrs. Johnstone called in response.

After he strode inside the room, Jon turned first to Mrs. Johnstone, offering his gratitude for her time and efforts. As he spoke, Belle's gaze trailed over the length of him. Rather than his usual wardrobe of fine wool trousers and expertly tailored shirt, he wore garments that resembled a workman's attire: trousers, unadorned cotton shirt, boxy jacket, and a workman's flat-brimmed cap. The unfussy garments presented Jon's essential masculinity without distraction. Indeed, the plain attire appealed to Belle.

She sipped her tea, fervently wishing that her cheeks had not flushed as her gaze traced the broad width of his shoulders. His dark eyes met hers.

"I will be heading out for the evening," he said without elaboration. "I've informed Mrs. Gilroy that I shall take my supper at the pub."

"Have you learned anything new pertaining to this situation?" Belle asked on the off-chance that a messenger had arrived unknown to them.

He shook his head. "Nothing of the sort." He turned again to Mrs. Johnstone. "Something has come up . . . something that requires my attention."

Chapter Nineteen

AT THE REINS of his phaeton in the brisk night air, Jon headed to the one place where he might work off the tension that had seemed to permeate every cell. Even the relaxed atmosphere of the Rogue's Lair would not do the trick tonight. No, he needed strenuous activity to unwind the stress that had seemed to coil within him.

Every corner of his world seemed to bring another source of tension into his existence. Planning for the latest acquisition planned by Mason Enterprises had stalled, leaving their most recent expansion with an uncertain timeline. He was losing patience with the snail's pace of the negotiations. But there wasn't a bloody thing he could do about it.

At home, his residence had transformed from a quiet—perhaps too quiet, in fact—place. For quite some time, his house had meant little more to him than walls and a roof over his head with well-appointed furnishings and possessions that held no sentiment. Now, the near-silent peace was gone, replaced by the sounds of singing and conversation and laughter, the sight of a child's genuinely joyful smile, the caring in Belle's deep blue eyes, and inexplicable powdery white pawprints on bookshelves in his study. For weeks, he'd looked upon the near solitude he'd previously found behind the closed doors of his home with a sense of nostalgia. He had wanted to return to the life he'd known—an existence free of distractions and messes and noise.

But now, the question tore at him. Since he was a very young man—perhaps even before he'd reached manhood—he'd had a clear picture in his mind of what his life should be. Many might've envied the wealth and status afforded to him as his father's heir. But at times, the expectations weighed on him.

In his life, efficiency was of prime importance. After all, only with an effective use of time could he oversee the operations of the company and maintain the business his father had worked so diligently to build. But now, suddenly, the prospect of structure and order and routine held far less appeal. A life that was a mere existence would be suffocating. Such a shell of a life might be bloody intolerable.

Tonight, he had to clear his head. And for that, he needed to use his fists.

Arriving at the Rogue's Athletic Club, a gymnasium he and Finn had installed in a building that came available beside the Rogue's Lair, he wasted no time before entering the ring. He faced off with his first opponent, a burly regular who stood half a head taller than himself. Despite the man's advantage in height and weight, Jon easily prevailed in their sparring contest.

His second opponent proved more of a challenge. But not by much. A brawny, puffed-up noble who'd had precisely enough liquor to think himself invincible, the man thought he'd get the better of him by fighting dirty. After taking one low blow that took the air out of his lungs, Jon set him to rights. Brought to his knees with a right cross, the baron glared at him, angered by the turn of events. He came to his feet and swung wildly, aiming low once more. This time, Jon knocked him on his noble arse. Bloody hell, it felt good to use his muscles and pent-up raw energy.

After several bouts of sparring that greatly helped to clear his head followed by a pint of Murray's best ale, he decided to call it a night. As he headed through the gaslit streets, his mind wandered. The questions he'd debated before he donned his gloves at the gymnasium flooded back over him.

None of the changes that had impacted the day-to-day order

of his household were permanent. The cat and the dog would soon return to their homes. Though he'd actually delayed Heathy's departure despite Logan's return home, it was only a matter of time. Carrie had grown so attached to the ball of fur on legs, it seemed only prudent to continue to have the dog in residence until Amelia's return.

By then, Carrie might well be in his sister's loving and attentive care. Macie and Finn would be kind and doting parents, and they'd embraced the prospect of adopting the girl. It was indeed the most sensible course of action.

Bloody hell, why did the very idea feel like a fist to the belly? Acting as the child's guardian had seemed a daunting task, given the demands he faced as the head of Mason Enterprises and his utter lack of experience with child-rearing. But now, he'd actually started to look forward to the girl's guileless smiles and off-key melodies.

And then, of course, there was Belle's unanticipated arrival. When he'd sailed out of New York harbor, he'd always known there was a chance they would encounter one another once again. A good chance, in truth. After all, they traveled the same circles, even if on the opposite sides of an ocean. But he'd prepared for a fleeting, cool interaction, a perfunctory exchange of pleasantries at best.

He had not been prepared for the sight of her smile, the melodic notes of her voice as she sang with a child, and her beauty even when her face was smudged with flour as she delighted Carrie with her impromptu art lesson. He had never considered what it might be like to have her within reach at night, with only a door between them. He had never thought to wonder what it would be like if he'd never walked away. Until now.

Bloody hell, he'd convinced himself he was over her. That was the way it had to be. He'd believed leaving New York was the only rational decision he could've made. After all, Mason Enterprises wasn't going to run itself. His father was getting on in years. It was his turn to take on the burden his father had long shouldered. His turn to prove himself worthy of the trust his family had placed in him. He hadn't really had a choice.

Or had he?

The question shook him to the bloody core.

In his life, he'd known his fair share of beautiful women. He had never been at a loss for the right words to tempt a woman into bed. No promises. No commitments. No regrets when one of them walked away.

Rogue. Once, a lovely young widow had flashed a particularly enticing smile as the word had dripped from her lips. At the time, she'd expressed her clear taste for a man like him—a man who would neither whisper sweet, meaningless promises nor harbor expectations she had no desire to meet. And above all, she'd wanted a man who would definitely *not* look upon her as a *wife.* She'd spoken the word with disdain, as if the mere thought of marriage was utterly distasteful. At the time, he'd been more than happy to be deemed a rogue. Though at some point in his life he would have to settle down and produce an heir, at that moment, he'd had no need of a wife. Nor could he have envisioned a time when he would look forward to spending his life with any one woman.

Until that night in Manhattan when he'd first laid eyes on Belle.

She is the one, he'd thought, swept up in the haze of passion.

Belle was special. Her heart was tender, far more vulnerable than she liked to let on. She deserved a man who would be there for her, through good times and bad, the true partner she wanted. The partner she needed. Perhaps someday, he might prove himself worthy of her.

But now, he needed to protect her.

IT WAS A rare occurrence indeed when Jon returned home before the witching hour. Generally, he arrived to find his home quiet. Perhaps too quiet. Rather ironic, that, given the genial chaos he tended to face earlier in the day. With Mrs. Gilroy sound asleep, Carrie tucked in snugly beneath her covers, and Heathy content in his bed by the hearth, his only companion on many late nights was Macie's cat. The feline typically regarded both Jon and Heathy's sleepy snores with a look of unvarnished disdain. But tonight was different.

On this night, he was not alone.

So much for clearing his head.

He'd entered the house through the rear entrance, intent on making his way straight to bed while he was still inclined to sleep. But the sound of Belle's quiet voice drew him with a magnetic pull to the sitting room.

The door was open, and he glanced in from the hallway. Holding an open book on her lap, Belle sat in an overstuffed chair with Carrie perched within the space between her body and the upholstered arm. As she glanced up, the relaxed set of Belle's mouth made it clear he had not alarmed her.

Given that she was still dressed in the white blouse and dark blue skirt she'd worn earlier that day, she had not yet begun to retire for the evening. She'd tied her hair loosely at her nape, while the few loose tendrils framing her face emphasized the gentle beauty of her features.

By thunder, she was lovely.

"Might I join you?" he asked, then entered without further conversation, so as not to disturb the moment. He primed the flames in the hearth, retrieved a small pad and pencil from a side table, and settled into the chair nearest the fireplace.

"Hello, Cousin Jon," Carrie said in a drowsy voice. "Did you have a bad dream, too?"

"Not yet," he said. That would come later, after he managed to drift off to sleep.

"A nighttime story is just the thing to chase away a bad dream," Belle said softly. "Isn't it, Carrie?"

Not the ones that come to me. Jon kept the thought to himself as the girl nodded her response to Belle's question.

"What story are you listening to?" he asked.

"Rapunzel," the girl said, her pronunciation of the name impressively precise. "Her hair is very long. And very pretty. Like Belle."

"Indeed," he said. If anything, Belle's honey-gold locks were far superior to anything Rapunzel might've used as a makeshift rope, but he would keep that opinion to himself.

"The prince is handsome," Carrie went on.

"That is a requirement for princes, isn't it?" he asked, sending Belle a wry look.

"Only in fanciful tales," Belle replied with the slightest of smiles.

Turning her attention to the book, she went back to reading the story in a gentle, animated tone.

At her side, Carrie covered her mouth with her small hand and yawned. Belle's calm reading of the fairy tale was working its magic. The child looked as if she could scarcely keep her eyes open.

Drawn to the image of Belle and the little girl sitting so contentedly, he picked up his pad and pencil. He'd intended to make notes of key points he needed to discuss when he attended a property negotiation the next day. But instead, he found himself idly sketching upon the blank page.

As Belle continued to read, his idle sketches turned to more. With each stroke of the pencil against the paper, he captured the image before his eyes. Years had passed since he'd last put pencil to paper for some purpose other than writing and performing calculations. He didn't spare a moment for such a frivolous use of time. After all, it wasn't as if he possessed true skill. But his ability to recreate a scene with strokes of his pencil was ingrained deep within. A natural talent, his mother had dubbed it, a true contrast to his father's assessment of any artistic pursuit as a *waste of bloody time.*

Moment by moment, the sketch took shape. He captured the essence of kindness he saw in her eyes, and the loving trust gleaming in Carrie's wide blue eyes.

As Belle declared that Rapunzel and her handsome prince—after all, what other kind were there in fairy tales—had lived happily ever after, Carrie grinned with happiness, then smothered her yawn with her hand.

"I never doubted it for a minute," the girl declared happily.

"You are a clever girl," Belle said as Jon agreed. "Now, let's get you back in bed before it becomes very, very late."

"I am sleepy now," Carrie agreed. She scooted out of the chair and bustled over to Jon's seat. He casually flipped over the pad, keeping the sketch out of sight. "Were you writing a story?"

"Nothing so clever as that," he replied truthfully. "Now it's high time you were in bed. It won't be long before Heathy is awake and looking for his friend to play."

Her expression scrunched into a little frown, but quick as it had come, the frown disappeared. "Goodnight," she said, standing on her tiptoes to give him a kiss on the cheek.

"Goodnight, little one."

"I'll tuck you in," Belle said as the child reached for her hand. Standing by his chair, Belle squinted a bit, as if puzzled. "You've been hurt."

He rubbed his hand along the line of his jaw, feeling a small cut by his cheek. He hadn't thought anyone would even notice.

"It's nothing."

"Did that happen during Mrs. Johnstone's training session?" Her brow furrowed. "I don't recall seeing it."

He shook his head. "I shall explain in the morning."

"Well, I do hope so," she said, then took Carrie by the hand and led her from the room.

Blast it, he could not recall the last time anyone had looked at him with any semblance of concern. He'd simply tell her the truth. In better light, she'd notice the cuts on his knuckles from sparring. There was no point in leaving her to worry over him.

He leaned back against the chair and closed his eyes. The interest in her expression had been genuine. *How bloody unexpected.* Despite the hurt that had gone between them, she still cared about him, if only for his essential wellbeing. That small truth warmed him more than the flames in the hearth.

Chapter Twenty

TUCKING SOFT QUILTS around Carrie, Belle pressed a quick kiss to the child's forehead, then settled into the chair by her bed and waited for her to fall back to sleep. The child's quiet, contented sighs as she drifted off brought Belle a sense of peace. Not quite a quarter hour earlier, Carrie had awakened from what must have been a horrid nightmare and come looking for her. The girl's muffled whimpers had left Belle a bit shaken, but she'd had no trouble calming the child. The little girl had experienced such loss. So much upheaval. Belle sighed to herself. If only she could find a way to offer the child stability and consistency and, above all, love.

No matter what happened in the future, she hoped she might have a presence in Carrie's life. It wouldn't be long before Jon's sister returned and welcomed the child into her family. With any luck, Macie would be receptive to Belle's visits. But for now, she would focus on the present. She'd fill Carrie's days with as much joy and learning as possible.

Satisfied that the child was sleeping peacefully, Belle returned to the sitting room. To her surprise, she was not alone.

Jon glanced up from the evening edition. "I went to check on Carrie, but I saw you had matters well in hand."

"She's sleeping now," Belle said as she went to the bookshelf.

"Thank you," he said quietly, catching Belle by surprise. "Carrie is very fond of you."

"As I am of her," Belle replied. Surveying the shelves on the towering case, she selected a volume of poems. "I must say, I did not expect to find poetry in your collection," she said. "Much less the works of the romantics."

"And why might that be?" A trace of amusement flickered in his dark eyes. "I am not a heathen."

"Surely there must be some unspoken rule or another against a decidedly practical man like you reading Byron."

He shrugged. "I cannot say that I recite his verse during a night at the pub. But I do possess a familiarity with his works."

"I suppose this might impress a female visitor?"

"Ah, you've deduced my secret." He hiked a brow. "Would that include you, Belle?"

"Most definitely not. After all, I know you far too well."

"You wound my pride. And there I thought you were drawn to my intellectual side."

"I might have been had you not kept it so well hidden."

He flashed a half-smile that once would've charmed her. "Well then, you've stumbled upon it now."

"I'm still not sure it truly exists."

"Is that so?"

Setting his paper aside, Jon joined her at the bookcase. He was dressed in casual attire—dark trousers, an unadorned white linen shirt unbuttoned at the throat, and a silvery gray waistcoat only partially fastened. The subtle spice of soap wafting from his skin betrayed he'd quite recently bathed. His dark hair was combed back from his face, emphasizing the angles of his cheeks and the carved edge of his jaw.

Somewhat irked with herself that she was so very aware of him, she pulled in a low breath. Why, she could even identify the familiar aroma of his preferred soap.

"A single volume of poetry proves nothing," she countered. "For all I know, this book might be one of your sister's possessions."

Jon retrieved a leather-bound book from the shelf and placed it in her hands. *Walden; or, Life in the Woods.* "This is more to my taste."

Her interest was piqued. "I'm quite familiar with Thoreau's works. Of course, my father would've preferred that I focus my attention on ladies' journals and such."

Taking a step back, she steadied herself to express a truth that had played in her thoughts. "There is something . . . something I've wanted to tell you."

A slight touch of humor played on his mouth. "You've decided to confess you've no more knowledge of how to bake a pie than I have training in how to properly curtsy before Her Majesty?"

"Truth be told, the matter of my baking ability is moot—I do not intend to lose our wager. But if I did wish to make a pie, I'll have you know you would savor every last bite."

"We shall see," he said, looking a bit smug.

"Jon, what I'd wanted to say . . . though I now question my better judgment . . . I wanted to tell you that of all the men in London I might've encountered that night, I am glad it was you."

He appeared to ponder her words. "Might I ask if you suffered a blow to the head during Mrs. Johnstone's instruction?"

"I assure you I did not."

His brows knit together. "You've helped yourself to more sherry than you can handle?"

"Not so much as a drop."

"Then perhaps the blows I suffered at Mrs. Johnstone's surprisingly brutal hands have altered *my* perception." Amusement brightened his brown eyes. "It sounded as if you were glad it was *me*—of all people—that you came upon when you were dashing about the city in that abominable gown."

"Your ears did not deceive you. That is precisely what I said."

He scrubbed a hand over his stubble-covered jaw. "By thunder, you do possess the ability to confound me."

"And why might that be?"

When he met her eyes, his expression had been stripped of

amusement. "When I left New York, you made your feelings clear. You thought I was a heartless cad."

"That is not correct," she said, biting back a smile. "An arrogant *arse,* perhaps. But never heartless. And not a cad."

"An arse, is it?" His eyes narrowed ever so slightly. "I might actually prefer *cad.*"

"I believe *arse* is a better fit. Besides, I rather like the sound of the way you Brits phrase it. It doesn't sound like a blasted mule."

"I must say, I like this spark in you." His eyes darkened as he met her gaze. "At first, I'd thought it might've been doused. But you're as feisty as ever."

"Much to your chagrin."

"Precisely the opposite." Again, he seemed to search for the truth in her expression. "I know things did not end well between us."

"That is true." She held her tone steady. It wouldn't do to give in to the emotion lurking so near the surface. "In my life, I've dealt with my fair share of bounders and scoundrels. Men who will sweet-talk a woman with pretty lies, without a shred of honesty. But you . . . you've never lied to me. If anything, you have been exceedingly truthful." She let out a little sigh. "Even when I didn't want you to be."

With a gentle touch, he tucked a rebellious curl behind her ear, searching her face for answers she wasn't ready to give.

"Belle, there's one more thing."

Seeing the intensity in his eyes, her pulse sped up. "What is it, Jon?"

He cupped a hand to her cheek. When he touched her like this, it was so very hard to reconcile this man with the cold-voiced tycoon who'd once walked away. Even now, she could hear the *click* of the door latch behind him as he'd taken his leave.

As one breath followed another, she savored the simple touch of his skin to hers. His gaze held hers.

"I wanted to tell you . . . the dress you're wearing . . . it suits you." He'd spoken the words with a hesitance. Instinct told her he'd thought to say something else entirely but had held back. It was better that way, she supposed.

Pulling in a breath, she affected a cheerful tone, when in truth, she felt a slight, dull ache in the region of her heart. "Thank you," she said. "Ellie was so very helpful."

His brows knit in a line. "I still cannot fully comprehend why Miss Blake now refers to herself as Ellie. Since she was a girl, she'd gone by Nell."

"I believe her new preference has something to do with a man she met while traveling on the continent. She told me the mere thought of her name on his lips made her teeth clench."

Jon offered a brisk nod. "I suppose that would do it."

"I do understand her reasoning."

He nodded again, more thoughtfully this time. "Do you, now?"

"Very much so. Though in my case, it was the memory of *your* name that set my teeth on edge."

His eyes crinkled at the corners. "Well then, we should consider it fortunate that we usually exist with an ocean between us."

An ocean was not far enough to make me forget you.

But she was certainly not about to admit that bitter truth. Even if they *existed*—as Jon had phrased it—on opposite ends of the earth, she would still hear the passion-roughened timbre of his voice in her maddeningly decadent dreams.

She shot him a little frown. "Don't go thinking I ever moped about over you."

"The notion never entered my mind."

My, the man is a poor liar, isn't he? "I suppose that is a relief. I wouldn't want you to think I wasted so much as a day in a melodramatic malaise."

"I have it on good authority that was not the case."

"Do you, now?" She echoed his question. "I am surprised our mutual acquaintances would inform you of my rather tame exploits."

"I can assure you they did not. On those rare occasions when

I did inquire about your wellbeing, their replies were cool. Stilted, in fact. But the New York press has been more forthcoming in their coverage of your charitable ventures."

"Oh, yes, that would be me, the Frost Princess of Good Deeds." She forced a smile. "You follow the American papers?"

"Given our expansion, it is imperative that I keep up with the happenings across the pond. Generally, my assistant provides a summary of relevant news in the New York press. At times, I will thumb through a paper or two. I understand your last gala was a smashing success. Not that I am at all surprised." He spoke with a tone of sincerity. "My sister also supports a variety of charities. Though after her shenanigans with Miss Blake at their last masquerade ball, I'd wager the founders of the charity would prefer that she simply offer a donation. Now, back to Miss Blake's new nickname; you say the change was tied to some gent on the Continent."

"She met the man in Paris. Given her light tone when she referred to him, I cannot say whether he caused any lasting heartache, or if his behavior became so irksome that she would prefer to forget him."

"I'd wager it was the latter," he said. "The change of name does rather fit her temperament. Nell—blast it, Ellie—has always been one to follow her whims of the moment."

"That certainly would not be your preference, but I see no harm in following one's instincts."

"You might be surprised." An emotion she couldn't quite read flashed in his eyes. "There are times when I've done precisely that."

She pursed her lips, regarding his statement with a skepticism she made no attempt to hide. "And to think I'd envisioned your life running with the precise efficiency of the gears on the Swiss watches my brother so admires."

"You, of all people, know there have been times when my actions have been neither precise nor efficient . . . I've pursued a course others would view as impulsive. Perhaps even rash."

"Rash?" She deliberately hiked a brow. "I think not."

"Then perhaps, you should think again." His voice was low and deliciously gruff. "I am certainly capable of *carpe diem*."

"You do realize that *seize the day* does not refer to the most efficient use of your time?"

"Ah, Belle, you wound me. My Latin tutors ensured I knew the meaning."

Again, she hiked a brow. "Making reference to your Latin tutors does not strengthen your case."

"I had not thought you so cruel," he said in a teasing tone. "Surely you have not forgotten the night we'd made our first acquaintance."

The memory of that moonlit gala flashed through her mind. "By midnight, you'd kissed me on the steps of the art museum." An unbidden warmth crept over her cheeks. "I suppose that might've been considered a bit impulsive."

"Only a bit?" An appealingly crooked grin played on his mouth. "If I were to kiss you—right here, right now—many would consider that rash."

"Most definitely."

His gaze held hers, speaking louder than his words. "Would you?"

She gulped a breath. "Perhaps."

Such a kiss would be impulsive. Rash. And utterly delicious.

She nibbled her bottom lip. As his attention drifted to her mouth, a sly smile crossed his features.

"It drives me a bit mad when you do that." His voice was low and husky.

She knew full well what he meant, but she wasn't about to admit it. "Why, Jonathan Mason, I have no idea to what you are referring."

"You expect me to believe that?"

She gave a little shrug. "I see no reason why you should not."

His brows knit skeptically. "You possess little talent for eva-sion."

"Much as it pains me to agree with you, I must on this particular point," she said. "My brother has advised me to never, ever play a game of poker."

"Bluffing is not one of your strengths," he said with a knowing nod.

She folded her arms at the waist. "You're sure of that?"

"Quite so." He spoke the words with vexing confidence.

She studied him for a long moment, taking in the carved lines of his features and the sable shadow emphasizing the contours of his jaw.

If I were to kiss you—right here, right now—many would consider that rash. Would you?

His question was bold. Unexpected. Perhaps even a bit provocative. But had it been nothing more than a bluff? Well, she knew precisely how she might call it.

Belle smiled to herself as a scandalous notion took shape in her mind. It was time she put his words to the test. She pulled in a steadying breath, as if that might shore up her courage. What she was about to do was impetuous. Scandalous. And perhaps, a bit risky.

"Something on your mind, Belle?" He took a step back, watching her with a touch of wariness. So, he knew she was up to something. "I see that look in your eyes."

She had to play this carefully. After all, she could not go too far. She could not risk falling for him. Again.

But somehow, she couldn't quite stop herself.

Taking a step closer—then another—she cut the small distance between them. Standing this near, she savored crisp notes of bergamot and shaving soap.

"Given that we are no longer involved in any semblance of a relationship, I find it somewhat curious that you would speak of kissing me."

His eyes narrowed as he gave a nod. "I believe I referred to the act as potentially rash."

"I would agree with that assessment," she said, affecting a

prim tone. "And impulsive as well." Fixing a sly smile on her mouth, she grazed her fingertips along the strong lines of his chin. "And might I add, utterly ill-advised."

His jaw went taut. His response to her touch seemed a triumph, if only a minor one.

"Indeed." His voice was edged with gravel.

She met his gaze. "While I am here—under your roof, day and night—I presume you will remain a proper gentleman."

"That is the plan." His eyes flashed with an emotion she could not quite read.

"Oh yes, of course . . . the plan." She brushed her fingers over dark bristles of new beard. "Frankly, Jon, I am not sure whether I should be relieved." She lowered her voice, her tone anything but prim. "Or disappointed."

"Perhaps you should tell me, Arabelle." He uttered her name in a deliciously husky rasp. "Tell me what you want."

Despite her best efforts to shield herself with a veneer of ice, the emotion in his dark gaze was all too clear. The flickers of primal hunger set her pulse racing.

He seemed to study her. "Arabelle, what is it that you truly want?"

You.

As she threaded her fingers through his straight, dark hair, her instinctive response sounded an alarm. My, she was playing a risky game—a game she could not win.

She'd taken her little ruse as far as she dared. She could not put her heart on the line. Not again. Taking a step back, she created a slight distance between them. But when she turned away, he reached for her. Gently, he caught her hand against his.

"Belle, is something wrong?"

She gave a brisk shake of her head, but he seemed to see through it. "When you spoke of a kiss, you seemed rather bold. I sensed that you were teasing me."

"Teasing, eh?" His brows quirked, betraying his sense of intrigue. "And if I was?"

"I thought I might call your bluff."

"Did you, now?" His mouth curved at the corners, not quite a smile. "I must admit, you had me going there. You're a far better actress than I'd credited you."

She hadn't been acting. Not really. But she certainly wouldn't tell him *that* truth.

Reaching for her, he drew the pad of his thumb over the curve of her face. Gently, he tipped up her chin. "It occurs to me that you never truly answered my question—would a kiss be rash, Arabelle?"

"Perhaps," she repeated her response, but this time, her heartbeat thudded in her ears and she could not bring herself to look away from his eyes.

"Shall we seek a definitive answer?" His query was far more civilized than the simmering heat in his gaze.

"That might prove a risky venture." Her pulse quickened. "Perhaps even a bit reckless."

"Indeed." He let out a low breath, as though he debated within himself. "But I am ready to take that chance." With a velvet-smooth touch, he traced the tip of one finger over the curve of her mouth. "Are you?"

Belle held his gaze as his question echoed in her thoughts. Could he feel the slight acceleration of her breaths? Had he sensed how intensely she reacted to his touch?

"Yes," she said on a whisper.

"Arabelle, if I kissed you—right here, right now—would you think me utterly mad?"

When he spoke her name like that, as a husky caress, it was all she could do to maintain a shred of coherent thought. All she could do to resist the impulse to fall into his powerful arms even as a voice deep within warned her to walk away. All she could do to hold tight to the strings to her heart.

"I would think you bold. Perhaps overly so," she said. "And most definitely impetuous."

"If I wanted to hold you . . . to touch you—would you think me a cad?"

"A cad?" She mused over the word. "I suppose that would depend . . . if you carry our risky little game a step too far."

His brow furrowed. "You think this is a game?"

"At this point, I don't know what is real." The truth tumbled from her lips before she could hold it back. "And what isn't."

She felt him drag in a breath. "I do understand," he said, his voice low and rough-edged. "The simple truth is this: I don't want to go another moment before I hold you in my arms again."

His words plowed into her with the force of a runaway train. She believed him. Every husky, searingly honest word.

Restrained hunger deepened the brown in his irises to a rich chocolate. His strong arms holding her close, he drew her to his lean, muscular body. "Arabelle, would you welcome my kiss?"

As she drank in the delicious warmth in his eyes, her heart beat with a long-dormant yearning. But still, she would present a rational response to his question. She was a woman. Not a skittish girl. She would meet his inquiry without hesitation. Without shame. If she wished to savor his touch, that was her prerogative, was it not?

Still, she wasn't about to let him know that after all this time, he possessed the power to make her heart soar. "I do believe I'd like that," she said. "It's not as if this would be the first we've shared. Not so very scandalous, really."

A touch of amusement on his lips tempered the look of desire in his eyes. "You haven't forgiven me yet, have you?"

"Not entirely," she said, holding her tone rather cool. "But you already knew that, didn't you?"

"I've had my suspicions," he said in that gravel-edged voice of his. "*Arrogant arse* might've given it away."

"Or perhaps it was when I told you the mention of your name set my teeth on edge?"

"Another clue," he said.

"My, Jon, I never realized your deductive powers rank with those of Sherlock Holmes."

"I make no such claim," he said. The amusement faded from

his expression. "My dear Miss Frost, something rather peculiar has occurred to me."

"And what might that be, Mr. Mason?"

"We are both still here, and I am still holding you. It is the damnedest thing."

"It is, isn't it?" A curious blend of hope and desire and wonder rippled through her.

With exquisite gentleness, he framed her face in his hands. "I want to kiss you, Arabelle."

"Do you, now?" she asked, if only to tease him.

"More than I've wanted anything in a very long time." He spoke the words as a confession, low and gruff and ever-so-tempting. His dark eyes gleamed with sweet challenge.

And then, he kissed her.

Dipping his head, he touched his lips to hers. Lightly, at first. The most gentle of caresses.

His hands curved over her upper arms, drawing her to his body. The heat of him warmed her, just as the heat in his kiss. Moment by moment, he deepened the delicious contact. Seeking. Exploring. Taking and giving with each tender touch of his mouth to hers. Slowly, his hands glided along her body, settling at her waist.

With a low groan in the back of his throat, he eased away, even as he still held her. For the span of several heartbeats, he gazed at her.

His touch exceedingly gentle, he framed her face in his hands. "By thunder, you are so beautiful." His words were spoken in a gravelly rasp, and instinctively, she knew he meant every word.

If she lived to be a very, very old woman, she would always remember the way she felt when he looked at her like that. When he kissed her. When the touch of his unshaven jaw to her face unleashed tingles all over her body.

Ah, yes, it was all coming back to her. The memories of tenderness and yearning and pleasure flooded over her. Yet this new longing was even deeper. The desire ever more profound.

"Oh, Jon," she whispered as she wrapped her arms around him. The powerful muscles on his back flexed beneath her touch, and he grazed his lips over the tender curve of her face.

Again, he kissed her. Hungrier. More filled with need. Pulling her to his body, his arms coiled around her in a possessive hold. The undeniable proof of his passion for her pressed against the softness of her belly. Instinctively, she canted her hips. She craved this contact, so primal and intimate and intense.

Another low, raw groan escaped him, and he eased away.

"My lovely Arabelle. You'll always be the most beautiful woman I've ever seen." His husky voice was like a caress. With a feather-light touch, he pressed another soft kiss to her lips. "It's best if I leave you now."

A heavy reluctance settled over her, but deep within, she knew he was right.

"Goodnight, Jon." Standing on her tiptoes, she kissed him, a sweet, delicious caress.

And then, she turned. With quiet steps, she left him. Even as she reached her bedchamber, she ached to go back. Ached to return to him. But she closed the door behind her and lay upon the bed.

It was too soon. Far too soon to tell the difference between memories and the possibilities of a future. Far too soon to have faith that this was not a rekindled passion that would burn itself out like a shooting star. Far too soon to give her heart to him. Again.

Lying on her back, she stared up at the darkened ceiling. She felt the rhythm of her pulse steady as her breaths slowed. But her heart still longed for him.

They'd been caught up in a moment of desire that had flared beyond what either had anticipated. She knew that much. Had the memories of what had once been drawn them together?

Or was this something more?

As she eased into slumber, a pleasant notion—wishful thinking, perhaps—drifted through her thoughts. *A new beginning.*

Chapter Twenty-One

THE YIPS OF Heathy's agitated barking roused Belle from what had been a thoroughly pleasant slumber. Still foggy with sleep, she left the warmth of the bed and slipped into her dressing gown. Still, the barks continued. It wasn't like Heathy to carry on without a reason. Something was wrong.

Hurrying to investigate, she rushed down the hallway, following the sound to the front window of the sitting room. Mrs. Gilroy stood by the curtains, peering out the window as Heathy finally quieted.

Rubbing her sleepy eyes, Carrie made her way into the room, clutching her rather ragged-looking doll. "What's wrong with Heathy?" she asked, punctuating the question with a little yawn.

"Now that is a good question," Mrs. Gilroy said, her brow furrowed, even as the look in her eyes hinted that she knew more than she was letting on. She turned to Belle. "Whatever it was that had him riled up, it's gone now."

Carrie went to the window and peeked outside into the morning haze. "The sun is rising."

"It is rather early," Belle said. "Would you like me to tuck you back in bed? You could sleep a while longer."

The child shook her head. "I'm not sleepy now," she said, even as she yawned.

"She'll be needing a nap this afternoon," Mrs. Gilroy predicted.

"I might as well," Belle said with a little laugh.

"Carrie, will ye take Heathy to yer playroom for a bit while I finish making breakfast?"

"Of course," Carrie said, sounding rather formal. Smiling proudly at her responsibility, she cheerfully led the pup away. As her footsteps skipped down the hall, Mrs. Gilroy settled onto a chair, a look of concern on her features.

"The dog was not barking at thin air," she said. "At first, I thought Mr. Mason had returned. He left for his office at the crack of dawn. But it wasn't him."

"Perhaps Heathy detected a rabbit or something of that sort in the yard."

"It is possible, I suppose." Mrs. Gilroy's mouth thinned. "Perhaps another dog is running about. I'll check with the neighbors to see if their hound went on an adventure."

"Or it might've been an amorous cat on the prowl," Belle said as Cleo strolled into the room. "That might well leave Heathy in a stir."

"One can hope it was only an animal." Mrs. Gilroy patted Belle on the hand. "In any case, these doors are stout, the bolts are strong, and I've got my rolling pin close at hand in case anyone does get in."

"Of course, we can't forget the parasols Mrs. Johnstone left," Belle said, forcing a smile.

Mrs. Gilroy made a scoffing sound. "I'll take my rolling pin any day over one of those gadgets. But ye might want to keep yer brolly nearby. Just in case." She turned to the window again, taking another searching look. "And Belle, promise me ye will not take the wee lass into the garden. Not until we can be sure it was, indeed, nothing to worry over."

"That would be the wisest course," Belle agreed.

"When ye take my advice, it always is, lass." The old woman broke into a grin that brought a smile to Belle's face. "Ye will not go wrong."

"Miss Blake is here. And she's brought a parcel for ye—quite an expensive one, from the looks of it." Mrs. Gilroy announced as she peered inside Carrie's playroom. Her careworn features creased into a warm smile as her gaze fell upon the girl's efforts to poke a threaded embroidery needle through the plain dress of her rag doll. "Ye're teaching those busy little fingers to be productive. I must say, ye're doing a fine job of it."

"Thank you," Belle said with a sincere smile. "As her doll is 'all better now' since I stitched it after its unfortunate encounter with Heathy, she's decided Anna needs a fancier dress. She's learning to embroider, one little stitch at a time." Pride in the child's perfectly imperfect stitchwork filled her heart. She turned to Carrie. "We shall have to show Miss Blake your handiwork after we take tea."

"And biscuits?" the girl added with a hopeful little grin.

"Of course," Mrs. Gilroy said. "Miss Blake is waiting in the sitting room. I'll bring the tea service there."

"Thank you," Belle said as she took the doll from the child's hands and placed her on a shelf, well out of Heathy's mischievous reach. "We'll leave Anna here, just for a while."

"I'll bring my new doll," Carrie said, taking a porcelain doll from the shelf. "She looks very pretty in her lace gown."

"She does indeed, lass."

"Mrs. Gilroy, you mentioned that Ellie has brought a package," Belle said. "Are you quite certain it's for me?"

Mrs. Gilroy shrugged. "I believe that's what the miss said." A sly smile played on her mouth as she turned to take her leave. "Ye'll find out, soon enough."

Carrie dashed down the corridor toward the sitting room. Belle wasn't sure what motivated the child more—the opportunity to see Ellie or the prospect of tea and biscuits.

"Well, there you are." Ellie smiled as Belle followed the little girl into the sitting room. "I suppose Mrs. Gilroy told you I'd brought you something new from the dressmaker."

"She did not reveal that detail," Belle said. "But really, I don't need anything else."

"When I stopped by the shop, I simply could not resist this." Ellie opened the box and removed a crisp linen blouse with perfect blue pinstripes. "It's perfect for you."

Belle held it up against her. "It is lovely, Ellie. But this does feel a bit indulgent."

"Don't be silly," Ellie laughed. "Of course, I simply had to take this as well." She held up an elegant cape of stormy blue wool trimmed with black velvet. "It will look striking on you. Every bit the governess . . . wouldn't you agree?"

"Most definitely," Belle said. "But still, I don't truly *need* it."

"Of course you do," Ellie replied. "Besides, I thought I might borrow it on some occasion when I feel the urge to appear prim and proper."

Belle ran her fingertips over the soft fabric. "This is on Jon's account?"

"Absolutely." Ellie grinned. "I wouldn't give it another thought. Believe me, the man can afford it."

"She speaks the truth," Mrs. Gilroy said as she returned with the tea cart. To Belle's surprise, Mrs. Johnstone stood by her side.

"I do hope ye don't mind me calling upon ye unexpectedly. I have news, something ye'll want to know." As Mrs. Johnstone crossed the threshold, she seemed to hesitate as her gaze pulled to Carrie, who sat on the rug, happily playing with her dolls.

"Mrs. Johnstone, it's a pleasure to see you," Belle said.

Ellie spoke up. "Is everything well?"

Mrs. Johnstone's drawn expression offered an answer to her question. "We will talk over our tea." She turned to Mrs. Gilroy. "I have something we need to discuss. Might I trouble ye to see Carrie to her playroom?"

Mrs. Gilroy nodded, taking her meaning. "I trust ye'll tell me what's happening."

"Of course," Mrs. Johnstone said, then took another sip of oolong. "This is certainly information you need to know."

With another nod of understanding, Mrs. Gilroy smiled down at the girl. "Carrie, let's see if ye can finish that pretty picture ye were drawing. And bring yer dolls, lass." She started for the door with Carrie close behind.

As soon as the child bustled out of the room, Mrs. Johnstone gently set her teacup on the table. "I take it Jon is not home at the moment."

"The man is up with the sun and out until dark most days," Ellie said, pouring tea for each of them. "He is dedicated to his enterprises."

"I suppose that's to be expected," Belle said.

"Perhaps too dedicated," Ellie observed as Mrs. Johnstone flashed a look of agreement. "He's done everything he could to follow in his father's footsteps."

"Indeed," Mrs. Johnstone said. "I've often wondered if he might have been less, how shall I say it, willing to mold himself into his father's image if he'd remained the second son."

"I'm afraid I don't follow. He is the oldest child." Belle said as the words swirled in her thoughts. "Isn't he?"

Ellie slowly shook her head. Her mouth pulled into a somber line. "Jon was not his parents' firstborn child. He and Macie had an older brother." She seemed to pull in a steadying breath. "He didn't tell you?"

"No," Belle said. "I assumed he was the eldest son and his father's heir."

"I suspect it is a painful subject for him," Mrs. Johnstone said. "There was a family tragedy, you see. Jon was quite young at the time, only about seven or so. Finn shared with me that no one in the family speaks of the accident."

"How very sad," Belle managed as emotion welled in her throat. "Will you tell me what happened?"

Mrs. Johnstone nodded. "One day, many years ago, Jonathan and his family were at the family's country home. He and his older brother had been climbing a tree which overlooked a stream. There'd been quite a bit of rain, and the creek was swollen. A limb cracked, and Jon fell into the water. Edward didn't hesitate to go after him. He managed to save Jon, but the poor lad was overcome by the current. He was swept away."

For a moment, Belle felt as though an invisible hand had squeezed her heart. "How awful."

"Macie once told me she has a hazy memory of her eldest brother," Ellie added. "She was quite young at the time, perhaps Carrie's age."

"She mentioned that to me as well," Mrs. Johnstone said. "Macie believes the loss of his oldest son changed her father. He threw himself into his enterprises. And as ye might imagine, he expected Jon to do the same."

"Jon has certainly followed in his father's footsteps," Ellie observed. "Macie suspects he has shouldered a sense of guilt over the accident, even though he was a child and had done nothing to cause it."

"His mum—my, she is a lovely woman—tried her best to comfort him," Mrs. Johnstone added. "Even through her own pain, she did what she could to ease his mind. Maggie once told me Jon had always been a conscientious lad, but after the accident, he felt a need to do whatever it took to meet his father's expectations. He dreaded the thought of letting him down."

Belle's heart sank. Jon had endured such horrible sadness at such a young age. He'd been so very young when he'd suffered the painful loss.

Suddenly, the rhythmic thuds of a man's boots along the length of the corridor drifted into the room. Belle felt the sudden stillness as they all heard the sound.

"I asked Jon to meet us here. I presume he has arrived," Mrs. Johnstone said while taking her weighted parasol in hand. She met Belle's gaze. "But one can never be too cautious."

He strode into the room with Heathy at his heels. Both man and dog appeared to hesitate as they spotted Mrs. Johnstone's defensive posture. "Well, I must say, that's not the greeting I'd expected."

"In these times, it is precisely the greeting ye should expect," Mrs. Johnstone said. The quiet steel in her voice unleashed a fresh wave of tension in Belle's chest. What had the woman learned that had prompted her visit?

Jon strolled toward the chairs where they sat. "I believe I've had nightmares like this—an alliance forming, with Ellie Blake as their leader."

Ellie laughed softly. "When Macie returns, I shall see if she would like to assume that role."

"For the time being, I suspect she will have her hands busy with other matters," Jon replied. "She's expecting her babe not long after they return."

Ellie gave a little shrug. "Knowing Macie as I do, I doubt that will stop her."

"Ye may be right," Mrs. Gilroy said with a little shrug as she rejoined them.

"I wouldn't doubt it," Jon said with a shrug. He settled into a chair near the fireplace and stretched out his long legs. "By the way, Miss Blake, I understand you had a fine time shopping."

"Miss Blake, is it?" Ellie chuckled. "Regarding your comment, I did have a grand time, indeed. There was something quite liberating about shopping for someone else. And with someone else's money. What could be more enjoyable?"

Mrs. Johnstone took a sip of her tea. "Now that we've enjoyed an exchange of pleasantries, I suppose I should tell you why I've come today."

Jon's brow furrowed. "What in blazes is going on?"

Her expression somber, Mrs. Johnstone spoke in a low voice. "I've made numerous inquiries about the city, and what I've learned . . . shall we say it is a most troubling development."

Chapter Twenty-Two

"WHAT IN BLAZES have you heard?" Reading the concern in Mrs. Johnstone's eyes, Jon knew that *troubling* had to be an understatement.

"To begin with the most immediate issue, it would appear that Belle's aunt has not stopped her scheming." Mrs. Johnstone poured herself another cup of tea and plopped in two cubes of sugar as she went on to explain the new intelligence she had gleaned. "The shrew has planted a rumor to explain Belle's sudden absence from society."

Jon considered her words. "And what might that be?"

Belle's face paled. "What sort of lies is she spreading?"

Mrs. Johnstone appeared to hesitate. "She is claiming that ye're no longer staying with her." Again, she hesitated. Her lip curled with a look of utter distaste for what she had to say. "The woman has implied that ye ran off with Kentsworth."

"Good heavens." Her face paled to the hue of freshly washed linen, but Belle remained steady. She met his eyes. "If these tales reach my family, my mother will be beside herself."

"Indeed." Jon thought to reach out to her, to comfort her, but held back. "I will send word to them."

"I believe they are in the midst of a river cruise at the moment. Mama's latest correspondence indicated they would depart for England following their tour of the Nile basin." Belle laced her fingers together, as she tended to do when she was on edge. "The telegrams were delivered to my aunt's residence. She and Gideon will be privy to whatever information my mother might relay."

"Your brother is in New York, is he not?" Jon went on.

She nodded. "Jeremy could not spare the time away from the business."

A situation with which I am well acquainted. Raking a hand through his hair, he did not give voice to the thought.

Jon caught her hand in his, reassuring her. "I will arrange a telegram. With discretion, of course."

"We will find a way," Mrs. Johnstone spoke up. "I also have contacts who will be useful in getting a message to yer family." She rose and went to the window, looking out into the twilight. "Mrs. Gilroy mentioned that Heathy was agitated this morning, but neither of ye could determine the cause."

Belle's mouth thinned to a seam. "Something had definitely stirred him up, but we did not see anyone."

"How frightening," Ellie said.

"I suspect the dog's barking scared them off," Mrs. Johnstone said.

Bloody hell. "You think someone was here."

Her expression taut with concern, she nodded. "I'm fairly certain of it. A quick stroll around the grounds revealed areas where the shrubs have slight damage, as if someone was looking for a way into the house."

"There seemed to be no cause for alarm. It wasn't as if there was an attempt at entry," Belle said. "We suspected a neighbor's dog may have gotten loose."

"That may indeed have been the case. But it is also possible that whatever set the wee beast to sounding the alert was not an animal." She made her way back to the window and motioned them to join her. "Do you see what I see?"

Jon surveyed the landscape surrounding the house. "A cluster of broken branches."

"It's entirely possible that someone was there," Mrs. Johnstone said. "The dog might've sent him running."

"Have you learned anything that suggests he knows she's here?" he asked.

"No," Mrs. Johnstone replied. "But he's still searching."

"He will not give up," Belle said.

"Ye're right," Mrs. Johnstone agreed. "It might be helpful if we understood precisely why yer aunt would spread such a lie. What is her part in their plan?"

"I'm convinced she is the one who put the scheme into play," Belle said. "Now that I know she was lying to me, she has a great deal at risk. My father will see to it that she pays for what she has done."

"Ye were wise to run from them," Mrs. Johnstone said. "There's reason to believe they are quite dangerous."

Belle stared down at the fingers she'd laced together in her lap. "I honestly do not know what they are capable of."

"I don't mean to pry," Mrs. Johnstone went on. "But I am wondering what ye know about Gideon Kentsworth." Her mouth tensed. "About the man's past."

"He told me he'd been married . . . some time ago, when he was quite young. But his wife took ill with a fever." Belle met the older woman's questioning gaze. "She did not survive."

"Her name was Fanny, and like ye, she was an American. But she did not die of fever. Her family suspected she'd been poisoned, but they could not prove it." Mrs. Johnstone seemed to hesitate, as if searching for the right words. "I don't believe she was the only one."

"Not the only one?" Belle said on a gasp.

"There's reason to believe the man has many secrets," Mrs. Johnstone said. "What I've been told may be little more than rumor. But my gut tells me to listen."

"What have you heard?" Belle stared at her as if she'd seen a ghost. "You must tell me."

"At this point in my inquiries, I have not yet verified much of what I've uncovered. But Belle, please, be very careful." Mrs. Johnstone directly met her gaze. "Kentsworth is dangerous. I feel it in my bones."

"Bloody hell. I'm taking you away from London." Jon reached for Belle, clasping her hand in his. "Out of that cur's reach."

"An excellent idea," Mrs. Johnstone agreed. Lines of strain framed her mouth. "In the meantime, I would strongly suggest posting a bodyguard at the premises when ye cannot be at the residence. Someone ye would trust with her life."

BELLE MOVED THROUGH the evening as if Mrs. Johnstone's words had not chilled her to the core. She assisted Mrs. Gilroy in serving the meal she had prepared. She sat down to supper, managing a light conversation, if only for Carrie's sake—after all, it wouldn't do to upset the child with uncharacteristic reticence, now, would it? After the meal, she helped Mrs. Gilroy with the kitchen tasks. Her skill in the kitchen might've been limited, but was certainly capable of washing dishes in the manner Mrs. Gilroy preferred. And when it was time, she ushered Carrie off to bed, tucking her in and reading her nighttime stories until the child nodded off.

She'd been thankful for the pleasant tasks she'd focused on, as they provided an excellent reason to avoid any further discussion of Mrs. Johnstone's revelations. During their time at the supper table, Jon had feigned a casual manner she knew was an act. His face bore lines of tension. Of responsibility. Her presence here had only added to the weight on his shoulders. Perhaps she should never have come here.

But that moment in time could not be undone. And now, she knew Jon was waiting for the time when they might be alone.

And soon, they would be. Ellie and Mrs. Johnstone had departed before sundown. Mrs. Johnstone was intent on meeting with Logan MacLain. She trusted her nephew—and Jon's business partner at the Rogue's Lair—implicitly, and with his connections, he might well be counted on to arrange discreet security for the house. She'd offered Ellie a lift back to her flat in her phaeton, a carriage she called The Spider, and Ellie decided the open-air ride would be more refreshing than a stuffy hansom. That left only Mrs. Gilroy as a distraction from the discussion Jon meant to have. When the housekeeper went to her room, as she customarily did immediately after the kitchen chores were done, Belle had no reason to avoid the conversation she knew they needed to have.

"Shall we go into my study?" He sounded rather formal, nothing like the man who'd kissed her so passionately the night before.

"I suppose we do need to talk. There's no more putting it off, is there?"

"I'd say not." He led her to the richly paneled room, closing the door behind them as Belle settled onto a comfortable chair. He went to the sidebar. "Sherry?" he asked.

"I'd like that."

He half-filled a crystal glass and poured whisky into a tumbler for himself, then joined her on the settee.

"Well, the last week has not gone according to plan for either of us, has it?" The slightest trace of a curve to his lips took the edge off his words.

"Now that, Jon, is quite the understatement."

"Belle, I know you're worried, but I need you to trust me."

"Trust?" She pondered the word. "I suppose it's ironic—given all that's gone between us—but I do trust you. As I told you, of all the men in London I might've run into, I am thankful it was you. But I don't know that this is right."

His brow furrowed. "I don't understand."

"It isn't right that I'm here." She allowed the words to tumble out of her. "I'd feared I was bringing trouble, perhaps even danger, to your doorstep. And now, it seems my concerns were well justified."

"Whatever this situation brings to my door, I will meet it

head-on. And I will handle it."

"But this isn't your problem to solve." She took a sip of her drink, savoring its taste and aroma. "I've made quite a mess of things, haven't I?"

"And if I disagree?" Jon's expression was unreadable as he took a drink. Setting the glass to the side, he met her eyes. "Whatever happens, I will see you through it."

"I can't bear to imagine what my parents will think if word of my aunt's vile rumors reaches their ears. Mama will be beside herself, and Papa . . . well, I don't even want to think about it." She let out a breath. "But if you send them a message, there may be repercussions."

Jon caught her hand in his. Gently. So very gently. "I don't give a damn about repercussions." He drew his thumb over her palm. "At this moment, all that matters is your safety. And your peace of mind."

"But if you inform my family that I am here, that I am with you, there may well be consequences."

His brow furrowed again. "After all that you've been through, you are concerned about a blasted scandal?" His voice was low and a bit raw.

She met his dark brown eyes. "And you are not?"

"I don't care about scandal. Or anything of the sort, for that matter." He regarded her for a long moment, a look of determination on his features. "As I told you that first night, if a complication should arise, it may be rectified with a few well-chosen words . . . with a proper proposal."

"This is not a conversation we should be having." She went very still. Her heart sped up, if only slightly. She would not—could not—see him forced into a marriage of mere necessity. Nor could she settle for such a hollow existence. She let out a low breath. "I should leave this house. I can arrange passage on a steamship home. Surely, he would not dare to follow me to Manhattan."

Jon's jaw hardened. "I won't stand back while you risk your neck."

"What alternative is there?" she said. "He will not give up. And now, Mrs. Johnstone has uncovered even more reason to fear him."

"Belle, I need you to trust me."

"This has nothing to do with trust. And everything to do with necessity." She took another taste of sherry to ease the scalding emotion in her throat. "It may be too late for me, Jon. Too late for my future. But it isn't for you."

"Too late?" He spoke the words in a husky, scoffing tone.

"You can still make a good match—a woman who will suit you well, who will be everything you want in a wife."

"Everything I want, eh?" He scrubbed his hand along the edge of his jaw, over the bristles of new beard. For a long moment, he studied her, his brow furrowed again. "Belle, might I ask if you've gone absolutely batty?"

She sat up straighter, nearly convinced she'd misunderstood. But in her heart, she knew she'd heard him correctly. Each and every word.

She faced him directly, forcing herself to meet his eyes. "I beg your pardon."

"You heard me, Belle. Now answer my question—have you gone batty?"

"I don't understand you at all." She took another drink, more than a sip this time. "But for the record, I will say that I most definitely have *not* gone batty, absolutely or not."

"Very good," he responded with a crisp nod. "Now, to cut to the chase. What in blazes would make you think I'd ever want any other woman?" Reaching out, he traced his fingertips along the curve of her face. "That I could ever want anyone but you?"

Her pulse quickened, and she could feel her cheeks burn with emotion. But she had to keep her head about her. "Well, it *is* said that you are one of the most eligible bachelors in London."

His eyes narrowed, a faint curve to his mouth brightening his expression. "In Cardiff and Edinburgh as well, for that matter. Or so I'm told."

She bit back a smile that surprised her, given the ache in her heart. "I see none of this experience has put a damper on your ego."

"I don't give a bloody damn about any of it." His voice had gone low and gruff, deliciously husky. "The truth of it is, I haven't cared about another woman since I left New York."

"Is that so?" She gulped against a surge of emotion.

"Damned right it is," he said. "Arabelle . . . *all* I want is you."

A delicious heat coursed through her whenever he spoke her name in that delicious low rasp of his. Searching his expressive features, she saw the raw depth of feelings he no longer tried to hide.

"My, I must say, you do know how to surprise me." Her eyes brimmed with tears she struggled not to shed, but she lost the battle. One warm teardrop trickled down her cheek. With exquisite gentleness, he brushed it away with the pad of his thumb. For the span of several heartbeats, he regarded her with what seemed a sense of amazement brightening his dark brown irises.

"Ah, my Arabelle." His arms enfolded her, and he drew her to his lean, muscular body. The subtle spice of soap and bergamot filled her senses. "Bloody hell, I want to kiss you."

"I'd like that too," she whispered.

His mouth curved at the corners, not quite a smile. So tempting. So very seductive. A ribbon of anticipation unfurled within her, all the way to her toes. When he cupped her chin and tilted it up just so—just perfect for him to kiss her oh-so-properly—she met his intense gaze.

"Arabelle Frost, all I'll ever need is you."

Chapter Twenty-Three

FOR FAR TOO many long, empty months, Jon had hungered for this moment. Now, the woman he had craved with every cell in his body was in his arms. And he was holding her. Kissing her. Savoring every moment. Every touch.

How could he have ever thought he'd want to live without her? How could he have been such a bloody fool?

I want to kiss you. He'd murmured the words like a plea, and the sweet honesty of her response drove him wild.

I'd like that too. She wanted him. Just as he wanted her.

How had he gotten so blasted lucky?

Tenderly, he pressed his mouth to hers. Lightly at first. Gently. Testing the waters of her desire.

Deepening the kiss, he drank in the sweetness of her plump mouth. God above, how he'd missed this. And then, as she melted her body into his, a quiet little moan escaped her. Whisper-soft, the sound was one of pleasure and desire and innate hunger. Bloody hell, had he ever heard anything as blasted erotic?

As he kissed her, she reached for him, lightly sweeping her fingertips over his cheek. The simple, nearly chaste touch struck him with the force of a lightning bolt. A primal hunger pulsed through his body. But he held back.

Easing from the kiss, he pressed soft caresses to the curve of her face, to her throat, to the tender spot just below her ear that always brought a little sigh of delight.

Longing he'd ruthlessly suppressed broke free, unleashing a heated need. But he had to tamp down his desire. He knew she wanted him. He sensed her passion would match his own.

But it was too soon.

He could not fully pursue this moment. Their bond was still tenuous. Perhaps even fragile. He would not—could not—take a chance that might well drive her away.

He dragged in air, as if that might clear his head. Instead, he breathed in a subtle blend of rose water and lemon infusing the long strands of her honey blond hair. Jon searched her face, seeking the answer he needed in her eyes.

And so, he kissed her again. Tasting her sweetness. Drinking in the subtle scent of lavender that perfumed her skin. Savoring the tenderness in her caress.

She is bloody perfect. And for this moment in time, she was his.

Gently, he led her to the settee. When the backs of her legs bumped against the upholstery, he slowly eased her down upon the plump cushions. Propping an elbow against the back of the settee, he indulged his desire to simply look at her lovely face, to drink in her beauty. Golden rays of lamplight cast a soft glow over her high cheekbones. With a feather-light touch, he traced the slightly heart-shaped contours of her face.

By thunder, the very sight of her took his breath away.

She gazed up at him, studying his features as though she'd found something she'd been seeking, something she wished to treasure until the end of her days. *How bloody wonderful.*

With Belle, everything was different. Utterly, completely, different. No other woman could compare to her. Never had he felt like this, the gentle thrill in his heart when he looked into her eyes. From their first glance across a crowded ballroom, she'd intrigued him. When Belle's gaze met his, he'd been drawn to her—to her utter lack of guile. He'd seen honesty and a radiant beauty all her own. One look into those gorgeous eyes that gleamed like rare sapphires, and he was hers. No other woman would do.

Only his beautiful Belle.

He leaned over her and cradled her head beneath one arm. Her honey-hued tresses flowed unbound against the upholstered cushions like spun gold. Relaxing in the moment, he traced his finger over the curve of her face. Down the pert slope of her nose. Along the curves of her tempting mouth—a mouth slightly rosy from his attentions.

Perfection.

The woman was sheer perfection. And tonight, he would savor every moment while he held her. Every moment while he kissed her. Every moment while he made her sigh against his mouth with delight and pleasure.

"Oh, Jon." When she murmured his name, Belle's voice was husky and low. Yet smooth as silk. "I love it when you kiss me."

"And when I touch you, darling?" he whispered against her mouth.

"Ah, sweetheart, you drive me wild." She pulled in a breath. "I do love it when you're a bit wicked."

"Only a bit?" he teased.

"Perhaps I do prefer you to be *very* wicked." She pressed a kiss to his mouth, a caress that was quite far from chaste.

Wicked. Ah, the word seemed a delicious challenge. What he wouldn't give to bring her pleasure, to take her to the very edge of reason. And beyond.

The mere thought of it unleashed a powerful hunger within him. He pulled in a breath. Then another. No matter how badly he wanted this—how badly he wanted her—he had to control his instincts.

Raw hunger coursed through his body. His passion for her transcended the physical. But he could not deny that his male body longed for her with a fierce need that went beyond ordinary desire. One night would never be enough.

No, he wanted Belle tonight. And every night.

But was it too bloody soon?

Blast the meddling voice within him that urged restraint, that asked too many blasted questions at a moment like this. But still, he could not ignore the inner warnings that told him he should not move too quickly. He had to think of Belle—of the pace that was right for her.

He couldn't allow his own need to run roughshod over what he knew was right.

Belle was a born romantic. He knew that. He always had. She wore her heart on her sleeve. She couldn't hide it. Didn't try, really. And in this moment, she was vulnerable.

She still had faith in him. And no matter the cost, he would not—could not—betray that trust. God knew he already had. He was damned if he would do anything to hurt her again.

He brushed a kiss over her brow, a feathery caress. He knew what he had to do. Anything else might well lead them down a path from which there would be no return.

Forcing himself to keep his rational thoughts in control, he eased back, putting distance between them. To his surprise, her forehead furrowed. A little worry line formed between her brows as she looked at him with a bit of confusion.

"Is something wrong?" she whispered. "Do you hear someone coming?"

"No," he said truthfully. "But the very fact that we have to consider that tells me we've taken this as far as we should. For tonight, at least."

"I suppose that is a rational consideration." A slight frown played on her full mouth. "But at the moment, I truly do not care for rational considerations." She glided her fingertips over the edge of his jaw, tracing a path along his throat to the vee of skin exposed at his collar.

"Is that so?" He pulled in a low breath, determined to rein in his hunger.

She toyed with the top button, releasing it. A tempting little grin played on her lips as her fingers went to the next fastening, working it free. "I'd much rather think about . . . this." She grazed her fingers over the newly bared skin. "I like the way you feel, Jon. Very, very much."

"Do you, now?" he said, hearing the husky strain in his own voice.

A hint of a smile curved her lovely, plump mouth, and she freed another button. Slipping her fingers beneath the linen of his shirt, she teased him with a butterfly touch. "I want to feel you, Jon." A seductive heat warmed her gaze. "I want to make you wild for me."

"Oh, love, you already do," he said, his voice sounding like a growl to his own ears.

"I want to feel the texture of your hair beneath my fingers," she murmured and pressed her lips softly to his. "Oh, Jon, I want to hear your voice grow rough with passion."

God above, she was intent on driving him to the edge of madness. The words on her lips. Her delicious kiss. The satin of her touch. Each drove him further toward the brink of restraint.

The subtle smile on her face told him the minx knew exactly what she was doing. And she was loving every moment.

He caught her hands in his, stilling them. "You know I want you, Belle. I always have."

Passion surged through him as his lips caressed her sweet mouth, releasing the restraint that had held him back. The sensuous touch left them both breathless, both hungry for more. Any doubt as to the depth of his hunger for her had fallen away.

A delicious smile curved her lips as she stared up at him. Her eyes filled with a dreamy expression that warmed his heart. Despite her temptingly bold words and her subtle touches, pure desire was still rather new to her.

Her voice was a throaty whisper. "I don't want anyone else, Jon. Only you."

Her words plowed into him. Framing her face in his hands, he drank in her loveliness for a long moment. And then, he kissed her again. And again.

But then, he stopped himself. "I need you, Arabelle. More

than you could ever know." He let out a breath. "But you deserve more than stolen moments."

"And if I believe that what I truly need is you? Under any circumstances . . . no matter how scandalous?"

"We will have those moments." He drew his thumb over her bottom lip, slightly puffy from his kiss. "But not now. Not here. You deserve more than a quick tumble in my study."

She veiled her gaze with her lashes, seeming to ponder his words. "I agree," she said, meeting his eyes. "This is not the time. And certainly not the place. I do understand you won't press this moment to what you believe would be your benefit. You possess a sense of honor, Jon. I do love that about you."

"So, finally, we are in agreement," he said, if only to lighten the intensity of the mood.

"Definitely." Her top teeth grazed her bottom lip, driving him ever so slightly mad. "But I still want you. I still want *this*."

He took her hand in his. "And we will have it."

"I will return to my chamber." Once again, her teeth grazed her lower lip. "But if I dare to come to you, as a willing woman who wants a man with all her heart, promise me that you will not hold back."

Her words stirred a fresh rush of desire. *Bloody hell.* He dragged in air, forcing himself to rein in his need. And she sensed it. He could see it in her sapphire eyes.

"If you come to me tonight, or any night, for that matter, I shall endeavor to be wicked. On that, you have my word."

"How delicious," she said. "Perhaps only a bit wicked?"

"A bit? I think not." Slowly, he shook his head. Perhaps, just perhaps, he would shock her away from even considering her bold—and maddeningly seductive—plan. "Ah, my Arabelle—rest assured, I shall be exceedingly wicked."

Chapter Twenty-Four

A S SHE TIPTOED to Jon's bedchamber, Belle felt as if butterflies were fluttering about in her stomach. Not quite an hour had passed since she'd left him in his study—not quite an hour since she'd asked him to make a rather daring promise—and now, her mind raced. Not with doubt. But with anticipation flavored by a slight bit of trepidation.

Once she'd returned to her chamber after making her bold proposition, Belle faced a reality she had lost sight of in the heat of the moment. What precisely did one wear to be seduced? Or, for that matter, to seduce the man her heart desired?

She'd scanned the wardrobe Ellie had selected for her not once, not twice, but three times before coming to the conclusion that she did not possess a single garment that might be considered alluring. That certainly had not been a consideration when Ellie had gone on her shopping spree for Belle's benefit. Tweed walking suits. Sensible dresses suited to teaching a small child and assisting Mrs. Gilroy about the house. A warm flannel nightdress. Belle simply did not possess any garment that a woman might choose for her first night with the man who'd captured her heart.

With a sigh, she'd settled on the only logical alternative. She'd undressed and soaked in a hot tub of lavender-scented water for a time, if only to relax herself, and then, she'd slipped into a white cotton chemise trimmed with a single delicate row of lace. It would simply have to do. Tying her dressing gown around her, she quietly left her room.

She rapped lightly upon the door and stood at the threshold to his bedchamber. Heart pounding. Mouth dry. Pulse beating in her ears.

It isn't too late, a little voice deep within reminded her. She could still change her mind. Jon would understand.

But she didn't want to give in to the nervous flutters deep within her. She didn't want to go back.

She only wanted to be with him.

The door opened quietly, without so much as a squeak of the hinges. Jon stood before her, wearing loose trousers and a robe he hadn't bothered to tie. As the garment shifted, she caught a glimpse of sleek, muscled abdomen.

Her mouth went dry—with longing or nerves, she couldn't quite be sure.

"So, it is you," he said with a sly smile. He toyed with the robe belt that dangled loosely. "Until I was sure, I didn't want to take a chance at shocking Mrs. Gilroy."

She hiked her chin and met his eyes. Despite the confident half-smile on his face, questions blazed in his dark gaze. "Did you doubt I would dare to come here?"

"I wouldn't say that." His shoulders lifted and fell in a shrug, further opening the robe, further displaying his lean, strong upper body. His gaze drifted over her, seeing to focus on the well-tied dressing gown that effectively shielded every inch of her below her chin from his gaze. "You're positive . . . positive you want to be with me?"

"I'm here, aren't I?" She struggled to keep her tone light, as if coming to a man's bedchamber at night when the rest of the house slept soundly in their beds was as ordinary as rising with the sun.

"Yes, you most definitely are." A charming look of amusement flashed in his eyes. "But if you cinch that robe any more tightly, you might not be able to breathe." He took the ends of her dressing gown tie in his hands. "You're entirely sure about this?"

"I am," she replied, even as her heartbeat quickened.

He leaned against the doorframe, looking quite relaxed. "I do see one problem, Belle."

Her brows hiked. Was the man actually stalling? "And what might that be?"

A grin pulled at his full mouth. "Isn't it obvious? You're still not in the room. I suppose I should do something about that."

Without warning, he took her in his arms, lifting her easily in his powerful hold. A thrill coursed through her at the feel of his sleek muscles tensing against her body, at the display of purely masculine power as he carried her over the threshold.

"I've never done that before," he said with a brief grin. "I could get used to this."

"Could you now?" she teased. Truth be told, so could she.

He quietly nudged the door closed behind him with his foot, then carried her across the room. Gently, he placed her atop his bed before returning to the door to fasten the lock. When he turned back to her, a spark lit his eyes.

"Perhaps I shall carry you to my bed each and every night. This might well become a habit."

What a wonderfully romantic thought. Belle nibbled her lip. *At least until we're both old and our bones are quite creaky.*

Oh, she was letting her hopes run wild, wasn't she? Envisioning a life with Jon—a life in which they would grow old and cranky and creaky together—was a pleasant daydream. But she had to be realistic. She had to focus on the present. On the moments they would share. On the sweet memories they would make on this one delicious night.

He shrugged off the robe and carelessly tossed it over the back of a chair. Watching him intently, she pushed herself up on her elbows. The sconce on the wall cast a golden illumination over the chamber, lending a striking contrast of light and shadows to the contours of his body.

Oh, my. It wasn't as if she'd never seen him without his shirt.

It wasn't even as if they'd never kissed or touched or tempted fate before. In New York, they'd shared many heady moments.

But never had she ever seen him look at her quite the way he looked at her at that moment. The intensity in his gaze made her mouth go even drier than the sight of his chiseled form and set her pulse racing. A primal anticipation coursed through her, tempered by a twinge of apprehension.

She gulped a breath, steadying herself. It wouldn't do for her to make him think she was frightened. After all, this was what she wanted. What she craved. What she needed.

But it was so very new. And a bit disconcerting. She knew the elements of what she thought was about to happen between them. Her mother had had *that* talk with her—brief and awkward as it had been—quite some time ago. But she didn't quite know what to do. What was the acceptable sequence of events? It wasn't as though Mama had described the precise manner in which to seduce a man. Or to be seduced by him, for that matter.

Lying there on his bed, she allowed her gaze to drink him in. By Athena's spear, he was a handsome man. A true feast for her eyes. The slightly wanton thought brought a little smile to her lips. And tonight, he would be hers. She would savor each and every delicious moment in his arms. And nature would take its course. Wouldn't it?

She watched him without shyness as he quietly stalked toward the bed. His dark trousers hung low, revealing carved hipbones and a line of dark hair—perhaps even darker than the hair that feathered over the muscles of his broad chest—that trailed beneath the waist of the pants. She couldn't quite explain why, even to herself, but she longed to touch the sleek muscle of his upper body, the strong biceps and powerful, athletic chest and flat, muscled abdomen.

She'd expected he would come to her then. She'd envisioned him joining her on the bed and making love to her.

Instead, he studied her, the slightest of smiles curving his full mouth. "Tell me the truth, Belle—are you nervous?"

She couldn't lie. He would see right through her. "Yes. I suppose I am."

"That's natural, love." His voice was low and edged with gravel. "I've had my own battle with nerves."

She blinked with surprise. He was a rogue. A man of the world. And yet, he was standing before her, telling her that he was not as unwaveringly confident as one might've thought. *How very surprising. And delightful.* "You have?"

"At this very moment, my heart is pounding." He prowled onto the bed, close enough that she could touch him. Very slowly and gently, he took her hand and pressed it to his chest. "Feel that, Belle. Feel the effect you have on me."

The strong throb of his heart radiated through his chest and against her palm. "At this moment, my heart beats for you." He pressed a kiss to the back of her hand. "Ah, my Arabelle. It's every moment of every blasted day."

His hands went to the tie on her dressing gown. He met her eyes, waiting. And when she nodded, he untied the robe. With exquisite gentleness, he peeled away the fabric that had covered her.

As she lay before him, she felt her nipples pebble against the delicate fabric of her chemise. When he spoke, his voice was husky and roughened with emotion. "I want to touch you, darling." He drew his fingers over the curve of her still-closed breast. "I want to kiss you, my sweet Belle."

"Oh, yes," she said on a little moan.

Slowly, he unbuttoned the tiny fasteners at the top of the thin gown. His gaze heated as he exposed her to his eyes. And then, he caressed her with his hands and his lips until she was wild with sensation. Wild with wanting.

"Ah, Belle, I want to see you." He kissed her, unleashing a fresh current of passion. "All of you."

"Yes," she murmured. "I'd like that."

As he eased the chemise over her, she shimmied out of the garment. With a little smile at the sense of freedom, she took the cotton gown in one hand and tossed it aside.

Never had she felt so very free. Lying on his bed, completely bared to his eyes, it felt so natural. So very right.

Heat warmed his gaze. He cupped his fingers beneath her chin and kissed her, a soft, lingering caress that spoke of wanting and adoration. "So, love, are you ready to be wicked?"

"Of course," she murmured. "Not so very wicked, I suppose."

"I won't do anything you do not want me to do."

"I know," she said, looping her arms around his neck and bringing him back to her.

"If you're not ready, you will tell me." He sounded so very serious, it warmed her heart. "Promise me that, love."

"I will," she whispered against his lips.

"You will like this." His voice was smooth as velvet and utterly tempting.

He began to touch her then. His clever hands glided over her body, kindling an instinctive heat. Caressing her breasts. The flat of her middle. Her legs. When she was thoroughly breathless from his sensuous attentions, he flashed a deliciously wicked smile.

As his hands wandered lower, shivers of pleasure rippled over her. The sweep of his fingertips against her skin was so very gentle. So very tender. He mastered her body with the most adoring of touches. When she moaned against his mouth, a gentle little plea for the release she knew he longed to give, he stilled and draped the bedsheet over them.

Nesting his body against hers, he held her for a long moment. She felt the beat of his heart, feeling its strong, steady pulse against the hand she'd splayed over his chest. Goodness, his body was hard. All sleek muscle and bone, he exuded lean, masculine power. Letting out a breath, she ran her fingers through the feathering of crisp hair on his chest, trailing lower over his abdomen. Then lower still, following the path of that single line of hair lower, to the hard ridge of his manhood pressing against his trousers.

He pulled in a low breath, almost a hiss, and rolled onto his side. Pressing a soft kiss to her mouth, he caught her hands in his own. And when he spoke, his voice was a sensuous rasp against her ear.

"Shall we be more wicked, still, my sweet?"

"As wicked as you dare," she whispered against his mouth.

His smile would've melted the hardest of hearts. And then, he kissed her again, a decadent caress. Long and slow and nearly mesmerizing with sheer pleasure.

"You'll like this, darling Arabelle," he murmured the words against her lips. "I promise."

Following the path of his hands, he explored her body with tiny, sweet, decadent kisses that drove her wild. Dancing over her belly. Anointing her breasts. Her inner thighs. Tempting her with tantalizingly gentle nips of his teeth against her skin. Stirring her need to a fever pitch. And then, he ducked his head beneath the sheets. Ah, so very wicked. So very bold. And so very tender.

She heard her own quiet moan of pleasure as his oh-so-clever mouth found that most deliciously sensitive part of her.

The sheer bliss of his caress coursed through her. Soon, she was utterly wild with hunger. Utterly wild for each wicked kiss. Utterly wild for *him*. Suddenly, it felt as if she were on the edge of a precipice. With each gentle touch, he nudged her further. And further. Toward the vortex of the pleasure she craved.

Suddenly, time stilled. She toppled over the edge. Spiraling down in a tide of sensual delight, she heard herself cry out.

And then, it felt as if she'd landed in powerful arms that held her with breathtaking gentleness. If only she could stay in that tender embrace all night. Every night.

Goodness, he'd certainly convinced her that being wicked in his bed was both decadent and delicious, hadn't he?

Basking in a sense of greater contentment than she'd ever felt before, she breathed in the heady scent of bergamot and savored the sleekness of the taut muscles beneath his skin. They reveled in their lovemaking with a passion born not of lust. But of adoration.

Cuddled up to Jon after they were both utterly and completely fulfilled, she drank in the heat of his body. While they'd made love, he'd taken the necessary precautions. But as she nestled her head against his shoulder, she closed her eyes and drifted off to dreams of a happy toddler with dark hair and mischief-filled eyes.

As the night ebbed, Belle lay in his arms until the first rays of morning peeked through the curtain. The rays pulled her from sleep, and she stirred. Reluctantly, she slipped out of his bed and pulled on the chemise and robe. She had to leave. After all, it wouldn't do to scandalize Mrs. Gilroy or confuse Carrie.

"Don't go," he murmured, half asleep.

She sat on the edge of the bed and drew her fingers over the curve of his face. Sable-brown stubble edged the firm edge of his jaw and chin. She couldn't help but smile.

Oh, Jon. You are so deliciously wicked. And you are mine.

Gazing down at him, she felt something shift within. A new awareness dawned on her, bright as the new sunrise.

I love him. She threaded her fingers through his hair, pressed a soft kiss to his temple, and watched as he fell back to sleep.

I truly do. I love him more than anything.

With that truth playing in her thoughts, she forced herself to leave him. With whisper-quiet steps, she made it back to her chamber, slipped beneath the covers, and fell back to sleep, dreaming of the man she would always adore.

Chapter Twenty-Five

IN BELLE'S EYES, the morning after her night in Jon's arms came far too soon. She'd have happily lingered beneath her bedcovers for another hour or so, relishing the very recent memory of his adoring touch. Of his heady kiss. Tenderness. Passion. Pleasure. All blended in each delicious caress.

Arabelle, all I want is you. Even now, while she lay alone in her bed, gazing up at the ceiling, the notes of his husky rasp played in her thoughts.

Out of all the pubs in London, she had run into the Rogue's Lair. And straight into the one man in London who'd captured her heart. Now, she never wanted to leave him. The hours she'd spent with Jon had healed the hurt of the past and soothed the grief over the time they'd lost. This was a new start.

Forcing herself out of the comfort of her bed and the thoughts of Jon that warmed her, Belle dressed and prepared for the day. It wasn't long before Mrs. Gilroy rapped lightly on her door.

"Just so ye know, ye have guests," she announced when Belle asked her to come inside.

"Guests?" Belle tried not to frown. "At this early hour?"

"Mr. MacLain has come to visit." Mrs. Gilroy tapped her cane a bit nervously. "He's brought a man with him. Says he's here to guard the place."

"What do you think of him?"

"He's a fine enough specimen of a man. I certainly will not mind having him around. He's easy on the eyes, he is."

"Why Mrs. Gilroy, you scamp," Belle teased.

"Before my dear George left this earth, I'd have never looked at another man. Well, at least, I would not have admitted to it." A wry smile brightened her features. "But now, my hair may have turned to silver, but my heart is still young."

"How long were you married, Mrs. Gilroy?"

"Nearly thirty years. Until my husband's heart gave out on him. We were in Cardiff, with the Mason family at their country estate. Ah, Mrs. Mason was an angel to me. She made sure I would always have a place with them. The woman has a kind soul, she does." A pensive expression fell over her. "Just like ye, Miss Belle."

The sincerity in the old woman's slightly scratchy voice touched Belle. "Well, thank you, Mrs. Gilroy. I consider that high praise, indeed."

"Ye haven't been around me for very long, lass. But I think ye've seen enough to know I speak the truth." A warmth lit her eyes. "That first night, I'll admit I was not pleased to see ye at the door. I'd thought ye'd be one of those high-brow snobs who think the sun and moon revolves around them. But now I see ye're exactly what the wee lass needed to brighten her days."

"Thank you," Belle said, moved by an unexpected rush of emotion. "She is a precocious little girl, isn't she?"

"That she is," Mrs. Gilroy said with a nod. For a moment, she looked as though another thought had perched on the tip of her tongue, but she did not give voice to it. Glancing about, she seemed to stall before she met Belle's gaze. "I should be getting back to the kitchen. I'll let the men know you'll soon be out to join them."

"I won't be long," Belle said, stifling a little yawn.

Appearing to spot Belle's telltale sleepiness, Mrs. Gilroy's mouth pulled a bit tighter. Was the old woman doing her best not to chuckle? Had she heard Belle tiptoe from Jon's bedchamber to her own not long before dawn?

The housekeeper smiled, the twinkle in her eyes suggesting Belle's suspicion was correct. "For now, I'm hoping our guest has a hearty appetite this morning. I'm looking to get to know him a wee bit better."

"Oh, Mrs. Gilroy, I think Carrie might need a bit more rest this morning. Please leave her to sleep a while longer," Belle said as the housekeeper went to the door. "I'll see that she's dressed and ready for the day after I've spoken with Mr. MacLain and the easy-on-the-eyes guard."

"A fine idea." Mrs. Gilroy gave a brisk nod then headed to the stairs.

Not quite a quarter hour later, Belle joined Jon and his guests in the dining room. At the first sight of Logan MacLain, she understood why the rumor mill had been abuzz with talk of the striking tavern keeper. While his reputed unsavory past remained a topic in London's gossip hives, most of the talk centered on the way a pretty librarian—of all things, as they liked to put it—had tamed the man they'd dubbed an outlaw, devil, and above all else, a rogue.

Tall, broad-shouldered, and dressed in black from his boots to the tie at his throat, he certainly did look the part of an outlaw. Logan MacLain might've passed for a buccaneer of old. With his sable hair and dark brown eyes, he was an undeniably handsome man. Though the twitters about his wild and woolly past might've been quieted if the gossips had witnessed the scene that met Belle's eyes as she entered Jon's study. As Heathy bounced about, yipping delightedly for MacLain's attention, the man scooped up the dog in his muscular arms and bestowed affection-ate pats on the pup's furry head, an image that certainly contrasted with the man's hard-edged reputation.

A man with salt-and-pepper hair combed back from his lean face and a neatly trimmed Van Dyke beard stood by the shelves, thumbing through a book. So, this was Mrs. Gilroy's easy-on-the-eyes gentleman.

As she entered the room, she saw Jon leaning against his desk, his legs stretched out and crossed at the ankles. Wearing black trousers and a plain linen shirt beneath a burgundy waistcoat, he might've been preparing for a day at his office. But this morning, he'd been dealing with a far different matter—protecting her and the others within his household.

As he met her questioning gaze, his lazy smile warmed her, a vivid reminder of what they'd shared the night before. "Good morning," he said, coming to her side. He'd managed a bland tone, but the subtle heat in his gaze was anything but proper.

"Good morning, gentlemen," she said, taking a seat on the loveseat as Jon went about the introductions.

The older man was an acquaintance of Mrs. Johnstone's. A former colleague, in fact, from her days as an operative for an agency that she'd been a bit hush-hush about. A taciturn man, Henry Northcutt possessed the skills of an accomplished bodyguard. And above all, he had earned the trust of Mrs. Johnstone, which evidently was no easy feat.

Listening to the man's tight-lipped description of his previous position, providing security for an industrialist's family in Glasgow, Belle could not help but feel a pang of sympathy for Mrs. Gilroy. If the woman had hoped to strike up a friendship with this man of very few words, Belle suspected she might well be disappointed.

Not that any of that mattered. Not really. For the next several days, Belle would be essentially a prisoner in this house. Even the garden was now off-limits. But there was nothing to be done about it. Given the strong possibility that someone had been snooping about the house, even the high wall around the terrace would not provide proper cover from anyone with an ounce of determination to find her. Even a local lad might be employed to spy on the place.

"Hello." Carrie's softly spoken greeting pulled them from their discussion. The child stood in the doorway, looking rather puzzled at the gathering of men whose faces she'd never seen.

"Who are you?"

Oh, dear. In that moment, Belle rather regretted her decision to delay Carrie's morning routine. The child had taken it upon herself to select her own clothing for the day. And she'd evidently decided to be as fancy as she could be. Decked out in a lace-trimmed velveteen dress, she'd topped it with what looked like fairy wings and a gleaming crystal tiara.

Jon's brow furrowed. "What in blazes—" He broke off the exclamation as Belle went to take the girl's hand and ushered her to the settee, wings and all.

"Well, ye don't see that every day, do ye?" MacLain said with a hearty chuckle.

"I wanted to dress up," Carrie said with a child's honesty, waving the crystal-tipped wand in her hand as if she were casting a magic spell.

"And you did," Belle said gently. "Perhaps the wings are not the best choice for breakfast."

Jon scratched his chin, as if deep in thought. "Personally, I think the wings are a smashing choice."

If he had declared his own intention to add a magic wand to his wardrobe, Belle might have been less shocked. For her part, Carrie grinned with delight. "You like them?"

"Of course I do," he said. "You found these in my sister's old steamer chest, didn't you?"

"In the wardrobe," Carrie nibbled her lip.

A look of pleasant reminiscence fell over his features. "My mother used to host costume parties every autumn. As I recall, Macie wore these wings at one of the balls, quite some time ago."

Again, Carrie chewed her lower lip. "Will she be cross with me?"

"Not at all," Jon said. "I think she'd be very happy. It's been far too long since we've had anyone wearing wings in this house."

"Indeed," Logan MacLain said, chuckling again. "Isn't that the wand yer sister used to teach some uncouth bloke a lesson at

Lady What's-her-name's masquerade?"

"I do believe it is," he said. "That was some time ago."

"Obviously before she'd spoken her vows with Finn," MacLain said. "He would've used his . . ." He glanced toward Carrie. "He would've taught the dolt a more memorable lesson."

"One he would not have forgotten," Jon agreed.

"Gentlemen," Belle spoke up. "Carrie does not need an education on lessons for the uncouth."

Still waving her wand, Carrie scurried over to the chair where Mr. Northcutt was seated. "Who are you?"

The bodyguard stared down at the girl as if his ears had deceived him. But when he spoke, his tone was calm and smooth. "My name is Mr. Northcutt."

"My name is Carolyn Marie Mason," she said, sweeping the wand over him as if she were casting a spell. "My mama called me Carrie."

"Then I shall as well," the man said, sounding every bit the gentleman. He turned to Jon. "I was not aware there was a young child in residence."

Belle spotted the housekeeper approaching just beyond the bowed door. Mrs. Gilroy rapped lightly against the wood. "Mr. Mason, if ye do not mind me interrupting, I'll ask Carrie to assist me with the cat."

"Thank you, Mrs. Gilroy," Jon said with a nod.

"Come with me, wee one." She motioned to the child. "Cleo is being cranky this morning. I could use yer help."

"She does like me." The girl grinned and hurried after Mrs. Gilroy, her legs swishing against the velvet of her dress.

When she was out of earshot, Jon turned to Mr. Northcutt. The expression in his eyes was flinty. "I am Carrie's guardian." His mouth hardened. "I presume Mrs. Johnstone briefed you as to the residents of my household."

"She did." Mr. Northcutt rubbed a hand against his beard. "I did not realize the girl was so young."

"Is that going to be a problem?"

The bodyguard shook his head. "I will need to refine my tactics. The child's presence is not truly significant. I will complete the job I've been sent to do."

TIDYING UP AFTER their midday meal, Belle bustled about the kitchen. With a glance through the window facing the garden, she spotted the new bodyguard squinting against the afternoon sun. Seeming to sense she was watching him, Mr. Northcutt turned toward her, his expression stony and unreadable. Since his arrival that morning, the man had kept a clear distance. He'd come inside briefly to eat the meal Mrs. Gilroy had prepared, taking hasty bites of the hearty sandwich before returning to his patrol. Now, he turned away from her, checked his pocket watch, and began to pace with long strides.

She couldn't quite put her finger on it, but the man seemed on edge. Of course, Mrs. Gilroy's attempts at conversation might've had something to do with that. The housekeeper had spoken to him in her usual, forthright manner, but Mr. Northcutt clearly had no interest in gaining any familiarity with those he'd been hired to protect. Perhaps he did not wish to risk any appearance of impropriety, especially with Jon out of the house. But still, what would be the harm in offering a nod or a chuckle when an old woman attempted to break the ice?

Something about the man didn't quite fit. She wasn't surprised that the bodyguard was somewhat aloof. But why would Mrs. Johnstone have felt this man who seemed downright cold was a good fit for a household which included a curious child, two mischievous pets, and a slightly saucy old woman?

Oh, she was letting her nerves get the better of her. She had faith in Mrs. Johnstone's judgment. What did it matter that the man's personality was as stale as week-old bread?

"So, Mrs. Gilroy, I was wondering . . . do you still think Mr.

Northcutt is—oh, how did you phrase it—easy on the eyes?" Belle asked while she and Carrie washed and dried the dishes.

"As a matter of fact, he is a rather handsome sort." The housekeeper's mouth pursed, rather like she'd tasted a lemon. "Pity the man possesses the disposition of an ornery goat."

Belle bit back a chuckle. "Oh, he's not so bad as that."

"The way he reacted to Carrie did not sit well with me," Mrs. Gilroy said. "And he was none too warm toward Heathy, either." Her lips pursed again. "As my dear old mum always said, if ye want to know the worth of a person, take a good look at how they treat the wee ones and animals. That will always tell the tale."

Belle took a freshly washed cup from the strainer. She'd scarcely had time to wipe it with her drying rag before Heathy suddenly began to bark. Without warning, the dog bolted from the room, the bell on his collar jangling wildly.

"Heathy's not happy," Carrie said, staring after the pup with the innocent eyes of a child. "I'll check on him."

As she rushed to follow the dog's path, Belle reached out to stop her, but she couldn't quite catch the girl as she scurried away.

The sound of Mrs. Gilroy's gasp stopped Belle in her tracks. "God above, you startled me," the old woman murmured, eyes wide with indignation. "Who are ye? Did Mr. Northcutt let you in?"

Turning to the doorway, Belle froze. The cup in her hand crashed to the floor, sending shards of glass scattering around their feet. For the span of several heartbeats, she stood transfixed.

She couldn't move. Couldn't speak. Couldn't gather her wits.

And all the while, the man she'd run from met her eyes with a piercing blue glare.

Gideon.

"Hello, Arabelle." His voice was as icy as a frigid January morn. "I've come to take you home."

Chapter Twenty-Six

THROUGHOUT MOST OF his life, Jon had trusted facts and figures and rational analysis above emotion-driven decisions. Yet, he'd learned not to discount his gut. The last time he'd done so, he'd boarded a ship out of New York harbor and made the most foolish move of his life. Even then, his instincts had warned that no matter the rational justification he managed to cobble together, leaving Belle would be a mistake. Like a dolt, he'd pushed that warning aside. Now, he would leave that one fateful decision in the past as he started his relationship with Belle anew.

He'd scarcely slept the night before. Holding Belle in his arms, he'd drifted off despite his best efforts to stave off sleep. He'd wanted to remain awake, wanted to experience every sweet moment of the night. The feel of her soft skin against his. The taste of her tender kiss. The delicious sound of her quiet moans as they'd reached the heights of passion. The wonder of it all could not be matched. Never in his life had he felt such contentment. Such utter satisfaction.

If everything went to plan, he would ask Belle to become his wife. For the rest of his days, he would cherish her. Adore her.

But first, he had to earn Belle's trust. Had to earn her faith in him. Had to erase any doubts in her mind that their lives should be forever intertwined.

Now, hours after their night together, a tonic for his weary soul, he'd strode into his office intent on retrieving the one thing he would need when he uttered the question he burned to ask. While the sun was high in the sky, eliminating the risk that an intruder might conceal himself in the shadows of his home, and an experienced guard stood watch within the house, the rational part of his mind had insisted Belle would be safe for the brief time of his absence. But an instinctive tension stirred in his gut.

"Bloody hell, ye look like ye need a drink, my friend," Logan MacLain marched into Jon's office with his usual blunt assessment of any situation. "I know what ye're thinking about doing. It takes a stout soul, but I know ye'll figure it out."

"Indeed, I will," Jon said, a bit more confident than he felt. He sat upon a leather chair near his desk and stretched out his legs. "Take a seat, will you, so I don't feel like a lazy dolt."

Logan pulled up a chair, his gaze settling on the small box on Jon's desk. "So, that's it, is it?"

Jon opened the velvet-lined box. For a long moment, he studied the sapphire and diamond band his grandmother had given him on her death bed. This was the ring his grandfather had slipped upon her finger when he'd asked her to become his bride. The ring she'd worn when she'd given birth to his mother. The ring she'd envisioned on the hand of the woman he would marry.

For years, he'd kept it locked away in his safe. It had seemed a precious reminder of a great love. His grandmother, wise woman that she was, had encouraged him to seek a greater reward in life than profits and losses and the like. At the time, he'd listened to her gentle entreaties with respect, but deep within, he'd dismissed her words. Someday, he would marry. He'd known that much. After all, he had to carry on the family name. But he'd doubted love would have much to do with it.

Until now.

Until he'd fallen for Belle.

"It's quite impressive," Logan said, taking a good look at the ring. "A part of yer family legacy."

"That was my grandmother's intention."

"Ye're edgy as a rabbit looking into the eyes of a hound,"

Logan observed with a chuckle. "Having doubts?"

Jon mulled the question for a long moment. "Not about Belle." He ran his fingertip over the ring, envisioning it on her slender finger. "Not about this."

"Then what is it?"

"I cannot put my finger on it, but there's something about Northcutt," he said. "Something about the man doesn't sit well with me."

"He's not a talkative sort. But if the Dragon referred him, ye can be confident he's up to the job."

"I don't doubt that." Jon considered his words. "He answered every question we posed with knowledge born of hard experience. His credentials are impeccable. By all reasonable measures, I should have full confidence in the man."

And yet, something gnawed at him. Something logic couldn't explain away.

I was not aware there was a young child in residence.

Why in blazes had Northcutt seemed taken aback by Carrie's presence? Surely Mrs. Johnstone had briefed him on the specifics of the assignment, including the members of Jon's household.

I will complete the job I've been sent to do.

A sudden chill coursed down his spine. Something was off. Something about Henry Northcutt didn't fit.

The sound of hurried footfalls along the corridor reached his ears. "Stop," his secretary called, her tone clearly agitated. "You cannot simply barge in—"

Mrs. Johnstone strode into his office. "I was hoping to find ye here," she said as Miss Smithson bustled up behind her.

"Mr. Mason, I tried to tell her you were not available," the secretary explained.

"Thank you," he said. "But she is welcome here."

"Very well." Miss Smithson turned on her heel and made her way down the hallway.

"There has been a most unfortunate development," Mrs. Johnstone said. "A true crimp in the plan."

"What are ye saying?" Logan said, rising to greet his aunt.

"As ye know, I met with the security agent yesterday evening. Preparations were in place for him to begin the assignment today," she said. "But there has been an incident."

Jon saw the lines of stress on her face. Heard the strained notes of her voice. What in blazes was going on?

"Last night, sometime after our meeting, Mr. Northcutt suffered an attack in his residence," Mrs. Johnstone went on. "The physicians believe he will recover. But—"

"Bloody hell," Logan swore under his breath.

An invisible fist plowed into his gut. By hellfire, why had he trusted the blighter to watch over Belle?

Jon bolted for the door. He had to get to Belle. He had to protect her.

Desperation coursed through his veins. In that moment, he knew the truth.

Not a bloody thing in the world matters. Only Belle.

IN HER LIFE, Belle had thought she'd known true fear. Once, as a girl exploring the woods behind her family's country home with her brother, she'd come frighteningly close to a bear. She'd stood frozen, pulling in ragged breaths as the large beast roamed past without a care. On another occasion in those very woods, she'd come too near a snake that had scared her silly. Heaven knew she'd run as fast as her legs could carry her that day. And then, there'd been the time she and her cousin walked along a gloomy street, only to encounter a knife-wielding thief who'd cut the strap of her handbag and torn it from her grasp.

In those days, she'd believed she knew what fear was. But nothing she had ever experienced could compare to the quiet terror that surged through her at the sight of Gideon standing in the dining room, watching her like a hawk stalking a field mouse.

The tight-lipped bodyguard who'd betrayed their trust strode toward her. He'd closed the door to the corridor, shutting Heathy out of the room, but the sound of the dog's vigorous barking provided a mild sense of relief. Heathy was alive and well, though Carrie didn't understand that each frantic *yip* was in truth a good sign.

"I want to see Heathy." The child gazed up at the treacherous guard with innocent eyes.

Dear God. The sight of the man who'd deceived them moving toward Carrie cut through the haze that had seemed to fall over her. She rushed to take the girl from his reach, to protect Carrie in her own arms, but he was quick.

Catching the child's hand in his own, he met Belle's desperate gaze with a quirk of his thin mouth. "She is safe." His expression hardened. "For now."

"Do something with that bloody dog, will you," Gideon said as Heathy's barking grew more insistent.

"Don't you dare touch that pup," Belle gritted through her teeth.

"Ye think to stop me?" Northcutt cocked his head. "Bold words, indeed."

"Enough." Gideon uttered the word as an order. Cold. Clear. Leaving no room for dissent. His narrowed eyes raked over her. "He will not hurt anyone. Or anything." His mouth curved into a serpent's smile. "Unless I say so."

Belle pulled in a low breath. It wouldn't do to show the extent of her fear. Gideon watched her with a hawk's gaze. A silent prayer for strength whispered in her thoughts as she squared her shoulders and hiked her chin.

"My, Gideon, am I to understand you would stand by while your hired man uses force against defenseless females?"

"I would prefer this to be a peaceful reunion." His eyes narrowed. "But if persuasion is necessary, I shall do whatever needs to be done."

The curve of his mouth was meant to be taunting. He knew he could use the safety of the others against her. How had she been so blind to the deceit in his eyes? If only she'd seen through the charming veneer Gideon had worn like a mask.

"I would think you might offer a greeting," he went on. "After all, I have looked high and low for you."

Praying she could hide the slight tremor in her voice, she forced a steady tone. Calm. And reserved. "Hello, Gideon." Each syllable tasted bitter on her tongue.

"A refreshingly civilized response." His gaze drifted over her from head to toe. His expression showed his undisguised contempt. "Might I ask what in blazes you are wearing?"

"I believe you are familiar with the term, Gideon." She forced a wan smile. "This is an apron."

"I certainly know *what* that thing is." His upper lip curled into a sneer. "But rather, why on earth *you* would don such a thing?"

Out of the corner of her eye, she spotted Mrs. Gilroy's rolling pin. The cagy woman had curled her fingers around the handle, slipping it out of sight within the folds of her voluminous skirts. Belle endeavored to keep Gideon's attention bearing down on her as long as she could.

She shrugged. "It's rather helpful when washing dishes. And cooking. And cleaning. But of course, you wouldn't know anything about that now, would you?"

He stared at her as if she'd grown a tail. "Am I to believe Jonathan Mason put you to work as a bloody maid?"

"Nothing of the sort," Belle replied. Sliding her hand over the pocket of her skirt, she felt the skeleton key she'd stowed there. In a pinch, it might well serve a purpose. "I rather enjoy it."

"God above," he said with a curl of his lips. "I had not realized this was a rescue."

"A rescue? Really, Gideon, you don't have a clue, do you?"

"Have you gone a bit mad then, Belle?" He met her eyes. "That might actually prove useful. A delirious wife in an asylum—why, I wouldn't even need to have you in my sight."

"I assure you, I am not mad, Gideon. I am not in need of rescue—I'm quite content, if you must know." She steeled her spine. "And I most definitely will *never* be your wife."

His mouth thinned to a slash. "Ah, you wound me, Belle. And there I thought you were eager to get down off the shelf."

"It's actually quite comfortable up here." She slid her hand in the apron pocket, feeling the tiny studs on the handkerchief Mrs. Johnstone had given her. The simple weapon might buy her time.

"You've put me to a great deal of trouble." His gaze hardened. "I expect to collect my due."

"If you think I will marry you, perhaps you are the one who has gone a bit mad. I know the truth." She dragged in a breath. "About you. And my scheming aunt."

"Blast it, you are nearly more trouble than you're worth. Had I known of your defiant nature, I would've pursued a malleable spinster. But Vera . . . bloody hell, I should not have trusted her."

"Go back to her." Belle forced a cool edge to her tone. "She is the one who wants you. Not me."

"Do you think I give a bloody damn?" he scoffed. "The woman is a useful, well-connected fool." His eyes narrowed. "She'll be out of the picture soon enough. My special blend of tea will see to that."

"Dear God." Belle gasped. "You would see her dead?"

His shoulders lifted and fell in an emotionless shrug. "Enough talk. You are coming with me." His gaze bore into her. "Now."

"I will not go with you." She glanced around the kitchen. If she could get to the frying pan on the stove, she might have a true defense.

"Do not try my patience, any more than you already have." He turned to Roderick. "Unless you truly don't give a damn about that sweet-faced little girl."

Belle's heart raced. "You would not sink so low as to harm a child."

"I have no desire to hurt her. Nor you, for that matter." He slanted Northcutt a glance. "That is his job."

Carrie squirmed against the jackal's hold. Until that moment, the child had been very quiet, taking in the scene with a wide, not-quite-comprehending gaze. But sudden understanding gleamed in her eyes.

The girl's look of instinctive fear tore at Belle's heart. She would never forgive Gideon for using the child as a pawn in his ugly scheme.

Wrenching against the man's unyielding grasp, Carrie let out a plaintive wail. But it wasn't a scream.

It was a word.

"Stomp!" Carrie belted out at the top of her lungs.

"*Ooof!*"

As Carrie slammed her hard-soled shoe into his instep, Northcutt grunted in pain.

"Kick!" The child sang out a heartbeat before her foot plowed into his shin.

"Bugger it!" the man bellowed.

Seizing the opportunity, Carrie ripped free. She dashed down the corridor as the blustering man chased after her.

"Do not touch her!" Belle cried out and took off running after the child.

She'd made it as far as the sitting room when Gideon caught her against him, hauling her nearly off her feet.

"Put me down, you bastard!" she screamed, desperate to reach Carrie before the brute could harm her.

"You're making this harder than it needs to be," he grated against her cheek.

Belle jabbed her elbow into his ribs.

Swearing beneath his breath, he staggered back. But his hold was solid as iron.

Another jab of her elbow, solid into his belly. Another muffled groan. But still, the taut restraint of Gideon's hold did not ease.

Concealing the rolling pin against the folds of her skirts, Mrs. Gilroy hurried after Northcutt. Each step as fast as her hobbled knee would allow, she pursued him. "Don't even think about hurting the wee lass."

Moments later, a muffled thump and an angry bellow of pain drifted from the dining room. Had Mrs. Gilroy's stout rolling pin connected with the man's thick skull?

"Bugger off, you little witch." Northcutt ground out the words a moment before another *thud* cut off a bitter epithet.

Belle's pulse thundered in her ears. Dragging in a fortifying breath, she pulled the weighted cloth from her pocket and snapped it as hard as she could over her shoulder, directly at Gideon's face.

"Bloody hell," he muttered against her ear. Taking hold of the cloth, he tore it from her hand and forced her to face him. He clasped her wrists tightly enough to cause pain, but she steeled herself not to give in.

"Belle, you are playing a dangerous game."

"Unhand me, you son of a bitch."

"Language, my dear," he said with a smirk as he dropped his hold. "Uncouth Americans."

"My father will destroy you," she bit off the words between her teeth.

"To the contrary, he will make me a wealthy man."

She gave her head a vigorous shake. "You won't extort a single penny out of him."

Gideon hiked a brow. "You are aware many in London believe the two of us have run away?"

"I'd heard some nonsense to that effect."

"I have proof, Belle." A viper's smile curved his mouth. "Proof that we've eloped."

"Impossible," she scoffed. "You have only Aunt Vera's lies."

He slowly shook his head. "A certificate of marriage locked safely in my personal vault—signed by a most cooperative officiant—says otherwise."

"You are despicable."

He shrugged. "Give me what I want, and no one will be hurt."

"And what is it that you want, Gideon?"

"You." He smirked. "More precisely, the hefty dowry I'm quite certain your father will offer to be rid of you."

"He will not give you a dime." She gritted out the words.

"You're wrong, Belle. After the news of our impetuous marriage spreads, I'm confident he will provide the funds I require," Gideon said in a tone that dripped venom. "At the very least, he will pay me handsomely to secure an annulment."

"I'll tell him the truth. He'll know . . . he will know you're lying."

"That won't matter," Gideon said. "After we've been together for a sufficient time, you will be compromised by any standard. At that point, your doting father will do whatever it takes to ensure your good name is not indelibly tarnished."

"I don't give a fig about my *good name*." She forced herself to meet his cold gaze. "I will not go along with your scheme."

"You still don't understand, do you?" Releasing her wrists, he turned to the door. "I am not giving you a choice."

Suddenly, Mrs. Gilroy cried out, a sound of shock and pain. *Good Lord, what's happened?*

Belle rushed to the doorway. Mrs. Gilroy stood with her back to Belle, glaring up at Mr. Northcutt. He gripped the rolling pin in one hand, regarding the old woman with snake-cold eyes while another man thudded toward them with heavy steps.

Dear God. No. Gideon's towering driver led Carrie into the room, his fingers encircling her small wrist. Belle's heart nearly skipped a beat.

Tossing Mrs. Gilroy a glance, Roderick chuckled under his breath. "The old woman has got a backbone, I'll say that."

"Let the girl go," Belle said, hearing the plea in her voice.

"This child is quite small, isn't she?" An ugly smile curved his mouth. "It would be a blasted shame if this sweet little girl had an accident, wouldn't it?"

"No!" Belle blurted out the word. Desperation filled every cell. She could not bear to see Carrie hurt. But she didn't want to frighten the child any more than she already was. "Don't do anything . . . please."

Gideon came up behind her. "I'd say this is checkmate." His hands curved over her shoulders. "Wouldn't you agree?"

Belle gulped against a burning rush of emotion. He was right. She was out of options. Even if she fought back, there was no way she and Mrs. Gilroy could deter three powerful men.

Gideon had left her no choice.

"Let the child go." Belle forced out the words. "I will go with you."

"Now see how easy that was," Gideon said. "So much ado about nothing."

"Miss Belle, no," Mrs. Gilroy said, her voice raw as Carrie began to cry. "Ye cannot give the rotters what they want."

"There's no choice, is there?" She turned to Gideon. "Tell him to let Carrie go to Mrs. Gilroy."

"Do what she said," Gideon coolly ordered the burly driver.

"Whatever ye say," Roderick said with a nod. Releasing his hold on the child, he nudged her toward the housekeeper. "Go now. She'll take care of ye."

With a cry, Carrie ran to Belle. The look in her tear-filled eyes threatened to break Belle's heart.

"Please," Carrie murmured between sniffled tears. "Please, I want you to stay."

"I'm sorry, dear." Belle choked back tears of her own. "I cannot."

The girl let out a hushed cry. As Belle felt the pressure of Gideon's hold tighten, she met Mrs. Gilroy's anguished eyes.

"Get Carrie," she managed to utter the words. "Hold her . . . please, hold her while I go."

"Ye're sure about this?" Mrs. Gilroy choked out as she took Carrie's small hand in hers and wrapped her arms around the child in a reassuring hug.

"He is right," Belle said as she steeled herself to leave. Summoning her dignity, she hiked her chin in defiance, even as she admitted the truth. "This *is* checkmate."

A sudden commotion erupted from the vicinity of the kitchen—a sound like a muffled curse, and then, the *thud* of something heavy landing on the floor.

Gideon threw Roderick a speaking glance. "Take care of that, would you?"

The man responded with a curt nod, but before he made it out of the room, he stopped in his tracks. Belle's pulse raced as she felt Gideon's muscles tense with what she suspected was fear.

Her knees felt a bit wobbly at the moment when Jon marched into the room. His hard-edged words allowed no room for discussion.

"Take your bloody hands off her."

Chapter Twenty-Seven

As THE LOW-GROWL of Jon's command reverberated through the room, Belle went very still. Her heartbeat pounded in her ears. Dear God, he'd come after her. Had he walked into a brutal trap?

Desperate to see Jon's face—to look into his dark eyes—she wrenched against the vise-tight clamp of Gideon's hands. But the strength of his hold only intensified. As the vicious pressure bit into her upper arms, a low sound of pain escaped her.

"Let her go, you son of a bitch." Jon bit out the words.

Struggling against Gideon's relentless hold, she angled her body to set her gaze on Jon. Her heart raced. He'd discarded his jacket and waistcoat, the linen of his shirt clinging to his lean, strong upper body, displaying the raw power in his sleekly muscled build. Determination blazed in his eyes. He had promised to protect her. And he'd meant every word.

Her gaze darted to Mrs. Gilroy. Shielding the child with her own body, the old woman held Carrie tight. Roderick stood within an arm's length, his cold-eyed expression making it clear he would harm them without so much as a qualm of hesitation.

Belle's pulse hammered in her ears. This seemed her worst fear, come to life.

"Let the woman and child go, you rotter." The unspoken threat was clear in Jon's low rasp.

"It's peculiar, really, how a child provides the ideal leverage,"

Gideon observed, his icy tone infused with contempt. "Everyone becomes so bloody emotional over the mere thought of a sweet little girl suffering an unfortunate accident."

A chill gripped Belle's nape. She'd never imagined the cold cruelty that lay beyond Gideon's eyes.

"If you touch that child, I will end you." A muscle in Jon's jaw clenched and unclenched.

"Will you, now?" Gideon shrugged. "You must forgive my lack of decorum. I had wanted to have a chat. After all, you've kept Belle from me for days."

"Kept me from you?" She could not hold her tongue. "I ran from you."

"An emotional overreaction." He shrugged. "Rather hysterical, really."

"You are a detestable man," she said.

"Again, you wound me, my dear. Not that I give a damn."

"Kentsworth, you are a coward." Cold fury gleamed in Jon's dark eyes. "Using women as a shield."

Gideon's eyes narrowed. "If you cross me, it will not end well for you."

"Take your hands off her. Now." Jon ground out the command. "Leave this house while you still can."

"You think threats will send me running?" Gideon questioned coolly, even as Belle saw the flicker of fear deep within his eyes. "I had not wanted this to descend into violence. But then again, it might be more interesting this way." He turned to Roderick. "Where the devil is Chauncey?"

The big man shrugged. "Hell if I know."

"I assume you're referring to the bastard who claimed to be Northcutt. He's taking a nap—of sorts—in the pantry," Jon said. "When he does come to his senses, he won't be much good to you."

"Bugger it," Gideon muttered under his breath. "The man wasn't good for much."

"That should make your decision easier," Jon said with steely menace. "Call your attack dog away from the women."

"You've charged in here, the knight rushing to the rescue." Gideon scowled. "I'd never taken you for a fool. Until today."

Jon met his cruel gaze. "She is not going anywhere with you."

"You think not?" Gideon gave his driver a nod. A mountain of a man, Roderick towered over them. With the build of a lumberjack and the wits of a worm, he would take little convincing to do whatever his employer demanded. Even if it meant killing a man.

Even if it meant killing Jon.

The mere thought sickened her. She could not stand there helplessly. She had to do something. Anything. She could not let this go on.

She had to stop this.

"Gideon, this is between you. And me," she said, mustering a strong voice. "Let them go."

"He will. I'll make sure of it." Jon grated out the words. "Get the hell out of my house, Kentsworth. Or you will regret it."

"Strong words. But can you back them up?" Gideon glanced toward Roderick, a serpent's smile playing on his mouth. "You may think you can stop me. But first—you've got to get past him."

IT WAS ABOUT bloody time. Jon had started to wonder if Kentsworth would ever tire of spewing his hollow threats. It would be a cold day in hell before the blustering jackal forced Belle to bend to his will.

He threw his housekeeper a glance. Holding Carrie huddled against her, the old woman stood with a look of clear defiance in her eyes.

"Mrs. Gilroy, take her away. Now." His gaze darted to Roderick. "This bastard has better things to do than to frighten a woman and child." He baited the oaf with a deliberate smirk. "Wouldn't you agree?"

"Aye," the man said, an ugly, half-toothless smile on his crude face.

Jon fairly itched to bury his fists in the ox's flabby middle. The key to taking on any opponent did not lie in strength. But in strategy.

A fair fight may bring honor, mate. But ye must know when to be ruthless—that, my friend, brings victory. Years earlier, a grizzled, bare-knuckled brawler had imparted that particular piece of wisdom.

Ruthless. Victory. The old fighter's words playing in his thoughts, he sized up the hulking bastard's weaknesses. He would keep them in brutal focus.

"I'm going to enjoy this, ye bloody fool," Roderick taunted.

Jon faced the ox with a half-smile. "I suspect I will as well."

Roderick canted his head, a look of confusion in his dull eyes. Jon's cocky expression had stirred uncertainty. *Blasted good thing, that.* A fight was as much mental as physical.

Resembling a bull spurred by a red flag, the big man charged forward.

He swung. Jon darted back. Avoided the blow. Another clumsy punch. Another dodge. Roderick was a burly fool, more accustomed to intimidation than combat.

Suddenly, the dolt got lucky. His fist plowed into Jon's upper chest.

"Damn."

As Jon groaned, he heard Belle's soft cry. The distress in her tone was like another blow. *Block it out.* He had to keep his full focus on the man who would grind him into the floor if given a chance.

He darted to the left. Avoided another punch. Roderick swung again. And again. Jon dodged the impacts, but then, the ox's thick fist landed. *Bloody hell.* Jon steeled himself against the pain.

He had a strategy. It would work. But he had to stay the course.

Red-faced and breathing heavily, Roderick grimaced. Sweat peppered his brow. Soon, the buffoon would be worn out. Facing an opponent with well-honed instincts, he was tiring. Fast. Soon, his strength would ebb. His resistance would falter. A few well-placed strikes would be all it took to take him down.

Jon slammed him with a fist to the ribs. Another. And another.

Riled up by the blows Jon had inflicted, Roderick struck at him. Another poorly timed punch. Grunting in frustration, the ox swung again. A powerful blow. This one connected. *By God, the pain.* Sucking in a breath, Jon powered through it.

Time to turn the tables.

Allowing no warning, Jon plowed a fist into the big man's ribs. *Crack.* Roderick groaned in pain. Another powerful jab. And then another. Jon pummeled him. The chest. The ribs. The gut.

Despite his pain-filled grunts, Roderick stayed on his feet. His massive fist found its target. *Bugger it.* The impact nearly ripped the breath from Jon's lungs.

Taking a step back, Jon aimed for the oaf's tender middle. For the solar plexus. He plowed his fist into him. Roderick moaned. There was no disguising his misery.

Time to close the deal.

A right hook to the bastard's jaw. And then, Jon sent an uppercut into the big man's chin.

Roderick collapsed like a puppet unmoored from its strings. Sprawled on the floor, he stared up at the ceiling. Incoherent groans spilled from his bloody mouth.

"Jon!" At the sound of Belle's cry, he whipped around.

Kentsworth no longer held her. Her eyes wide with terror, she stared at the revolver in the cur's right hand. *Blast the cold-blooded bastard.*

"God above, such a tiresome display." Kentsworth leveled the gun directly at Jon. "I have always found mutual combat to be the stuff of brutes. A weapon is far more effective."

Jon felt his jaw clench. Blast it, he knew Kentsworth's kind. He should've known the rotter would be armed. The man was a coward. And now, he was getting desperate.

"Gideon, please, put down the gun," Belle pleaded. The fear in her voice sliced into Jon like a knife.

"If the two of you make the right decision, I'll see no need to use this." Kentsworth made a show of brandishing the weapon. "Come now, Belle. It's time to leave."

Jon met his icy gaze. A muscle ticked in the bastard's jaw. Despite the cool malice in his words, Kentsworth could not hide his fear. That made him all the more dangerous.

"She's not going anywhere with you." Jon stalked toward him. He had to get Belle away from him. And he had to get the weapon.

"You've been a thorn in my bloody side." Kentsworth eyed him with cold malice. "Now, it would appear you have a death wish."

"If you pull that trigger, you will hang," Jon said, deliberately calm. "Not a pleasant death, or so I've been told."

"I'll be long gone." Kentsworth's words held a note of false confidence. "And you will be—"

Jon lunged. "Run, Belle!" he ground out as his hands closed around the gun.

Fighting fiercely for control, Kentsworth tilted the barrel toward Jon's torso. Toward his heart.

Jon blocked the trigger guard. Leveraging his weight, he forced the gun down. Away from his heart. Away from his chest. Battling to wrench the weapon from the cur's hands, he held nothing back.

But Kentsworth fought hard. And he fought dirty, driving his elbow into Jon's sore ribs.

By Hades, the pain! The blows came fast. And with agonizing fury. Dragging in a breath, Jon staggered to stay on his feet.

Suddenly, the cur's strength seemed to surge. Kentsworth

tore the revolver away. He raised the gun. Took aim.

Within Jon's heart and mind, no fear registered. Only raw instinct.

God above, I will not fail her.

Jon reared back. His fist slammed into the bastard's jaw. Rattling his teeth. Knocking the sneer from his mouth. Sending him into oblivion.

The gun clattered from Kentsworth's hand to the floor below.

Bloody hell, it was done. Jon stared down at the unconscious man. *He'd kept her safe.*

Over his shoulder, he heard Kentsworth's hired oaf mutter an epithet. *Bugger it.* Roderick was on his feet, lumbering towards him. Jon dragged in a low breath and braced himself for another round.

Out of the corner of his eye, he saw Belle. What in blazes was she up to? She crept quietly behind the hulking fool. Too blasted close for her own good.

Bloody hell, was that a skillet tucked behind her apron?

Run! The word played in his thoughts like a litany, but he couldn't risk drawing the oaf's attention to her.

"Back for more?" Jon taunted the man in deliberate distraction.

Roderick slipped a folding knife from his trouser pocket. With a flick of his wrist, light gleamed off the honed metal blade. "I'll see ye dead, ye rotter."

"Tough talk." With a quick beckoning motion of his hands, he kept Roderick's attention on him.

The hulking bastard sneered. "I'll gut ye."

Belle took a step back. She raised the iron frying pan in her hands.

And then, she swung the skillet as if it were a cricket bat. Straight at the bloke's thick skull.

Roderick let out a sound of pain, more of a moan than a cry. Utterly dazed, he stared at Belle with dull eyes until his knees buckled.

He collapsed.

"Dear God, Jon," she murmured. "Is he . . . is he alive?"

Jon rushed to her side and crouched at the big man's side. His burly chest rose and fell with even breaths. "I doubt you've done him any lasting harm. He and Kentsworth will both live long enough to see the inside of the prison."

"Well done, lass," Logan's hearty brogue announced his presence. He strode in, revolver in hand, his gaze darting to Roderick. "I was prepared to put this to use." He smiled at Belle. "But damned if ye didn't beat me to it."

"Thank God you're here," Belle said. "Have you seen Carrie and Mrs. Gilroy?"

"They are safe outside the house. Mrs. Johnstone is with them," Logan said. "Thanks be to God the child was spared this sight."

"Indeed." Jon pulled Belle close and kissed her with all the feeling in his heart. "Ah, my sweet Arabelle. Tell me you'll always be mine."

"Always, Jon." She stared up at him, her eyes glimmering with emotion. "Always."

Chapter Twenty-Eight

NOT QUITE FORTY-EIGHT hours after Gideon and his hired thugs had invaded Jon's home, Belle joined Ellie and Mrs. Gilroy on the garden terrace for tea and biscuits. All in all, she and the housekeeper were in remarkably good spirits. The ordeal had seemed a testament to their inner strength. They had met danger head-on. They had survived. And they had triumphed.

While taking tea and enjoying a bit of pleasantly bland conversation, they welcomed Mrs. Johnstone upon her arrival. As she settled in with a cup of piping hot oolong, Belle uttered the question that had been weighing on her mind. "Have you any word on Mr. Northcutt—the true Mr. Northcutt, that is?"

"The physicians are confident he will make a full recovery," Mrs. Johnstone replied, stirring sugar into her tea.

"It's distressing to think the poor man suffered an assault at the hands of Gideon's horrible lackeys." Belle stared down at her hands, gathering her thoughts. "I would never have imagined Gideon was capable of such ruthlessness."

"The man is a viper who possesses a false charm," Ellie said.

"He is a skilled deceiver." Mrs. Johnstone met Belle's gaze. "From what I've unearthed, the man has left a trail of heartache. Thank God ye realized he was a fraud before it was too late."

Belle drew in a calming breath. "Indeed, I regret ever making his acquaintance."

"Ye could not have known the man was a snake in disguise,"

Mrs. Gilroy said. "He put ye through a nightmare. But I must say, if I may be so bold, I do believe something good has come of it."

"And what might that be?" Mrs. Johnstone said lightly.

"Ye know full well what I'm getting at," Mrs. Gilroy replied and took a bite of a scone with jam.

"Of course I do," Mrs. Johnstone replied. "Belle, ye've been good for Jon. I can see it in his eyes."

"Indeed. As a matter of fact, his sister is of the same mind on the subject," Ellie said as Cleo slinked past the small sofa where Belle and Ellie sat. The midnight-black feline eyed the saucers on the table with mischief in her golden eyes.

"Macie?" Belle sat up a bit straighter. "She's back in London?"

Ellie smiled. "She arrived last night. Macie is quite excited at the prospect of meeting the woman who finally took the starch out of her brother's collar."

"How delightful. I've been looking forward to making her acquaintance," Belle said. "Though I certainly do not see that I've taken any starch out of Jonathan Mason. I do know if it is even possible."

Mrs. Gilroy chuckled, a hearty, happy sound. "Ye cannot see it, lass. But we can, and believe me, there's a change in him. And in my opinion, it's for the better."

"I must agree," Mrs. Johnstone said. "I'm quite positive Macie will as well."

"She and Finn are planning to stop by shortly after supper," Ellie went on. "She's excited to see Carrie again. And, of course, she wants to retrieve Cleo. She truly misses that minx of a cat."

"Carrie is taking her afternoon nap, so she'll be refreshed when they arrive," Belle said. "You know she gets a little cranky when she's tired."

"Don't we all?" Ellie said with a light laugh. "I don't believe Macie has seen Carrie since she was a babe in arms."

After Miss Macie and her husband return from their travels, they'll take the child into their home.

Mrs. Gilroy had explained the plan for Carrie's guardianship soon after Belle had arrived. Belle had known all along that she wouldn't have much time to watch over the girl. Yet now, the housekeeper's no-nonsense explanation felt like a fist in her belly.

Taking a sip of tea, she steeled herself against the inevitable sadness. It was for the best, wasn't it? If she remained in London—if she and Jon were indeed on a path toward a future together—she would still be able to spend nurturing time with the child.

But in truth, she didn't really know what the future held. Oh, she knew what was in her heart, and she didn't doubt that Jon cared deeply for her. He'd risked his life to protect her from Gideon's vile scheme. But since Gideon's arrest, she and Jon had scarcely carved out a moment alone. Between interviews with the Metropolitan police detectives, tearful moments of reflection she'd shared with Mrs. Gilroy, quiet hours with Carrie to return a bit of calmness to the child's life after what she'd experienced, and well-meaning visitors who wished to offer their support, she'd had little time with Jon to discuss anything beyond the day's events. No moments alone when they might look ahead to the path they would follow together. Or, perhaps, travel on their own.

She took another sip and plastered on a smile. It wouldn't do to let the twinges of sadness show through. This was supposed to be a time of happiness. She certainly should not dim the pleasant moments.

Mrs. Johnstone met Belle's gaze, seeming to study her. Had the keen-eyed woman read the conflicting emotions playing in her thoughts?

"Belle, I do hope this is not an inopportune time to broach the subject, but Jon has dispatched two of his employees to gather yer things from yer aunt's residence," she said. "Evidently, since the police put Kentsworth behind bars, Lady Willsbury has become quite cooperative."

"I'll be thankful to have my books and journal again. I'd left them all behind." She turned to Ellie. "Since your shopping spree,

I have not missed my wardrobe nearly so much."

"A lady can never have too many dresses," Ellie replied with a cheeky grin. "Or shoes or hats, for that matter."

"I used to believe that, but now, I'm not so very sure." Belle spoke the truth. There were so many things that mattered more to her, precious things no amount of money could buy. But she wasn't about to say that and dim Ellie's smile. So instead, she spoke another truth. "I'm rather concerned that my oak chest will never, ever hold so many garments. The doors might well pop off their hinges."

Ellie grinned again. "Now that, my friend, is an excellent problem to have."

"It certainly is," Belle said. Pity that was not the problem truly weighing on her heart.

"MY GOODNESS, IT'S true, isn't it?" Macie Mason Caldwell flashed a grin. "My big brother has been hiding the fact that he's quite the hero."

"I wouldn't go that far," Jon replied. "You do realize Belle prevented a towering fool from putting a knife in me."

"A fitting heroine for my dear brother." Macie wrapped her arms around him in a hug. "I'm so proud of you."

"Are you now?" he asked, suddenly serious.

"Very much so." Macie beamed. "Now, enough of this admiration society. I wish to take this time to get to know Belle."

As the women entered into a robust conversation, Finn pulled Jon aside. "Miss Frost is a beauty, Jon. Clever, too. So, why doesn't she have yer ring on her finger?"

Jon took a drink of the whisky in his tumbler. "Logan's been talking, has he?"

"He told me ye've got yer grandmother's ring." Finn drummed his fingers over the edge of the table. "When are ye going to inform the lass she'll have to put up with ye for the rest of yer days?"

Jon took another drink as he set his gaze on Belle. She looked especially beautiful tonight. She wore a dress in a rich shade of blue that brought out the sapphire hue of her eyes, while her honey-gold hair, swept back and held in place with mother-of-pearl combs, framed her lovely oval face.

"I'm going to ask her to marry me tomorrow night. I've made a reservation at the most elegant restaurant in town. After dinner, a walk along London Bridge in the moonlight should set the mood. And then, I will propose."

"Impressive," Finn said. "So ye've worked it all out, have ye?"

"You know me well, my friend. Never without a plan."

"I wouldn't say that," he said with a chuckle. "I've heard yer beauty showed up most unexpectedly."

His gaze wandered back to Belle. "That is an understatement."

"Aye, sometimes the best things in life come to us when we have no bloody expectations."

"Indeed." Picturing Belle's drenched dress and hair, Jon smiled to himself. She'd been a true diamond, even sopping wet in a muck-caked gown. "Wiser words have seldom been spoken."

They embarked on a spirited discussion as Finn recounted the months he and Macie had spent on the road, photographing everything from Egyptian monuments to flower stands in the heart of Paris. Finn and Macie had the time of their lives, and now, with their honeymoon behind them and a new babe on the way, they were ready to settle into their new London home.

Delighted to see Macie again, Mrs. Gilroy had joined in the reunion. For all of her grumblings, the old woman was at her happiest in the company of the women who now chatted amiably in his sitting room. Why, she'd even warmed up to Cleo. Over time, Mrs. Gilroy had become much more than a housekeeper to him. She'd come to feel like family.

Carrie had also joined in the cordial gathering. Intrigued by the photographs of Macie's travels, the child was eager to learn how to use a camera. She and Macie had taken to each other with a natural ease, though it was Belle the girl ran to for comfort when she became a bit weary of the excitement.

Soon, Carrie would be living with his sister and her family. The little girl would have a baby to dote on and a loving home. Macie and Finn would be nurturing parents. And he and Belle would certainly have the opportunity to visit as frequently as they wished.

He knew it was for the best. His sister was settled into her life with Finn. She was delighted by the prospect of bringing the little one into her fold.

So why did the thought of Carrie living somewhere—anywhere—other than under his own roof feel like a punch to the gut?

Blast it, he didn't need to think about that now. First things, first. He had to know what was in Belle's heart. Above all, he had to be certain she wanted a life with him. Just as he yearned for a life by her side.

Again, his gaze was drawn to Belle. Her appeal was utterly magnetic. A wide smile lit her features, brightening her blue eyes. She'd laughed softly at something Macie had said, her tone light and without artifice. By thunder, she was lovely.

Suddenly, he wanted her alone. He wanted Belle to himself, if only for a few stolen moments.

Concocting a reasonable excuse, he asked her to join him in the kitchen. As Belle met his eyes, he knew she'd seen through the blatantly false pretense, but she flashed a cheeky little grin that threatened to drive him mad with longing. He had to kiss her.

And that was precisely what he did. The moment he had her alone, he enfolded her in his arms and tasted her sweet mouth. God above, she was temptation come to life.

And, soon, she would be his. For the rest of their lives.

"I just had to see you," he whispered against her lips. "Had to kiss you."

Her arms curved around his back, and she drew his head down, close to her lips. "Your timing is impeccable. I was thinking about a moment like this," she said. "Thinking about you."

"You look so beautiful tonight. How is it possible that you are even lovelier than you were in New York?" He lightly touched his hands to her cheeks and kissed her again. "I wish I could tell you how much you mean to me."

He'd spoken the words clumsily. Blast it, he was a man who could wield the English language skillfully in an argument or negotiation. But with Belle, he felt suddenly as if he were a schoolboy again, clumsy and uncertain.

"The truth of it is," he said, drinking in her beauty. "You take my bloody breath away."

"I might say the same, Mr. Mason," she replied moments before she raised up on her tiptoes and kissed him, a sweet, delicious caress. "I am so glad I'm here." A lovely smile played on her lips. "Here with you."

A sudden noise pulled him from the blissful moment. Heathy was barking. Not the sound he made when he sensed an intruder. But rather, the dog's excited yips announced the arrival of someone with whom he was quite familiar.

"I suspect Mrs. Johnstone has arrived," Belle said with the slightest of smiles. "I knew she could not resist a visit with Macie and Finn."

"When I spoke with her earlier today, she was nearly popping with excitement. She and Macie have grown quite close."

"So she's told me," Belle said. "We should greet her now, shouldn't we?"

Jon considered the question. "I'd rather slip into the pantry and kiss you senseless."

"Quite an appealing prospect." She flashed a cheeky little grin. "But I suppose you must be a proper host."

He shrugged. "If you insist."

She glanced about the kitchen. "Shouldn't we bring out another tray of finger sandwiches or something of the sort? After all, that's what they're expecting."

Jon could not resist pulling her close and kissing her again. "Actually, I'd wager no one here, save for Carrie, believed my reason for calling you in here had a blasted thing to do with food." He grinned. "Besides, one look at your lips, and the truth will be told."

"Oh, you are incorrigible," she said, taking a tray of cookies from the counter. "We should at least pretend, if only for Carrie's sake."

As they returned to the sitting room, they greeted Mrs. Johnstone, who'd already perched on the edge of a chair by Macie's side. Her solemn expression took him aback. When he'd met with her that afternoon, Mrs. Johnstone had been eager to see Macie and Finn after their months' long sojourn. But now, the woman's features were drawn, her mouth set in a tight line. Something was wrong. Bloody hell, had Kentsworth or his hired men escaped?

"As much as it pains me to say this, I am not here on a social call." Mrs. Johnstone met Belle's eyes with a look of concern. "It is a matter of some urgency."

"What in blazes is going on?" he said.

"When we retrieved Belle's personal items from her aunt's home, Lady Willsbury admitted that she had withheld a message from her—an urgent telegram that arrived several days ago." Mrs. Johnstone went on. "I have it with me now."

Belle's complexion went pale. "What has happened?"

"A member of yer family has taken ill."

Belle's face paled. "Mrs. Johnstone, you've got me a bit frightened. Please, tell me what is going on."

"Of course," Mrs. Johnstone said. "This is a difficult message to convey." She removed a folded paper from her bag and presented it to Belle.

As Belle's gaze trailed over the typed words on the creased

paper, she began to tremble. *Bloody hell.*

"Oh, dear," she murmured. "I have to return to New York."

"I am so sorry, my dear," Mrs. Johnstone said kindly. "I understand how much yer grandmother means to ye."

He wrapped his arm around her. Drawing her near. Comforting her. "Belle, tell me what's wrong."

She gazed up at him, her eyes brimming with tears. "My brother sent a message from New York." Belle choked back tears. "He wanted me to know our grandmother has taken ill. Her physicians are hopeful that she will recover, but she faces a difficult road ahead. She needs me now." Belle swiped away a tear and squared her shoulders. "I need to be there with her. To comfort her. To help her find the strength to go on." She met his gaze with a look of anguish. "I must go home."

Chapter Twenty-Nine

A TORRENT OF emotions swept over Belle. This evening with Jon and his family had been a time of happiness, a time of looking to her future—a future she'd wanted with all her heart to spend with Jon. But now, the terse words on a single scrap of paper had upended everything.

At the news, Jon had taken her hands in his, comforting her with his strength. Sensing her distress, Carrie rushed to Belle, wrapped her arms around her, and gave her a sweet hug, while the others offered words of reassurance. Belle could only pray that Grandmama would have faith that Belle would be there as soon as the ship could carry her across the Atlantic.

As they calmly discussed Belle's intention to return home on the first available voyage to New York, a hush fell over the room. The joy that had filled the air not long before had evaporated, replaced with a sense of inevitability. Soon, Belle would be an ocean away. At the moment, it felt as if she was planning to leave them all behind. Forever.

Jon had continued to comfort her in the face of the distressing news, though his demeanor had shifted. A muscle clenched and unclenched in his jaw, even as he held her hand so tenderly. Belle knew that expression. He was bracing himself for a loss. She'd seen that look before—in Manhattan, before he'd left her behind.

This time, it was her turn to leave.

The thought plowed into her like a blow.

Heaven knew she didn't want to leave him. Didn't want to cast aside the tenderness and passion they'd found in each other's arms. But she had no choice. She could not forsake her grandmother. No matter what, she would be there with the darling woman who had always loved her without condition. Surely, he could understand.

For her part, Mrs. Gilroy had grown quiet. Was the old woman genuinely dismayed by the prospect that Belle would leave? Saying little but giving Belle a supportive squeeze of the hand in the face of her sadness, she'd taken Carrie to her room and tucked the girl in for the night. But the child was unsettled. Understanding more than Belle had hoped, Carrie had returned to the sitting room as they discussed Belle's options. Standing in the doorway, clutching her rag doll to her heart, the pout on her little face had nearly shattered Belle's heart. Belle went to the child, taking her back to bed and reading her a story so that she might drift off to sleep.

"You've been so good with her," Macie said warmly as Belle returned. "I can see that she adores you."

"I must say, I feel the same about her," Belle said, gulping a breath against the scalding tears in the back of her throat. "She is a sweet and clever little girl. She will soon be a wonderful new addition to your family."

Finn nodded. "Aye, we'll be happy to have her with us." He slanted Macie a glance. "Our little one will have a sister."

Belle caught a tear before it could make it down her cheek. "And she will be a doting sister, I'm sure."

Throughout the conversation, Jon had gone very quiet, that single telltale muscle betraying the tension coursing through his body.

"I suppose I should take Cleo home," Macie said, readying the cloth traveling bag she'd brought for her cat. "I have missed the little dickens."

"Cleo will be happy she no longer has to tolerate Heathy," Jon said, sounding a bit cold.

Macie frowned at him. "My, Jon, I doubt she bothered to *tolerate* him. She's quite independent, as you know." She slanted Belle a smile. "If anything, the poor dog was likely outsmarted by my clever girl many a time."

"I'd have to agree," Belle said. "At least, from my observation, brief as it was."

"Belle, I will return in the morning," Macie said, offering the warmest of hugs and a kiss on the cheek. "I'll help you prepare for your voyage in any way that I can. And perhaps, I will convince you to come back . . . just as soon as you can."

"I do not believe I will need to be convinced," Belle said.

"I'll be here as well," Mrs. Johnstone said. "I will assist in making the necessary arrangements."

"Thank you," Belle said as Mrs. Johnstone put aside her reserve to also offer a hug.

And then, they were gone. Mrs. Gilroy closed the door behind Mrs. Johnstone as she departed the residence. Turning to Belle, she regarded her with a careworn expression.

"I am off to rest these weary bones," she said. "This has been quite a day."

"Indeed," Belle agreed. "I'll soon be off to bed myself."

"Sleep well," the housekeeper said. "Ye've got a busy day ahead of ye."

With that, Mrs. Gilroy headed to her room.

"She's very fond of you," he observed. "A rare thing, indeed."

Taking Jon by the hand, she led him to the settee. They were alone. Finally.

"We must talk," she said, summoning her courage to face the prospect of a truth that might well rend her heart in two.

"Indeed," he said. "Belle, I understand you have to leave. But first, there's something . . . something I must tell you."

"I think you know how I feel . . . how I feel about you. But I've never said it." Pulling in a deep breath, she caught his hands in hers. "I love you, Jon. Truly, I do."

"And I love you, my beautiful Arabelle." His eyes darkened

with emotion. "More than I've ever loved anyone in my life."

"I was hoping you would say that." A flicker of hope warmed her heart. "Now, I have an idea. I suppose it is rather impetuous. Perhaps a bit unconventional. But then again, so is everything about our relationship."

His brow furrowed. "Belle, what are you saying?"

Steeling herself, she pulled in a low breath. "I don't want to do this alone, Jon. I don't want to leave you." She looked into his eyes, drawing strength from her hope for a future with the man she loved. "Come to New York with me."

"To New York?" He raked a hand through his hair, holding her gaze. Reading his expression, she could envision how his mind was racing. "Now?"

"Yes, Jon. Now." She reached for him, taking his right hand between her palms, feeling the warmth of his skin against hers. "Sail away with me, darling. We can start our life together there. A new beginning, filled with love."

He went very still, not saying a word—not even making a sound for the span of several heartbeats. His jaw hardened again, that expression that told her he was bracing himself for what he had to do. For what he had to say. Again.

"Belle, you know I want to be with you." His gaze was warm as he studied her face. But his words bore a flinty resolve that warned he was about to break her heart. "But you also know I am nearing the end of crucial negotiations. The investors will not wait. If I leave—much less to sail to New York and be away for God knows how long—the bargaining will end. The deal will fold. It will all be over and done."

Negotiations. Investors. Deal.

The words seemed to reverberate in her ears. Somehow, the way he spoke so rationally, so calmly, while she was desperate with worry over someone she loved felt like a slap to the face. When she'd spent hours in his arms—in his bed—he'd whispered words of adoration, words of love. He had risked his life to protect her from Gideon's machinations. Afterwards, he'd held her tenderly and caressed her with sweet kisses. Why, just moments earlier, he'd told her he loved her.

But yet, in his world, none of that mattered at this moment. At least not more than his duty to his family's company. Nothing they'd experienced these last few days outweighed his need to carve out a deal at the negotiating table and meet his responsibility to the enterprise his father had founded.

"Belle, darling, I know this is hard. But we will get through this." He held her hands with a gentle touch. "You must understand. If I leave now, everything I've worked for these last months . . . it will all be lost."

Lost.

Indeed. Belle gulped a breath. She steadied herself against a fresh wave of emotion. *Everything has already been lost.*

"I do understand, Jon." She felt her heart beating in her chest, heard the beat of her pulse in her ears. "Believe me, I do. Better than you might think."

"After this deal is done, I will join you in Manhattan."

He brushed his lips over her cheek, a tender, sweet kiss. It wasn't fair, really, how this man could move her with the simplest caress. But he held that power. At least now, she understood it was all rather fleeting.

"I will be waiting for you," he murmured against her ear.

"Will you?" She blinked back stubborn tears.

"Of course, my sweet Arabelle." He cupped her face in his hands and kissed her again. "Soon, this blasted deal will be settled. It won't be long, darling."

"But won't there be another deal?" She studied him for a moment. "Another negotiation?"

"Of course," he said. "That is the nature of business. You know that as well as I do."

"I suppose I do," she said.

He drew her closer, the heat of his lean body warming her. "I don't like to let you down, my love."

"If I am disappointed, that is not truly your fault, now is it?"

She cocked her chin, meeting his eyes. "I suppose I should have learned my lesson in New York."

His eyes narrowed as he studied her. "What are you saying?"

"You know full well what I mean," she said. "I thought you had changed . . . I thought *we* had changed. But I was wrong. It's all the same."

"Arabelle, I love you. Surely you don't doubt that." His voice was low and husky with emotion.

Ah, how she wanted him. How she adored him. Heaven knew she wanted to spend her life with him. Pity destiny might well have something else in mind.

"I love you, Jon. But I'm not quite sure loving you is enough." Squaring her shoulders, she met his eyes. "Nothing can change the bitter truth: I know where your heart lies. And it isn't with me."

"You know that's not true." He scrubbed his hand over his bristled jaw. "There's no one else."

She choked back tears she refused to shed. Heaven knew she'd cried enough over this man in New York. "I think this is a fine time for me to get some rest. Mrs. Johnstone will be here bright and early in the morning, and I have much to do." She forced herself to meet his eyes. "I am going home."

"Belle, I love you." The rawness in his voice cut through her like a blade.

"I believe that you do love me. But I know what is in my heart." She pinned him with her gaze. "In the morning, I will seek accommodations outside of this house. And then, I will sail to New York. I shall wait for you, for a time at least. But for now, I prefer to be on my own."

"Darling, don't be angry." He followed her to the door, but she turned away from his embrace.

"I am not angry. Far from it," she said, forcing her voice to remain steady, her tone cool. "For now, I need to clear my head. This has all been a bit too much to bear." She reached out to him, tracing her fingertips over the dark stubble on his jaw. "I will wait for you in New York. You have my heart. But it's up to you to claim it."

Again, he raked his long fingers through his hair. "Arabelle, I love you so bloody much."

"I love you, too, Jon. More than you know. But for now . . . I need a bit of distance. Perhaps an ocean's worth." She turned away. "Good night, my love."

Chapter Thirty

THREE DAYS HAD passed since Mrs. Johnstone had arrived at his home, intent on assisting Belle with the logistics of her return to New York. In that time, Jon had gone about his duties as if each hour that passed by was no different than any other in his life. And not one moment closer to the time when Belle would board a train to Southampton, and then, the steamer for the transatlantic crossing which would take her home.

The very thought of Belle being an ocean away robbed him of his ability to concentrate. Stripped away his ability to focus on something—anything—besides what he might well be losing. Even sleep provided no respite, not with the agitated dreams which tore him from his rest.

He had no real cause to feel as he did. Or so the logical voice in his thoughts tried to convince his heart. It wasn't as if Belle was leaving him forever. She would wait for him in America. Those words had come from her own lips. This was not a parting intended to last for the rest of their days.

This time, he would come to her. But despite his rational reasoning, his gut instinct argued that he was wrong. A frost had formed between them. He saw it clearly when he looked into Belle's eyes. When he did join her, would the spark still flare between them? Or would the ice have become impenetrable?

I should have learned my lesson in New York.

Her words had struck him harder than the blows the ox-of-a-man Roderick had hammered into him. *Bloody hell.* He'd let her down. And he'd hurt her. Again.

But still, he went about his routine. At his office, he conducted business as usual. But when he returned home at the end of each day, the truth slugged him like a dirty punch to the gut.

Belle had accepted Ellie's offer to reside in her flat until she was set to leave for the dock at Southampton. There, she spent her days preparing for the voyage and devoting precious hours to visiting with Carrie at his sister's home. They'd all agreed it would be best for the girl to come to know her soon-to-be adoptive parents and grow comfortable with the house which would be her new home. After all, that had been the plan.

This had been what he'd wanted all along. Wasn't it?

Now, the place was so blasted quiet. The genial chaos that had greeted him for weeks had suddenly disappeared. Even Heathy had returned home with Logan after the Scot came to the realization that he actually missed the *ball of fur on legs*, as he'd put it.

And just like that, his home was peaceful again. And orderly. *So bloody orderly.* Even though the place was as it had been before Carrie and Belle had walked through its door, the house now seemed like a well-appointed tomb. It was all so very different now. In forty-eight hours, everything had reverted back to normal.

And he bloody well hated it.

At times, moving through the day, and especially at night, he felt as if he were in a fog. But he couldn't show it. Didn't dare admit to it. He was only doing what he had to do. Any man with a company to run and responsibilities would do the same. Wouldn't he?

It wasn't as if he hadn't seen Belle. They'd even had dinner, a rather civilized and proper gathering at the Rogue's Café with Macie and Finn on the very night he'd planned to ask her to marry him. He'd envisioned his grandmother's ring on her finger. But this didn't seem the time. God knew he didn't want to make the process of leaving to return to her own grandmother any harder than it already was.

Something had shifted between them. A veil of tension had drifted between them.

And he didn't know if he could ever repair the damage he'd done.

And now, sitting in his office, he leaned back in his chair. Catching his reflection in the plate-glass window, he looked every bit the part of the proper, successful man of industry.

Man of industry. Since he'd been a lad diligently applying himself to the dry curriculum deemed necessary for his success in the world, his father had applied the term to him. For so many years, he'd promoted the image of the man he expected his son to be.

Jon, you are my heir. Someday, this will all be yours.

His father's voice played in his thoughts. He'd wanted the best for him. In his heart, Jon knew that truth. But had his reluctance to question the path set before him when he was still a boy been a mistake?

"Well, Jon, why am I not surprised to find you here?" His sister's sharply enunciated question startled him so, he nearly tumbled backwards out of his seat.

He turned to her, affecting a bored expression. "Might I ask who let you in?"

"Will you be upset with them?"

"That goes without saying," he said.

"In that case, I shall not betray their trust."

"I've no doubt it was Bennett. You've always been able to twist the man around your little finger."

She flashed an impish grin. "I must admit, it *is* a talent. But that isn't why I'm here."

"An excellent point. So, why have you ventured away from your doting husband to pay me this unexpected visit?"

"I'll have you know Finn is in the building. He stopped to chat with Mr. Bennett. Besides, I wanted a moment alone with you." Macie took a step back, folded her arms at the waist, and sent him a glare. "I wanted to say—and I will keep it brief—that of all the blockheaded things you've ever done, this mess you've made of things with Belle takes the cake."

"Blockheaded, eh?" Jon came to his feet. "I've always said the money Father paid for your fine education might've been better spent at the racetrack. Marital bliss has not tempered your colorful way with language."

"I would tell you what you might do with your observation, Jon. But I *am* a lady." A thin smile played on her mouth. "Besides, I would not take the chance that my babe might overhear something shocking before she's even born."

"She?" Jon cocked a brow. "Wishful thinking?"

"Intuition," she countered. "But don't attempt to change the subject. I am here on a mission of mercy."

"A *what?*"

Her smile widened. "Precisely what I said—a mission of mercy."

"What in blazes are you saying?"

"You already know why I'm here, Jon. You're my brother, and I will not bite my tongue while you make the most colossal blunder of your life."

"Would you like to sit?" Jon motioned to a chair. "Or do you prefer to stand while you lecture me?"

"I will stand, thank you." Macie clipped the words between her teeth, as she did when she was fit to be tied. "This is not a lecture. But you need to hear the truth."

"She's right," Finn said as he marched into the room and closed the door behind him. "If ye have a brain in that thick skull of yers, ye'll listen."

"So far, she's informed me that I'm a blundering blockhead. What's next?"

"I suppose dolt will do, but I'd envisioned an even more colorful term." A hint of a grin tugged at her mouth. But then, the smile faded, replaced by a look of concern in her eyes. Blast it, he hated it when his sister looked at him like that, with that look of what seemed almost like pity.

"What is it, then, Macie?" He leaned against his desk, stretching out his legs as he folded his arms over his chest. "Belle and I have discussed this matter, I'll have you know. She has agreed to wait for me in New York. I shall meet her there, after this deal is done."

Macie slowly shook her head. "It all sounds so very civilized, Jon. The way you tell it, it's as if the two of you sat down and negotiated yet another deal."

"What would you have me do?" He searched his sister's face. "Shall I abandon my responsibilities in favor of . . ."

"Your own happiness," Macie supplied.

He shrugged. "In a manner of speaking."

"So, am I to understand you feel you must make sacrifices for the sake of the company?"

"Of course," he said. "Goes without saying."

Her eyes narrowed. "Has it occurred to you that you are making a mistake our father did not?"

"He worked tirelessly to build this company to what it is today."

"True," Macie said, her tone a bit hushed now. "But there is one crucial difference. Papa had our mother by his side the entire time. He would not have put anything ahead of her. Not even the all-important *family business*."

Jon let out a breath. "Might I point out that our father and mother had wed before he made his first shilling?"

"Quite so," Macie agreed. "As Mama tells it, he stood tall against any obstacle to their love. Even when Grandfather tried to steer her toward a match he considered more suitable, Papa would not give up. And now, they have forged an unbreakable bond. Do you truly think our father would've given up what they have together for anything, much less a blasted contract?"

His sister's softly spoken words plowed into him. He turned to Finn. Surely his friend and partner would understand the decision he'd had to make.

To the contrary, Finn regarded him with a slow shake of his head. "Tell me this, Jon. Ye faced a man who pointed a gun at ye—at yer heart—and ye did not flinch. Ye did not run. Ye thought only to protect Belle. And yet, now . . . now ye're risking the happiness ye've found with her. And all for the sake of a negotiation others could pull off." Finn's expression spoke louder than his words. "Am I understanding this correctly?"

Jon walked over to the window and stared down at the hustle and bustle of the street below. The bleak skies and drenching rain fit his gray mood.

"Ye say the two of ye have come to an understanding," Finn went on. "But Belle needs ye now. More than ye might know."

"She is not one to make a scene," Macie added. "She knows you're torn. I do believe Belle intends to wait for you, at least for a time. But she's hurting. She hasn't spoken much about it . . . about what has happened between the two of you. Still, I can see it in her eyes, Jon. She's trying to put on a brave face, but she is hurting. And she is frightened. Someone she loves quite deeply is very ill, and she's worried to tears she won't make it home in time."

"The lass needs ye now, Jon. Not in two months. Not even in two bloody days." Finn was blunt, as usual. "Even if ye do actually make it to speaking yer vows, do you really want her to carry the memory of this—a time when she wanted ye by her side, and ye were not there? And all for the sake of a blasted deal."

The unvarnished truth of Finn's words shook him, hard as a bare-knuckled blow to the chin. Good God, Macie was right. He'd mucked it all up, hadn't he?

Belle wanted him by her side. She needed the simple comfort of knowing she wasn't alone, that she wouldn't have to face this difficult time on her own. So why in blazes was he standing here in his office when all he really wanted was to hold her in his arms and reassure her that he would always be there for her, no matter what?

He loved her. And by thunder, he would be there with her.

Chapter Thirty-One

*T*HE LASS NEEDS *ye now.*

As Jon prepared to walk away from his home—perhaps for quite some time—Finn's words played in his thoughts. He'd certainly spent many weeks and months away, but this time was different. For once, he was seeking something far more enduring and valuable than any business venture might produce.

This time, he would build a life with the woman he loved.

Bustling about like a mother hen, Mrs. Gilroy dangled his boxing gloves over his traveling case. "Shall I pack these?"

He shook his head. "I cannot imagine I'll have need for them on the ship."

No, he had far more pleasant pursuits in mind.

"I've packed yer black bowler," she went on. "And one of yer flat-brimmed caps."

"Thank you. If I find myself in need of more hats, New York has no shortage of haberdashers." Touched by how the old woman fussed over him, he smiled to himself. "Oh, and there's one more thing, Mrs. Gilroy. You can expect Mr. Bennett to pay a call this evening. He will need the folio I've left on the desk in my study."

"I'll be sure he gets it."

"Thank you. He will be taking over the negotiation on the contracts."

"Ye trust him to work out the details in yer stead?"

Jon nodded. "Bennett has earned this promotion."

The old woman glanced around, sniffling a bit. "My, it is going to be awfully quiet around here, isn't it?"

"For the time being, perhaps," he agreed. "But I'd think you would enjoy the peace."

As her thin shoulders lifted and fell in a shrug, a sheen of tears brimmed in her eyes. "A while ago, I might've danced a jig at the prospect of an uncluttered house. But now . . . now it will truly feel empty."

"You won't be alone for long," he said, feeling a decidedly unexpected reluctance at the thought of leaving behind the woman who'd been his housekeeper for nearly a decade. "Macie will appreciate your help as she readies her home for her child. Once the baby arrives, she will truly require your assistance."

"It will be pleasant to be near a babe again." She sniffled. "And I'll assist her with the wee lass. Perhaps I will even teach Carrie to make my lemon cake. It was always Macie's favorite."

"And one of mine as well." He regarded her for a long moment. "I don't know what I would've done without you these last months. I do appreciate all you've done."

Were his eyes deceiving him, or had the old woman actually blushed? "Ye're a good man, like yer father."

"Thank you. That is high praise, indeed."

"And if I may speak my mind, ye're a lucky man to have had this second chance with Miss Belle. She's a good woman, she is. She never puts on airs, and no matter what, she was eager to help. It's hard to believe she's one of those dollar princesses." Mrs. Gilroy planted her hands on her hips. "If ye ask me, she's a true gem."

"I agree," Jon said with a smile.

"Treasure her," Mrs. Gilroy regarded him with a solemn expression. "Just as yer father has treasured yer mum all these years. If ye do that, ye will have a happy life."

"Believe me, I will. The question is: will she want to spend her life with me?"

"She'll give ye the answer ye're looking for. The lass loves ye. I've seen it in her eyes."

"By thunder, I hope you're right."

"Ye know I am," Mrs. Gilroy said, her smile fading as the door chimes interrupted the moment. "I should get that."

"No need to trouble yourself," he said. "I'm expecting Macie and Finn. I'll see them in."

"JON, I AM so very excited for you." Perched on an overstuffed chair in the sitting room, his sister peered over the cup of tea in her hand and regarded him for a long moment. "I knew the day would come when you'd finally meet your match."

"Is that so?" He met Macie's warm gaze.

"She's perfect for you," Macie said without a single note of doubt. "Belle makes you smile—a genuine smile, at that. A rare thing, indeed."

"Now to hope she'll still have your dolt of a brother."

"Ye might need to do some convincing," Finn spoke up. He sent Macie a speaking glance. "A perhaps a bit of groveling. I know something about that myself."

Mrs. Gilroy brought in a tray of scones. "I know how much ye like them, Miss Macie."

"Why, thank you," Macie said, taking a pastry from the tray. "So very thoughtful."

"I'll prepare a few for ye to take home. The wee lass has a fondness for them."

"Oh, she'll be delighted." Macie met Mrs. Gilroy's careworn features. "She misses you."

"Ah, and I miss her, too. Her giggles could make Scrooge himself smile," Mrs. Gilroy replied. "I'd best put on another pot of tea. It won't be long before ye'll be wanting another cup."

As Mrs. Gilroy headed back to the kitchen, Jon cleared his

throat. The conversation he needed to have might well be difficult. But he had to follow his gut. And his heart.

"I'd like to talk to the two of you . . . about Carrie."

Finn reached for Macie's hand as she sat up straighter on the loveseat. "Is something wrong?" she said.

"No. Nothing is wrong," Jon said. "I'm quite sure Carrie is very happy. But I feel . . . I feel your dolt of a brother has made another blunder."

"A blunder?" Macie repeated thoughtfully, even as he spotted what looked like understanding in her eyes.

"There was a time, not very long ago, when I did not have the slightest notion of how to be a father to the girl. But now, I see—"

"You see the truth, don't you?" Macie said, her voice quiet, yet direct. "You've been a fine brother to me. And you will be an even better father."

His sister's words caught him by surprise. "You really mean that, don't you?"

Macie's gentle smile warmed his heart. "Could you ever doubt it?"

"That means the world to me," he replied truthfully, then strategically cleared his throat. "I know Carrie has a wonderful life with the two of you . . . she is loved and content. I would never do anything to interfere with her happiness."

"The young lass *is* happy," Finn said. "With one exception."

Macie met his eyes. "Jon, she misses you terribly."

"There's no denying it," Finn agreed. "The child has a bond with ye . . . and Belle . . . that should not be broken."

"Quite so," Macie agreed. "Are you aware that Belle spoke to me about spending time with Carrie when she's in the city?"

"She did mention something of the sort," Jon said. "She's developed a true fondness for Carrie."

"Such a true fondness that she's decided to become a frequent visitor to London," Macie pointed out. "She misses her time with the girl. That much is abundantly clear."

"Bloody hell, I miss the little moppet, too." Jon glanced at the framed photograph his sister had given him. She'd captured an image of Carrie clutching her atrocious-yet-beloved ragdoll. The child's eyes were wide with wonder as she'd looked into the camera's lens. "If anyone had ever told me I'd miss the sight of ugly dolls and blasted mudpies, I'd have thought them quite mad."

Finn's forehead creased. "Mudpies?"

"I'll explain later," Macie said with a little chuckle.

"The house is so blasted quiet now. It seems empty without her little songs and laughter." Jon raked a hand through his hair. "I don't know an eloquent way to say what's on my mind, so I'll just speak the truth. I would like another chance to be a father . . . to Carrie."

"You're sure of this?" Finn said, even as Macie's smile lit her face.

"I've given this a great deal of thought, and I have no doubt," he said. "Belle loves Carrie, just as I do." He considered his next words carefully. "If Belle and I are to start our life together, I want Carrie to be a part of it."

"The two of you will be so good together . . . you'll be marvelous parents." Macie clapped her hands together in excitement, even as her husband seemed to give Jon's words more consideration. "Finn and I adore Carrie, but I know she will be so very happy with you . . . as her father."

Finn lowered his gaze, seeming to study the patterns on the rug beneath his feet. When he looked up, the set of his jaw betrayed his train of thought. "It might be best to keep this notion from the girl until everything is settled between you and Belle."

"I've hurt Belle. I know that better than anyone." Jon met the concern in his friend's eyes. "There's no guarantee that she will forgive me . . . that she will accept my proposal. But I know this—I want to be a father to Carrie. No matter what."

"The girl will be delighted to have you as her Papa." A slight sheen brightened Macie's eyes. "And Belle . . . well, after speaking to her, I'd wager my last shilling she's wild for you."

"By thunder, I shall be the luckiest man in London if that is true," Jon said as the chimes at the front door sounded again.

"You're expecting someone?" Macie asked.

"Mr. Bennett is due to stop by, but not until later in the day."

He stood to greet the unexpected visitor, but Mrs. Gilroy had already met Mrs. Johnstone at the door.

Offering brisk greetings, Mrs. Johnstone bustled in. "Good afternoon. I do hate to interrupt, but I've come with news ye need to hear."

"What's happened?" he said, searching her expression.

"Nothing's wrong, but there has been a change in plans. I did not speak to her myself, but Ellie has informed me that Belle has decided to leave considerably earlier than we'd expected. She is already on her way to the station.

Bloody hell. "She's leaving tonight?"

Mrs. Johnstone nodded. "She has booked passage to Southampton. The train is scheduled to depart at six o'clock." Her features taut with concern, she retrieved an envelope from her handbag. "I do realize ye've only an hour to reach the station. It may not be feasible."

He shrugged. "I shall depart on the six o'clock train as well."

"Very good. I was hoping ye would say that." Mrs. Johnstone's mouth pulled into a faint smile as she handed him the envelope. "I've taken the liberty of purchasing yer ticket."

Chapter Thirty-Two

WITH FINN AT the reins, Jon joined Mrs. Gilroy and Mrs. Johnstone in his coach as they hurried to the train yard. Setting a brisk pace, Finn deftly navigated the crush of traffic—coaches and carts and pedestrians filled the streets, going about the ordinary business of their lives on a rainy afternoon that was far from ordinary for Jon. It was as if he'd finally awoken from an existence that wasn't entirely whole. He knew now what he'd needed all along—the love of a spirited, bright-eyed woman who somehow still cared about him despite the fact he'd been an utter arse.

Belle was the woman he loved. The woman he needed. And she loved him. At least, she had.

You have my heart. But it's up to you to claim it.

She'd spoken the words in cool, even tones, even as tears had filled her eyes. The days that had passed since then had only thickened the ice between them.

An invisible weight landed in his gut. He simply had to see her before she boarded the train. But was it too late? Had he already damaged their bond beyond repair?

If he had—if she did not want him to accompany her, he would honor her wishes. If she desired more space and time to clear her head, as she'd put it, he would allow her whatever she needed. And if she'd come to a realization of her own—if he'd extinguished the spark of passion she'd held for him, he would have no choice but to live with that truth for the rest of his life. But first, he had to tell her what was in his heart.

The carriage slowed. Then stopped. Each passing moment felt like an eternity. Still, they made no progress. He heard Finn swear an epithet from the driver's bench, and Mrs. Gilroy peered from the window.

"I don't see what's causing the problem," she said with a shrug.

"Accident ahead," Finn called from the bench. "A blasted wagon has overturned. Take a look for yerself."

Jon opened the door enough to survey the scene. *Bollocks.* Not only had a wagon overturned in the middle of the street, but its cargo—sacks and more sacks of potatoes, from the looks of it—strewn about the pavement. Adding to the chaos, some of the burlap bags had split, their contents spilling over the road.

Finn pulled his hat lower to shield his face from the pouring rain. Seated on the bench, his raincoat offered some protection from the deluge, but he still looked to be getting soaked.

"I don't see an opening. The wagon's blocking the whole blasted road," he said. "There's no way to proceed."

Rain pelted Jon's face. "How far are we from the station?"

"At least ten blocks, by my estimate," Mrs. Johnstone spoke up.

He smiled to himself. Finn was wrong. There *was* a path. And he was going to take it.

Pulling his flat-brimmed hat lower, he eyed his traveling bag. The cumbersome satchel would only slow him down.

"Surely ye're not thinking to proceed on foot," Mrs. Johnstone said.

"Of course he is." Mrs. Gilroy turned to Jon. "I always knew ye had spirit. Now, go get the pretty lass."

"That, Mrs. Gilroy, is precisely what I intend to do."

"Ye'll be drenched and in no condition to travel," Mrs. Johnstone cautioned. "A bit of patience might be in order."

"Patience is highly overrated," he said. "Goodbye, ladies.

Wish me luck."

"Ye will not need it," Mrs. Gilroy said, her eyes bright with encouragement. "Miss Belle is over the moon for ye."

"Now *that* is a thought which inspires a man to get going." He grinned at the old woman. "Mrs. Gilroy, there's one more thing—please tell *the wee lass* I'll be coming back for her soon."

He jumped to the ground, his feet hitting the pavement as Mrs. Gilroy called after him.

"Coming back?" she said. "Are ye saying what I think ye're saying?"

"Indeed, I am." With that, he turned from the carriage.

And he ran.

The downpour had intensified as the wind picked up speed and the sky darkened to a stormy gray. Wind-driven drops of rain slapped against his face. But he didn't give a damn.

He heard the sound of his boots pounding against the cobbles. He felt the cool, heavy drops penetrate his layers of clothing, soaking him to the skin. As he pictured Belle in his mind's eye, he quickened his pace, even as he dodged a carriage and a man walking an exceedingly small dog. She was all that mattered. He had to get to her. He couldn't spend another day—and night—without her.

BELLE IMPATIENTLY TAPPED the tip of her umbrella against the floor of the train station. She'd only been waiting an hour or so, but her nerves were on edge. And she was eager to get going. It was difficult to leave London as it was, but delaying the inevitable would only worsen the pain.

"It seems appropriate that even the sky is cross today," she said, turning to Ellie. "This dreary rain rather fits my mood."

Her friend looked up from happily knitting a scarf she would likely never wear. "Mine as well," she said. "I do hate to see you go, Belle. It's a pity I cannot travel with you, but my aunt—not the one in Paris, but the one who's heading off to Egypt—is in need of a companion. With any luck, I'll discover an archaeologist of my own on the expedition."

"I don't doubt you'll find yourself a handsome explorer."

"I do hope so," Ellie said, her tone a bit dreamy.

"Take care, my friend," she said. "And promise me you'll soon come to New York."

"Of course," Ellie said. "I look forward to visiting the Metropolitan Museum."

"You'll love it. The collections are—"

Belle saw him then. The sight took her breath—and by extension, her ability to speak—away.

"Are you alright?" Ellie asked.

"Yes, I do believe I am." She stared at the man who'd walked into the station—or perhaps, sloshed into the place wearing rain-soaked shoes was a better description. *My goodness, he looked as if he'd been in the rain for far too long.* "Goodness," she murmured.

Leaping to her feet for a better look, her gaze locked with his. Her eyes were not deceiving her. The man was, indeed, Jon.

Drenched. Soaked to the skin. And utterly irresistible.

The straight, dark strands of his hair were plastered to his head while raindrops beaded his forehead, his cheeks, his face. His wet clothing clung to his lean, muscular frame like a second skin.

Oh, my. Her pulse raced. She dragged in a breath, as if that might calm her. There were many reasons why Jon might be at the station. But only one would make her heart sing.

"Good heavens. Why in the world . . ." Ellie made a sound that was a cross between a giggle and a gasp. "Such a pity Macie isn't here to capture this moment with her camera. I doubt we'll ever again see anything like it."

Curious onlookers scrunched their foreheads and hiked their brows at the sight. Undeterred by the questioning stares, Jon cut through the crowd on a direct path, his gaze set firmly on his destination. On *her*.

Belle's heartbeat sped up as Jon came to stand before her. He didn't reach out. Didn't touch her. Didn't even take her hand. Instead, he searched her face, seeming to seek an answer to a question he had not yet asked.

"You're still here." He sounded both a bit out of breath and relieved.

"Hello, Jon," she said. "Might I ask why you look as though you've been walking in the rain?"

"I wasn't walking," he replied matter-of-factly. "I was running."

"Has something happened?" Her gaze trailed down to his soaked shoes. "Something urgent?"

"Extremely urgent." His eyes darkened as he held her gaze. "I realized I'd left something unfinished—a matter of the utmost importance."

"I see," she said, steeling herself. It was quite possible, after all, that this *matter of utmost importance* had nothing to do with what was in his heart.

He gave a solemn nod, even as his eyes gleamed with something that looked like hope. "Arabelle Frost, the dolt standing before you has finally come to his senses."

She met his eyes, seeking the truth. "Jon, I don't understand."

"But you will." The slightest of smiles played on his full mouth as he fumbled about in his sopping wet jacket. When he found what he'd been looking for, he appeared to cup something in the palm of his hand.

"Oh, my. He's going to do it," Ellie commented in a breathless whisper. "He is actually going to do it."

Belle stared at him, a sense of confusion blending with a rekindled ember of joy. "Jon, what is happening?"

"I want to be with you until I take my last breath." A keen intensity gleamed in his deep brown eyes. "Arabelle Frost, love of my life, will you marry me?"

Joy crashed over her like a rogue wave. Her knees wobbled,

and Ellie came to her side, propping her up by the elbow.

"This is so . . . so very unexpected." Belle gulped a breath, then another. This was the moment she'd waited for. The moment she'd longed for. But there was a truth they both had to face before she could speak the word perched on the tip of her tongue. "But I cannot stay in London. I must return home."

"I know." Jon's husky rasp seemed a caress. "I don't give a damn if we are in London or New York or on the blasted moon, for that matter. All I need is you, Belle. By my side. Every day . . . for the rest of my life."

"And if I say 'yes'?" Nearly overcome with emotion, she heard the quaking of her own voice.

"If you do, I will accompany you to Southampton. And then, we will marry in New York." His eyes gleamed with promise and hope. "If you will have me, that is." He extended his hand, presenting a ring, perhaps the most beautiful Belle had ever seen. The breathtaking sapphire at the center gleamed with an intense hue, accented by the brilliant diamonds flanking it on both sides.

"Oh, my," she gasped in a little whisper. Of all the things she'd expected might happen on this day, she could not have anticipated this moment. Her heart raced even as it soared.

"Please say 'yes,' Belle, so that I might kiss you." His low voice was rough with the emotion he made no attempt to hide. So very tempting. So very irresistible.

"Well, when you put it like that," she said with a little smile. "How could I possibly resist?"

"Say it, my Arabelle." A muscle in his jaw went taut. "Say you'll always be mine."

"Yes," she said. "Yes, yes, and yes again. Oh, Jon, I cannot wait for the day when we speak our vows."

His gaze intent, he slipped the ring onto her finger. And then, he framed her face between his hands. His fingers threaded through her hair as he kissed her, a slow, tender caress that spoke of passion and love and a lifetime of promise.

When he released her, he looked at her as though she were

the most precious treasure he'd ever seen. "I had planned a far more romantic proposal than this," he said, his voice gruff and tender. "I'd selected an elegant venue with musicians and candles and such, rather than standing here, dripping all over the floor of a train station. But I simply could not help myself. I had to tell you the truth." He caught her in his arms, gazing down at her, not giving a damn about the gawking passengers who looked on eagerly. "I love you, Arabelle. I always have. I'll love you until I take my last breath, and beyond."

"Oh, Jon," she whispered against his lips. "This is a moment I will always remember."

"I'd wanted to make this a memorable proposal." He grinned. "I suppose I succeeded." He glanced around. "For these good folk as well."

A familiar voice cut through the whispers of the crowd. Finn strode toward them, a satchel in hand. "Looks like ye'll be needing this," he said with a broad smile, handing Jon the traveling bag. "By thunder, ye didn't leave any rain in the clouds, did ye? From the looks of it, it's all in yer shoes."

"If I were not in a deliriously happy state of mind, I'd tell you what I think of your observations," Jon said lightly. "But instead, I would like to introduce you to the future Mrs. Mason."

"In that case, I'll wish ye all the good fortune in the world." Finn gazed down at Belle, a twinkle in his eyes. "He's a lucky man, lass. The bloke will make ye happy. Of that, ye can rest assured."

"I am over the moon." She clasped Jon's hands in hers. "I cannot wait until I am officially your bride."

"Safe travels, my friends," Finn said as he strolled away with jaunty steps. He threw a glance over his shoulder. "Macie and I will see ye at the wedding."

Epilogue

New York, December 1897

NEW YORK AT Christmastime held a special place in Belle's heart. As a girl, she'd delighted in ice skating in the park and singing festive carols. Now, introducing her young daughter to the many wonders to be found in the city brought a special sense of joy. Gathered with friends and family on a cold and snowy day following an enjoyable excursion to the remarkable toy store in Union Square, she smiled to herself as Carrie sat by the hearth, hosting a pretend tea party, serving sweet cakes instead of mud pies to the MacLains' toddler son, Finnegan. The boy eagerly nibbled one of the tasty treats, while the other guests—Carrie's new stuffed elephant and her treasured Anna—looked on with make-believe eyes.

"My, that is certainly a well-loved doll," Amelia MacLain observed, rocking her infant daughter on her lap. Her blue eyes sparkled as she lowered her voice to a whisper. "I've brought your little girl a gift from London, a collection of Robert Louis Stevenson's poems for children. I acquired the most beautiful illustrated edition for my library, and I thought she might enjoy one as well."

"How very thoughtful," Belle said. "She will love it, and so will I."

"Finnegan was enchanted by trains at the toy store. We shall have to pay another visit." Amelia brushed a wayward ginger-gold curl behind her ear.

"Carrie cannot wait to return," Belle said. "She had her eye on a stuffed rabbit in a beautiful paisley print."

"That was quite an appealing creation," Amelia said, brushing her fingers through her baby's strawberry blonde curls. The girl bore a striking resemblance to her mother, while little Finnegan was the very image of his father, with deep brown hair and eyes as dark as midnight.

Mrs. Gilroy strolled in from the kitchen, bearing a tray of scones and a fresh pot of tea, then joined them in the sitting room. In the months since she'd arrived in New York, she'd grown very close to Belle. The woman had become a friend, a sage advisor, and, most of all, a part of their family.

Mrs. Gilroy poured herself a cup of tea and took a bite of scone. "Have ye had a chance to take a look at the ornaments on the Christmas tree, Mrs. MacLain?" She went to the decorated spruce and retrieved one of the salt and flour ornaments that dotted the branches. "The wee lass has been busy," she said with a touch of pride.

Amelia examined the ornament cut in the shape of a candy cane. "Carrie made this?"

"It's become a holiday tradition," Belle said. "Carrie enjoys making them as gifts for birthdays as well."

"She made me a lovely one for my special day last month." Belle's grandmother walked slowly into the room, lightly tapping her elegantly carved walking stick against the floor. She beamed as her doting gaze settled on Carrie. "I have it hanging over the dresser in my bedchamber."

"Grammy Pru, would you like to see my new tabby?" Carrie hurried to greet Belle's grandmother. With a grin, she displayed the stuffed animal Belle had purchased for her at the toy store. "Isn't she pretty?"

"That she is, dear," Grammy Pru gave her a hug. "What is her name?"

"Pru . . . Prudence," the girl said. "I named her after you."

"Did you now?" A twinkle lit Grammy Pru's eyes. "What a special honor." Her attention returned to the table where Carrie had been having her little pretend party. Little Finnegan gazed up at her, his mouth dusted with sugar from the cookie he'd been enjoying. "Have you forgotten you have a guest, dear?"

"Oh, my," Carrie said in a rather dramatic fashion. "I must be a good hostess, mustn't I?"

"Most definitely," Grammy agreed. As Carrie returned to join Finnegan, Grammy made her way to the settee. "Oh, Belle, I'm so delighted to see children playing in this house." She clasped Belle's hand within hers. "I'm over the moon to spend this Christmas with you." She glanced toward Mrs. Gilroy and Amelia. "And your dear friends."

"It's my pleasure to be here with you," Amelia said. "I understand we will be able to a Christmas pageant together later this week."

"I do think you will enjoy it. It's a marvelous production," Grammy replied.

Her grandmother's attention turned to the tree. "I must say, Belle, you've decorated the tree quite beautifully."

"I'd say we've all had a part in it," Belle said, joining Grammy on the small sofa. "Some might think it's a bit, well, a bit much, with the eclectic array of ornaments, but they're all quite special to me."

Grammy clasped Belle's fingers in hers. "Carrie's handcrafted pieces are a wonderful touch." She smiled warmly. "I've brought something for you, dear. I have kept this for a very long time. But now, I want you to have it."

Her grandmother presented her with a small box. Belle slowly lifted the lid, revealing a snowflake ornament made of lacy yarn.

"Grandmama, I don't quite understand."

"Don't you remember, my sweet girl?" Her grandmother's eyes brightened. "You made this for me a very long time ago." The most adoring of smiles curved her mouth. "You were about Carrie's age at the time."

"You . . . you've kept this?" Emotion swelled in Belle's heart. "All this time?"

Her grandmother nodded. "All this time." Her tone was filled with love. "I did not merely *keep* it. I treasured it. And many years from now, you will look back upon the handmade ornaments on that tree, and you will cherish them more than the most elegant spun glass bauble."

"I know," she said. "Just as I treasure these memories we're making now."

"You are a dear girl, Belle. You and your mother and your brother are the greatest gifts of my life. And now," she said, looking at Carrie. "Now, you've given me another to treasure. A great-granddaughter—how very wonderful."

Tears filled Belle's eyes as she hugged her grandmother. She would not have traded these precious days for the wealth of a queen.

As she sniffled against her handkerchief, the sound of Logan MacLain's hearty baritone pulled her attention to the doorway. Moments later, Logan made his entrance. Dressed in a black wool coat, hat, and scarf, he cut quite a dashing figure. His attention went straight to his wife. They exchanged a long glance, and then he offered greetings.

"Might I ask where my husband is?" Belle asked, sensing some plot or other was afoot. Judging from the hearty smile on Logan's face, she had reason to believe she would be pleased by the surprise.

"He's on his way. He had one last stop to make."

Belle hiked a brow. "Are you telling me he actually went to a shop rather than sending his assistant?"

"That would be the case," he replied blandly. A brief grin played on his features. "It's a surprise." He helped himself to a scone and joined his wife on the sofa.

"A surprise?" Belle pressed.

"Ah, lass, ye will not pry the truth out of me. I'm made of sterner stuff than that."

"He is," Amelia agreed with a chuckle. "A true keeper of secrets."

"Well, I suppose I should brace myself," Belle said.

"That might be a good idea," Logan agreed. Changing the subject, he said, "I believe Mrs. Johnstone will arrive tomorrow. The Dragon is still in Boston."

"Dragon?" Grammy repeated with a hint of a grin. "How intriguing."

"I'll explain later, Grandmama," Belle said. Turning back to Logan, she took a sip of tea. "I do hope her train has not been delayed."

"Actually, she is staying by choice. Her message mentioned exploring Boston Harbor. She's quite the aficionado of history."

"So I'd gathered," Belle said. "When she arrives, I'll be pleased to show her the sights in New York."

"I suspect the woman could take ye to parts of Manhattan ye've never seen," he said. "She was quite an adventurous sort when she was with the agency."

"Somehow, that does not surprise me," Belle said. *Not very much, in any case.*

An unexpected sound tore her attention from the conversation. A series of yips and small barks, coming from the direction of the front steps to their house.

Hearing the noise, Carrie stood up and ran to the window. "Papa is home."

Papa? Belle had not expected Jon's return to be announced by the sounds a dog—a young dog, at that—might make.

Precisely what is the nature of our surprise? Belle wasn't sure whether to be delighted or fit to be tied.

Moments later, Jon strolled through the door, bearing a green traveling bag that bore a striking resemblance to Heathy's blue case. What was going on?

"Hello, my darling wife," Jon said, greeting her at the door.

"Hello, Jon," she said. "Might I ask what you're carrying?"

"I believe you already know the answer." He grinned. "A gift that will require care and feeding, and perhaps, a pair of earplugs for me."

Carrie bounded to him. "Oh, Papa, is it—"

Crouching low, he set the case on the floor and gave her a hug. "I've been doing some thinking, and I realize there's one thing we need to make this family complete." He grinned. "Take a look at our newest addition."

Carrie peered into the case and let out a squeal of delight. "Oh, Papa, he's so cute."

"He is, isn't he?" Jon flashed Mrs. Gilroy a winning smile. "Might I have the morning edition . . . just in case."

With a quick nod, Mrs. Gilroy went to fetch the paper.

"You brought home a puppy?" Belle looked on in open amazement as her grandmother chuckled.

"I did," Jon said. He met her eyes. "I wanted it to be a surprise. I suppose I didn't think to consider that you might not be pleased."

"To the contrary, Jon." She threw her arms around him. "I could not be more surprised. And delighted."

He pretended to wipe imaginary perspiration from his brow. "By thunder, that is a relief. You had me fooled for a moment."

She pressed a kiss to his cheek. Another kiss—much more than a quick press of her lips—would come later, when she had him alone. "This is a wonderful gift."

As soon as Mrs. Gilroy returned, he spread out a few sheets of newspaper and opened the case.

A small pup dashed out and ran straight into Carrie's waiting arms.

Good heavens. The dog was a younger, even fluffier version of Heathy.

"In case ye're wondering, Heathy is the pup's sire," Logan said with a chuckle.

Belle could not take her eyes off the precious puppy. "Why, that little dickens."

Amelia looked a bit guilty. "I wanted to tell you. But Jon made me promise to keep it a surprise."

"And a marvelous surprise it is." Belle's heart swelled as Carrie cuddled the tiny pup. "By the way, where is Heathy?"

"He's home with our housekeeper," Amelia explained. "At his age, he's not fond of traveling."

"The furry mop on legs is getting a bit creaky in the joints," Logan said matter-of-factly.

"Believe me, I understand," Mrs. Gilroy said. "These old bones can be contrary at times."

"We'll have to be careful to keep the pup from getting underfoot," Belle said. "We wouldn't want to repeat what happened with Heathy."

"Ah, it was not such a bad thing." The old woman lifted her gaze to Belle. A cheeky little grin played on her mouth. "Truth be told, I might've put that mishap to good use."

Belle hiked a brow. "What are you saying?"

Her smile broadened. "Well, to tell ye the truth, I may have played it up . . . just a bit."

Jon's brow furrowed. "What's this about?"

"It's simple, really," Mrs. Gilroy said. "When Heathy got underfoot that day, I did twist my bad knee. But as ye know, the other one's not much better. I've had twinges in my joints for years now." She turned to Belle. "When I saw how the wee lass brightened up after ye came to stay, I didn't want ye to leave."

Belle bit back a grin. "Mrs. Gilroy, you scamp."

The old woman met her gaze with kind eyes. "As it turns out, my achy bones were a bit of a blessing, now, weren't they?"

With a smile, Belle caught the woman's work-worn hands in hers. "I would most definitely have to agree."

Carrie brought her puppy over. "Mama, what shall we name him?"

"We'll need to ponder that a bit," Belle said.

Logan chuckled. "I'd suggest Mop-on-legs, but Amelia would poke me in the ribs."

Jon scratched his chin, appearing deep in thought. "Carrie, I have an idea."

"What, Papa?"

"He looks like his father, doesn't he?"

When Carrie nodded, he went on. "I suspect he will act like his father as well. So, why don't we call him Rascal?"

"Rascal," Carrie repeated. She beamed at the name. "I love it. So now, I have my Rascal."

Logan chuckled. "If he's anything like that like the little ball of fur he's descended from, ye can consider it a fitting name, indeed."

"Well, Jon, since you've already presented your surprise, I have one for you as well," Belle said. "Though it's not nearly so special."

"A surprise, eh?" Jon sat in a wing chair and stretched out his long legs. "And it's not even Christmas yet."

"Not quite. But you'll enjoy this." She nibbled her lip. "I presume you recall our not-quite-friendly wager."

"I do," he said. "Obviously, you won the bet quite handily."

"I did," she said. "But I wanted to clear up one point."

A smile tugged at his mouth. "And what might that be, my love?"

"You doubted my ability to bake a pie."

"I did." He shrugged. "I suppose I still do."

"Is that so, my darling husband?" She sent him a cheeky grin, then went into the kitchen and brought back a covered silver plate. "Perhaps you might want to think again."

Uncovering the plate, she showed off a perfectly baked apple pie.

Jon leaned back and folded his hands behind his head. "Am I to believe that you—a woman who had never peeled an apple, let alone baked one—made something that looks and smells as delicious as that?"

She nibbled her lip. "I didn't know how when I made that wager."

"But she learns fast," Mrs. Gilroy said. "Ye were an eager student."

"And you, Mrs. Gilroy, are an excellent teacher."

Jon came to her, cupped his hand to her chin, and looked into her eyes. "Ah, my Arabelle. As always, you amaze me."

And then, as always, he kissed her.

FOLLOWING A BUSTLING day filled with winter festivities, conversation, and delicious food, Belle joined her husband in their bedchamber. Relaxing on the settee near the warmth of the hearth, she sipped chamomile tea while Jon enjoyed fine Scotch. Carrie had been happily tucked into bed, eager to awaken with the dawn to discover what Santa had left in her stocking, while the adults had retired to their respective bedchambers. The day had been one of joy and togetherness and celebration, but as the clock approached midnight, Belle welcomed the quiet, the warmth, and the prospect of a night spent in Jon's arms.

Gazing at her husband, she battled a sudden whisper of nerves. For days, she'd been harboring an inkling that something she'd always dreamed of was on the horizon, and now, she had good reason to fully trust her instincts.

"Penny for your thoughts," Jon said, lightly draping an arm around her. "You seemed preoccupied at dinner. Is anything wrong?"

"Wrong?" She shook her head. "Quite the opposite, really."

"Belle, what is going on?" He kissed her lightly, grazing his lips over the curve of her cheek. "Will I find another surprise under the tree?"

"Well, darling, I do have another surprise," she murmured, keeping her tone light and teasing. "But you will not find it under the tree."

He looked rather puzzled. "It's in here, then?"

"In a manner of speaking," she said with a cheeky little smile. "When you brought Carrie her puppy, you said there was one thing we needed to make this family complete." She took another sip of tea, if only to prolong his suspense. "Darling, there is *one* more thing that will add to our family."

He stared at her for a long moment. He downed a drink of Scotch and set the tumbler on the table.

"Are you telling me . . . what I think you're telling me?"

She nodded. "I do believe I am."

"Good God, Belle," he murmured as he searched her eyes. "A baby."

She nodded again. "I wanted to wait until I was certain before I told you."

"When?" The word tumbled out of his mouth.

"In the summer, darling."

He looked like he wanted to shout the news from the street, but instead, he became very quiet. "By thunder, I don't have the words."

She sat up straighter. "Perhaps you might start by telling me you are happy about this rather significant development."

"Happy?" He slowly shook his head. "My love, *happy* is in no way adequate to express my feelings."

His arms slipped around her, and he drew her close. With one hand, he tipped up her chin. Looking into his eyes, Belle felt as if she were lost in his gaze. My, the man she'd wed—the man she loved with all her heart—was handsome. As long as she lived, she'd never tire of looking into those intelligent dark brown eyes. Relaxing against his warm, strong body, she heard herself sigh, drawn into a sense of bliss that enveloped her.

"Belle, you're so beautiful." He searched her face, as if she were a lost treasure he'd found. "How bloody amazing that you're mine. And now, we're going to have a baby."

Belle blinked back tears of joy. "Carrie will be delighted to have a little brother," she said. "Or a little sister."

"I don't know how I got so bloody lucky," he whispered against her ear. "A beautiful wife I'll cherish until the day I die, and beyond. A beautiful daughter who calls me Papa. And now, a little boy or a little girl who will lay claim to my heart, just as you and Carrie have."

How she adored this man. And she knew she would until she took her last breath.

"I love you, Jon," she murmured, drawing in the spicy scent of his shaving soap. "I'll always be yours."

"Oh, my Arabelle," he said. "I love you more than any words can say. And I always will."

"Then show me," she teased.

He framed her face in his hands, seeming to drink her in. "An excellent idea, my darling wife."

And then, he kissed her. Tender. Searing. Hungry with need. His kiss spoke of passion and promises and true devotion—a kiss of love that would nurture their future, a love that would endure and grow ever deeper.

True love.

The essence of their unbreakable bond filled every touch, every caress. Belle whispered words of love against his lips as pure joy washed over her.

She was his. And he was hers.

Forever.

THE END

About the Author

Award-winning author Tara Kingston writes historical romance laced with suspense and intrigue. She lives her own happily-ever-after in a cozy Victorian with her real-life hero and a pair of deceptively innocent-looking cats. When she's not writing, reading, or burning dinner, Tara enjoys movie nights, cycling, hiking, DIY projects, and cheering on her favorite football team.

Visit Tara at her webpage, www.tarakingston.com. If you'd like updates on new releases, historical romance news, excerpts, and more, please sign-up for Tara's newsletter at www.tarakingston.com/newsletter-signup.